For Beth —

TUNNEL VISION

Follow the light!
All the best —

GARY BRAVER

TOR®

A TOM DOHERTY ASSOCIATES BOOK • NEW YORK

This is a work of fiction. All of the characters, organizations, and events portrayed in this novel are either products of the author's imagination or are used fictitiously.

TUNNEL VISION

Copyright © 2011 by Gary Braver

All rights reserved.

A Tor Book
Published by Tom Doherty Associates, LLC
175 Fifth Avenue
New York, NY 10010

www.tor-forge.com

Tor® is a registered trademark of Tom Doherty Associates, LLC.

ISBN 978-0-7653-4855-5

First Edition: June 2011
First Mass Market Edition: June 2012

Printed in the United States of America

0 9 8 7 6 5 4 3 2 1

ACKNOWLEDGMENTS

Several people have helped me with technical matters in the writing of this book, and I would like to thank them for their generous time and expertise: Dr. James Stellar, provost of Queens College; Dr. James F. English, Mount Auburn Hospital, Cambridge, Massachusetts; and Karen Zoeller, R.N., Massachusetts General Hospital. Thanks also to Cathie Gould for her insights on spirituality.

As always, thanks to Barbara Shapiro for her keen suggestions in making this a better book.

One book that was indispensable in writing this novel is *The Near-Death Experience: A Reader,* edited by Lee W. Bailey and Jenny Yates (New York: Routledge, 1996).

Also, a special thanks to Kathy, Nathan, and "Diamond Dave" Goshgarian, my ace in the hole.

As ever, thanks to my editor, Natalia Aponte, and my faithful agent, Susan Crawford.

Lord, I do believe; help me in my unbelief.

—MARK 9:24

ONE

PROLOGUE

....

Karen Wells was at the computer behind the ER desk at
Jordan Hospital when a call arrived in from an ambulance unit. It was nearly three A.M., and EMTs were
bringing in an unidentified male about fifty years of age
with minimal vital signs, possible cardiac arrest. She
alerted the other nurses, the on-duty physician, Dr. Brian
Kennedy, and two residents. They readied an empty cubicle specially equipped for cardiac patients.

It had otherwise been a slow night—a couple of victims of minor accidents, a drug overdose, a sprained
foot, an elderly woman being treated for acute diarrhea—
atypical for a Saturday night in spring. Just two weeks
ago the place was bedlam, with a packed waiting room
and patients from infants to seniors in various states of
distress. The ward was so quiet, it was almost spooky. So
the possible cardiac would get fast and full attention.

Within seven minutes of the call, two paramedics burst
into the ER with a man unconscious on a stretcher in full
CPR mode. They rolled him into the bay, where the resuscitation team transferred him to a bed, intubated him in
seconds, and wired his chest to an EKG machine.

"Come on, guy. Hang in there," the EMT said, still performing CPR.

Karen hooked him up to a blood pressure cuff while another nurse inserted an IV into his arm. "Shit. Seventy over palp."

"I can't get a pulse," said Barbara, another nurse.

The EKG showed agonal rhythm—slow, irregular complexes often seen as the heart dies.

"Come back to me, buddy!" the EMT shouted.

"Paddles!" Dr. Kennedy said.

Instantly, they slammed his chest with four thousand volts. The body lurched upward, but still no regular heartbeat, no pulse. Nothing.

They continued pumping and paddling the man until it was clear they could get no electromechanical activity at all. Dr. Kennedy then jammed a cardiac needle of epinephrine between the man's third and fourth ribs and directly into the heart. No response.

They continued the CPR, and the doctor called for another intracardiac injection. Karen pushed a second needle back into the right ventricle of the man's heart and depressed the plunger, sending another bolt of epinephrine into him.

Again, nothing. No crisp spikes on the EKG. No pulse. No obtainable blood pressure. Respiration negligible. Body temperature was eighty-two. His skin had assumed the bluish, mottled look of a dead man.

"Was he this cold when you found him?"

"Yeah."

"Was he breathing?"

"Hard to tell. His BP was seventy over palp, but he had a pulse. I swear."

"Well, he hasn't got one now," Karen said.

"We worked on him all the way over."

"Where did you find him?"

"Some kids spotted him on the side of a road near White Cliffs and called 911, and we got the dispatch."

"Any booze containers or drugs with him?"

"Not that we found. But he looks like street."

It was the face of dozens of others she had treated over the years—weathered maps of lives gone amok—fiftyish, unshaven, mottled skin, pupils dilated, eyes bloodshot. A face interchangeable with chronic druggies and alcoholics. He was dressed in black pants that looked relatively new. His top had been removed by the EMTs and sat in a belongings bag. His feet were bare and raw.

She could find no needle tracks in his arm. However, on the back of his right hand was a pinprick over a vein. "Looks like he injected himself."

"That, or he'd been hooked up to an IV line."

No, he looked like heroin to Karen. His skin resembled gray Naugahyde and was covered with scabs and nicks, as if insects had feasted on him while he was exposed to the elements.

"He's gone," Kennedy said. "Time of death . . . three twenty-five."

Kennedy left, and they unhooked the man from the monitors. As Karen put away the equipment, she barely registered how jaded she had become to dead people. In her seventeen years in ER, she had seen every manner of death that could claim human beings—cardiac arrest, drowning, domestic abuse, gang shootings, drug overdoses, stabbings, fire, mangling car crashes—people alive but so disfigured that you had to check for limbs to be certain the carnage was human. When she was in her twenties, it had been much harder to detach herself from the blunt reality of death—to view the dead not as human beings but as bodies, husks of whom they had been. She would look at victims and think that not too long ago they were living, breathing, thinking entities, animated, ensouled with whatever it was that defined life. And now they were tissue, organs, and bone in the process of decaying.

As consolation, she told herself that the real person had departed, gone to a better place where the suffering had ended. But even after seventeen years of ER nursing, it saddened her when the victim was young—even this guy, who died far short of his three score and ten. Sadder still that he had no identity, no name she could put on the toe tag.

She and Barbara cleaned him up. They put his shoes and shirt into a belongings bag and laid the bag on his thighs. They disconnected his monitors and left in the IV, the arterial lines, and the intubation tube for postmortem confirmation that nothing they did in the ER had caused his death.

Because only a physician could legally pronounce a patient's death, Karen left to check her other patients. When she returned, Dr. Kennedy had completed the death certificate. The official time was listed as "3:25 A.M." Karen entered the data into the computer. Later, the body would be delivered to the medical examiner's office, where it would be held until identified and autopsied.

Karen prepared the toe tag and headed into cubicle four, where their John Doe had been left on the gurney. The gurney was still there and the lines were still connected to the IV and monitors, but the body was gone.

Karen shot out to the desk. "Where's the dead guy in four?"

Barbara looked up from her paperwork. "Huh?"

"The John Doe. He's gone. Did someone move him?"

"No. What are you talking about?"

Barbara dashed down the hall with Karen to find the other nurses. Nobody had moved the man. And Dr. Kennedy said he hadn't touched the body. The same with the orderlies. "Who would have taken him?"

"You think somebody took him?" Barbara asked.

"Well, he didn't walk out on his own. Somebody stole him."

Karen ran to the reception desk in the emergency room lobby. The waiting area was empty, and the desk attendant had just returned from the restroom and had seen no one wheel out a body.

Karen buzzed security, and in seconds a guard showed up. "We've got a missing body," she said, and explained what had happened.

"Who the hell would steal a corpse?" the guard said.

"That's *my* question." Then Karen went into the nurses' office, where the video security system was stored. She typed in "3:20 A.M." and hit the playback button.

The image was a long shot of the row of cardiac bays. At 3:27, Dr. Kennedy left cubicle four. Two minutes later, Barbara and Karen left as they checked patients in adjacent cubicles. Then Karen headed down the corridor to the nurses' station to enter the dead man's data into the computer. There was no other activity until the digital clock said 3:43 A.M., when a man emerged from cubicle four.

It was the dead man—Karen's John Doe, his toe tag in her pocket—still naked from the waist up, still barefoot, EKG electrodes still visible on his chest—shuffling down the empty corridor toward the exit with no pulse, no heartbeat, no blood pressure, no body functions, flat-lined and moving on his own power.

Karen watched and bit down on a scream.

1

"Thought I'd died and gone to heaven."

"You did. Two jacks staring at you from Anthony's hand, and you draw another. Don't you believe in counting?" Damian said. "Bro, you take some wild-ass risks."

"But I won," Zack said.

"Yeah, on pure luck. 'Least you don't have to play beer money for a while."

"More like blood money. Found a clinic that pays thirty bucks a pint."

"You mean you're selling your blood?"

"I'm down thirty-six hundred on my Discover card, and they're threatening court action."

"Maybe you should stop gambling."

It was a little after one in the morning, and a mantle of clouds made a hefty underbelly in the Boston sky. Although it was midwinter, the temperature was above freezing, and the streets were free of snow. Zack Kashian was heading to his bike, chained at a light pole near where Damian Santoro had parked his car. They had just left a friend's apartment where a Texas hold 'em game was still going on. After four hours, Zack had drawn a high-win hand—a full house, queens over jacks—and walked away with a $300-plus pot that put him in the black for the night.

"What about your mother?" Damian said.

"She thinks I've got a gambling problem."

"And she refuses to support it."

"Except I don't have a gambling problem. I've got a losing problem."

They crossed Tremont Street to his bike. Zack's apartment was on Hemenway on the other side of Northeastern University's campus. Because it was so close, he didn't bother with his helmet, just a knitted cap. He unchained his bike and rolled it to Damian's car.

"Whatever, get some sleep," Damian said.

Zack patted his breast pocket. "And on Anthony. He sold me half his Lunesta."

"Maybe you do have a gambling problem."

"I'm not sleeping because I've got debts up the grunt, not because I'm gambling."

"That's nuts. You're borrowing to pay down your debt. And now you're selling your blood. I'm telling you, man, you might want to get off those online games. That stuff's dangerous."

Zack put out his hand. "Thank you, Dr. Phil. Or is it Father Damian?"

Damian took it. "You know what you need?"

"No, but you're going to tell me anyway."

"You need to consider finding God again."

"I never found Him to begin with."

"Then the first time. It doesn't have to be a church. Just go where you can find enlightenment, some kind of spiritual enrichment."

"I'll think about it."

"You won't, but I wish you would. I'm visiting a Buddhist temple on Sunday. You're welcome to come."

Damian was a devout Christian who went to different churches in Greater Boston each week. Sometimes even non-Christian places of worship. "I've got another commitment."

"Yeah, the God grumblers."

He meant the Secular Humanist Society Zack belonged to. "We're not God grumblers, man. We don't sit around making fun of religions. We're planning an outing to the Museum of Science for inner-city kids. If there's a God, He'd approve." They had met as roommates in their freshman year at Northeastern. Despite the fact that Zack was an unapologetic atheist, they were still fast friends, held together in part by sniping at each other's dogmatism.

"Whatever, you're too much the rationalist. You need enlightenment."

"Would Foxwoods qualify?"

"A casino's the last thing you need." Damian gave him a hug and drove off as Zack began pedaling home.

Zack had never been to a casino. He preferred home games and the poker Web sites. Perhaps a little too much. Some weeks he'd rack up thirty hours, missing classes and staying up all night, running three and four hands at once. Yes, he made money because he played low-ante games—$25 buy-ins. He'd often win, but it took hours to amass a decent haul. With his face buried in a flash poker site, an easy seduction was an occasional $250 buy-in or a $500 game. And each time he felt the rush that came with laying money on the next card, telling himself that his time was *now*. But that was the problem: getting into a twilight zone of your own adrenaline, convinced of beating the odds. Unlike at table games, online you can't read faces. Instead, you're locked in a cubby with a dark goddess and no good sense. And his debt to friends, bank, and credit card was what he had to show for it. Maybe Damian was right.

You're a congenital screwup, pal. Twenty-four years old and going on fourteen.

Zack glanced up at the sky, wishing he had a father he could call for advice. He dismissed the thought and turned up Ruggles Street, thinking that tomorrow he'd head to Mass General Hospital's blood bank, hoping they didn't screen for poker.

His apartment was only a few blocks away off Huntington Avenue. But a cold drizzle began falling and chilling his face. Another few degrees and the road would be a skim of ice. As he pumped his way onto the avenue, he felt the wad of bills slide up his pocket. With his right hand he pushed down the lump to keep it from working its way out. But doing so left only his other hand to steady the handlebars against an uneven, slick surface.

In a protracted moment, Zack saw the fatal error. His front tire slammed into the jagged edge of a pothole. In the next instant—played out in weird slow motion—the front wheel snapped to the left, sending him flying over the handlebars and coming down dead smack on the top of his head into the base of the crosswalk lights.

In a fraction of a second, Zack was suddenly looking down from someplace above, seeing himself lying crumpled across the curb with his head at the base of the pole and his bike on its side, the front wheel at a crazy angle. In that sliver of awareness, he knew he was viewing things from an impossible perspective. And just as he tried to make sense of it, the moment blinked to total black.

2

··

Maggie Kashian was in a deep sleep when the telephone rang.

She jerked awake. The digital clock glowed 3:28 A.M. Panic filled her chest. No call after midnight was a good call. Not since that night thirteen years ago when she was told that her firstborn son, Jake, had been murdered by two homophobic thugs.

Please, make this a wrong number, she begged the dark as she reached for the phone.

"Mrs. Kashian?"

"Yes?"

"Are you the mother of Zachary Kashian?"

She felt an ice pick pierce her heart. "Yes."

"This is Kyle Kerr. I'm the resident physician at the emergency center at Beth Israel Deaconess Medical Center. Your son Zachary is here. Unfortunately, he was in a bicycle accident and is in our intensive care unit."

"Oh God, no!"

"The good news is he's alive and breathing. But he sustained a head injury. He's unconscious. Is there someone there who can drive you to the hospital?"

"Is he going to be all right?"

"We don't know at this stage. But if you can get someone to drive you in, that would be good. If not, we can have the local police come for you."

"How bad is he?"

"He has a concussion and there's been some subdural bleeding which we're working on."

"No, God. This isn't happening."

"I'm very sorry to call with such news. But can you get someone to drive you here?"

She tried to concentrate on the question. The only neighbor she was close to, Ginny Steves, was away for the weekend. "No."

"Then we'll call the Carleton police."

She agreed and hung up. Barely able to maintain control, she called her sister, Kate, who lived south of Boston, to meet her at the hospital. She dressed, and within minutes a Carleton squad car showed up in front of the house.

Maggie had only a vague recollection of the drive—sitting in shock in the rear of the cruiser, lights flickering, no siren, no conversation with the officer behind the wheel—her mind iced with fright.

Twenty minutes later, the car pulled up to the entrance of the emergency room. The officer escorted her inside to the reception desk. In a matter of moments, the resident physician, Dr. Kerr, came out.

"How is he?" Maggie said.

"The good news is that there are no broken bones, no damage to his spine or internal bleeding," the doctor said. "We've secured his airways and stabilized his blood pressure. But he experienced trauma to his parietal lobe," and he put his hand on the left side of his crown. "The CAT scan showed intracranial bleeding, so we performed a procedure to lower the pressure."

"A procedure?"

"We put a burr hole in his skull to relieve the subdural hematoma." Dr. Kerr continued, but Maggie nearly passed out at the thought of their drilling a hole in her son's skull.

"We implanted a pressure bolt to monitor the swelling. It's normal procedure for this kind of injury. We're also hyperventilating him to keep his blood pressure augmented."

"Is he going to have brain damage?" She could barely articulate the words.

"At this point, it's hard to tell. But he's young and healthy, and that's in his favor. But we can't get a full assessment of brain injury until the swelling subsides. We induced a barbiturate coma to lessen the activity. And we'll be attending him aggressively to be certain that there's no swelling."

While they spoke, Maggie's sister, Kate, arrived. They hugged, and Maggie told her what the doctor had said.

"I want to see him," Maggie said. "I want to see him."

"Certainly."

"How did it happen?" Kate asked as they headed down the hall.

A Boston police officer took the question. "He was bicycling home and hit a pothole at the corner of Huntington Avenue."

"He was less than a block from home."

The officer nodded woefully. "There wasn't any ice or snow on the streets, but this time of year they get chewed up pretty bad."

They brought them into the ICU and past a few beds to a cubicle. When they pulled back the curtain, Maggie nearly fainted in horror. Zack lay in a bed, his face bandaged and tubes and wires running from his wrists, neck, and skull to a cluster of beeping monitors. An IV hung above him and a catheter tube ran down his leg to the other side of the bed. His eyes were discolored and swollen closed, and he was breathing on a respirator that was hooked up to an intratracheal tube. His right arm was also bandaged from the fall. For an instant, Maggie could not process that this was her son, not some unfortunate stranger. Then she broke down.

A nurse came in and put a chair beside the bed for Maggie. When she was able to compose herself, she rested a hand on Zack's arm. "Zack, it's Mom. I'm right here, honey. You're going to be all right."

"The good news is that he's stable now," the nurse said, "and his vital signs are strong."

Maggie nodded. Then she whimpered to herself, "I can't lose him."

"You won't," Kate said.

"Zack, you'll be fine. You're going to wake up soon." As Maggie said that, she had a fleeting flash of her getting him up for grade school.

Please don't let me lose him, too.

Thirteen years ago, Zack's older brother, Jake, was left to die in a pool of his own blood, his face reduced to pulp. He had been at a Cambridge club, frequented by gays, and was set upon in a dark parking lot by two brutes named Volker and Gretch who were high on beer and pot. Apparently one of the men had shouted slurs to which Jake was heard shouting, "Go to hell, asshole!" Then they were upon him. Because the only witnesses were a female cousin of one of the killers and their friends, everybody lied, claiming that the two were elsewhere. A slick lawyer managed to dismiss DNA analyses as faulty. After the acquittal, one of the killers said justice had been served, adding that it was too bad about Jake's death, but that may have saved some little kid from sexual molestation.

Jake's death had all but killed Maggie's husband, Nick,

who lapsed into a profound depression. Eventually he said that he could not go on with life as it was and renounced the world, joining an order of Benedictine monks at the other end of the state. They divorced, and in so doing Nick had left a gaping hole in Zack's young life and Maggie full of grief and contempt. Three years ago, Nick died of cardiac arrest and was cremated.

Volker and Gretch.

Even after all these years, the very syllables of the killers' names made Maggie's stomach leak acid.

For maybe twenty minutes, she and Kate sat by Zack's bed without speaking. Then Maggie said, "I don't even know him anymore. Since Nick died, he barely talks to me. He's like a stranger, like someone else's son."

"He's on his own now," Kate said. "He's got school, he lives in the city. Kids do that. They grow up and go off on their own. It happens to every parent."

"Does it? Weeks after he and Amanda broke up, he finally told me. I'm like the last person to know what's going on in his life. I sometimes feel childless."

"What was he doing biking in the middle of the night anyway?"

"At a friend's house playing cards." Then she added, "He's got a gambling problem." The moment the words hit the air, she wished she could pull them back.

Kate glared at her in dismay. "He has?"

"He's in debt. I don't know how much, but he's been trying to gamble his way out."

"How do you know that?"

"Bills and overdraft notices used to come to the house till I spoke to him." She shook her head. "I'm a lousy mother."

"No, you're not. And you're not responsible for his financial problems."

"I wish I believed in God so I could pray. I really do."

At the foot of the bed, she spotted Zack's backpack with his laptop in it. He brought it wherever he went because he was working on his master's thesis to meet a deadline. The topic was the influence of Darwinian theory on Mary Shelley's *Frankenstein*. As he had explained it, he was using a core argument in an early Darwin essay, that revenge is the strongest human instinct, and applying that to understanding character motivations in the novel. His main argument was that revenge drove Victor Franken-stein to create life artificially in hopes of killing death.

Maggie looked at the backpack, knowing how much he had put into the paper. Then she began to sob again. Kate put her arm around her. "He'll be back."

Maggie's eyes roamed over the monitors, coming to rest on the orange squiggle monitoring his heart. As she fixed on it, she sent up a silent prayer that there would be billions left in that big stallion heart. "The last time I was here was when he was born. Twenty-four years ago. June six, seven eleven at night. I can still remember when they handed him to me."

"Of course you can," Kate said.

Zack had arrived a week early, while Kate and her husband, Bob, were in California on business. "Did you know he was born with a caul?"

"A caul?"

"Part of the amniotic sac had covered his head. The nurse gasped. I guess she was new and hadn't seen that before. The doctor broke the sac and removed it from his face. Later he said that in olden times a caul was a sign that the baby would have mystical powers."

"I never knew that."

"Others believed it was a sign the child would grow up to be a demon."

"And like most legends, it's just that—an empty legend."

"I suppose, but I wish I hadn't heard that." She glanced at Zack. "Like maybe there's some kind of curse or something."

"Pardon my French, but that's plain bullshit."

Maggie squeezed her hand again. "What if he doesn't wake up?"

Please bring him back, she prayed.

But, ironically, Jake's murderers killed God for her. For a year or more she had stumbled along with her life on autopilot, her will all but extinguished. Eventually she moved out of near lethal grief to a state of semi-numbness in order to raise Zack. Three years after Nick secreted himself in his monastery, a Brother Thomas Albani from the same order showed up with an urn of Nick's ashes. To add insult to injury, the ashes sat on the fireplace mantelpiece at home at Zack's request.

"What if this is punishment?" she asked.

"Punishment for what?"

"For not believing. What if this is God getting back at us?"

"My guess is that this was an accident pure and simple," Kate said. "You're a dedicated teacher who does volunteer work for abused children. If God's in a punishing mood, He's got the wrong person."

3

....

Maggie spent the night in a chair beside Zack's bed. She didn't sleep much, dozing off and waking in fits. Zack did not move throughout the night—his face remained pale and inert, his eyes sealed shut. His only movement was the rise and fall of his chest to the respirator. The only signs that he was alive were the pulsing and squiggles of the monitors.

At one point during the night, the resident doctor asked her to step outside while he, a nurse, and an aide examined Zack. When they were finished, the physician spoke to her. "The good news is that he's still stable and there are no signs of intracranial bleeding."

"Thank goodness," she said. "But when's he going to wake up?"

"He's in an induced coma, so it's hard to predict. He did sustain a serious concussion so we have to wait until the pressure and swelling come down. Then we'll back off on the barbiturates and ventilation."

The word *coma* sent a shard of ice through her heart. "But he will come out of it, right?"

"We certainly hope so."

"You mean he could still remain in a real coma?"

"Well, there's a slight chance, but we don't expect that."

She studied the doctor's eyes and thought she saw another hideous possibility. "What about brain damage?"

"We see no signs at this point, but it's still hard to tell," he said. "But we'll be treating him aggressively."

....

Later that day, the doctors reported that the swelling had gone down in Zack's brain and that they would reduce the barbiturates. It was the best news so far. At Kate's insistence, Maggie overnighted in a hotel nearby instead of commuting to Carleton. Meanwhile, Kate drove to Maggie's place and packed a suitcase of clothes for her.

Sometime before noon, Damian Santoro called Maggie to ask if he, Anthony Lawrence, and his roommate, Geoff Blessington, could come for a visit. She agreed. They arrived in the early afternoon and sat around the bed, staring in disbelief at Zack, who looked like a battered corpse in the bed. Maggie explained how the accident had happened and summarized what the doctors had said.

The news was sobering, but they found solace in the fact that Zack had suffered no internal injuries.

Maggie looked at the three of them. "You're his best friends," she said, "and I'd appreciate you being straight with me. I know he gambles more than he should. I also know that he's fallen into arrears on rent and other matters. I don't mean to put you on the spot, but does he owe any of you money?"

They glanced at one another, each hoping another would take the question. Finally Anthony responded, his eyes fluttering. "No, not much."

"How much, exactly?"

"I don't know . . . maybe . . . four hundred dollars."

Maggie looked to Geoff. "What about you, Geoff?"

"Only about three fifty. But it's not a problem."

"Damian?"

"I think a little over six hundred."

Maggie felt a small stab in the chest. "I'll take care of it." Then she asked, "Besides borrowing from you all, how does he get by?"

"I'm not sure."

"Please, this is no time to cover for him. He's in serious debt."

There was hemming and hawing, then Anthony said, "I think he sometimes sells stuff."

"Sells stuff? Like what?"

"Like his books. Sells them back to the bookstore. Clothes. I don't know for sure."

Maggie did her best to contain her shock. She had regularly sent Zack money, and he was borrowing from friends and selling textbooks. "I appreciate your candidness." She pulled out her checkbook.

"You don't have to do that, Mrs. Kashian," Damian said.

"Thank you for your generosity," she said, and wrote them each a check. "Please be honest with me. Do you think he . . . he has a gambling problem?" She stumbled as she nearly worded the question in the past tense.

Anthony's eyes widened in exaggerated surprise. "Oh no, nothing like that." And he looked to Damian and Geoff for help.

They shook their heads. "It's not like we played every night or anything," Geoff said.

"But something must account for all his debts. Please, if you know something, I'd appreciate your telling me."

After an awkward silence, Damian said, "He may be playing online poker."

She nodded and imagined Zack during the wee hours

of the morning huddled over his laptop, half-deranged to beat the odds.

As if reading her mind, Anthony said, "Mrs. Kashian, I really don't think he's got a gambling problem. It's more like his back's to the wall and he plays to pay down creditors. But I seriously don't think he's addicted."

"Hi," said Kate as she entered the room.

She said hello to the three visitors, then went over and kissed Zack on the forehead. She then convinced Maggie to have lunch downstairs, leaving the three friends to sit with Zack. Anxiety had killed Maggie's appetite, but she realized that she was becoming light-headed from hunger.

....

Half an hour later, they returned to the ICU. When she entered the cubicle, Maggie let out a cry. "What happened?"

Damian was leaning over Zack with his hand on Zack's forehead. "I'm just putting some holy water on his forehead."

"Holy water?" For a shuddering moment, the figure of Damian dabbing Zack's forehead filled Maggie with horror that Zack was being given last rites.

"He's okay," Kate said. "He's still asleep. Look at the monitors."

Maggie stared stupidly at them until her mind caught up. Then she snapped her head at Damian. "Please don't do that," she said. "We're not religious."

Before she could continue, Kate cut in. "That's very nice of you, Damian. Thank you." She put her arm around Maggie, giving her a squeeze to cool it.

Maggie said nothing, but she eyed Damian and the small vial with apprehension. Her disdain for all things religious was palpable. And religious people made her uncomfortable.

A nurse burst into the room. "Is everything all right in here?" She had heard the commotion.

"Yes, everything's fine."

The nurse studied everybody, then checked Zack and the monitors and IV and straightened out his covering as an awkward silence settled over the scene like a skim of ice. Breaking the silence, Kate asked the nurse if there was anything she could do to help.

"Actually, it would help if the next time you brought in a pair of sneakers."

"Sneakers?" Maggie said.

"To protect his feet. God forbid, if his condition persists, his feet will contract. We exercise them, of course, but the shoes keep the toes from balling up."

"But he'll wake up, won't he?" The syllables choked out of Maggie.

"I'm sure he will. It's just a precautionary measure."

Maggie nodded and gave the woman a toxic look to leave the room. She did, and a menacing silence resettled on their collective horror of Zack remaining in a state of indefinite unconsciousness, wearing Nikes to prevent his feet from curling into claws. After a spell, Anthony nodded to Geoff and Damian and announced they were going to leave.

"No offense," Damian said, "but I'm wondering if first we could say a little prayer for Zack."

Before Maggie could respond, Kate said, "I think that would be very nice."

Maggie nodded. "Fine." A little prayer wouldn't hurt, she told herself. And it would make up for her overreaction.

"Thank you," Damian said, then asked everyone to join hands around Zack's bed.

The moment was awkward, and Maggie felt a tinge of discomfort, uncertain if it was guilt for her falling away from her Catholic upbringing or for betraying her conviction that religion was a sham.

"We join our hearts to thank You, Heavenly Father, for Zack's salvation. He lies in a coma, and we pray that You show Your healing powers and restore him . . ."

While he continued, Maggie glanced around the room. Anthony and Geoff were standing with their eyes closed, hands joined to Kate, who also kept her eyes closed. As Maggie's eyes came to rest on Zack, she wished Damian would wrap this up.

"We also pray that You protect his mother and other family members and friends and bring them comfort and hope as they wait and suffer in uncertainty."

Despite herself, Maggie let out a whimper of despair.

"We know that Your Holy Spirit can work miracles and we ask that You restore Zack from his sleep to pursue the great plans You have for him. We ask in the name of Christ Jesus—"

Suddenly Maggie broke. "What miracles? There aren't any. There is no God. Only dumb, stupid luck." She was crying freely now.

Damian hesitated for a moment in shock. Then in a low voice he said, "You really can't be certain of that."

"Where was He for Jake, huh? I prayed with all my heart that God would protect him, and he was killed by two monsters. Where was God then?"

"Maybe for prayers to work you have to believe in them."

"I *did* believe in them, and nobody answered them," she sobbed.

"I have faith."

"Well, I *don't*."

Kate tried to cut her off, but Maggie continued. "If

prayers worked, every coma patient in the world would wake up. Every cancer patient would heal. Every cripple would walk."

"God's healing is not always evident."

Kate tried again to interrupt, but Maggie could not let go, her despair morphing into anger. "It's never evident. Show me a real miracle—make Zack wake up—and I'll believe."

"There's always hope," said Damian.

"Bull."

"Maggie, that's enough!"

But she disregarded Kate. "If something good happens, people claim their prayer was answered. If something bad happens, it's because your prayer wasn't good enough. It's all a sham. God's a sham."

A stunned silence fell over the room as the others gawked at Maggie and Damian. Finally Kate put her arm around Maggie.

Maggie looked up to see the dull hurt in Damian's face and felt the malice drain from her. "I'm sorry," she said. "You meant well. I just . . ." But she could not finish her statement.

Damian smiled weakly. "I understand, and I'm sorry."

Maggie lowered herself into the chair and put her face in her hands as the three visitors mumbled good-byes.

Damian put his hand on Maggie's shoulder. "He'll wake up," he said. "God has faith in him."

Then he exited the room behind the others, his words echoing in Maggie's head.

4

....

Roman Pace swallowed hard. "Forgive me, Father, for I have sinned."

"Would you care to confess your sins, my son?" said Father Timothy Callahan.

"I will if you assure me that what I confess will be held in strict confidence."

"My son, confessional priests are bound by the holy sacrament of penance to be sworn to secrecy. Your sins are between you and God, and I am an intermediary who has no legal obligation to report anything beyond this confession booth."

"You're saying I have your word, because I don't want any repercussions."

"Yes, you have my word. Our vows are sacred. Feel free to make your confession, my son."

There was a moment's pause as the silence of the church filled the dim space. "I'm guilty of murder."

"Of murder?"

"I killed nine people."

"You killed nine people! Is that what you said?"

"Yes, Father, and I'm very sorry."

"Was this in military combat?"

"No, it wasn't."

"Are you a policeman?"

"No."

"So what were the circumstances?"

"Business."

"Business?"

"I used to be a professional assassin."

"A professional assassin?"

"Yes. I was a hit man for criminal organizations."

A long pause filled both sides of the grate.

"Why did you kill these people?"

"For money."

"This is very, very serious. Murder is a mortal sin."

"Yes, I know."

"Did you know the victims personally?"

"No."

"Did it bother you to . . . to take their lives?"

"At the time, not really. I was doing a job."

There was another long pause as the priest turned something over in his head. Then he said, "I assume you no longer need the money and feel contrite?"

"No, I still need money. It's just that I'm concerned about, you know, what's going to happen when I'm gone. To be perfectly frank, I had a mild heart attack a few months ago, and that made me think about dying—you know, about the afterlife and stuff. I just don't want to go to hell, is all."

"I see. Do you believe in hell?"

"I don't really know, but if there is one, I don't want to end up there."

"Do you believe in God the Father Almighty?"

"I think so. And just in case there is a God and a heaven, I want to open up a clear path, if you know what I mean."

"You'd like to make amends."

"Yeah, I want to be forgiven if I can."

"The men you killed, were they bad?"

"To the people who hired me they were."

"Are you a member of this parish?"

"No."

"Another church in the diocese of Providence?"

"I'm sorry to say this is the first time I've been in a church in years."

"I see." Then, after another long pause, the priest said, "What's important is for you to regain God's love and forgiveness."

"I would like that, Father. Very much."

"Fine. I would like you to return in three days so we can talk again. Can you do that?"

"Yes, Father."

"In the meantime, say ten Hail Marys and ten Our Fathers."

"Thank you, Father," said Roman Pace.

"Together we will find a way to salvation for you."

"That's all I ask."

And Roman left the church feeling buoyed in spirit.

5

....

On the fourth day after the accident, they moved Zack to a step-down unit in another ward of the Shapiro Building.

Maggie met with a neurologist, Dr. Peter McIntire, and the head nurse, J. J. Glidden, in a small lounge near Zack's room. Dr. McIntire, a handsome man who looked too young to be a physician, led the discussion. "The good news is that the pressure in his brain has finally normalized."

"What a relief," Maggie said. Yet she could sense a "but" coming.

"We are going to keep him ventilated, however, at least until we're certain he can protect his own airways."

"To breathe on his own," Nurse Glidden added. "At that point, we'll extubate him—remove the respirator."

Maggie nodded.

"Unfortunately, we've taken him off the barbiturates, so it's still a waiting game."

"Isn't there anything you can do . . . you know, some kind of stimulation to wake him. I mean . . ." And she trailed off.

"If there were, we'd do it," Dr. McIntire said. "Technically, he's still in a coma, which is not like being asleep. The brain wave activity is completely different, and we really don't fully understand the comatose state. The thing is, you can wake the sleeper but not the coma patient."

"But," Nurse Glidden added, "Zack could wake up any day now."

Or he could remain in a vegetative state for twenty years, Maggie thought.

Later that day, Maggie rented a room in a nearby motel and came in every morning, despair and hope racking her soul.

Concern for Zack and Maggie poured in. An article appeared in the Northeastern University newspaper about Zack. The school president sent out a global e-mail expressing the university's hope for a speedy and complete recovery. Well-wishers sent flowers and cards. But Maggie allowed only a few close friends and relatives to visit—not until he woke up, she kept saying.

....

The next week passed, and Zack remained in a coma. But because he was stable, his medical staff had him moved out of intensive care to a private room on another floor.

On the tenth day there was more good news: Zack was breathing on his own. Also, because the swelling had subsided, the doctors removed the intracranial pressure gauge; and the bone and skin of his scalp were beginning to heal over. They shaved him regularly and changed his diaper as if he were her baby again.

But he was still in a level two coma. Although he could respond to stimuli—pressure to his fingernails or a sharp poke to the bottom of his feet—he wouldn't respond to spoken commands or open his eyes or squeeze his fingers when asked. Because he was still unconscious, a gastric feeding tube was inserted into his stomach through a small incision in his abdomen. As the doctors explained, this was standard for patients unable to feed normally. He was also put in a special bed that inflated and deflated to prevent bed sores. Braces were attached to his joints to prevent contraction. As requested, Maggie had brought in a pair of Nikes.

By the end of the second week, Maggie could barely restrain panic attacks that Zack would remain in a persistent vegetative state, wasting away while she kept endless bedside vigil like the parents of Karen Ann Quinlan and Terry Schiavo, waiting for him to wake up or die. Already he was gaunt, sunken, and void of the flush of life. But to remind herself of the gorgeous young man he was, she brought in a framed photograph of him she had taken last year at his graduation party. Posed with Damian, Anthony, and Geoff, he glowed with vitality. With his thick ringleted black hair, smooth, high-cheekboned face, and green starburst eyes, he looked like a young Zeus—the same beauty that a long time ago had first attracted her to Nick.

Despite Kate's claims that he could break through at any time, Maggie felt herself slip into dark fears that went back to early motherhood, when she was alert to every potential threat to her children—too high fevers, toys they could choke on, plastic bags. When they got older, she and Nick would take them to Canobie Lake Park, where they would stroll down the lanes thronged with other parents and kids. While they appeared to be having a happy family time, Maggie's mind tripped over the possibilities of her sons being thrown from the Flying Mouse or suffering brain damage from a centrifugal ride or frightened into cardiac arrest in the Haunted House or choking on a candy apple. When they became teenagers, a whole new buffet of horrors presented itself—drugs, alcohol, AIDS, car accidents, school shootings.

With Jake's murder, all her nightmares came true. Adding to the horror, his killers got away with murder, and Nick had descended into an abyss of despair, disappeared into monastic silence, only to die. And now Zack lay in a coma that could go on indefinitely.

It seemed to Maggie that she had become defined by grief in a world that no longer made sense.

6

....

Jenna Emmons could not believe what she had seen. It was bizarre, horrifying, and the image would smolder in her brain for years.

Her first thought was that it was all the beer from the Theta Chi party—maybe four pints. But those were spread over four hours. She was groggy, but not delusional.

She had returned to her dorm around two thirty and changed for bed. As usual, she went to the window to take in the fabulous night view of Boston. Her room was on the fourth floor in MIT's Building W1, at the corner of Massachusetts Avenue and Memorial Drive, in the tower peaked by a cupola shaped like the helmet of Kaiser Wilhelm. It was one of MIT's trophy dorms and a choice locale she had won in the housing lottery.

From that height, she took in the full span of Harvard Bridge, which carried Mass. Avenue across the Charles River into Boston, whose glorious skyline burned like jewelry boxes stacked up from the river's edge to the top of Beacon Hill. Tonight a full moon had risen over the eastern horizon, leaving a rippled disk riding the river's surface.

What arrested her attention were two men walking

on the western side of the bridge from Boston. They stopped a few times to look down at the water, then proceeded until they were about three-quarters across, no more than fifty yards from her window. One man wore a hooded jacket. The other was bareheaded and leaning with his back against the rail. The hooded man gesticulated with his free hand, as if trying to convince the other of something. Then the hooded man helped his companion get up on the rail, where he found his balance. Jenna's first thought was that the hooded man was going to take pictures of his friend with the river and skyline as backdrop. But they continued talking, the hooded man appearing to hold something in his far hand while pleading with the other, who rocked back and forth on the rail like a primate in a too small cage.

Suddenly the men embraced each other for a long moment. The sitting man then braced himself on the rail with his hands. When the hooded man was certain that no cars or strollers approached, he raised a baseball bat and smashed the other on the head.

Even through the closed window, the blow made a sickening crack that sent the victim over the rail and into the black water.

Jenna cried out in horror and disbelief. But what sickened her was the hideous realization that the victim had waited for his companion to bash his head in. That it was on purpose—that they had walked together to just the right spot and waited for the traffic to clear so one could put the other out of his misery.

Before the hooded man walked away, he flung the bat into the water, then looked down to where his friend had fallen and made the sign of the cross.

....

7

On the evening of the twenty-second day, Damian and Anthony stopped by the hospital. They had been back a few more times since the prayer incident, for which Maggie had apologized. And being the gentleman that he was, Damian said he had no hard feelings. He had even brought her a bouquet of flowers.

Zack was still breathing on his own, with his vital signs holding normal. But he was still at level two.

They chatted for a while. Maggie asked how they were doing in school, then told them how physical therapists came in daily to exercise Zack's arms, legs, and feet and how she helped. Anthony was in the middle of a funny story about something that happened at the local mall when Zack suddenly rolled his head and made a strange cawing sound.

"Omigod!" Maggie cried out. Instantly she was on her feet and gripping his hand. "Zack! Wake up. Wake up."

"He's saying something!" Anthony said.

"He's breaking through," Damian said.

"Zack! Zack, wake up!" Maggie cried. "It's Mom. Please, honey. Open your eyes."

Zack's mouth moved as guttural sounds rose from his throat—the first sounds he had made in three weeks. "Get the nurse," Maggie said to Anthony, who bolted from the room. She rubbed Zack's hand. "Zack, it's Mom. Wake up!"

"His eyes are moving," Damian said. "I think he's trying to open them."

"Zack! Open your eyes. You can do it. Open your eyes."

While she continued coaxing him, Zack's eyes rolled under his lids as if he were having an intense dream. But he didn't open them, just kept muttering nonsense syllables.

A few moments later, Anthony returned with a nurse and an aide. The nurse began to rub Zack's cheek. "Zack, it's Beth Howard, your nurse. Talk to me, Zack. Talk to me. Open your eyes."

Zack winced as if registering her voice. He continued muttering unintelligible sounds, but he didn't open his eyes. "Zack, it's Mom. Wake up. Please."

"What's he saying?" Anthony asked Damian.

Damian didn't respond but stood transfixed, studying Zack's face.

"Whatever it is, it's a good sign," said the nurse. The aide agreed, her cell phone in her hand presumably to call the resident. "Hey, Zack, your mom's here. So are Anthony and Damian. Time to wake up. You can do it. Open your eyes."

More mutterings from Zack as his head rolled slightly on the pillow. Maggie put her ear close to his mouth as he continued muttering strange syllables. "He's saying something. He's saying words."

"Does he know a foreign language?" the nurse asked.

"He took a year of Spanish, but that's not what it sounds like."

Anthony leaned over Zack. "Hey, bro, it's Anthony. Come out of there. We got some partying to do."

But Zack made no response to the promptings, just continued muttering.

"It's just gibberish," Anthony said. "I do that when I sleep, too."

"No, it's not," Damian whispered. "He's speaking in tongues."

"Tongues. What's that?" Anthony asked.

"Glossolalia."

"Glossowhat?"

"Glossolalia," Damian said in a voice barely audible. "The Holy Spirit is speaking through him."

"Cut the crap," Anthony said as the nurse's aide gawked at Zack. "It's nothing."

Damian nodded and fell silent.

Through a broken voice, Maggie continued to beg Zack to wake up, but after several minutes he fell silent again.

And anguish raked through her soul as Zack's mouth stopped moving and his eyes fell still and he sank back into a deep sleep.

Although there were no changes in him, the nurse said it was a good sign that he tried to talk, tried to break through. There would be another time.

She and the aide replaced his IV and checked the monitors. Then the others resumed their vigil around Zack in his coma as acceptance settled over them like snow.

"False alarm," the nurse said, and left the room.

8

....

No false alarm. He could hear voices.

His first thought was that he was dreaming. That he was in bed in his apartment, and faceless people were in his room telling him it was time to get up and go to class, to work on his thesis—his deadline was closing in—to get a job, to stop gambling . . .

Voices. Lots of them, some he recognized. His mother. Aunt Kate. Anthony. Damian. Geoff. Beth Howard, his nurse. Also voices he didn't recognize telling him dumb stuff like to wiggle his toes and squeeze their fingers and open his eyes. He tried to tell them that he was stuck in a foolish dream, that he'd wake soon and get hustling.

But as in all dreams, he had no control. He could hear them but couldn't respond. Couldn't open his eyes. Couldn't move. It was as if he had become afflicted with some kind of paralysis. But that happened in dreams, like his legs freezing when he was being chased. He couldn't just shake himself awake. And just as weird was how things moved in dreams, how the familiar world took on non-Cartesian logic, non-Euclidean geometry, and how gravity could be suspended.

Like the snap of a finger, he found himself bodiless and floating above his bed—

no, not his bed, not the one in his apartment, with the blue paisley spread his mother had bought, but a bed all in white in a strange room with colorless walls and IVs dripping and flickering, beeping machines—

and all those people were standing around him making demands. He could see them. And he could see himself in the bed, but from above, as if he were some kind of ectoplasm hovering in the air, and below was himself: dead asleep, eyes shut, face colorless and shrunken, head roughly shaven and cocked on a pillow, arms gaunt and limp by his sides, with tubes and wires running from them and his gut to drips and bags and monitors like so many umbilical cords.

A hospital room, of course. He was asleep in a hospital room for unknown reasons.

And his mother was holding his hand and weeping. Also Anthony—a big guy with pecs like gladiator plates and biceps like muskmelons, fidgeting over his bedridden pal—and beside him Geoff, whose big toothy grin and exuberant face had given way to a solemn mask as he, too, beheld the sleeping figure. And Damian—pale, lean, angular Damian with that sincere ascetic face and premature bald spot, looking like a monk in a medieval painting before the reposed figure in sainthood.

"Glossowhat?"

"Gibberish."

Anthony. He recognized the voice, but the view outside was wrong. Nothing lay beyond the window. No buildings, no grasslands, no river, no woods—as if fog had clotted the view. Then someone in a low voice said, *"This is good. Right here."* The next moment, the wind blew sand in his face, filling his eyes and mouth. And his chest felt as if something were threatening to press the life out of him.

Can't breathe. Can't breathe, and mouth filling.

"Open your eyes. Open your eyes."

Can't. Got sand in them. Can't breathe. Chest crushed. Heart's stopped.

Why was this happening? What did they want from him?

Then the lights went on and they were all around him, dressed like picture cards—jacks and kings and queens, black and red, spots all over them—as if he were being hauled away by creatures from some Lewis Carroll looking-glass world. And one jack raised his spade and brought it down full force onto his face, disintegrating into granules that filled his eyes, mouth, and ears. And all went black.

It's God's punishment.

He floated above the scene and could see the bloody knob of his head, a broken bicycle on the street, lights, and people swarmed around the twisted body in the gutter.

"Wake up. Please wake up."

His mother. She was calling to him over the vast expanse. She wanted him to open his eyes. But every time he did, they would fill with sand.

Then he found himself alone again, moving down a gauzy, featureless corridor. But, strangely, he couldn't feel his feet or solid ground under his shoes (a bright white pair of Nikes!). Yet he was moving through a dim tunnel as if traversing some realm between consciousness and unconsciousness—or maybe this world and the next. As he moved toward the light, he became aware of how totally alone he was. No more voices, no more people, no more sense of his family and friends by his side. Alone in this funnel of mist.

Then that changed.

Suddenly he became aware of another's presence—as if someone had sidled up to him. He looked around but saw no one, just the gray nothingness. Yet he knew in his heart of hearts that someone else was near him just beyond the threshold of perception.

As he proceeded, he heard a voice, a familiar voice, saying something in a language he couldn't decipher. And it was coming from the bright end ahead of him. He picked up his pace, and the harder he listened, the more familiar the voice sounded, but the words were meaningless.

As the light got brighter, he stirred, feeling the softness of the bed beneath him. Summoning every fiber of will, he forced open his eyes. Caked with matter, they cracked open to the light. Bright white light. White walls. White ceiling. White sheets. The impressions of his legs running down the length of the bed. Tubes. Wires, beeps. The same hospital room, of course. And with a burst of air he woke himself up.

"Dad?"

The room was empty. Soundless but for the muffled beeps of machines. But the single syllable resonated in his ears. Alone, he closed his eyes to get back. A moment later, he slipped back into the tunnel, now lost in darkness.

False alarm.

9

On the third day, Roman Pace returned to St. Pius Church just outside of Providence. He had no idea why he had been asked to return for his penance or to further confer with the priest. But he feared a setup.

It was a Tuesday morning, and he showed up two hours early. The church parking lot was empty, and so were the few cars parked on the street of the residential neighborhood. He drove around the block several times, finally convinced that cops weren't staked out anywhere. He entered the church fifteen minutes before ten. The interior was empty, and two candles burned up front. The only other light streamed through the stained-glass windows.

He walked the full length of the nave to be certain that he was alone. No one, not even the priest, was in sight. He went outside again and saw nobody. And the sixth sense that years in his trade had honed did not alert him to an ambush. When satisfied, he went back inside and entered the confessional to wait for the priest. Even if police were staked out, he had not incriminated himself.

He carried no weapon. In fact, he had not carried one

since his last kill. That was four months ago, when he had suffered a heart attack and decided to give up contract work. Yes, he missed the money because the recession had hurt his auto body business as people stopped coming in with dings, dents, and fender benders. Furthermore, as an independent, he could not compete with chains that cut pricing deals with insurance companies. Nearing his fifty-second year, he reminded himself, while sitting in the confessional, that his father had died of a coronary thrombosis at fifty-five and his mother a year later of a stroke.

What had brought him to this booth the other day was his reaching out to God. Lying in that hospital bed four months ago and fearing he was going to die, he had sent up a prayer from the bottom of his soul that he would give up the killing if God would spare his life. The next night, he could have sworn that Jesus had appeared to him. It was probably just a dream, because he looked like the Jesus in the picture his mother had on her bureau—a tall figure in white standing on a hillside with people gathered around his feet, listening. And beneath it the Ninety-first Psalm. He could still recall the words:

He shall call upon me, and I will answer him:
I will be with him in trouble;
I will deliver him, and honor him.
With long life will I satisfy him,
And show him my salvation.

But as Roman sat in the dim light waiting for the priest, he recalled the promise of those words and the bargain he had made. He had fully recovered, certain in the belief that God had answered his prayer and forgiven him. Certain that while he lay in his hospital bed, God had visited him like one of the guys from the body shop or softball team. And he knew because he could feel something happen inside his soul—something that told him that God was real. And that God had actually loved him enough to have intervened, telling him, *You still have some work to do, so let me help clean you up.*

A little after ten, Roman heard someone enter the other side. Because of the low light and screen, he couldn't see the profile of Father Callahan.

"Good morning, my son."

"Good morning, Father," Roman said. Then he began: "Forgive me, Father, for I have sinned." The words tumbled out of his mouth like gravel. It was the second time in forty years he had uttered them.

"Would you care to confess your sins, my son?"

The voice did not sound like that of Father Timothy Callahan. This was a different priest. "I was here three days ago."

"Yes, I know," the voice replied. "But I still need to hear your confession."

Roman felt his chest clench. A setup—the guy on the other side was a fucking cop, his backup hiding in the pews or behind the altar. "You're not Father Callahan."

"No, I'm not. I'm a brother in spirit and am bound by the same vows of confidentiality. Father Callahan is a new priest and shared with me the special circumstances. But I can assure you that what is said in this confessional is strictly confidential."

Brother in spirit? "What about Father Callahan? How can I trust that he's not shared my confession with others?"

"He hasn't. He's bound by the holy sacrament and his sacred vows."

Maybe Roman's sins were so awful that the young priest had to call in a heavy hitter—a bishop, maybe, or even a cardinal. "I've committed mortal sins."

"God will hear your sins."

"I killed some people and want to redeem myself."

"I see. It's good that you want redemption. Let us pray that God forgives you for your sins and gives you guidance and strength."

Through the decorative grate, Roman could hear the man praying. The last time Roman was in the presence of a priest was when he was a teenager. His mother had made him go to church, and he'd hated every moment of it—an hour plus of mumbo-jumbo, half in Latin, half in bloated threats. The only matters that held his attention were stories about saints being crucified or roasted alive. For more Sundays than he cared to count, he sat numb-butted on hard pews that smelled of Murphy's Oil Soap. But instead of losing himself in it all, he watched others lock into complex rituals of praying, kneeling, standing, and crossing themselves. And never once did he feel any mystery or peace—just near terminal boredom, surrounded by a lot of people going through the motions out of duty, fear, and hope. As for confession, he went because Father Infantino insisted he go. That had always struck him as silly—a way to shed guilt and get a free pass to sin some more.

Now, sitting in this oaken box, he could not repress a deep unease that took him back to those days at St. Luke's at the south end of Hartford, where Father Infantino tried to pound the fear of God into his adolescent brain.

"Were you were raised Roman Catholic?"

"Yes—early on."

"So, you strayed from your faith."

"Something like that."

"What made you choose this parish to return?"

"I guess it's like the traditional Catholicism I grew up with."

From what he knew, St. Pius Church still held sacred pre–Vatican II dogma, resisting efforts to modernize the Church—holding fast to the sanctity of the literal Bible, the Latin mass, the dress codes for women, the firm stand on divorce, and the conviction that there was no salvation for those outside the Roman Catholic Church. The parish also rejected reconciliation with the Jews. From what Roman had heard, St. Pius Church was a small, white, conservative enclave of traditionalist worshippers who upheld Catholic purity within a Church that had become too liberal and a culture that rejected God's Word. Given his sins, Roman figured that he needed a ministry of severe unction.

"Then we welcome you back, my son, but know that your sins are very heavy."

"I know and I'm asking forgiveness."

"Good, and no matter how heavy, there is a way back to God, my son."

"Thank you, Father."

"But for such special circumstances, special sanctions are necessary. Do you believe in God the Father Almighty and his son Jesus Christ our savior?"

"Yes."

"Do you believe that God answers prayers?"

"Yes, and I ask that He save my soul."

"He will because God sees you and He loves you. And He will welcome you home."

Roman took in the comfort of those words. "Thank you, Father."

"Do you believe in evil?"

"Evil?" The question caught him off guard. "I guess. There's a lot of it out there."

"So it seems. Do you believe in the devil?"

"No, not really."

"So you believe only people are evil."

"Yeah. Because evil is what people do, what gives them pleasure."

"I see. Did you get pleasure from your profession?"

Roman picked up on the careful wording, though he was beginning to wonder about the direction of the interrogation. "It was a job, and I was good at it."

"You did it for money, correct?"

"Yes."

"And what do you think are the motivations of evil?"

"I never thought about that. I guess lots of motivations—power, money . . ."

"No, only one: revenge. It is the one true source of evil in the world. All other motivations—power, money, lust—they're mere variations. Revenge. It's what Satan taught mankind. It's his sole motive: getting back at God. You plied your trade to get back at the economic inequities in your life, correct?"

Plied your trade. The guy was being discreet, knowing that Roman was looking for any sign of a trap. "I guess you can look at it that way."

"Revenge against higher forces," he whispered. "It's the same motive behind Satan's attempt to overthrow God. It's what Satan did to get back once ousted from heaven. It's still what he does, filling the world with evil in vengeance against God. If you believe in God, my son, belief in Satan is only a half step away. He's as real as you and I."

All Roman could think to say was, "Okay."

"Would you like to reinstate your soul with God?"

"That's why I'm here."

"Would you like to reconcile your life of sin with God, to make up for your transgressions?"

"If I can, yeah."

"You can, but you must believe completely. And if you have any doubt in God's love and forgiveness, you must ask yourself if your disbelief is worth forfeiting eternal life in paradise. And that's what hell is—never waking up, being dead forever and not knowing it. But for those who believe, heaven is living forever in the eternal awareness of God's love."

Roman was losing him. "Okay."

"And you are wrong about evil being solely the acts of man. The greatest evil is the handiwork of Satan—Satan, the Great Deceiver. Satan, who leads man astray. Satan, whose greatest trick was convincing the world that he doesn't exist. Satan, who stands in the way of your own salvation."

Now the guy was going off on a tangent.

"Do you know about Saint Michael?"

"No."

"Saint Michael was the perfect Christian soldier, the archangel of God who led forces against the darkness of evil led by Satan. He is the defender of God and the protection of the Holy Catholic Church."

"Uh-huh." Roman wished the guy would give him his Hail Marys and let him leave.

"Your being here is not an accident. God sent you to earn your way to salvation by following the path of Saint Michael through the darkness into the eternal light of heaven."

"I'm not sure what you're telling me."

"I'm telling you that a mission of salvation is before you."

"What mission?"

"To be a warrior for the Lord God Almighty, Mr. Pace."

Mr. Pace. "How do you know my name?"

"That's not important."

Roman wondered if maybe a security camera outside the church had recorded his license plate and they had somehow had access to the RMV database.

"What is important is that you accept this mission to redeem yourself in defense of the Lord Jesus Christ."

More silence filled the booth. "What are you asking me?"

"To ply your trade in the name of the Lord."

It must have taken the better part of a minute for Roman to absorb what the man was saying. "You want me to whack Satan?"

"No, one of Satan's doormen. Someone who's blasphemed against the Lord God Almighty."

"This is crazy. Who are you? How do you know me?"

"None of that's important." Then the small door at the base of the grille slid back and the priest's hand slid through a plain brown envelope that was as thick as a brick. "Please open it."

Roman did. Inside was $15,000 in three banded five-grand packs of hundred-dollar bills.

"This is yours, and so is salvation should you accept this mission."

Roman looked at the money, feeling the heft. He placed the pack on the sill between them. He still could not see the priest's face—if he was a priest. "This isn't what I came for."

"I'm sure, but your coming was a godsend."

"That's a lot of money," he said, feeling his resolve slip. "So, what exactly did he do?"

"He and his associates are offending the Lord in the worst possible way."

Roman muffled a chuckle with a *humpf*. "What's worse than murder?"

"Blasphemy against the Holy Spirit. And God is asking you to be His warrior and is offering you a second chance at life eternal."

A second chance at life eternal.

"Right." As a result of all his years of contract killing,

Roman had lost the capacity for surprise, but this was a first—hired by a priest to be a hit man for the Lord.

He had a dozen questions, but in private contract work you didn't ask why someone had to be whacked. The hit was strictly business. But he was intrigued. He was also cautious. "How do I know this isn't some kind of setup, you have a recorder in there taking it all in?"

"It's not a setup, and nobody is recording this exchange. Besides, you have confessed to no specific killing—so there's nothing that has incriminated you."

Roman hadn't confessed to any killing. He looked at the packs of bills. "Let's say I decide to do this, I'll need information and stuff."

A second, thinner envelope appeared atop the packet of money. Then that was topped by a cell phone. "Full instructions as well as a cell phone to call with your report."

Jesus, this was a fucking sting. But unlike anything he could have possibly dreamed up.

"Whether or not you believe in the devil, you have been called to the highest service of the Lord to defeat him. You have been chosen to soldier for the Lord, and in so doing earning your way back to Him. Do you accept this mission?"

Roman looked at the fat wad of hundreds and the cell phone waiting for him. He could not determine if the guy was serious or nuts. "You haven't told me who you are. I don't know what the hell I'm dealing with here."

"You're dealing with a servant of the Lord who will remain anonymous."

A second chance at life eternal.

"And this guy is really bad?"

"In the eyes of God, the worst."

Roman picked up the envelope of bills, and in his head he heard the words of the psalm in his mother's voice: *Because he hath set his love upon Me, therefore will I deliver him: / I will set him on high, because he had known My name.*

"Fine," Roman said, and pocketed the envelopes and phone.

"May the Lord bless you in this mission. May He show you the lighted path back home and grant you eternal life."

"Thank you, Father," Roman said, and left the confession booth and walked out of the church and into the warm glow of the morning sun.

Even if the mission stuff was all bullshit and Father X was wired, there was $15,000 in the envelope, and Roman had said nothing to take to the cops.

10

....

It was Good Friday, and Maggie had sat with Zack throughout much of the night. There were no changes, and he had not repeated his mutterings. She was exhausted, and on the nurse's suggestions, she went down to the café on the ground floor. She had coffee and a muffin, feeling numb, as if the core of her body had been infused with Novocain. While in the cafeteria, she tried to get lost in a copy of *The Boston Globe* that someone had left on the table.

The news of the wars and the economy filled most of the front pages, so she turned to Section B and the local news. A strange headline caught her eye: SUICIDE BY FRIEND: VICTIM HAD RARE PUFFER FISH TOXIN IN HIS BLOOD.

The story went on to explain that a homeless man was found dead with the toxin in his system. He had been killed with a baseball bat while sitting on the rail of Harvard Bridge. Because of surveillance cameras, the batman had been apprehended, claiming that his friend had asked to be killed because he had been plagued by "demons" in his head, the result, according to the assailant, of scientists doing experiments on his brain. How he had acquired "tetrodotoxin" was unknown, but authorities assured the public that it was not a new street drug, nor was puffer fish legal in American cuisines. "The perpetrator could not give any explanation of who the scientists were or what experiments were performed on the victim, only that they paid well."

Maggie folded the paper, thinking how she, too, had a demon in her head—the sick certainty that she would never have her son back.

After half an hour, she finished her coffee and walked to the elevators. Ahead of her were a middle-aged couple and their teenage daughter in a wheelchair. The girl appeared to be a victim of some neurological disorder. Her mouth hung open and her head moved loosely on her neck, and she made inarticulate sounds. Clutched in her fingers was a string of rosary beads.

Maggie went to push the button to the seventh floor, but it was already lit.

"Are you here to see Zachary?" the father asked.

The question caught Maggie off guard. "Pardon me?" *Zachary?* No one called him that. And how did they know about her son?

"Zachary Kashian. Are you going to him?"

"Yes," she said, wondering about his strange wording. He was about fifty and was dressed in brown pants, blue blazer, and plaid shirt buttoned to the top. She did not recognize him. "Do you know him?"

The elevator door closed as they started to ascend. "We're friends with Zachary in Jesus. We're here to pray for him."

Before Maggie could respond, the woman looked at Maggie. "We're bringing Agnes to him."

The man held out his hand. "I'm Burt Wickham, and this is my wife, Judy, and my daughter, Agnes. Are you here to be healed?"

"I'm his mother, and I don't know what you're talking about."

The man made a sheepish smile. "Oh well, we'll pray for you too in your suffering. The Word of God penetrates where nothing else can go."

"Look, I don't know your intention, but my son is in a coma in a private room and no visitors are allowed."

"But this is very important," he said. "We've been praying for a sign like this for years."

"What sign?"

The man looked at her in surprise. "How can you not know? God is speaking through your son, announcing to the world that he's been chosen to do God's healing."

"What are you talking about? My son's in a coma."

"We know. We saw him."

"What do you mean you saw him?"

Then the daughter muttered, "On YouTube."

The elevator door opened and they stepped into an empty foyer. "YouTube?"

"He's a chosen," the wife said. "He's got the power."

The mother produced a BlackBerry and held it up to Maggie. On the small screen was a brief and shaky video of Zack in bed muttering nonsense syllables. The moving banner beneath the image read: "God Speaks Through Coma Patient."

"He's speaking the tongue of the Lord."

Maggie looked at the image, dumbfounded. Her first thought was Damian. He had shot the footage of Zack muttering nonsense syllables with his cell phone. How could he do that to Zack? Violate his privacy in his most vulnerable state?

"God chose Zachary to work His miracles, which is why we're here," the wife said, and she looked toward her daughter in the wheelchair.

"I'm sorry for your daughter, but you cannot visit my

son. He's in a private room, and no one but family are allowed. Is that clear?" She ran down the hall to the nurses' station to ask for security, but the station was empty. Then she heard a commotion down the cross-corridor. Her heart nearly stopped. Outside of Zack's room was a small crowd of people arguing with Nurse Beth Howard, two other nurses, and a resident physician, all trying to keep people from pushing inside.

"What is going on?" Maggie said to Beth. "Call security."

"We did."

Maggie pushed her way inside the room, where maybe a dozen people were pressed around Zack's bed—elderly, young, old, white, brown. A small woman with Down syndrome was pawing at Zack's arm as a camera flash went off. Through the bodies, she could see with relief that Zack was still breathing and that the monitors still registered his vital signs. But his blanket was covered with rosary beads, prayer cards, religious trinkets, statues, and photographs. And around him were people muttering prayers and crossing themselves, touching his hands and face.

Maggie felt insane. "Get out of here!" she screamed. "This is my son. Get out of here!"

"I have a tumor," one woman said. "All I want is to be healed." Her mouth quivered as she pleaded.

Another beside her said, "Jesus is here to make me better. I don't want to die."

A man pressed against her insisted that a divine presence was in Zack. "We want Jesus to save my wife. She's very sick."

"Then get a doctor and leave my son alone." As Maggie pushed her way deeper, she spotted a tall white woman looking out of place in a navy blue suit. She stood in the corner behind the others, staring at Maggie intently.

There was a reddish birthmark on her cheek or maybe a melanoma.

The shouting of security guards filled the room. "Okay, everybody clear out." Half a dozen guards were pulling people out of the room as protests rose up.

"You have no right," one woman cried.

"The Lord Jesus Christ is speaking through Zachary," cried another. "It's in the video. I saw it with my own eyes."

But the guards cleared the room in spite of the pleas and protests. As the people were led out, one woman grabbed Maggie's arm. "She's here! She's here!" The woman's eyes were huge.

"Who?" Maggie asked.

"The Blessed Virgin. I smell roses. They're her flower." The woman looked crazed.

Maggie pulled away toward the bed when a guard caught her arm. She turned. "I'm his mother!"

From the hall, Nurse Beth shouted confirmation to the guard. He let Maggie go and continued removing the others. She gasped when she reached Zack. He had not been disturbed by the melee, and the monitors blinked stable life functions. But the bedcover was strewn with religious objects and dozens of photographs of people, making it look like the shrine of a dead saint.

Beth took her arm. "I'm so sorry. We'll clean it up. They must have come up through the back stairwell."

"There's a video of him on the Internet."

"Shit."

Less than twelve hours had passed, and a fifty-second YouTube video of his nonsense mutterings had summoned a small mob hungering for miracles. "I think it was Damian."

"No. It was Stephanie, my aide."

"What?"

"She had her cell phone, but I thought it was to call the desk. I'm sorry. I don't know what she was thinking, but I can't believe she did this."

"Where is she?"

"It's her day off, but we'll report her to the chief administrator."

"I want him moved to an undisclosed room with guards."

"Of course."

Beth took Maggie's arm and led her outside while orderlies began to remove the stuff from the bed. The halls had been cleared, and several security guards patrolled the corridors. Maggie walked with Beth to the nurses' station, where someone handed her a coffee.

As she made her way back down the hall, she spotted the tall, stylish woman with the birthmark at the elevators. The woman glared at her. A moment later, the elevator light went on and the door opened. Before stepping inside, the woman said something.

"Pardon me?"

"I pray that your son is a miracle child."

Before Maggie could respond, the woman entered the elevator and was gone.

11

....

Satan's doorman lived in a large Tudor home on Green-dale Road in Falmouth on Cape Cod. Roman Pace sat in his car on a small parallel street beside a vacant lot that allowed a clear view of the rear of the house.

Roman never met those who hired him—just anonymous telephone calls and cash delivered to a drop spot. It was a good arrangement, since anonymity kept things discreet and simple without the chance of compromise. Roman had no idea if the guy on the other side of the confessional booth was a priest, a bishop, or Friar Tuck. But he wasn't Father Timothy Callahan. And after a week it made no difference, because a part of Roman began to believe that he was, in fact, in service to God. The same part that began to believe that God Himself had directed Roman to that confessional booth in the first place.

Your chance to reinstate your soul with God.

It was a promise that he latched on to.

The rear end of a detached garage had a window that allowed a view of the interior, not that he cared about the contents. The garage door was open, and twenty minutes ago the headlights of a white Lexus had lit up the window as the owner pulled in and then entered the house through the rear door. The neighbors looked to be away, maybe because it was Easter weekend.

After fifteen minutes, Roman exited his rental and walked to the front of the house. Lights burned on the first floor and in one bedroom room on the second. The entrance was flanked with leaded windows through which he could see a foyer, but no movement. He rang the doorbell, and an outside light went on. A moment later, an old guy opened the door. "Sorry to disturb you, but are you Dr. Thomas Pomeroy?"

"Yes."

He was listed as seventy-one and looked it. His face was lean and pale, with loose flesh under the chin. He had dark, baggy eyes and receding gray hair. He was dressed in chinos and a long-sleeved T-shirt. His expression projected annoyance. "My name is Roman Pace, and I've got a message from Thomas Infantino."

"Who?"

"Thomas Infantino." And with his left hand, Roman handed Pomeroy a stiff manila envelope with his name printed in bold letters. As Pomeroy took the envelope, Roman pulled a pistol from his jacket and pressed it against Pomeroy's middle. "I think we best discuss this inside."

"W-what are you doing?"

"Inside, and not a peep." Pomeroy's face froze in shock and horror, but he backed into the foyer, and Roman closed the door behind him.

"What do you want? Who are you?"

"I'll ask the questions."

A red Oriental carpet filled the foyer, which was lit by a glass chandelier. A set of dark stairs ran up to the second landing, where a light burned in the room at the top right. "Is anyone else in the house?"

"No."

"Your wife?"

"My wife is dead."

This was true, and his daughter lived in Arizona, and he had no other children according to the spec sheet. "Other relatives? Live-in housekeeper?"

"N-no. I'm alone. Who are you? You want money? I can give you some." He made a move toward the staircase.

But Roman stopped him. "I don't want your money." He nudged the man into the living room—a space with dark-wood bookshelves, a black baby grand piano, and a maroon leather sofa and matching chairs—and directed Pomeroy to the sofa.

Pomeroy did as he was told, his face ashen with terror. Roman sat on the leather chair facing him. "I want you to tell me stuff," he said. "And if I like your answer, I'll make this easy for you."

Pomeroy looked into the stolid eye of the Beretta. "Okay, but please don't—"

Roman raised his finger. "Shhh. Cooperate, and nobody'll get hurt. Okay?"

"Okay, okay."

"Are you a religious man, Dr. Pomeroy?"

"What?"

"I asked, are you a religious man?"

Pomeroy hesitated. "No."

"Have you had any dealings with St. Pius Church in Providence, Rhode Island?"

"No, I've never even heard of that."

"What about the name Timothy Callahan?"

"No."

"Do you believe in God?"

"No."

"Okay. Do you believe in Satan?"

Bafflement clouded Pomeroy's face. "No."

"Look, you're a big-time physicist with awards up to here. So how come someone in the Catholic Church wants you dead?"

An involuntary squeal rose from his lungs. "I don't know. Please don't kill me. I'll pay you anything you want."

According to online sites, Pomeroy was celebrated for solving some problems involving magnetic resonance, resulting in hospital machines that improved the imaging of cancer cells. Apparently it was a big breakthrough, because several news releases announced articles he had coauthored in the *Journal of Chemical Physics* and elsewhere. Roman grasped the importance of Pomeroy's work, though he couldn't imagine why in the eyes of the Catholic Church it was an abomination.

The man continued to beg.

"You have cash in the house?"

"Yes, yes, in a small safe upstairs."

Roman snapped on a pair of latex gloves. "Let's go." He kept the gun to the guy's back as he followed him up to a bedroom, where he opened the door of a closet. On the floor sat a small safe, the kind you'd find in hotels. "If there's an alarm trigger, consider yourself dead."

"No, no alarm up here. Just the back door."

Roman watched as Pomeroy twirled through the combination, opened the safe, and pulled out four packs of bound fifties and hundreds—$5,000.

Roman took them and put them into his jacket pocket. "Fine. You just bought the rest of your life. Downstairs."

They walked down the stairs and back into the living room.

"We're going to make this look like a break-in, so I need to tie you up. I'll call 911 from the road. *Capice?*"

"Yes."

He then bound Pomeroy's legs together with plastic ties. The same with his wrists, but over his shirt to avoid marks. He put a washcloth across his eyes, then secured it with a small bungee cord. He then had him lie flat on the floor with a sofa pillow under his head.

According to the spec sheet, Pomeroy had a history of arrhythmia and was taking medication for high blood pressure and cholesterol. Actuarial statistics would give him a higher than 70 percent chance of dying by cardiac arrest. That narrowed the options to one.

And that came from a plant that grew four thousand miles south of Cape Cod in the rain forests of the Amazon—curare, a vine whose compound was used by local Indians to poison their arrows and blowgun darts. Also known as tubocurarine chloride, the substance upon injection caused paralysis of skeletal muscles, resulting in respiratory failure and death. With the standard autopsy, no trace of the compound would be detected, and the cause of death would be listed as cardiac arrest.

You're a warrior of God, a voice whispered in Roman's head. *Like St. Michael.* "Okay, lie still." For a man of 170 pounds, it took about seven minutes. In that time, the victim would remain conscious but incapable of sucking in a breath of air. He would die of asphyxiation. To appear natural, the body could not have any marks of struggle. And because the toxin had to be injected, not even the prick of the needle could be visible on the autopsy table. Special circumstances demanded special strategies.

Roman moved into the next room and filled a syringe with 4cc curare. When he returned, he knelt beside Pomeroy on the couch. "Before I leave, I have a couple of questions. Is there anything in your research that would be a problem to the Catholic Church?"

"No, I told you that."

"How about any government agency or whatever?"

"No."

"Any personal enemies or associates?"

"Not that I can think of."

He could see Pomeroy relax into the expectation that it would be over soon, that Roman would wrap up the break-in scene and leave. In his head, Roman rehearsed the next step. "One more thing . . ."

"What?"

"Shouldn't have lost your faith." In one smooth move, he threw himself full length onto Pomeroy's body, jamming the needle deep into his left nostril and depressing the syringe with his thumb. Pomeroy's body jolted under Roman as he let out a thin scream. Roman pulled the needle out of his face while trying to keep his body from bucking him onto the floor. The washcloth and bungee slid off Pomeroy's face in the thrashing, and Roman did all he could to prevent the man from leaving any telltale bruises for the coroner to ponder.

Because the compound was rated six out of six in toxicity, in less than a minute Pomeroy's torso and legs stiffened. His eyes bulged like cue balls and his mouth went slack, incapable of sucking in a breath. In seconds he had turned into a warm corpse, his legs giving an occasional twitch and his eyelids settling to slits of jelly.

Roman spread him out on the couch. He removed the tethers and adjusted Pomeroy's clothing and feet until he looked like a man who had died from a heart attack while reading a magazine. He removed a copy of *Time* from the coffee table and positioned it on the floor. When he was finished, Roman looked back at the dead man. "So how come you're Satan's doorman?"

Whatever, Roman did not feel closer to God, just twenty grand richer. He disarmed the rear door and slipped out into the night.

Half an hour later, he pulled into the scenic parking area along Route 6A.

During the day, dozens of fishermen would be perched on the rocks below, casting their lines for stripers. At ten at night, only one diehard kept at it. Motoring down the canal from the waters of Boston Harbor was a long, sleek sailing vessel. One of these days, he would buy himself a piece like that and set course for Bermuda. Roman pulled out the secure cell phone provided him by the guy in the confessional and punched in the number given to him.

A male voice answered with a simple, flat, "Yes?"

"Mission accomplished."

"Good. And in the manner prescribed?"

The voice sounded like that of Father X. "Yes."

"We're very grateful for your service. And so is the Lord God. You're cleansing your soul and moving closer to eternal life, my brother."

Roman felt something quicken inside, and it wasn't the priestly kind of talk that embarrassed him as a kid. "Mean we're not done?"

"In a few days you'll hear from us. Thank you, my son." And the man clicked off.

For a moment, Roman stared at the dead cell phone in disbelief. Then he folded it and slipped it into his jacket pocket. So there was more.

Below, the fisherman reeled in a striper. Working in the lights of the parking lot, he held the line with one hand, netting it with the other and hauling it onto the rocks. It looked under regulation size, twenty-nine inches, but after removing the hook from its mouth, he tossed it into a cooler.

Roman took a swig of his bottled water. As he watched the yacht slide down the dark expanse of the canal, the thought of a second assignment set off a giddy sensation in his gut. Maybe another fifteen grand. And maybe another millennium in paradise.

He looked out over the water, the shore lights on the far bank reflecting off the black surface. He thought about how interesting life had become of late. He raised his eyes to the sky. Above the black eastern horizon, stars began to emerge in the dark as if blown in by the sea. He sucked in the crisp salt air and took in the night. Above the far horizon, he saw a shooting star.

Thank you, God.

12

....

"The last thing I need is a bunch of religious fanatics flocking around him like he's Our Lady of Lourdes," Maggie said.

"Well, they won't get to him anymore," Kate said.

They were sitting in the hospital café the morning after the incident. Zack had been moved to another room in a different ward, known only to a handful of staff and family. At Maggie's insistence, the hospital had posted a guard outside his room around the clock. "If he was such a healing force, you'd think it'd occur to them that he'd wake himself up."

"Logic doesn't appear to be their strong suit," Kate said, sipping her coffee.

"Whatever. I'm not sure I'll be by Sunday." That was Easter, and Kate usually hosted a meal, less as a religious celebration than as an occasion for a family gathering.

"Maybe you can stop by for dessert after the hospital."

Maggie nodded, distracted by something in her sister's manner. And she was certain that missing Easter dinner wasn't the issue. "Is everything okay?"

Kate looked at her for a moment as she turned something over in her head. "Yesterday Bob dropped in on a friend, Art Avedisian, in Harvard's Department of Near Eastern Languages."

Bob taught French literature at Wellesley College. "Yeah?"

"Well, he showed him the video of Zack."

Maggie was suddenly alert. "Yeah."

"It wasn't glossolalia."

"Of course not. It was plain gibberish."

"Actually, it wasn't gibberish. It was Aramaic."

"Aramaic? Isn't that some ancient language?"

"Yes, and the native tongue of Jesus Christ."

"What?"

"According to Bob's friend, who's a scholar and an expert on Aramaic, it's still spoken in small parts of the Middle East. He says Zack spoke it in an older dialect."

All Maggie could say was, "What?"

Kate nodded. "That's what he claims."

"Well, that's not possible. He's wrong. Zack doesn't know any ancient languages. That's absurd."

"I'm just telling you what he said. He also translated what he could make out." She removed a notepad from her handbag. "I guess he was repeating several phrases: 'Father, with You everything is possible. Take this cup from me. Yet not what I will, but what You will.' Then Zack recited the Lord's Prayer in Aramaic."

"I don't believe this."

"I know. But according to Avedisian, that's what it was, an excerpt from the Sermon on the Mount in the original dialect."

"W-what? . . . How?"

"I don't know," Kate said. "As far as you know, did he ever take a course in Aramaic?"

"No, and why would he?"

"I don't know. And I guess it's not your basic college elective. According to Art, the only place you can find such a course in New England is the grad school at Harvard. And we know he never did that. Nor is Aramaic something you can pick up on Rosetta Stone."

"Then the guy's wrong. That's not what it was," Maggie insisted.

"I guess. Even if you wanted to, where would you find Aramaic versions of Jesus's sermons?"

Maggie felt a rash of gooseflesh flash up her arms. "He's not even religious."

"I know, but how do you explain it?"

"The guy is wrong. Dead wrong."

Kate nodded and sipped her coffee.

And Maggie rubbed her arms against the chill.

....

Later at home, Maggie listened to the tape over and over again. She could make no sense of the language, of course. It sounded a bit like Arabic crossed with Greek. But what stayed with her as she lay on her pillow in the dark was not the language, but the voice.

All she could hear was Nick.

13

....

Beetles were eating his brain.

He could hear them just inside his ears—a high-pitched electric chittering as they munched their way through the gray matter to the core of his head.

Hundreds of them. Maybe thousands. He could feel their thrumming just below his skull, nearly blinding him with distraction. He could barely restrain himself from making a scene in the back of the bus, from screaming and ramming his head into the balance pole.

As he did every morning at daybreak, he walked to Harvard Square from Boston and boarded the number 350 bus that took him down Massachusetts Avenue to the Alewife stop at the Cambridge/Arlington line, where he'd get off and walk half a mile to the intersection of Routes 16 and 2, his territory to panhandle the line of cars at the stoplight. It was a good place for handouts—maybe a buck or two for every twenty cars.

But this morning was the worst. The crackling and high-pitched chit-chit sounds and images of their little pincers boring tunnels had grown worse over the last week, so much so that he could barely hold up his cardboard sign:

PLEASE HELP
SICK AND HOMELESS
GOD BLESS

He could barely concentrate on his little walk up the worn path from the traffic lights along the line of stopped cars. Usually he'd eye the drivers, hoping they'd not pretend he was invisible and lower the window with a handout.

The lunatic scrabble on the inside of his skull had been going on for days, but today it was worse than ever—as if he had been slipped some bad tripping mushrooms. Then last night, he had a dream about falling off his bed and into a large dark funnel, moving at breakneck speed toward a misty gray light at the end. But it didn't feel like a dream because he heard an electric crackling sound that got louder as he shot down the tube toward an end that he did not want to reach. As he neared the light, he tried to stop himself by dragging his hands and feet against the sides but broke through the end into a black pit buzzing with beetles.

When he woke, he stumbled his way to the bus stop, trying to shake the sensation that they were inside his head and threatening to eat their way out of his ears. By the time he got off at Alewife, the chittering had intensified to an insane level, leaving him rubbing his face and batting his ears. His whole world had been reduced to those little shiny bodies with pincer jaws beginning to stream out of his ears and nose.

He stumbled along the traffic line, frantically trying to wipe the things off his face and head, spitting and gasping for air against the hot drilling buzz.

He stumbled to the ground, totally unaware of the drivers trying to watch the lights while not being distracted by the spectacle of Wally, yelping and insanely tearing his hair from his scalp and skin from his face.

Through the crack of his eyes, he saw a huge green dump truck idling at the light, the large double wheels filling his vision.

At the moment the light changed and the traffic began to move again, Wally scuttled onto the road and pushed his head under the rear tires.

14

....

Maggie had no idea how Zack ended up muttering Jesus's words in Aramaic.

The only thing that made sense was that somewhere in his studies he had read it or heard a tape and committed it to memory, consciously or unconsciously. But that raised even more questions, like where did one find such recordings? Even if he could, why would Zack, who took pride in being a secular humanist, be interested? Or commit to memory the Lord's Prayer in the original? Not to mention how and why he'd muttered the passages from a coma.

The other possibility was Nick. During his decline, he had become fanatically religious, maybe to the point of reading the Bible in Aramaic. Possibly without her knowledge, he had taught it to Zack as a child.

Whatever the explanation, Zack was now in an undisclosed room with a staff sworn to secrecy and an around-the-clock guard—an arrangement made by the hospital, which was terrified that Maggie might sue for violation of her son's right to privacy. Stephanie, the nurse's aide, had been fired for posting the video.

Although the major media had by now dropped the

story, online religious groups complained about people being barred from divine healing. Photographs of Zack still circulated on the Internet, as did the video. There was also a fuzzy shot of a water stain on the wall above his bed that was reported to be the face of Jesus.

To Maggie it looked like a water stain. A dead dull water stain.

15

....

The death notice of Thomas Pomeroy was on the obituary pages in the form of a lengthy article about the man and his life. And Roman read it with interest.

Pomeroy had been found dead on his living room couch by a housekeeper. The autopsy report claimed that he had died from "cardiac arrest"—words that filled Roman with pride.

According to the paper, Pomeroy had been lauded for his role in the "development of high resolution of magnetic resonance imaging, or MRI. Although MRI instruments have been available since the early 1980s, Dr. Pomeroy's contribution greatly enhanced the imaging capabilities for viewing individual clusters of brain cells, which aided the monitoring of the progress of brain tumors. . . ."

Colleagues and family members went on to say that his contribution to medical physics and the practice of radiological diagnostics was invaluable. All his fancy schools and awards were listed among his accomplishments and how he left a daughter and three grandchildren in Phoenix, blah, blah, blah.

Roman took a sip of Red Bull, thinking how good he was at his trade and how he hadn't lost the touch after all these years. He could still dispatch a subject without qualms or mercy, made all the more resolute now that he was working for a higher cause. The highest, in fact. Like St. Michael himself.

In the past, Roman maintained professional respect for client privacy. He rarely knew those he was working for. Likewise, he never inquired into the lives of those he dispatched. Not only was he disinterested, he understood that it was not a good idea to know his targets. Curiosity might weaken his resolve about putting a bullet through the brain of some guy who was a Little League coach and had a bunch of kids. Likewise, asking about a target's background could endanger his own life. So he had plied his trade with total anonymity.

But the Pomeroy assignment began to eat at him. Why would someone want to assassinate a famous medical physicist?

And why someone in the service of God?

16

....

Emma Roderick did not personally know Stephanie Glass, the nurse's aide she had replaced, but she had heard about the firing. Until the other day, Emma had been on a gerontology ward, where most of her patients were suffering dementia and a laundry list of physical ailments associated with advanced age. The patients here were under fifty and in various stages of rehabilitation from an assortment of neurological afflictions—strokes, aneurysms, head injuries, drug overdoses.

What she knew was that on orders of upper administration, Zack Kashian had been moved here to hide him from the press and public, because religious fanatics had crashed his room last week, claiming that God was talking through him and dispensing miracles. She had seen the cell phone video and believed none of the claims. Like her dementia patients, the poor guy mumbled nonsense syllables and people overreacted, claiming it was God and the face of Jesus on the wall and a statue of the Virgin Mary crying tears of blood, the air thick with the scent of roses.

Unfortunately, people will believe what they want to believe, Emma told herself. But the hard fact was that

Zachary Kashian's Glasgow coma rating was level two, meaning he would probably remain in a profound sleep for a long time, if not until death. Already caseworkers were talking with his family about moving him to a private rehab facility.

Because Emma was new, she worked the eleven-to-seven graveyard shift and on holidays such as today, Easter Sunday.

It was midafternoon, and she would celebrate the holiday in the evening this year. Her parents were completely understanding, especially her mother, who would appreciate not having to get up at the crack of dawn to prepare the meal—the traditional leg of lamb and homemade mint jelly. Her sister and sister-in-law would bring the baked beans, potatoes au gratin, asparagus, and carrots, plus a rhubarb-strawberry pie, her father's favorite.

"Dad."

For a moment, Emma thought she had uttered the syllable without awareness.

She turned her head toward the bed, and a bolt of electricity shot through her chest. Zack Kashian's eyes were open and staring at her.

"Dad," he whispered.

"Oh, my God!" she gasped, as if the guy had emerged from the grave. "Wait. Wait," she said, and bolted from the room to get Heather, the duty nurse, and Seth Andrew, the resident physician.

When they returned, Zack was still staring ahead.

Heather had been on the ward for years and had seen patients wake from comas before, so she instantly took over. "Hi, Zack. My name is Heather and I'm your nurse. And this is Seth, he's your doctor, and this is Emma. Can you hear me?"

Zack looked straight up at her but gave no response.

"Zack, I want you to listen to me, okay?" She moved

from side to side to determine if he was tracking her. He was. "Good, Zack. I know this is confusing to you, but I want you to tell me your name."

Incredibly, Zack looked directly at Heather and said in a voice rough from disuse, "Zack."

"That's great. Now tell me your full name, last name, too."

"Zachary Kashian." Then he rolled his eyes toward Emma. "Where's my dad?"

Emma tried to repress the tremors passing through her. "Your dad?" she squealed.

"He was just here."

"There was nobody else here," Heather said.

"I think you were dreaming," Dr. Andrew said.

"No. He was here." Zack closed his eyes again and turned his head away.

"Zack!" Heather cried. "Open your eyes. Please open your eyes again."

Zack didn't respond.

"Zack," said Dr. Andrew, "don't be alarmed, but you're in a hospital. You had an accident that left you unconscious for a while. But you're a lot better, and the great news is that you woke up."

Zack slit open his eyes again. And Dr. Andrew was quick to catch them. "Zack, look at me, okay? Move your feet."

His feet, still in new sneakers, stuck out from the bottom of the bedding. Zack rocked them back and forth, knocking the shoes together.

"Good job. That's terrific. Now I want you to tell me where you live."

"Magog Woods."

"Where?"

Emma knew from his chart that he lived in Boston near the Northeastern University campus.

"Magog Woods."

"Where's that?" Heather asked.

Zack closed his eyes again.

In a sharp voice, Heather said, "Zack, open your eyes. Come on, keep them open and talk to me. Tell me where you go to school."

No response.

"Zack," the doctor said, "you had an accident on your bike and were brought to the hospital. Remember that?"

"Sand."

"Sand? What about sand? Did you skid on sand? Tell me about it. Zack, please open your eyes. You can't go back to sleep again. Please. You're doing great."

"Hit my head." He opened his eyes.

"You hit your head? Tell me what you remember, Zack. Tell me how you hit your head."

He closed his eyes again and rolled his head away.

"Come on, Zack, open your eyes. You can't fall asleep again. Tell me how you hit your head. Did you fall off your bike?"

But Zack kept his eyes closed, and Heather and the doctor continued coaxing him to open them again, fearing that he would slip back.

But after several seconds, his eyes opened again. He looked at his arms with the IV connections and the monitors attached to his chest and tubes running from his body to bags and feed tubes. "How long?"

"Well, it's been a few weeks."

Zack stared at her, his eyes blank but his mind working on what she had just said. He winced and closed his eyes again.

Heather moved closer. "Zack, keep your eyes open."

"He's here," he whispered.

"What's that? Who's here?"

But Zack had slipped back into sleep.

17

....

At eight the next morning, Nurse Heather came into Zack's room. "Hey, Zack, how you doing?"

"Okay."

"You ready for company?" Heather was beaming. "Your mother's here to see you."

Several hours had passed since Zack had woken up. He felt more centered and less fatigued. They had kept him awake by plying him with questions to assess his cognitive functions. It took a while to sink in that he had been in a coma for twelve weeks—that he had missed spring break and March madness, not to mention nearly three months' work on his thesis, which had been due April 1. (He'd have to get an extension.) What amazed him was how in so short a time he had lost nearly twenty pounds. More startling was how weak he was. Lifting his arms took effort. But the nurses said that was expected, and because he was young he'd be back to normal after a few weeks of physical therapy.

Nurse Heather rolled up the bed slightly and gave him a few sips of orange juice. In a day or so they would remove the G-tube so he could eat normally, beginning with soft foods and milkshakes.

"We'll keep it short so you won't be too taxed. Ready?"

He nodded. "Send her in," he said, a little anxious at seeing his mother because she was an emotional woman.

Heather left, and a few moments later she returned with Zack's mother. As she entered, his first thought was that she had lost weight. She was dressed in pale green slacks and a white sweater and a necklace he had given her last Christmas. She rarely wore makeup, but today she did. "Hi," he said through a raw windpipe.

For a moment she stood at the doorway, frozen. Although she had probably kept steadfast vigil at his bedside, he imagined how she saw him—gaunt, ashen, hair roughly chopped, scabs, scars, his arms like broomsticks. He smiled as best he could and raised his hand toward her. She burst into tears and came to him, taking his hand. He was weak but did his best to give her fingers a squeeze.

Sobbing and trying to smile, she said, "Thank goodness. I love you," she whispered.

"Love you, too." His voice was hoarse.

The nurse helped her settle into a chair by his side. She clutched his hand as she tried to compose herself, wiping her face with tissues.

He knew that she felt some degree of guilt—and not just the residue of her Roman Catholic upbringing, something she carried like a low-grade fever. Or a maternal thing for not protecting him better. It was deeper layered. For some ineffable reason, she believed that Zack had blamed her for Nick's abandonment. It was totally irrational. Jake's death had caused that, not Maggie.

She took Zack's hand, now crying for joy.

"Menino's revenge."

"What?"

"The mayor. They tell me I hit a pothole."

When she regained control, she said, "You shouldn't have been riding your bike so late. And without a helmet."

"Mom, I live only a few blocks away. I just didn't see the hole."

She kissed his forehead. "Thank goodness you're okay."

"But I got a great sleep."

"Yeah, for eighty-six days."

"But who counts?" She leaned over and kissed his cheek and forehead. And he could feel the press of tears behind his own eyes.

When she settled in the chair again, she said, "Good news. Your thesis adviser gave you a six-month extension. So the pressure is off. Isn't that great?"

"That means I get my degree in January. No June graduation."

"We can live with that." She smiled and kissed him again.

"I think I heard you talking to me while I was asleep."

"You did?"

"You kept telling me to open my eyes. But every time I did, I got sand in them. I think you also asked me to clean up my room and take the trash out."

She laughed and squeezed his hand.

He could feel the warmth of her grip. It felt good. It was a relief to see her laugh again. She must have been gnarled with fear and grief these past three months. As he lay there, he resolved that once he got out he'd spend more time with her, get closer, do more to make her life better. She had suffered too much in the last ten years.

"I also had dreams of Dad." As he'd feared, the mere mention of him caused her smile to sag.

"Dreams? What kind of dreams?"

"Mostly from Sagamore Beach, I think."

Maggie nodded, trying to appear interested.

"It felt so real, even the heavy fog. I'm surprised the bed isn't all wet."

She didn't say anything but looked at the IV connection on the back of his hand.

"I think Dad was in it, but I couldn't see him, just sensed he was there. It was weird."

"Well, you were in a coma."

She said nothing else but glanced away, probably thinking how characteristic that was of Nick—barely there. She never forgave him for leaving them, then dying, and now Zack was having dreams of him. And he knew she resented that. He had abandoned her at her lowest. He had abandoned him at his neediest. Yet Zack remembered him as a quiet, private man who was also warm and loving. He never missed one of Zack's soccer matches or Jake's Little League games. And he'd cheer with wild enthusiasm and pride in his boys.

But Jake's death changed him profoundly, sucking the vitality from his soul, leaving him a husk of his former self, barely able to communicate. By the time he and Maggie got divorced, his depression had rendered him insubstantial. He had moved to an apartment in Waltham to be closer to the engineering firm where he worked. That was when Zack was in high school and caught up with a heavy college prep load. Then Nick announced he had quit his job to become a lay monk in the Berkshires, making his retreat permanent. And for all practical purposes, Zack's father had died.

On some basic level, Zack still loved him—or some former him. But he could hardly recall what he had looked like. He never told his mother, but during his school years, Zack had made up tales about him—cool things like his traveling all over the world as a professional photographer, scuba diving in Australia and Papua

New Guinea. He'd even once claimed that his father had disappeared trying to land in a storm in Tonga. Those ended by the time Zack entered college. By then his father had died for real. And the only sign that he had once partaken in his life were a few photos and the urn on the fireplace mantel.

"They'll probably tell you, but when you woke up you called for him."

"I did?" Zack was surprised, though he could see she was flushed with resentment.

"You also were reciting something the other day while you were under."

"Reciting something?"

"A prayer in Aramaic."

"Aramaic? You've got to be kidding."

"Do you know any Aramaic?"

"No, and how would I? Isn't that a dead language?"

She removed her BlackBerry from her handbag, hit a few keys, then turned the screen toward him. There he was lying in a bed, his eyes closed, but moving beneath the lids. His lips were glistening with some hydrating balm, and in a strange guttural voice he muttered something totally unintelligible but what sounded like actual language from the rhythm and pattern. The recording lasted for maybe a minute, then he ceased muttering and resumed his coma state as if nothing had happened. "I don't know what that is. That's not even my voice."

"I know. Which makes it even weirder. But a language expert confirmed you were speaking Aramaic. Actually, the Lord's Prayer. Maybe you memorized it for a paper or something?"

"I'd remember that. And what kind of course would that be?" Suddenly he felt overwhelmingly tired.

"Maybe your father taught it to you as a child."

"Maybe."

She made a dismissive gesture with her hand. "Whatever. The nurse wants you to get some rest." She kissed him on the forehead. "I love you."

"Love you, too." He watched her leave the room, fatigue overtaking him. The last thing he wanted was to slip back into sleep and dream.

But, thankfully, he fell into a deep blank for the next six hours.

18

....

Killing for God took all the pressure off. No issues of conscience or morality. No worry about a bad afterlife. Plus you did good by doing well, just as Father X had said.

A week after dispatching Thomas Pomeroy, Roman Pace got another call on the secure phone. In the same feathery voice, Father X said he had another assignment. Another of Satan's henchmen. Would he accept the mission? Yes. For the same fee? Yes.

Life was good.

The instruction was for Roman to drive to the parking lot at the Burlington Mall at eight fifteen that morning, where at the base of a particular light pole he would find a small bag containing another payment and another cell phone, which he was to answer when it rang at eight twenty. Like the other, this one was secure. Nonetheless, he was to remove the battery and to discard it and the phone separately to avoid tracing.

At precisely eight fifteen, Roman drove to the parking lot, which was vast and empty at that hour. He spotted a security car moving in the opposite direction, so whoever had hired him knew he wouldn't be noticed pulling up to the pole to snatch the brown bag.

In it was the money, three banded packs of hundreds, and another cell phone. Minutes later it rang with Father X calling to confirm pickup. Roman then drove off, humming with curiosity as to why a man of the cloth had advanced him another fifteen grand to pop another scientist.

This one was a Dr. LeAnn Cola from the Department of Neurology at the Dartmouth-Hitchcock Medical Center in Lebanon, New Hampshire. Her death was to look accidental and without similarities to Pomeroy's. According to her biography, Cola was divorced and living with her fifteen-year-old daughter. They owned no pets because the daughter was asthmatic.

Before he returned home, Roman violated protocol and called back. "I've not done women before, so I'm just wondering about her."

"I can't go into details, but let it suffice to say that in the eyes of the Lord she has committed acts of abomination against heaven itself."

"Can you give me a hint like what?"

"No, I'm sorry. But rest assured that you will please God in this service."

....

Number 147 Forest Street in Cobbsville, New Hampshire, was a brick garrison that was nestled in shrubbery on a quiet street with deep lawns. The house next door was lightless. The house on the other side was hidden by hemlocks. Across the street was conservation land. Nearly perfect.

Roman parked down the street and waited two hours until the lights went out, another hour to be certain that mother and daughter were asleep. It was an unusually warm spring night, making him wish he could turn on the AC, except that might draw attention. So he waited in the warm interior, reminding himself that a few months ago he had been saved from dying for this mission. That it wasn't blind luck, but that God so loved him that He intervened, giving Roman another chance, as if God were saying, *You can redeem yourself by doing something for Me.* And *this* was that something. And even a woman could be an abomination against God.

Roman slipped out of his car and cut to the rear of the house. There were four rooms on the second floor; two of them had air conditioners that were turned on. Perfect.

But there was no AC in the downstairs family room, where a screened window was open a couple of inches. He wedged the blade of his pocketknife under the frame, slid that up, and raised the window. No wiring on the window and no motion detector in the room. It always amazed him how most people left themselves so vulnerable. A brain doctor living alone with her daughter. You'd think she would get an alarm system or at least lock the windows.

He slipped inside a family room, where sectional sofas faced a flat-screen TV. All was quiet. He passed through a hallway to the kitchen. No motion detectors anywhere or alarm panel. But he did spot a shiny six-burner gas stove. He moved to the front of the house and the staircase leading to the second floor.

At the top of the landing was a door with a sign, "Victoria's Room." The daughter. Across from it was the master bedroom. He inched open the door. In the orange light from a lava lamp he saw the hump of the girl asleep on her back. The AC hummed in the window, chilling the air. That was good, because the girl slept under several blankets, and the machine would drown out sounds.

But first the mom.

He closed the door and cut across the landing to the

master bedroom. All he could hear from within was another air conditioner. He opened the door. The woman
was asleep in a king-size bed to the right. The AC was
blowing chilled air from a window on the left. He closed
the door and in the ambient light moved to the woman's
side of the bed. She was making feathery snoring sounds.

He clamped her mouth with a gloved hand and put
the gun to her head. "Wake up."

The woman's eyes opened, and for a frozen moment
she glared at him. Then she jolted and screamed into his
hand.

"Your daughter's in the next room. You scream, I'll
kill her. Do you understand? I will kill your daughter if
you make a peep."

She nodded and moaned that she understood.

He let go of her mouth.

"What do you want?" Her voice was a tightly stretched
wire.

"I want you to tell me your connection to Thomas
Pomeroy."

"Thomas . . . Tom Pomeroy?"

Tom.

"How did you know him? What's your relationship
to him? And keep your voice down."

"W-we worked together. Who are you?"

"Doing what where?"

"A project."

"What kind of project?"

"We were working on MRI machines. Magnetic resonance imaging."

"For hospitals."

"Yes. He helped develop hardware."

"That tells me nothing."

"We were doing high resolution of the brain."

"Who was paying you?"

"We had a private grant."

"Who was it?"

"I don't know."

Roman lowered his face and pressed the barrel into her temple. "Tell me the truth."

"I'm telling you the truth, I swear. Please don't hurt my daughter."

Roman said nothing for a moment. "The project. What were you trying to do?"

"Trying to get better control over atoms for quantum computing."

"In fucking English."

"To get precise images of active brain cells."

"Someone murdered Tom Pomeroy and I want to know why."

"Murdered?"

"What were you doing to get him knocked off? Tell me and I'll spare you and your daughter. And no mumbo-jumbo bullshit."

The woman nodded, and Roman pulled back the gun. In spurts she told him things that he had difficulty processing, but not because of the scientific jargon. "And that's the truth?"

"I swear to God." She whimpered not to hurt them.

"You believe in God?"

"What?"

"Do you believe in God? You just swore to Him."

"I—I don't know."

"How can you not know if you believe or not? It's yes or no."

"I—I . . . no."

"Do you believe in Satan?"

"Satan?" Her eyes filled with terror. She shook her head.

"Doesn't matter. I'm going to tie you up, and in half an hour I'll call 911."

"Okay, but please don't hurt my daughter. I beg you."

"I'm not going to touch her."

He rolled her onto her side, then put loose cords around her ankles and hands. When she was in place, he slipped a sleep mask over her eyes. "Okay, open your mouth. For a gag."

She opened wide. And in a flash, he pulled from his jacket an aerosol can of methane gas used to test gas leak alarms, and he jammed the nozzle into her mouth and released a continuous spray. She tried to snap her head away, but he clamped down on her face with his other hand and continued to force-fill her lungs until she passed out. It took less than half a minute. When she was still, he removed the tethers and gag, positioned her on the pillow, then turned off the AC and left the room with the door ajar.

He returned to the daughter's room. She was still asleep. As he stared at her darkened form, he rehearsed how he'd dispatch her without a clue. Before she knew what hit her, he'd straddle her body, lock her with his knees, then with his gloved hands clamp her carotid arteries, stopping the blood flow to her brain. In under a minute, she'd pass out. Then he'd close her eyelids and while her lungs still functioned fill them with gas from the aerosol.

But something held him back. His mission was Satan's handmaid, not her kid.

He closed the door, then slipped down the stairs and into the cellar, leaving the door wide open. With a penlight, he found the furnace and extinguished the pilot light. He removed the batteries from a fire-and-gas alarm and disconnected a contact wire from the alarm at the top of the second landing. In the kitchen, he extinguished the stove pilot light to prevent an explosion. By morning, the place would be full of methane gas, including the master bedroom, but not the daughter's room with the AC.

Perfect, and another fifteen thousand in the green.

If true, he also had incredible information that could be worth a king's ransom to the right buyer. Although he knew nothing about those who bankrolled him, what the woman revealed had explosive implications.

In fact, by the time he arrived at his condo, Roman was so wired over the possibilities that he needed a double hit of vodka to compose his mind to rest. But as he dozed off, like a closed loop in the back of his brain, he heard the lulling whispers of Father X's promise play over and over again:

A second chance at life eternal.

19

....

Miracle? Coma Victim "Resurrected from the Dead"

A 24-year-old Northeastern graduate student who had spent 12 weeks in a coma regained consciousness yesterday at the Beth Israel Deaconess Medical Center.

The case is being described by some as "a miracle." Zachary Kashian, who lost control of his bicycle the evening of January 28, sustained serious head trauma and remained in a "persistent vegetative state" until Sunday. According to Dr. Seth Andrew, head of neurology at MGH, he was completely unresponsive to stimulation efforts by the medical staff. "The sudden awakening of coma patients sometimes happens," said Andrew. "But given the severity of his trauma and coma level, the odds were slim." He added, "I'm not sure if his waking up is a bona fide miracle, but it's as close as it gets."

Others, however, are convinced. "Of course it's a miracle," claimed Richard Rossi, one of several people who had earlier flocked to Kashian's bedside. "He remained comatose for 3 months. Then on Good Friday he speaks the words of Jesus in Aramaic and wakes up on Easter. If that's not a sign the Lord's working through him, I don't know what is. . . ."

Kashian gained notoriety three days before his emergence when he allegedly recited passages in the ancient language. According to Arthur Avedisian, Harvard professor of Near Eastern languages, his recorded words came from the Sermon on the Mount, a compilation of the sayings of Jesus from the biblical Book of Matthew. . . .

Although dialects of Aramaic are still spoken by a small number of speakers in the Middle East, it is not known how Kashian could have recalled those passages. . . .

Maggie stuffed the paper into her briefcase and headed up the elevator to the seventh-floor ward. He had woken up two days ago and had remained alert as the doctors made mental and physical assessments. But he had not been told about the religious fanatics crashing his room, claiming that God was speaking through him.

"He's doing well," said Dr. Andrew. "His cognitive functions look normal. We've done memory tests as well as verbal, analytical, and visual tests, and he passed them all with flying colors."

"Thank you," Maggie said. "I can't tell you how grateful I am for all you and your staff have done. . . ." She trailed off, to keep from breaking down.

The doctor gave her a hug. "Of course, he'll need physical therapy. The PT people were pretty vigorous keeping his muscles exercised. They're setting up a schedule."

Because of their efforts, rehab would be no more than a few weeks. And he could be released in a couple of days.

"We'd like to observe him a little more up here before sending him to PT."

"Is there a problem?"

"Well, we're not sure."

Maggie's heart froze. "What?"

"The MRI shows that he suffered some trauma to his parietal lobe. That's the area associated with physical orientation. Usually, patients with posterior superior parietal injuries have some difficulty determining their spatial limits—where they end and the external world begins, so to speak. In preliminary tests, he seems fine. But we'd like to make sure he's a hundred percent—that he can navigate on his own. We'll be working in conjunction with PT, of course."

"But you don't see a problem." It was more of a statement than a question.

"No, but we want to be certain there's nothing we aren't aware of. It'll be only a few days."

"Okay." But she sensed something in the doctor's hedging.

"I do have a question," he said. "On the admittance form, it says Zack's father had passed away. When was that?"

"Three years ago. Why?"

"Well, when he emerged from the coma, he looked at the aide and said, 'Dad.' Apparently he'd been dreaming about him when he woke up."

"He told me. Is that a problem?" She tried not to sound defensive.

"Well, we were constantly monitoring blood flow and electrical activity, and the most active sectors weren't in areas associated with dreams."

"I'm sorry, but what are you telling me?"

"I'm not really sure." He paused a moment to think something over. "Is your son a religious person?"

"Religious? No, and what does that have to do with anything?"

"Well, while he was under, we did some scans and

found unusual electrical activity in the areas of his temporal lobe—sectors associated with abstract concept, but also mystical experiences. What some people call the 'God lobe.'"

"My son's not religious or mystical. And as far as I know, he's never taken psychedelic drugs."

"I'm not implying that. But given the trauma he experienced, the neurocircuitry appears to have undergone some reconfiguration—cross-wiring, if you will."

Maggie simply nodded, feeling tension constrict her throat.

"Was he close to his father?"

"Not particularly." She felt her resentment return. "Can I see him now?"

"Of course. And I know how you feel about all the religious fervor regarding the video."

"Doctor, is there something wrong with him?" She began to wonder if he'd be prone to seizures.

"No, I don't mean it that way. It's just that the rest of his brain was in deep sleep, while his parietal lobe was processing information like crazy."

"What kind of information?"

"I don't know. Nor do I know where it came from. Areas associated with vision and auditory activity should have been dormant."

Maggie could feel her anxiety spike. "What are you telling me? What's wrong with him?"

"I don't think anything is wrong with him. He's back to normal. It's just that while he was comatose, his parietal lobe was extraordinary, as if he were awake and receiving input."

"Meaning what?"

The doctor shook his head. "I've not seen anything like it before. But from the little literature on the subject, I'd say he was having a spiritual experience."

20

....

"'Miracle? Coma Victim "Resurrected from the Dead.'"

"He has no memory of being in a coma, no meeting the dead or finding God. He's a professed atheist, so he probably wasn't exposed to the scriptures, especially in the original." Elizabeth Luria removed her glasses and handed the newspaper back to Warren Gladstone. "Maybe there's a rational explanation."

Warren Gladstone made a steeple with his fingers. "St. Paul tells us that God sends signs and wonders to capture our attention. A professed atheist reciting the Lord's Prayer in Jesus's language while in a coma *and* on Good Friday and then waking up on Easter Sunday—those are signs enough for me."

"Well, given all those who showed up, you're not alone. I was there. I saw them."

He looked over his glasses at her. "But you don't share their conviction."

His statement was almost accusatory. "Warren, those people who'd flocked to his bedside were blue-collar people, some from third world countries, all ardent Christians, desperate for miracles."

"And you're an enlightened Harvard University neuroscientist whose Episcopal upbringing no longer has a hold on you."

"Warren, believe me that I want to believe. I want there to be an afterlife and God and all the promise of that. Why do you think I've invested so much of the last six years in this?"

"And we'll reap our rewards and maybe show you the light at the end of the tunnel."

Elizabeth smiled at his wording and took a sip of her tea. "We can only hope."

"Then take heart in the signs and the theological possibilities."

Elizabeth Luria and Warren Gladstone were sitting in the sunroom of her waterfront home in Arlington, overlooking the lower Mystic Lake. It was a beautiful home with four bedrooms and lovely views—views that still reminded her of all that had been taken from her. "I suppose," she said. "But given the imprecise calendar dates over two thousand years, who can say exactly when Jesus died and was resurrected?"

"Except those are spiritual dates—dates of believers. And the boy's breakthrough falls precisely on them."

"So, God uses the same Gregorian calendar as the rest of us."

"If God wants to get our attention, then yes, He does." He picked up the article. "From the look of things, He's gotten the attention of lots of folks, including mine."

"Well, the mother's not buying it. And clearly her son wasn't raised on the Word of God."

"The more powerful the message: The Lord spoke through a nonbeliever," Warren said. "And another confirmation that the ways of God are mysterious to man."

Warren Gladstone was an unwaveringly godly man and a good man. Elizabeth had met him through her late husband. Both had been raised in an Evangelical Christian tradition in Tennessee, Warren following his faith into a mainline Protestant seminary to become a televangelist. A dozen years ago, he'd founded the GodLight Channel— a satellite network that brought to the Northeast his ministry, now encompassing most of New England and parts of New York. Much of his success had to do with his enlightened social theology. Unlike most Evangelical preachers, Warren was a political liberal—a pacifist opposed to capital punishment and supportive of gun control. He also promoted the legalization of gay marriage and laws protecting abortion. It was his progressive views that drew liberal New Englanders, amassing him a tidy fortune that he hoped would expand coverage of his cable *GodLight Hour* into greater markets. He once told Elizabeth that he dreamed of building the first megachurch in the Northeast—a version of the ten-thousand-member Crystal Cathedral in Garden Grove, California. And Elizabeth, he believed, could make that happen.

Warren also was a godsend for her, embarrassing as it was. Owing to the nature of her research, she had been denied grant money even though she was a highly published tenured professor at Harvard Medical School. Critics accused her of abandoning serious neurological research for questionable pursuits. It was Gladstone and company that made possible her current quest and one that could lead him to the Promised Land.

"When you met the mother, what exactly did you say to her?"

"Nothing, really."

"You didn't tell her . . ." And he trailed off.

"No, I didn't tell her I'd lost a son, too. That would have suggested a more disturbing bond."

"Of course. And what was her response?"

"That she didn't believe in miracles, but she thanked me. And that was that."

"And you didn't mention our . . ."

"No, of course not." She walked to the window. Already the magnolia tree was fat with buds. Of all the trees in the world, she loved best the pink magnolia with their big fleshy leaves and intoxicating scent. But, sadly, full glory lasted only a week.

"Did you speak to anyone else?"

"No."

"Emerging from a coma is not extraordinary. It's what he uttered on the video that fills me with wonder."

For a moment, she was taken back to the double funeral—a day that she had managed to get through only because of the consolation and compassion that had radiated from Warren Gladstone.

He had spoken of spiritual dates. Could any be more brutally ironic than her own "spiritual" date? Fourteen years ago, on a warm Sunday in May, she had announced that she wanted the day off just to hang around the house and not work, not to do chores, not do things for other people—just a day to and for herself. The weather was beautiful, and under the delft blue sky the lake looked like liquid sapphire. All she desired was to languish on the deck with a good book. The Red Sox were playing a home game, so she sent her husband and son to Fenway Park. But on the way home, their car was hit head-on by a drunk driver, and her son and husband were killed. While the faith of her Christian upbringing kept her from total despair, she could never reconcile that loss or the hideous irony of losing her family on Mother's Day.

"His mother dismisses that," Elizabeth said. "The rumor is that he might have written a paper on religion and found an Aramaic recording on the Internet and committed it to memory."

"So you're skeptical, too."

"Yes. A lot of people were convinced that Jesus was

present and was speaking through him. Except that the faithful are always seeking miracles and find them in unlikely places. Their yearning made him a spiritual figure."

"And maybe he is."

"And maybe it's wish fulfillment," she said, thinking that she'd kill to know there was an afterlife and that her child and husband were all right.

"Did you know he had an older brother who was murdered?"

"Yes, but I was not about to mention that."

"What would you have said if you were?"

"That we both were robbed of the happiness of watching a son grow up. That we can't bring them back. But . . . you know the rest."

"Yes."

"I have no explanation for what I saw. He spoke in a voice that apparently wasn't his and in words that could never have been." She gazed out the window. Maybe twenty feet in the water sat two rock islets. When Kevin was young, those rocks were the humps of giant turtles that would sing to them while they picnicked under the magnolia as the setting sun enameled the lake in gold. They'd sit until the stars came out and tell stories until Kevin dozed off, her heart roaring with joy. Now those creatures were rocks in the water, and her heart merely pumped blood.

"But this isn't a case of bleeding statues or visions of the Virgin Mary," Warren said. "We have a video of him speaking the words of Jesus. And from all reports he's a nonbeliever who never enrolled in religion courses or wrote a paper on Jesus Christ. I see no other explanation. The young man was channeling the Lord."

"It's pretty to think so, but remains to be seen."

"And we should do all we can toward that end."

"We are."

"I appreciate that, in spite of your skepticism," he said.

They were quiet for a moment. Then Elizabeth said, "I have some sad news. Tom Pomeroy had a heart attack the other night. You didn't know him, but he was instrumental in our mission." The *Boston Globe* article on Pomeroy was a glowing review of his accomplishments as a biophysicist, perfecting software for interpreting data produced by magnetic resonance imaging, making it possible to observe individual human cells. "He was a good man."

"I trust you'll get on all right still."

"Of course, and thanks to your generous support."

"Dear Elizabeth, no one has ever accused you of being subtle."

And he handed her an envelope containing a bank check for $1 million.

21

··

At nine thirty the next morning, the nurse came smiling into Zack's room. "Some of your friends are here to visit. Think you're up for it?"

"Absolutely." He felt better than he had yesterday, more lucid and stronger.

A moment later, in walked Anthony, Damian, and Geoff. "If it isn't Zack Van Winkle," chortled Anthony Lawrence.

"Hey," Zack said, and greeted them all with hugs.

"How's the head?" Damian asked.

"Better than it looks." The headaches had subsided, but his crown was still tender to the touch. His hair was growing back and covering the scabs, and the facial bruises had nearly disappeared.

"Your bike's feeling a lot better, too. Got the front wheel and the wires replaced. Good as new." Anthony showed him shots of the repair job on his BlackBerry.

"You guys are the best."

They chatted some more, catching up with what they were doing. "My mom says you helped keep the rust off the joints." And he mentioned how he was scheduled for having physical therapy.

"So, what are they saying about getting back on your feet?"

"Thanks to you guys, maybe two weeks with a cane. Back to normal in a month."

While they talked, Anthony fidgeted with his Black-Berry, taking photos of them. "By the way," he said, "you were talking in your sleep."

"I was?" Zack played dumb.

"Some kind of ancient language," Geoff said.

"What're you talking about?"

Anthony pressed some buttons and held up the Black-Berry. The image was fuzzy and the reception weak, but Zack could hear himself muttering. "Sounds like nothing."

"Father Damian here thinks you were channeling God."

"Huh?"

"I said you sounded like you were speaking in tongues."

"Tongues?"

"It only sounded like glossolalia," Damian said.

"You mean like when people babble at religious revivals?"

"Yeah. But it turns out you weren't babbling," Damian said. "Believe it or not, you were reciting passages of the Sermon on the Mount in Aramaic."

"What?"

"The truth, man," Anthony said. "They got some ancient language scholar from Harvard to confirm it."

"That's bullshit." He played the video clip again. "I've never heard that before."

"Then maybe it was God," Geoff said, giving him an electric grin.

"Give me a break."

"Just kidding. But it is wicked weird," Geoff said.

"You're not gonna start preaching or anything?" Anthony said to Damian.

"No, but you might consider the possibility that the Holy Spirit was passing through you. In fact, a lot of other people did."

Then they told him how religious zealots had flocked to his bed for miracles. They also told him that for security reasons he'd been moved to this undisclosed room.

"That's crazy. I had no idea."

"You were in a coma, man. But it's pretty much blown over now."

"But still." How odd that his mother hadn't mentioned all that.

"Whatever, I'll send it to your phone so you figure it out," Anthony said. "So, when are they letting you go home?"

"Hopefully a few days. They still want to run tests."

"Any problems?"

"Just some minor problems with math calculations."

"There goes your poker game."

"The doc thinks it's only temporary. If nothing else, my mom will be happy. She's convinced that Texas hold 'em is hastening the decline of Western civilization."

"Well, you don't need math to pull down the slots," Anthony said. "Maybe when you're out we can whoop it up at Foxwoods."

"From the frying pan into the fire. I'm already in debt up to my ass."

"We'll keep an eye on you. Your mom has brought you to zero with us."

"How about that?" *Thanks, Mom.* He remembered that he owed his Discover card a small fortune. He didn't want to think of the interest compounded during his coma.

They chatted until the nurse came in to say Zack had to rest. They said their good-byes, and the nurse led them out, but not before Damian said a prayer for Zack's full recovery. He watched them leave, thinking he was lucky to have such friends. Thinking that he owed his mother big-time. And thinking something else.

Anthony had left Zack's iPhone on the night table. He picked it up and played back his coma mutterings.

The first time, all he heard was meaningless mumblings—not even distinct syllables or patterns, which made him think that the claims were even loonier than suspected. He didn't know what Aramaic sounded like, but this was pure deep-sleep blather.

He played it a few times with his ear pressed hard against the tiny speaker.

Suddenly the string of nonsense morphemes took on a vague familiarity. He couldn't determine if it was real language or not; and he knew that he didn't understand a syllable of the mutterings. But just beneath the skin of things, he sensed that what he had uttered was embedded deeply in his brain.

TWO

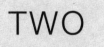

22

....

From a distance, it appeared as if the Emerald City had fallen out of Oz and into the middle of the Connecticut woods.

Foxwoods Resort Casino was a series of towers pressed into a huge multilayered structure blazing with lights. According to Anthony, it was the largest casino in the world, with nearly five million square feet, two-thirds of which was devoted to gambling and serving fifty thousand people per day. Apparently the Pequot Indians were making up for the bilking their cousins took on Manhattan Island.

Three weeks had passed since Zack's release from the hospital. But for a slight headache, he felt normal. He no longer needed a cane and was back at the NU gym regaining strength. He was also back at his apartment and working on his thesis. He didn't tell his mother, but he still owed nearly $4,000 on his Discover card. He had put on weight, his hair had grown back, and he sported a closely trimmed beard to discourage public recognition. The likelihood of that was low since in the YouTube video he looked like roadkill. Fortunately, no crazies had stopped him on the street for a miracle. A few reporters had met him on his release. He'd explained politely that he was not a miracle, that coma patients sometimes wake up, and that the Easter date was pure coincidence. As for reciting Jesus's words in Aramaic, he had no explanation.

A week later, he was a nonstory.

Zack had never been to a casino, so as celebration of his "rebirth," Damian and Anthony drove him to the Mashantucket, Connecticut, resort. Despite his mother's worry, this wasn't going to jump-start an addiction. He had sworn off online poker. This was simply an outing with pals. And maybe, if he was lucky, he'd make a few bucks to pay down Discover.

Stepping into the casino was like entering a hysterical penny arcade. Machines jingle-jangled, whistles blew, sirens wailed, coins tumbled, lights pulsed. Roulette wheels, gaming tables, and one-armed bandits were running at lunatic speed. The place was a full-scale blitz on the senses for the sole purpose of creating an adrenaline rush to toss about one's money. And it was working that Friday night. The place was mobbed, with people moving up and down aisles holding plastic tubs of quarters. This was nothing like the movies with women in elegant sheaths and men in tuxedos with martinis. This crowd could have been right out of the bleachers at Fenway: baggy jeans, tight pink shorts on fat bottoms, bandannas, tattoos, Hawaiian shirts, Red Sox tees, Bud Lights. "Not exactly *Casino Royale*," Zack said.

"Lucky for us," Damian said.

"Look around you, man," Anthony said. "What you see all comes down to this: They want your money and you want theirs. The rest is just excuse."

"You cynical devil, you."

"It's the truth," Damian said. "The place is a temple to mammon."

"But it's not going to stop you from dropping a few bucks."

"Heck, no. When in Rome, et cetera."

"Think there's gambling in heaven?" Zack asked.

"I'm counting on it."

They walked a few crowded aisles as the jangling of slot machines brought to mind the Wordsworth line: "The still, sad music of humanity."

Most players looked like regulars, feeding coins and pressing buttons, undeterred when a pile of winnings didn't jingle down. Or when they did. They settled at different machines, Zack finding one next to a middle-aged woman with freeze-dried yellow hair and a black Harley-Davidson T-shirt, smoking a cigarette and drinking what looked like a Pepsi. She had just won a small pile of coins.

"That's the one you want," she said, nodding at a "Double Diamond Deluxe" across the aisle. "I've got a sixth sense."

He thanked her and deposited four quarters into the slot and hit the button. The machine made a lot of noise, but the rollers turned up nothing.

"Keep doing that," the woman said, and left.

Four more times he fed the machine. Four more times he lost. "Nice sixth sense," he said. He found Damian and Anthony and headed into the poker room, which boasted over a hundred tables open 24/7 with limit and no-limit games all the time.

Anthony and Damian wandered off while Zack moved to the Texas hold 'em area, where he floated from table to table. He had about $400 in cash, which kept tugging at him to settle somewhere. After a few minutes, he fell in with a gallery around a foursome—a young black male in a red T-shirt and tinted goggles; two white guys in their forties, one wearing a plaid watch hat with a ruddy Irish face, the other a round guy with a smooth face and quick eyes. The fourth player was a heavyset Asian in his thirties with chips stacked like castle turrets. He glanced at Zack, then went back to the game.

Throughout the hands, the other players were loose, commenting on the cards. But the Asian guy was without affect. He didn't engage in the banter, nor did he fidget, perspire, or yield the slightest expression. He looked like a Buddha in a black golf shirt whose only communication was finger flicks to the dealer. Zack watched a few hands until the black guy sensed Zack's interest and asked if he wanted to join in. But Zack said, "No thanks," and quickly moved away.

He could barely get out the words because something strange had happened. He had watched four hands, getting a mental flash of the Asian's pocket cards. The first occurrence he discounted as a mere hunch that the guy had a pocket pair of nines. When, in fact, the guy did turn over nines, Zack told himself that he had unconsciously registered some microexpression or a body cue. During the next hand, it happened again. The guy peeked at his cards, and Zack saw an ace of clubs and a three of hearts. Both the turn and the river cards were aces, and the guy won on three of a kind.

It was the third hand that spooked Zack.

The blinds went in, and the dealer dealt the two down cards to each player. Bets were made, then the dealer laid down the flop, a ten and three of clubs and a queen of hearts. The first guy folded, leaving three others and the Asian. The bet was the black guy's and he slid $50 onto the table. The Asian and the other guy called him, and the turn card was a three of diamonds. The Asian bet a weak fifty, and the next guy hesitated, then met the fifty and called. The river card was an ace of spades, which got the black guy to fold, leaving the Asian and his opponent, who bet $200—raising the pot to about $600. When the Asian did a quick recheck of his pocket, Zack's mind glimpsed the corner spots—two queens, diamonds and spades—as if seen through the guy's eyes.

The guy looked up at Zack as if sensing the weird link. But the other player snapped him out of it. "To you." The Asian broke his hold on Zack and bet another fifty. When the final bets were made and the cards were dealt, the Asian guy turned over his pocket cards and claimed the pot with three queens, two in the down cards.

Zack quietly slipped away from the table and headed for the men's room. His head had a weird buzz, and his heart rate had kicked up. At the sink he splashed cold water on his face and glanced in the mirror at himself. *What the hell was that? Just a fluke. A statistical anomaly,* he told himself. *This whole place is a temple to flukes. But three times in a row? Maybe it was some kind of déjà vu in reverse. When the guy turned up his pocket, you only thought you had seen what he had. Let's not forget that four months ago, you did a blunderbuss with your head and a telephone pole.*

He left the men's room and went back to the poker tables. He thought about going to a different gaming room—watch the craps tables and wheels for a while. Or maybe find Anthony and Damian at the blackjack games. But something pulled him back to table thirty-three.

The Asian guy caught Zack's eye as he approached, then looked away.

Two more hands passed when the black man announced he was quitting while ahead. He tipped the dealer and got up. He asked Zack if he wanted to play, and without thinking, Zack said, "Sure," and sat down.

"You have a name?" asked the white guy on his left.

Zack told him, and the guy said his name was Jeff DeRonde. The others introduced themselves—Ralph, and another guy who joined the table was Sammy. The Asian guy was Winston Song. Zack bought $400 in chips. His abdomen felt as if a bird were trapped inside. He kept glancing at Winston, half anticipating some weird connection, but there was none. The first hand went by, and he and Jeff DeRonde dropped out early. Winston did the same. Zack had picked up nothing from the guy when he'd looked at his cards. It was as if the radio had gone dead. By the second hand, Damian and Anthony found him.

"Hey, man," Damian said. "Playing the big boys, huh?"

"Until they clean me out." Two more hands went by, reducing Zack's holdings to $200. Still no more imagined glimpses.

But on the next hand, it was back. The dealer dealt the pocket cards, and Winston open-raised to $15. Zack had been dealt a three of diamonds and a jack of spades. He called, as did the others. The flop was jack of diamonds, two of clubs, and six of diamonds. Winston bet $50 into the growing pot. Zack called, and two others also called. The turn was a nine of diamonds, and Winston bet $75. Zack raised another $50. The river was a queen of diamonds, leaving a final board with four diamonds. With the diamonds on the table, his three gave him a flush. The guy named Jeff on his right had nothing and folded, leaving Zack and Winston. And about $400 in the pot.

Winston looked at his down cards. Zack saw a deuce of diamonds and an off-suit king. He felt himself shudder at the core of his body. He had the guy. Anthony nudged him to show his pocket cards, but Zack shook his head. That caught Winston's eye. Zack pushed most of his chips into the pile. Winston looked at him for a chilled moment. Then he pushed in his chips, raising

Zack another $50. Zack pushed in his remaining chips. Winston flicked over his pocket. A king of clubs and the two of diamonds.

Zack turned over his cards. A "Whoa" rose up from the table as the crowd took in Zack's cards. And for the first time all night, Winston's face broke its mold. His eyes expanded as he took in Zack's three of diamonds. Zack had beaten him with a three.

"Thought I was bluffing?" he said as Zack raked in the chips. "Took a hell of a chance."

"Jesus, man! That was sick," Anthony said in disbelief. Damian just shook his head.

Zack had won a pot of over $1,100.

The next three hands yielded nothing, and he folded early. So did Winston. Again Zack thought he had fugitive flashes of his down cards, but since he never turned them up, Zack had no way to confirm. A little after midnight, Anthony joined the game while Damian stood beside him with a beer. Zack still was up about $900. The cards were dealt, and Zack pocketed two nines. The flop was a jack, a four, and another nine, launching Zack with three of a kind. Everybody stayed in as the pot approached $500. Winston had something because he smooth-called as Zack ran up the pot, scaring away two of the others, including Anthony. The turn was another jack, and the river was the last nine, giving Zack four of a kind. Winston stayed to the end, narrowing him at best to a spade flush, a full house, or four of a kind. The other possibility was a bluff. The pot was nearly $2,000, including about $700 from Zack. Winston looked at the river card, then pushed onto the table a stack of chips totalling $500, which equaled Zack's chips. He looked at Zack with that flat, expressionless face as the people around them—now twenty strong—buzzed in anticipation of Zack's response.

For a long moment Zack held Winston's eyes, which were unreadable flat onyx ovals. Not a giveaway tic in his face. "I fold," Zack announced.

A murmur hummed from the gallery of onlookers. "Had me going there," Winston said as he raked in the chips.

"What did you have?" Anthony said.

Zack didn't respond.

"No, really, man. Musta had the flush." Before Zack could stop him, Anthony flipped over Zack's two pocket nines. The gallery let out a gasp. "What the fuck!" Anthony said. "You folded with four nines?"

"Nobody folds with four of a kind," Damian said. And the crowd agreed.

Damian looked at Zack. "You were priced in to call, man, and you folded."

Winston gave Zack an intense glare and turned over his winning cards—two jacks, giving him four of a kind.

The crowd let out cries of dismay. "I don't believe it," someone said. "Holy shit!"

"This is sick, really sick," someone else said. "He folds four nines, and four jacks takes the pot." The crowd continued to buzz over Zack's wild hunch that saved him the rest of his money.

Zack stacked his chips and got up. "Time to go."

Winston picked up the river jack and turned it over, looking for giveaway marks. Then he flipped it down. "I don't know about you, kid," he said. "You've been doing that all night."

Zack felt his chest tighten. "Doing what?"

"Reading me. Nobody folds with four nines."

Zack could not think of a comeback, so he shrugged and gathered his chips. As they started away, two men in dark sport coats came up to Zack. Before he knew it, the three of them were being led away to an alcove where security guards asked to see each of their IDs.

"What did we do?" Anthony asked.

"I don't know what your scheme is, but you're counting cards and that's a violation."

"We weren't counting cards," Anthony protested. "I swear."

But the guards looked about as negotiable as a firing squad. They handed them their driver's licenses, and one guard went to make photocopies and check their database while the other guards held them against the wall, discreetly avoiding attention. When the first guard returned, he returned their IDs. "Your names have been entered into a database, shared with casinos from here to Las Vegas."

"Meaning what?"

"Meaning you're banned for life from stepping into a casino on American soil." His finger pointed toward the exit. "Out of here."

"But I wasn't counting cards. I swear."

"Whatever you were doing, you're not coming back ever."

"What about my chips? I want to cash out. Cash out and leave."

They walked them to the cashier, where Zack redeemed his chips for a $533 check. The guards then escorted them to the parking lot and waited until they moved to Anthony's car. "Were you counting?"

"No."

"You see him check out the river jack? Like he thought it was marked."

"How could it be?" Damian said. "The dealer changes decks every game."

"Don't know, man. You played that guy like a friggin' shark. The hell were you doing?"

Zack sucked in the night air as if to drain the atmosphere.

"Hey, you okay?" Anthony said as they moved to the car.

Zack nodded but could hardly catch his breath. When he didn't answer, Damian took his arm. "Sure you're all right? You're sweating like a pig."

"Yeah," Zack said. *I saw his cards. I saw his buried jacks.*

"Probably spooked by the security guards."

Zack nodded as they reached the car.

"So what were you thinking?" Anthony asked.

"I don't know. It was just a weird hunch he had me beat."

"Weird hunch he had four jacks to your nines? You're either wicked lucky or psychic, is all."

Zack said nothing and got into the car.

23

During the next four days, Zack tried to sort out what had happened that night and settled on a rational explanation. His brain had suffered considerable trauma and rewiring over the last four months. As a result, he had deluded himself into thinking he had mind-glimpsed the guy's cards. But in hindsight, it was no more than auto-suggestion crossed with pure dumb luck. Since then, he had experienced no more weird fugues.

Earlier that day, Damian had called Zack to join him at Uno Chicago Grill at Huntington Avenue and Gainsborough Street, just off the NU campus. Damian said it was his treat. Zack was still a charity case. His Discover bill was now $4,200 and growing by the hour.

"So, what did you do with your winnings?" Damian asked, sipping his Coke.

"Paid off half of next month's rent."

"What about the other half?"

"Anthony."

"Maybe it's a good thing they banned you."

"Those days are over, online and off. Gone cold turkey." He took a bite of pizza. "My postcoma resolution."

"Hear, hear!" Damian raised his glass. "To cold turkey."

Zack clinked him. "Except I can't live on everybody's dole. Twenty-four friggin' years old and I'm drowning in debt," he said. "I'm going to have to get a job."

"You can't do that and finish your thesis."

"Maybe I'll put in for another extension."

"Your adviser could die of old age before you're finished." Then Damian pulled something out of his shirt pocket. "This is what I called you about. From a notice board in the union." He handed Zack the flyer. "They're looking for research volunteers."

The announcement was written in bold letters. And under it was an 800 number.

IF YOU CAN READ THIS, YOU CAN MAKE MONEY (!) AS A PARTICIPANT IN A SLEEP STUDY. CALL THE PROTEUS RESEARCH CENTER AND LEAVE YOUR NAME AND PHONE NUMBER TO SCHEDULE A TIME.

"Some kind of sleep study. I called and they pay two fifty a session."

"Just to go to sleep?"

"I think it's an insomnia study. Might even be a twofer—figure out your sleep problem and pay you for it."

"Probably not a university project with the 800 number."

"They're looking for volunteers between the ages of twenty-one and fifty. No drug or alcohol dependency, no history of mental disorders. And two hundred and fifty dollars if eligible."

"Did you say you were interested?"

"Yeah, and I asked if they could use another, and they said yes. They're interviewing tonight down the street at the Colonnade. What do you think?"

"Can't hurt."

Damian paid the bill, and they walked to the Colonnade. When they asked at the desk about the Proteus interviews, the clerk directed them to a suite of rooms on the third floor. As they approached, a male and female about their age came out the door. Damian asked if this was for the sleep study, and they said it was. They tapped the door, and a man with fuzzy gray hair and a white shirt let them in. He introduced himself as Dr. Morris Stern and asked them to wait a few minutes, then disappeared into another room.

A minute later, he emerged with a tall woman who introduced herself as Dr. Elizabeth Luria. Splashed across her right cheek was a red birthmark. She thanked them for coming, then checked her watch. "If you don't mind, we'd like to begin immediately."

They agreed, and Stern led Damian into one room while Zack followed Luria into another that had a desk with a laptop and printer. Luria directed Zack to take a seat across from her. She looked to be about sixty and had quick, dark eyes behind perfectly round glasses. The birthmark began an inch or so under her right eye and ran down her cheek, making her look as if tears of blood had dried on her face. "So, what exactly have you heard about us?" She spoke in a sharp, clear voice that went with her quick, dark eyes.

"Just that you're doing sleep studies." He unfolded the flyer from his pocket.

"Yes, we do a variety of sleep-related projects, including assessment of disorders. You and your friend are students, so I needn't explain how loss of sleep can impact the way you function both physically and mentally."

"I thought sleep studies were done in hospitals."

"They are. And some are in universities or private research centers. Let me say right off that we cannot take volunteers with a history of drug or alcohol dependency."

"I'm fine there."

"Good, and no history of seizures, epilepsy, schizophrenia, bipolar disorder, psychosis, or other mental problems, including hallucinations."

Zack shook his head, trying to keep his expression neutral. "None of the above."

"Fine, but we still will require full medical records before we begin."

Zack felt his insides slump. If they learned about his head injury, they'd probably dump him. His school medical records predated that, and hopefully she didn't read the newspapers. "I can provide those."

"Good." She adjusted her glasses. "We'd like you to fill out a questionnaire. It's rather lengthy, so to expedite matters, the form is in a Word file." She nodded to the laptop and printer. "Shouldn't take more than half an hour."

"Okay."

"Good. Any questions?"

"Well, actually, if you don't mind . . ."

She read his expression and smiled. "Compensation. This is merely the application stage. Should things work out, we'll give you a call for the study, for which you will be paid."

"I heard two hundred and fifty dollars."

"Correct." She moved to the laptop and called up the application. "When you're finished, just tap the door." Then she left the room.

Zack paged through the application, which had several sections. The first asked for standard demographic data—age, gender, education, marital status. The next, "Family Relations"—parents' age; if they were alive, separated, divorced; any siblings and their ages. The third asked about any neurological disorders—migraine headaches, epileptic fits, seizures, brain injuries, and so on. He entered "NONE" to each of these.

The next section, "Religious/Spiritual Background," seemed superfluous—which religion, if any, was he raised in; if he currently practiced religion; the importance of religion or spirituality in his life. Irrelevant as they seemed, he answered each with "NONE." Then followed two questions: Where do you go to feel most connected with yourself (e.g., home, work, elsewhere)? He entered, "Hiking in woods." Where do you go to feel most connected with universe/God (e.g., religious center, mountaintop, ocean, etc.)? Zack entered, "Sagamore Beach, Cape Cod"—where they vacationed each summer.

The next section, "Sleep and Dream Patterns": the average number of hours he slept each night? The quality of sleep (good, fair, poor)? How often did he dream the same dream? How often did he have nightmares? Describe it (them). The final section asked about his most memorable dreams: the people in them; the emotions he felt; his worst nightmare. Did he ever dream of someone who had died? Or of an evil or demonic presence? Or an encounter with a religious being? Did he ever have a mystical experience? He guessed that the application was screening out fullmooner types. He typed in "NONE" and did not mention the casino episode.

When he was done, he printed up the form and tapped on the far door. Luria returned and scanned his answers, then thanked him and said they'd get back to him. "If you don't mind," he said, "I'm curious why all the questions about dreams."

She seemed momentarily absorbed in his answers. "Because some sleep disorders are caused by recurring dreams or nightmares."

"So why all the questions about religion?"

"We're interested in emotional or psychological sources of one's dreams."

"Sounds like you're more interested in dreams than sleep disorders."

"I suppose it does." But she didn't elaborate, and her birthmark seemed to flare.

"If I turn out to be eligible, just what will the tests entail?"

"If you don't mind, we'll cross that bridge if and when we get to it." She led him to the door. "And please send us your medical records." She handed him a card with a Boston post office box. "We'll contact you should we proceed to the next stage."

Zack didn't like the abrupt dismissal, but he said nothing.

Damian was in the lobby waiting for him. "How'd you do?"

"I'm still in debt," Zack said as they walked outside.

"Yeah, well, maybe that'll change."

The air was cool, and Boston glowed against a dark indigo sky. Before they parted, Zack said, "Meanwhile, they'll check to see if we're New Age freaks or junkies."

"At least they won't do a credit rating."

"There may be a God after all."

24

....

Warren Gladstone inspected his face in the mirror. He checked that his teeth were clean, his shave was close, all hairs were in place. He adjusted his gold tie peeking through the collar of his sky blue robe and flashed the GodLight smile that would light his way to the Promised Land. He then stepped to the podium and beamed at the cameras. The studio was small, and technicians crowded behind the two cameras. On cue from the video producer, Warren began.

"And it came to pass that the world once lived in peace and happiness. All loved God, and God loved all. Then one day Evil came into the world. Yes, men of a different god invaded the world and brought with them a false deity. Under a banner of 'true authority,' these invaders claimed the new land as their own, armed with their books and documents of iron words that promised false freedom and false peace."

As he read the teleprompter, Warren could feel the heat of his own conviction.

"And these men dreamed of unifying all God's children under this false idol that promised freedom from what they called *delusion*. Freedom from what they called *oppression*.

"And they filled the world with believers, not in the one true God, but worshippers of their false god, reciting so-called truths. And the one true Creator who feeds, clothes, and protects them was rejected. They cursed His gifts and piled them into trash heaps. They scorned and derided God's true people. And the false god ruled, and his book of lies was worshipped."

He took a sip of water, his veins throbbing with heavenly purpose.

"And their book is called *Science*. And their false god is called *Reason*. And their followers have taken the true God's world without valid authority. And they teach the belief that science provides the answer to every question and liberates the mind from ignorance. And that anyone who believes in the Almighty God is backwards and stupid.

"But I tell you that the rise of secularism has so hollowed out Western society that it gave rise to moral relativism, which regards all beliefs and principles as equal. This secularism has resulted in the junking of moral codes that have sustained people for twice a thousand years, leaving Western religion vulnerable to attacks of radical fundamentalists from afar."

He judiciously avoided naming Islam so as not to politicize his message of global unity.

"You've heard me say countless times that God doesn't require us to understand His will, just obey it, unreasonable as it may seem at times. You've also heard me paraphrase Mark Twain, When scientists explained the rainbow, we lost more than we gained. But the truth is that the more science unravels the mysteries of the world, the more mysterious the world remains. As many scientists have proclaimed, there need not be a conflict between religion and science.

"We've all heard the expression 'Fight fire with fire.' I believe it was Shakespeare who first said that. And there is great truth to that. And soon, yes, soon we will fight fire with fire and show how reason and science can be enlisted to verify the Word of God.

"No, I can't say when exactly that'll happen, but *soon*. Soon, my brothers and sisters. Soon we'll demonstrate to all the world the truth of God's promise to you. The truth that has sustained the faithful for twenty centuries. Truth that has driven this ministry. Truth—irrefutable truth right from the hands of science itself.

"It is coming, my brothers and sisters. It is coming. Hallelujah, the great day of the Lord is coming."

A moment later Warren stepped into the office, puffed up and beaming. "So what do you think?"

"You could sell condoms to a priest," said Morris Stern, whose small eyes flickered at him behind his glasses.

"What's that supposed to mean?" Warren gave Stern a hard glare. The man was a brilliant scientist, but an insufferable infidel. God only knew where Elizabeth had found him.

"Just kidding," Stern said. "You'll have them eating out of your hand."

"At first, you had me a little nervous making science sound like the God killer," Elizabeth said. "But you came around nicely."

"I'm not about to feed the hand that smites me."

"You are the wordsmith, Warren."

Gladstone seated himself at his desk. On the wall behind him hung a plaque that replicated the mission bannered on their GodLight Web site: "Ours is a covenant with the Lord God Almighty to spread the Gospel of the

Messiah by means of mass communications to the whole world."

Warren's plan was to continue making these teasing little broadcasts, priming the spiritual pump until they had the evidence they sought—evidence that would reconcile religion with science and once and forever put an end to the rancor and enmity between the two camps.

"By the way, did you find someone to replace what's-his-name . . . Pomeroy, you know, how to process all the cellular activity or whatever it is?"

"No," said Stern. "But we have Sarah Wyman, a former student and very competent woman who's working on that."

"What's her philosophical position?"

"She's a dedicated scientist."

Stern's code phrase for *atheist*. "As long as she can do the work."

"That she can."

"Then how come you look like you've just come from a funeral?"

"Well, we have a bit of bad news."

Warren stiffened in his chair. "What happened?"

"We lost another contractor. LeAnn Cola," said Stern.

"What happened?"

"Gas leak while she slept. Luckily her daughter had the air conditioner on."

"What a terrible shame, and poor child. Will that affect us?"

"No, not really."

"There's something else," Elizabeth said, and handed him a news article. "Police are investigating two dead males with high levels of tetrodotoxin in them."

"How were they identified?"

"An illegal alien from Haiti, found dead on a back street in Charlestown. The other, a homeless guy fished out of the Charles with his head crushed. Before he fell in, a witness saw him on the rail of the Harvard Bridge in the middle of the night while another man smashed him on the head with a baseball bat."

"Good God," Warren said.

"A witness claimed the victim appeared to wait for the other to hit him. A mercy killing."

Warren scanned the article. "We're hoping to send them to heaven, instead we created a living hell. This is terrible."

Stern cut in. "Before you get all worked up, he was a drug-addicted nobody."

"That's not the point. We can't be sacrificing people to find God even if they're street people."

"Well, science often moves from the bottom up."

Warren felt his face fill with blood. "These people talk, they have friends. What if the police trace them to us? Good God, we could be put away forever."

"That won't happen," Elizabeth said. "We've taken every precaution imaginable."

"But you don't know?"

"Warren, calm down. There'll be no more mistakes," Elizabeth said. "We've turned the corner with a whole new category of test subjects—younger, cleaner subjects whose brains aren't rotted out by drugs and booze and suffering delusions."

25

....

"Hey, brother, we passed."

"There's a claim to fame," Zack said. "We're qualified to sleep."

It was a little before noon when Damian called. It was Friday of the Memorial Day weekend, and three days had lapsed since Zack had sent Dr. Luria his medical records. In that time, Zack had received another overdraft notice from Bank of America for a check he had written just before his accident. The coma had cost him $125 in fines alone. He was now nearly $5,000 in debt.

"Yeah, but if you're really tired, it might get the dogs off your butt." Someone had called Damian to say that a car would pick them up at seven to take them to the center. Then he read off the restrictions: "No caffeine drinks after two P.M. No stimulants, alcohol, or sedatives. We can shower, but no use of conditioners, gel, mousse, and skin lotions—something about having good electrode contact with the skin. Eat normally and bring a change of clothes."

A little before seven, Zack met Damian at the corner of Huntington and Massachusetts Avenues. "Nice T-shirt," Damian said.

Zack's front was the ancient Christian schematic of a fish, but with rudimentary feet and the word DARWIN fashioned like bones inside its body. "I can lend it to you if you ever experience existential doubt."

Damian smiled. "Not going to happen, bro."

At seven sharp, a black Cadillac SUV pulled up to the curb. A stocky man in a white shirt and dark pants got out and came around. "Is one of you Damian Santoro?"

"Yes."

The man nodded, said his name was Bruce, and opened the rear door of the limo for them to get in. When they got in and Bruce closed the door, Zack noticed that a Plexiglas partition separated them from the front seat.

As the driver pulled away, he turned on the sound system, filling the car with classical music. They made a U-turn at Gainsborough and headed northeast down Huntington and onto the MassPike at Copley Square. After maybe twenty minutes, they pulled onto 95 South for another twenty minutes, then turned off at the Dedham exit and onto twisty country roads through Medfield and to a large white garrison originally intended as a private home.

Bruce escorted them through the main entrance, which had been converted into an office lobby with a receptionist. They passed some offices and through a door with steps to the basement. At the bottom, things changed into sterile white walls and fluorescent ceiling panels. Zack did not see the rear of the building when they entered, but it was clear that it had been extended to accommodate the corridor flanked by windowless doors.

The third door opened onto a spacious office crammed with desks, computers, shelves of manuals, books, and the like. Waiting for them were Drs. Luria and Stern and a black man introduced as Dr. Byron Cates. Also a younger good-looking young woman named Sarah Wyman, who said to call her Sarah. Zack guessed she was a medical or grad student somewhere.

Once again Zack and Damian were separated, Zack meeting with Sarah Wyman and Dr. Luria, Damian with the others. They moved across the hall to a small bright space with shelves of books and periodicals and a desk holding two large computer monitors. Across from it was a smaller desk where Luria sat. Zack took a seat across from her. On a table behind her sat a framed studio photo of a smiling little boy.

"We checked your medical records, and all looks fine," Luria said. "But on your questionnaire you say here you've had recurring dreams of dead loved ones."

"A few dreams of my father. He died three years ago, but my parents separated when I was ten, and I didn't see him much."

"I'm sorry to hear that," Luria said. "Can you elaborate on those dreams?"

"Sometimes it's stuff we did in the past. Other times he'd show up at the door."

"If you don't mind me asking, how exactly did he die?"

Zack could not see how this was relevant to a sleep disorder project. "Heart attack."

Sarah said, "I'm sorry to hear that. Do you dream of any other deceased relatives?"

"No, and I thought this was a sleep study."

Luria's birthmark lit up again. "It is, and a primary component is the neurophysiology of dreams—the electrical activity that takes place when they happen. So we'd like to get a mapping of your brain."

"Will I be put to sleep?"

"No, you'll be completely awake," Sarah said. "We'll fit you with a helmet with electrodes inside, creating a weak magnetic field to stimulate different sectors of your brain."

"Will I feel anything?"

"Not physically."

"Then I will feel something."

"That's what we'd like to determine."

She was vague so as not to influence his reaction. "But my brain won't fry."

"Hardly. The magnetic field is no more than that of an electric shaver."

"Before we start," Luria said, "we'd like you to sign nondisclosure and consent forms. Also, because we make a video recording of each session, a release should we use them in further studies or publications."

Zack read the forms, then signed.

"If you feel even the slightest discomfort, let us know and we'll stop."

"Okay."

Then Sarah led him out of the office and to a small, dim chamber with an observation window. In the space was a softly padded recliner with a pillow. He removed his shirt as Sarah attached contacts to his chest and to an EKG machine in the observation room. On his head she placed a motorcycle-like helmet with wires running from it to monitors and a computer in the other room. He was grateful his hair had grown to cover the pressure-gauge scar on his skull.

"This is a more highly sensitive electroencephalographic system than the standard device," she explained. "There's also a wireless sensor that communicates directly with the computer to analyze data and produce an electrical profile in real time."

"Okay." He watched her check the connections, admiring her clean good looks.

"We'll put a sleep mask on to avoid visual distractions. Again, if you feel the slightest discomfort, just let us know. A microphone's attached to the helmet to tell us anything you experience."

"Like what?"

From the observation booth, Luria responded, "We'll be applying magnetic stimulation to areas associated with different emotions and perceptions. So you may experience nothing at all or some sensations. So, just relax and narrate any change you experience no matter how subtle."

"Okay."

"You'll be just fine," Sarah said, and patted his arm.

"How long will this take?" Zack asked.

"Less than an hour."

When he was ready, Sarah slipped a mask over his eyes and adjusted the helmet, turned off the light, and left the chamber. Several minutes passed as Zack sat in the black silence. They had said they'd start low, so he would probably not register anything for a while. And maybe nothing at all. In the soundless dark and womblike chair, it crossed his mind that this was as close to sensory deprivation as he had ever been.

For a while he detected nothing but the throb of his heart. He counted beats, trying to concentrate on something—anything. Then he recited pi to fifteen places. In high school he'd memorized it to fifty. After a few more minutes, yellow amoebas floated across the inside of his eyelids—the kind of visual white noise the brain produced in darkness. But soon the blobs became haloed in orange and blues and began swirling around one another. "I'm seeing colored blobs."

"Okay," said Dr. Luria.

His parents used to take turns lying down with him at bedtime. One night he asked his father about the little floaters he saw with his eyes closed. His dad joked that they were tiny UFOs. Zack locked on one and began drifting upward until he was certain he had separated from the chair as if he were filled with helium. "Feel like I'm rising up."

"Okay."

The O of her response became a bright and rapidly expanding ring. He rode it as it expanded in a featureless void. Suddenly all went black.

Someone was in the chamber with him.

His first thought was that Sarah had entered to check a connection. He thought about removing the mask, but his hands wouldn't obey. "Who's there?" he whispered.

"What's that?" Dr. Luria.

"Someone's in here with me."

"Who's there with you?"

He hesitated for a spell, trying to identify the sensation, which kept fading and returning. Suddenly it got very strong, and he turned his head as if trying to track the intruder. He didn't feel fear or pleasure, just the awareness of a presence—like entering the woods and feeling as if you're being watched. The next moment he was at a great height, like a bird riding thermals. He wanted to narrate but couldn't. Then he began to dive through the gloom—zooming downward through space toward a pinpoint of light. As he glided closer, the spot took on form— a young boy atop a flight of stairs wearing a red shirt and holding a baseball glove—himself. And climbing toward him with open arms was a man.

"*Hey, sport, want to play catch?*"

"*Dad.*"

The sound of his own voice startled him back to the moment—sitting blindfolded and wired in a chair with a contraption on his head. He pulled off the blinders as a light went on.

A disembodied female voice said, "Are you okay?"

He could see her standing before him, and for a split second he had no idea who she was or why he was in a

chair in a booth. Then it all rushed back. And the swelling joy of seeing his father so full and vital suddenly
turned black, like a film exposed to light.

Sarah Wyman was asking how he was. He nodded
but couldn't speak. Grief turned his chest into a hollowed cavity.

They unhooked him and led him out and into the office, where he took a seat. He had been in the booth for
a little less than an hour, but it seemed timeless. Sarah
got him a bottle of water, and he sipped on it while he
found his center again. Then he forced a thin smile. "What
did you do? I felt like I was on an acid trip."

"We stimulated sections of your temporal and frontal
lobes."

Dr. Luria entered the office. "You said you sensed
someone in the room with you."

He nodded.

"Did you recognize who it was?"

He guessed that the various monitors had picked up an
emotional change, blood pressure or EKG quickening or
whatever, so there was no point in denial. "My father."

Luria gave him a penetrating look. "Your father? Can
you elaborate? Where were you? What he was doing?"

He described the image of his father climbing the
stairs to him.

"And how did your father look? How was he dressed?"
Luria asked.

Zack didn't know why that was important. "Happy
to see me. I don't remember how he was dressed. But
normal, I think—shirt and pants."

And he was alive.

"How did you feel seeing him?"

He took a deep breath to center himself. "Happy at
first." Zack felt the press of tears behind his eyes. "I was

glad to see him. Then he seemed to disappear as he got closer."

"Closer to you. And then?"

"And then I was standing all alone." His throat thickened by the second. He took in a deep breath and in his head began reciting the value of pi to keep from breaking down.

"Are you okay?"

He nodded, but his eyes filled up as melancholy hollowed out his chest. No, grief—what had assaulted him whenever he dreamed of his father, leaving him with deep, racking sobs and an aching in his soul. The dreams were all similar—his dad making a surprise return home, or showing up after school let out, or climbing the stairs where Zack waited for him.

"Hey, sport, want to hit a few?"

"Sorry we put you through that," Dr. Luria said, her eyes black with pupils. She looked fascinated with the results.

A sudden weariness weighed on him. "Think I'm ready to go home," he said, trying to sound neutral.

"Of course. But if it's okay, we'd like to run some more tests on you. Of course, at the same fee."

Zack nodded. *Only if you could put me back on those stairs.*

"What are good times for you?"

"Tuesdays and Thursdays."

She handed him a check and led him out. Damian was already in the car with the driver. "So, how'd it go?" Damian asked as the car pulled away.

They had signed a nondisclosure form and sworn not to talk about their experiences even with each other. So all Zack said was, "I could barely stay awake."

"You mean you didn't get anything?"

"Just a little dizzy." Zack didn't want to talk. He just wanted to fall into a deep sleep. "What about you?"

"Nothing, nada," said Damian. "But I'm two hundred and fifty bucks better off."

Zack nodded. At the moment, he was too drained to think about money. Whatever had occurred had left him with a sadness not felt in years. And something else: a weird and disturbing sense of his father's presence that went beyond dreams.

26

....

"'When little men cast long shadows you know the sun is setting.'"

Norman Babcock couldn't recall where he had heard that, but it described to a tee Warren Gladstone, whose fat evil face filled the screen of his laptop. He was at the wheel of the *Dori-Anne,* his forty-six-foot powerboat, late out of winter storage in Newport, Rhode Island. It was a glorious May day, and he was trying out his sea legs.

Norm had been boating since he was eleven, learning to sail at St. Andrews Prep. But it was powerboats that he loved. And this was his third. Beside him sat Father Timothy Callahan, newly appointed priest of St. Pius Church. Tim was half Norm's age and thirty pounds lighter. He had a full head of chestnut brown hair, whereas Norm Babcock was as bald as a cue ball. Today Father Tim was dressed in a green golf shirt and shorts. His usual attire was all black with a white collar. Or clerical robes, which some weeks ago Norm had donned to hold "confession" with one Roman Pace.

"The man is a bloody snake," said Babcock, looking at the monitor.

"Yes," Father Tim replied, his voice weak, barely audible.

While Gladstone pounded on his podium in perfect Evangelical self-righteousness, Norm turned up the volume so his sermon could be heard over the groan of the engines.

"The day of the Lord is coming, I'm telling you. Hallelujah. Hallelujah. No, I'm not talking about the so-called End time, the Day of Doom. I'm talking about the Day of Jubilation. A day we will all rejoice. A day of eternal light."

Norm veered toward Peddocks Island as they headed out to open sea. He knew all about Gladstone—a rube from the backwoods of Tennessee who followed in his father's footsteps to become a backwoods preacher. In time, the established clergy—other Protestants and Catholics alike—called him a fraud: just another Bible-thumping "evanghoul" getting fat and powerful off the dollars of destitute trailer parkers desperate for hope. His following at first was small because he was competing with dozens of other teleministries around the country and had no distinction—no hook.

"The day of greatness is coming, and you and I will be there to bear witness."

But then his sermons shaded into the occult—near-death experiences. Hundreds of books on the subject had been written over the decades—and all basically the same blather. Someone is pronounced dead from a heart attack, an accident, gunshot, whatever. The victim floats out of his or her body to go moving down a tunnel toward a celestial light, where he or she meets spirits of dead relatives and "beings of light." To bolster "authenticity," Gladstone claimed to have suffered a near fatal asthma attack; then, while paramedics attended him, he reported moving down a tunnel to a garden where the Lord Jesus

Christ himself welcomed him to paradise. He woke up in a hospital, alert to the glorious possibilities, and wrote a book, self-published, of course, and peddled it to his congregation as evidence of God's truth—for only $9.99. The same old charlatan but with spiritually toxic snake oil.

"I'm talking soon, within weeks. I can't be more specific, but when that day comes, you'll see with your own eyes, hear with your own ears, the living testimony to the presence of God on earth. On that day, all shall rejoice. Every Christian, Jew, Muslim, Hindu . . . every human, godly or not."

"There it is," Norm said, stabbing his finger at the screen. "Devil's blasphemy, point-blank. The son of a bitch."

Father Tim nodded, but his face wore a hangdog expression. "I still don't like it, Norm. We're complicitous to murder."

"Tim, what he's doing is an abomination. You heard with your own ears."

"Yes, but hiring a hit man makes us murderers in the eyes of the law and God."

"Let me remind you that the Jesus Christ he met with open arms was *not* the Lord Jesus Christ. It was a counterfeit, the same fake Christ met by all near-death claimants. That was the avatar of Satan, because the real Jesus doesn't teach that redeemed and unredeemed sinners alike go to heaven. Paradise doesn't have an open-gate policy."

"I can't be more specific, but we shall have proof, glorious proof of the Holy Spirit. Peter says in verse eleven that all true believers shall witness the sacred light. The great day of the Lord is coming."

"Now the bastard enlists the Holy Word in service of Lucifer," Norm growled. "Sacred light. Let's not forget that Lucifer's very name is a lie—Bearer of Light."

"But I'm still not comfortable with this whole thing."

"Look, these people have taken it into the laboratory. He and his scientist pals are trying to do what nobody's dared before—or had the means to. And once he has his so-called proof, he's going on TV to show the world. And then what? Bloody Armageddon, that's what."

"But murder."

Norm paused the video. "Review your book of Matthew, my friend—every sin and blasphemy will be forgiven, but not blasphemy against the Holy Spirit. Need further consolation? Then consider Ecclesiastes: 'To everything there is a season, and a time to every purpose under heaven,' including 'a time to kill.' This man is evil, and what he promises is an abomination against God and the Holy Spirit."

"Are you going to send this Pace after him, too?"

"That would attract too much attention. Just those doing his bidding. And then all his legions will see that the emperor has no clothes."

Tim was only two years out of the seminary and still wet behind the ears. But Norm was not reticent about telling him, made easier by the fact that he was Tim's uncle, with considerable clout with conservatives in the local Catholic community. At Boston College he had considered the seminary to become a Jesuit priest but went on for an M.B.A. Wise real estate investments made him a fortune, allowing him to generously support conservative Catholic organizations, schools, and businesses needing legal protection against liberal social movements and the ACLU. He was also a director of the ultraconservative Fraternity of Jesus, which was dedicated to preserving pre-Vatican Catholic orthodoxy and to promoting the inerrancy of the Bible and the Gospel of Jesus Christ as the only means to eternal life. This small but powerful brotherhood was not recognized by the Vatican. That was no problem for Norm and his colleagues because they didn't recognize the current pope or the last several.

Father Tim nodded in agreement. And Babcock unmuted the television.

"But we can't do this without your partnership," Gladstone continued. *"We can't bring you the Word of God without your help. Our operating ability depends on partnering with you, our viewers. With your support, the GodLight Channel reaches into people's homes via television, cable, satellite, and now the Internet and will be virtually worldwide. . . ."*

"First the snake oil, then the pitch." While Gladstone explained how payments could be made through all the major credit cards and so on, Norm muted the video. "We're fighting to save the Church herself from this lying son of a bitch. He's mimicking the real Word of God only to lead the flock away from the true Jesus, the true Holy Spirit, and the true authority of the Church. He's evil and he must be stopped. Period. And we've got the right man for the job—a master at stealth, a latter-day Saint Michael. And this dragon will be cast out—this silver-tongued serpent with his bloody 800 number."

"I cannot tell you any more at this time. But the day comes—the day of the Lord's truth. And ye shall all behold with your own eyes the proof of His glory." The camera closed in on Gladstone's face, his eyes raised to heaven and his palms turned up.

"He's turning the Holy Word inside out," Norm continued. "Jesus teaches that death be feared; they preach that death be embraced. Jesus says the Lord hates sins; they claim that sin's not a problem—that anyone can go to heaven. Jesus says fear hell; and they preach there is no hell, only divine light at the end of the tunnel. Jesus says only those who embrace God's Word will see heaven; and they preach that all are welcome—Christian, Muslim, Jew, or atheist. This is nothing less than the grand deception of Satan."

While Gladstone continued soliciting donations, Father Tim said, "But if you want to stop the snake, go for the head, no?"

"No, you just get the mouth. It's those behind the scenes, those fuzzy-headed scientists and their fancy machines and computer programs—Satan's doormen. That's where the danger lies. Stop them and their machinations, and this little man will have no shadow to cast."

"Thy will be done."

Then Norm pressed a few buttons on the laptop and a still photograph with a name under it appeared.

"Who's that?"

"The next doorman."

27

....

Zack took an MBTA train from Copley Square to Alewife station, where his mother picked him up. He hadn't
visited her since leaving the hospital. All their get-togethers
had been in town at restaurants or walking the streets, at
first with his cane, then without. They went to a few
movies and spent an afternoon at the Museum of Fine
Arts—as if making up for lost time. And he felt a bond
begin to renew itself.

About twenty minutes later, they arrived at the white
colonial on Hutchinson Road in Carleton, the house
where he and his brother were born and where he'd lived
until he'd started college. "Feels strange being here." He
hadn't slept over since last Christmas vacation.

"It's nice to have you back, even for a night."

For the last six years he had lived in dorms and apart-
ments, so that entering his own room was like slipping
into a time warp. Nothing had been changed—the same
movie posters; same photos of him, high school friends,
soccer teams; same collection of paperbacks, travel shot
glasses, high school wrestling trophies. Also a photo of
Amanda, his first girlfriend. They had met during soph-
omore year and dated for four years. But, sadly, last year

that ended when she and her family moved to England. They had kept up telephone and e-mail contact, but eventually their remoteness could not keep things alive. They broke up, and he was left with another hole to live around. His life seemed pitted with them.

Maggie had prepared Zack's favorite dinner, chicken parmigiana with a mixed salad and blue cheese dressing, fresh baguette, and pecan pie with coffee ice cream. She, too, was making every effort to strengthen that bond. He'd once overheard her tell a friend how he never shared things with her; how other mothers were "good buds" with their twenty-something kids and did things together. She felt cheated—their conversations reduced to her asking questions and his responding in monosyllables. She was right, of course. And their estrangement was rooted in a child's irrational blame for not preventing his father from leaving. Mothers were supposed to make things better. Of course, it wasn't her fault, but his distance had become habitual. His postcoma life would be a turning point.

To add to his guilt, she handed him a check for $500 to pay bills. He gave her a hug, thinking how she had no idea what a hole he had dug for himself. "You'll be happy to know that I applied for a part-time job."

Maggie's face lit up. "You did? That's good. What is it?"

"I don't want to say too much until it happens. But it's at a local lab."

"Good for you. Let me know if it comes through."

After dinner, they settled in the living room. He sipped some juice, she a glass of the Cabernet he had brought. As they chatted, his eyes moved to the fireplace mantel and the simple blue-and-white urn with his father's ashes. Near it was a clutch of framed photographs—a family portrait in front of the house, shots of Jake and him, one of Zack and his father at Sagamore Beach. Zack was beaming over a huge striper, his father smiling proudly next to him. Behind them was the breakwater jetty that formed the western flank of the Cape Cod Canal. For two weeks every summer, they'd rented the same cottage on the dunes looking over the bay, the canal less than a mile down the beach to the east, the Manomet cliffs a mile to the left, the vast blue bowl of the Atlantic spread before them. "I miss those days."

"I'm sure you do."

He could see that she wanted to avoid reminiscing. His eyes slid to the urn—what the Benedictines had given them. "What happened to him?"

She looked nonplussed. "Who?"

"Dad."

"You know what happened."

"I mean after Jake died. He changed."

"Why are you asking? That was a long time ago."

"Maybe because it's Memorial Day weekend. Plus he was my father, and I'd like to know."

"What difference does it make?" She sipped her wine. "He changed. We all did."

"He became different, withdrawn. I used to think he would have preferred that I had died, not Jake."

"That's ridiculous. He loved you both equally. . . . I think he felt guilty."

"Guilty for what?"

She hesitated for a moment. "Frankly, he blamed himself that Jake was gay."

"What? That's ridiculous."

"Of course, but he thought he should've been a stronger male model, doing more masculine things with him, with you both. Then he wouldn't have been gay, and he wouldn't have gone to that bar."

"Because he wasn't a jock didn't turn Jake gay, for God's sake. It's genetic."

"I know that, but I think that's how he saw it. Also, the Church viewed homosexuality as a sin. It still does."

"The Church. The bloody friggin' Church."

She waved her hand. "Please, don't get started. We did our best. We went to family counselors and support groups . . ." She trailed off.

"Instead he became born-again and fell off the earth."

"There's no point in being bitter."

"Hard not to be."

"He had a terrible time with it," she said. "The court dismissal only made it worse. Even medication didn't help. But religion did. Like it or not, he found solace."

"Yeah, abandoning your wife and kid to become a monk. Nice religious values."

"I suppose it was better than a life of grief and violent fits."

"But it's just the kind of hypocrisy that turns me against religious people. They fortify themselves with pious abstractions, but aren't there for the important things."

"Let's please change the subject."

But Zack disregarded her. "Did his parents bring him up religious?"

"Yes."

"What about when you got married?"

"Why are you so interested in his religious background?"

"Because I am. Because I never really knew him well. Because I'm wondering what the hell made him give up family for a fucking monastery."

Because something happened in that lab booth the other night.

He could feel her measure her language.

"He was a very spiritual person. I wasn't, so I guess I couldn't relate. On Sundays he went to St. Agnes, and I went to the Unitarian church in the center. He didn't like that because of the secularist-humanist mentality. They didn't talk about God."

"You mean he was more interested in heaven than earth."

"Can we please change the subject?"

They were quiet for a few moments as he stared at the photos of him and Jake.

"They're still breathing and living their lives," she said.

"Who?"

"Those bastards. Volker's a carpet salesman in Waltham. The other one moved to Connecticut. I can't even drive that way without my stomach filling with acid." She began to cry. Zack went over and put his arms around her. "I'm sorry," she said, her mouth trembling. "It's just so unfair. So unfair."

He kissed her on the forehead. "I know." And he felt the heat of rage rise up in him as it always did when he thought about Jake's killers. They had beaten him with a tire iron.

"He'd done nothing to them."

While he held her, his eyes rested on the urn. When the monk delivered it, he said that Brother Nicholas had died in his sleep, clutching his crucifix. A few weeks later, insurance money began arriving in bank checks. "He took the coward's way out."

His mother sat up. "Who?"

"Dad. It's like one of those tabloid headlines: MAN LOSES GAY SON TO KILLERS, LEAVES FAMILY, JOINS MONKERY, FINDS GOD. DIES."

....

They watched the evening news until Zack got tired and announced he was going to bed. He gave her a hug and kiss good night, then took a shower and got into bed. Someplace he had read that the average adult took about eight minutes to fall asleep. He probably dozed off in less than two. He slept deeply and dreamlessly until sometime after midnight, when he woke up. For some reason, his room was totally dark—no light seeping through the window blinds, no glow of his clock radio. Not even a light strip under his door from the hall night-light his mother still kept. Stranger still, he could smell the heavy salt air of the ocean. He could even hear waves gently lapping the shore in the black.

He tried to move, but his arms and legs wouldn't respond. He strained his muscles to push off the blanket, but he couldn't. *What's wrong?* Then a thought shot up: He had had a stroke. Or an aneurysm. His brain was so screwed up that while he slept he'd suffered some kind of neurological collapse that had rendered him blind and paralyzed. He tried to call his mother, but only a faint cawing sound escaped him. *What the hell is happening to me?*

He let a moment pass, then tried to scream but couldn't get his lungs to respond. All that came out was a pathetic click. He tried again and this time couldn't suck in air. Couldn't fill his lungs.

A thought sliced across his mind like a blade: *I'm dead.*

No. If you're dead, how can you even think that? Death was being completely nothinged. Worse than a coma, where voices filtered through. Being dead had none of sleep's awareness of sleep. He wasn't dead, because suddenly things changed.

And it wasn't a dream.

Cold. Shivering. The core of his body had turned to ice. Fishy night air against his chest. Electrode suction cups. But this wasn't a reality he recognized. A clammy alienness filled him.

Suddenly the sucking silence was shattered by a banshee blast.

Hands on him. Hands carrying him. Laying him down. In a hole. Then something landed on his face.

Sand.

28

....

Zack woke up spitting sand.

The room was dark but for the glow of the clock radio, which said 2:17. He was chilled but pushed off the blanket and sat up. He planted his feet on the rug and spit more sand. It peppered his skin and filled his scalp. He got up and flicked on the lamp, then pulled up the cover, expecting the sheet to be covered with beach sand. It wasn't. And he had spit only air.

But his head was swimming, and his heart was jogging. He flopped back down, feeling cold and clammy. After several minutes, his head stopped whirling and he got up, slipped on a sweatshirt, and stepped out of his room. The landing at the top of the stairs was still dark but for the night-light that had burned since he and his brother were kids. He gently opened the door to his mother's room. She was sleeping soundly. He closed the door and walked downstairs, steadying himself on the banister. Inside he was trembling.

He padded into the kitchen, flicked on a light, poured himself a glass of milk, and warmed it in the micro—something his father had taught him when he couldn't sleep.

His father.

Since that day in the chamber when they deep-stimulated some lobe, he could not stop thinking about him, reliving sweet memories before everything turned horrible—days of playing ball, fishing in the canal, getting buried in the sand . . .

Outside, the streetlamp turned into a blinking red beacon across the water. In the distance he heard the moan of a foghorn.

He looked back at the kitchen, trying to get out of that dream. The foghorn faded, and he was leaning against the polished granite counter and trying to lose himself in the stainless-steel stove and fridge and other appliances. It worked. He glanced outside, and the red light was the old streetlamp again.

He leaned against the sink and took a few long breaths until he felt his insides settle back into place. Then he gulped down a mouthful of milk. Instantly, he spit it out, gagging over the drain. It was thick with salt. He sniffed it. Like fish water. He dumped the rest into the sink and opened the fridge. He removed the carton of orange juice. It smelled normal. He poured some in a glass and made a test sip. Orange juice. He guzzled a glass to flush the taste of ocean.

He headed back upstairs and dry-swallowed two tablets of Lunesta, hoping they'd knock him into a dreamless sleep. He closed the door and got into bed, lying in the dark, his body clenched against a sudden assault of visions.

But there were none, and relief soon passed through him.

He cleared his mind and tried to concentrate on the dark slurry seeping into his brain. He thought about Sarah Wyman and wondered if she was dating anyone.

He snuggled into the goose-down pillow, the filling

making a soft cradle for his head. He pulled the blanket under his chin, then gave a little kick into the void. He would sleep undisturbed, he told himself as the heaviness spread throughout his body and the warm black cocooned around him.

The last thing he remembered before blacking out was a shovelful of sand landing on his face.

29

....

After closing the doors of his shop, Roman retired to the backroom office, where he went online and Googled LeAnn Cola and Thomas Pomeroy.

They had coauthored several articles on neurophysiology with long, complicated titles that meant little to him. The writing was highly technical, and he had to look up several phrases to get a general sense.

From what he learned, their research was aimed at perfecting ways of detecting microchanges in the electrical activity of the brain by use of a helmetlike device for the skull. Their objective was to help scientists better understand the function of different brain areas to diagnose and monitor diseases like epilepsy and dementia, but the same techniques could be used for personal identification. Signatures. The article went on to suggest security applications.

So what did that have to do with God or Satan?

He didn't have a clue. And it really didn't matter since he was thirty-five grand richer and didn't have to worry.

And God's in His heaven and all's right with the world.

30

....

Zack's brain was still tender from the nightmare when he awoke the next morning. It was seven thirty, and his mother had left to do some errands but had made him a breakfast of potato pancakes, turkey sausages, fruit compote, and a pot of French roast, which helped clear his head. He cleaned up and left her a note of thanks, thinking how she had gone through the fire and hadn't run off to a nunnery. He took public transportation into town and spent the rest of the day at the Northeastern library working on his thesis.

That night he received a call from Dr. Luria. She wanted to do another test on him next Tuesday evening, if he was free. He was. In advance of that, she asked him to e-mail sample photographs of his family members, friends, pets, his home, and favorite places. Her explanation was that they were going to use them to establish a baseline for brain scans. Zack didn't know what that meant, but he complied.

He also went online and Googled each of the key people in the lab.

Elizabeth Luria was a professor emerita of microbiology at Harvard Medical School with a long list of publications on brain plasticity and imaging in prestigious-sounding journals such as *The National Review of Neuroscience, Neuron, The Journal of Neuroscience*. A few were on functional MRI imaging with meaningless titles like "Temporal-Lobe Bursts and 'Transcendent' Experiences" and "Total Deafferentation of Posterior-Superior Parietal Lobules PSPL and Self-Transcendence." The words *transcendent* and *parietal* jumped out at him.

Morris Stern was listed as a professor of behavioral neuroscience, Department of Brain and Cognitive Sciences, Tufts University School of Medicine. He was an expert on brain imaging and directed a lab investigating the neural basis of learning and memory. He had a long list of publications in the journal *Neuroimage and Neurobiology*.

Byron Cates was a professor of computational neuroscience and health sciences and technology at MIT. From what Zack gathered, he was an expert on "neuropsychological recordings" and "mathematical modeling to establish definitions of anesthetic states." That was as meaningless to Zack as was an impressive list of published titles.

They each had research and/or teaching jobs, so this sleep study was something they did on the side during the evenings.

Sarah Wyman's Web site listed her as unmarried and a former nurse who was doing postdoctoral studies at Tufts. On a list of her publications was a paper called "The Role of Serotonin 5-HT (1A) Receptors in Spirituality," published in *The American Journal of Psychiatry*.

Spirituality? That did not seem like a topic for a doctoral thesis in neurophysiology. But he was too sleepy on Lunesta to speculate and went to bed thinking of her.

31

....

At six P.M. that Tuesday, the same unfriendly Bruce picked up Zack at the corner of Huntington and Massachusetts Avenues. Same trip to the lab. Same ensemble music. But this time Zack was alone. Damian had not passed the screening. He said he didn't mind. He also wasn't drowning in debt.

Zack arrived a little before seven, this time prepared to sleep over. Again Drs. Luria, Stern, and Cates and Sarah Wyman met with him in the same office. Dr. Luria explained the evening's plan. "This is going to be a different kind of procedure. We're going to establish a baseline recognition pattern of various images, but we're going to do it in a functional MRI machine. Have you ever had an MRI scan done?"

"Just on my shoulder some years ago."

"What about on your head?"

Not while I was conscious. "Nope."

"Are you at all claustrophobic?"

"Not that I know of."

"Good, because we're going to position your head and shoulders in the MRI with a visible monitor that will project a series of randomly selected visuals. All you have to do is simply look at them. Okay?"

"How long will I be inside the tube?"

"Maybe forty minutes."

"No problem."

"If you feel the least bit uncomfortable, let us know," Sarah said. "What we're doing is trying to determine neuroelectrical signatures of your emotional states."

"For what purpose?"

"Well," Dr. Luria said, "in our next session—and hopefully you'll agree—we will give you something to let you sleep, then do a scan of your brain activity."

She went on with more technical language that didn't clarify much. Zack's main concern was another $250. "Fine," he said, and followed them to another room.

Zack was startled by the size of the MRI machine—a giant white cube with a tube magnet and an attached gurney that slid into the bore. It must have taken some creative engineering to get it down here.

He changed into loose-fitting pajama bottoms behind a small screen, then lay on the gurney at the opening of the MRI tube. A computer monitor was attached to the lip of the tube for viewing from inside.

"The images will change every five seconds," Sarah explained. "All you have to do is look at them. Don't say anything, don't move, just look at them. Okay?"

"Easy enough."

Before they rolled him inside, Sarah and Byron Cates taped electrodes to his chest, chin, and scalp. A sensor was attached to his upper lip to measure temperature and airflow from his mouth and nose. Other sensors would measure body functions as well as the oxygen and carbon dioxide blood levels, his heart rate, breathing rate, and blood pressure. Elastic belts were placed around his chest and stomach to measure respiration. A clip to his earlobe measured oxygen levels.

Sarah positioned a videocamera on a tripod. "As with all subjects, we're going to record the procedure. Again, if you're at all uncomfortable, just say so. We'll be right here."

"Okay."

"One more thing," Sarah said. "We're going to fit plugs in your ears with a muffler so the sounds of the machine won't distract you."

He agreed, and when she was done, all ambient sound disappeared. He then signaled that he was ready, and she pressed a button, sending him into the tube up to his chest. They adjusted the monitor for his viewing.

For the next several minutes, bright-colored images flicked across the monitor: sunsets, cats, beach scenes, mountains, cityscapes, a disturbing war image, product logos, cars, and so on. There were also a few of the photos he had sent Luria—shots of himself, his parents, and his dog, Coco, a cocker spaniel that died when Zack was seven. The ordering seemed totally random. And after countless minutes he felt himself become bored and sleepy, although he kept his eyes open as instructed.

Toward the end, a few photos of his father appeared, including some that had been cropped from family shots, isolating just him. Also the same photo of his father posed with Zack and the striper, taken a year before his father disappeared. Eleven years before he died for real. Then more shots of sunsets, dolphins, flowers, churches, sports cars. But it was the shots of his father that touched him to the quick.

When the session was over, they rolled him out of the machine and removed the mirror and laptop. "How are you feeling?" Sarah said.

"A little tired." But his eyes filled up, which, he told

himself, was ridiculous since he had supplied the photos in the first place.

She put her hand on his shoulder in comfort, clearly seeing him holding back. So as not to embarrass him, all she said was, "You did fine," then walked him to the changing screen.

When he was dressed, Dr. Luria came over to him. "We'll need some time to analyze the data. But if it's all right with you, we'd like to do another session."

He nodded, hating the stranglehold of emotions in front of everybody. In his head he recited the value of pi to twenty places, knowing that if anyone tried to comfort him, he'd crack.

"Is this Thursday evening good?"

He nodded and choked out, "Yeah."

Luria handed him a check.

He thanked her, and Sarah walked him to the door, where Bruce waited.

"See you soon."

"Yeah."

He got into the car and settled into the comforting dark of the empty rear seat. As they drove in silence, Zack felt anger well up inside. Sarah knew they had cut him at the knees with those cropped and enlarged shots of his father. They were calculated to give them the spikes they were looking for. Maybe it was that helmet the other day. Maybe they had zapped some nostalgia node, leaving him vulnerable. Whatever, he was certain that tonight it was spiking in the red zone of grief.

So what the hell did that have to do with insomnia?

32

....

A little after seven the next morning, Sarah called Zack to say that she was meeting a nurse friend at Beth Israel Deaconess Medical Center just down the street from him and was wondering if they could grab a coffee before that.

He agreed, and they met at My Place, a small café on Gainsborough. They each ordered a coffee and muffin and sat at a corner table. Sarah had a beautiful smooth face with large golden brown eyes and a thin, sharp nose. She wore her hair short, exposing her long white neck. In the slant of the morning light, she looked like a saint in a medieval painting.

"I just want to apologize about last night. Sometimes these sessions can stir up emotions."

"I guess I was caught off guard."

"I understand."

He took a sip of his coffee. "Do you? I'm just wondering if you were baiting me."

"Baiting you?"

"The only shots that were cropped and enlarged were those of me and my father."

She looked surprised. "Weren't they photos you'd sent Dr. Luria?"

"Yes, but they were altered to just focus on him, and they were repeated several times in the sequence."

"I wasn't aware." She was silent for a moment as she nibbled her muffin. Then she asked, "So how was that baiting you?"

"The other day, with the helmet test, you found a soft spot." He was too self-conscious to admit that he had actually uttered "Dad" as if he were that ten-year-old at the top of the stairs. "So was that the point—to lower my guard to confirm a sadness signature?"

"We were trying to get a broad profile."

"Well, you went for the kill."

"I'm sorry about that, really."

They were quiet for a long moment as he sipped more coffee. "The thing is that experience in the booth was eerie, it was so real. I swear I felt my father's presence."

"That's the effect of the helmet. The stimulation targets emotion centers of the right hemisphere, and to make sense of them the left parietal lobe creates those sensations."

Parietal lobe. Where he got slammed and sent into a twelve-week coma.

"So, you're saying the electrical impulses created the illusion of his being there."

"Yes. Something made you think of your father, and the electrical impulses simulated an illusion of his presence."

"The ghost in the machine."

"In a manner of speaking."

They were quiet for a few moments. "That's kind of disappointing."

"I can understand that," she said.

"Are you bothered by what you're doing?"

"Bothered? I don't follow."

"I'm not spiritual, but I guess I still carry some fuzzy sense of God from childhood. I'm just wondering about religious people—those who claim to have spiritual experiences." *Like those who had flocked to my bedside for miracles.* "Or even not-so-ordinary people, you know, shamans, mystics, priests, saints—Joan of Arc."

"I'm not sure what you're getting at."

"You're saying their claims of feeling God or seeing Jesus or whatever are no more than electrical discharges in the brain?"

She played vague again. "Neuroscientists are interested in understanding the neurological basis of human experience."

"'The Role of Serotonin . . . Receptors in Spirituality.'"

Her eyebrows shot up. "You've been checking."

"That's right." He had found a complete copy of her article online. "I'm just wondering if your theory doesn't make you feel a little guilty."

"Guilty about what?"

"I'm not religious, but I know people who are. And I respect their faith. I also think that with some people, religion fills a human need. It gets them through crises."

"Okay," she said.

"My point is, were I doing what you and your colleagues are, I think I'd feel bad."

"Why?"

"Because the object of your research seems to be the elimination of the divine from the universe, reducing it to brain chemistry."

For a microsecond, he felt the shuddering awareness of being in Winston Song's head, reading his cards.

"That's quite a charge."

"But isn't that what you're doing—reducing spiritual highs and religious ecstasy to an endorphin rush?"

Her face flushed, and he couldn't tell if she was about to burst into tears or toss her coffee at him. She did neither but took a sip to collect herself before responding.

"That really isn't my objective. In fact, elsewhere we applied the same diagnostics to self-proclaimed mystics—people who'd reported intense religious experiences, including Carmelite nuns. They gladly signed on and left feeling that their heightened experiences only confirmed their faith. When nuns were shown religious images—medieval paintings of Jesus, Michelangelo's *Pietà*, the Vatican, et cetera—nearly every one of them said they felt the presence of God in the booth."

"So what's your conclusion?"

"That just because mystical experiences can be associated with specific neurological activity doesn't mean those experiences are illusions. Likewise, nobody can say that the neurological activity you're experiencing eating that muffin caused the muffin to exist."

He nodded. She had a point.

Then she checked her watch and downed the rest of her coffee. "Gotta go." She got up and put her bag over her shoulder. "See you Thursday."

He stood up and watched her hustle out the door, wondering just what this tryst was all about.

33

....

Zack could tell that something was different the moment he arrived at the lab that Thursday. He couldn't put his finger on it, but a heightened sense of anticipation charged the air. Sarah regarded him with a little gleam in her eyes, and Dr. Luria's birthmark was glowing. Stern's and Cates's faces were in a forced neutral mode, but he saw something in their manner as they met in Dr. Luria's office.

"Zack, the fMRI data the other day has been analyzed, and we're rather impressed."

"Because I got emotional over a few old photos?"

"Yes, in fact. Last week you asked about the nature of these tests, and we said that part of our investigation was the neurobiology of dreams. Well, the truth of the matter is that you fulfilled the requirements to proceed to the next level. Our concern is not so much with dreams or sleep *per se*, but with the subjective experience a person may have in a state of *very* deep sleep."

Zack sensed the careful wording, but the last three words hovered in the air like plovers.

"We asked you back because the electrical activity in

the temporal lobe is quite high, making you an ideal candidate for our investigation."

"So all that was just a screening."

"Yes, which most subjects don't pass," Luria said. "With your consent, we'd like to move to the next phase. We'd like to lower your metabolic activity so that your brain will be in a state of total repose, where the electrical activity is minimal."

"How minimal you talking?"

Nobody responded for a moment. Then Dr. Luria said, "We'll administer an anesthetic compound that will temporarily shut down the electrical activity of cell axons—the circuitry between brain cells. The individual cells will still be alive and healthy, of course. They'll still have their enzymes, metabolisms, and ATP, adenosine triphosphate, which supplies energy to cells. But while you're under, individual neurons will cease communicating with each other."

"You're going to stop the electrical activity in my brain?"

"The intercellular activity, and only for a short while. And as soon as we're done, and you're revived, cell communication will return."

It was as if his ears had suddenly cleared. "You're talking about near-death experience."

"That's the popular terminology."

"Like that movie *Flatliners*."

"But with a lot better results," Sarah said.

Dr. Luria continued. "We're investigating the few moments of time between near death and real death, which is when brain cells begin to die. But because we'll closely monitor cell activity, we know precisely when to stop before that happens. So it's perfectly safe. We can guarantee that."

They stared at him—four big-deal scientists with fancy degrees, surrounded by fancy equipment and stacks of fancy journals. He couldn't believe what they were saying. "You want to flatline me just this side of death, then bring me back? How can you guarantee that?"

"Because we've done it many times before. And because our methodology's been through rigorous trials, first with mice, then higher primates. And, of course, humans."

Stern added, "We'll be monitoring your blood pressure and heart rate—all your vital signs—very closely and can revive you almost at once. It's perfectly safe, believe me."

"Has all this been approved by the FDA or whatever?"

Luria nodded. "It's been cleared by the State Medical Board."

"Then why the cover story about sleep studies?"

"Because we don't want the public knowing what we're doing here. In fact, should you agree to proceed, we'll ask you to sign a nondisclosure statement."

"But why?" Zack asked.

"Because of our objectives."

"Which are?"

"To see if there's anything to claims of near-death experiences."

"Like what?"

"Like an afterlife."

The coordinates of the room seemed to shift. "And I was hoping you'd cure my insomnia."

"The local drugstore can help you there," Sarah said. "What we're doing is looking to see if there's anything that lies beyond or if all the claims are reducible to neurobiology."

"But you're asking my consent to kill me."

"Not at all," Stern said. "Zack, we've developed a

wonderful sedative that safely simulates brain death. In other words, we'll fool your brain's electrochemistry into thinking it's terminal. You'll effectively enter a flat-line state for a few minutes, then we'll give you a stimulant that immediately fires up full brain activity again."

He looked at Luria. "It will?"

"Absolutely. There's no way we'd endanger your life."

"But what if my brain really thinks it's dying and begins to turn off the rest of me?"

"That won't happen," Sarah said. "We'll be monitoring you every moment."

"What if you have a power failure?"

"We have generators that'll kick in instantly," she said. "Believe me, you'll be fine."

He took refuge in the promise of those tawny brown eyes. "And what about side effects—my memory, my ability to think . . . ?"

"There are none," Luria said. "Your memory will return. You'll remember family, friends, your own name, language. Your cognitive powers will be normal. Think of it like a Novocain shot. An hour later, all sensations are back."

"But while I'm under I'll be brain-dead."

"No, while you're under you could *pass* for brain-dead. Your brain cells will still be healthy and alive, just silent."

"And then what?"

"Then we wake you and ask you about any experience you may have had."

"You mean like moving down a tunnel toward a light, angels or whatever."

"That's the prototypical notion, though the experience may be entirely different."

"But if I'm flatlined, how can I remember experiencing anything?"

"Excellent question," Dr. Luria said. "If you do have an NDE, those areas of the brain where the neuroelectrical activity takes place will inform other areas of your brain once you're awake. In other words, your experience will be a kind of residual memory once your whole brain is in synchronicity again."

Were their manners not so sober and serious, he would have thought they were joking. "This doesn't even sound like something scientists investigate."

"You're right," Luria said. "In spite of all the fascinating claims in books and the popular press, nobody has ever demonstrated if the phenomenon is real or fantasy. And one reason is that all NDE claims are untestable reports of people who survived heart attacks and accidents et cetera. But here, we conduct NDE experiments under controlled scientific conditions."

"Of course," Stern interjected, "we could end up discovering that it's all in the head, which is what some of us believe."

"Or that there's no such thing as death," Luria said with a flicker in her eyes. "Just a change in state—from physical to spiritual, for lack of a better term. Think how extraordinary that would be."

Zack's mind was spinning. "Okay. Say I agree and go down a tunnel or whatever. How would you know that's the afterlife and not some dream thing?"

"Because once you're under, your brain cells can't produce the necessary electrical activity. In short, you won't be able to dream."

"So what will you look for?"

"Anomalous neuroelectrical activity," Stern said. "The key reason this hasn't been done before is that the diagnostics didn't exist. The MRI machine we used on you the other day is one of a kind. Its resolution power can distinguish individual brain cells."

"We also have the software to make sophisticated mathematical analyses of any electrical activity," Cates added.

"But I still don't get how there can be any electrical activity if I'm anesthetized."

"What the anesthetic does is to turn off intercellular activity, the long axon connections," said Dr. Luria. "However, there may still be microelectrical activity in the channels between individual cells—what we refer to as analog communication, driven by cell-body-based properties. That's what we'll be looking for. And if there is any, we'll need to analyze and explain that stimulation."

"Such as what?"

"Such as human consciousness separating from the brain," Luria said. "Mind transcending the body. To some that would be evidence that the afterlife is real."

Zack was quiet for a moment as he tried to process what they were telling him. "And what would be proof of that?"

"The sixty-four-million-dollar question," Luria said. "I suppose the ultimate test would be if someone comes back from an NDE with secrets only the dead possess."

"However," Stern added, "more skeptical people—me included—believe that the phenomenon is pure neurobiology—that is, the brain creating electrical-chemical reactions to impending death."

"Religion versus science," Zack said.

"Yes," Dr. Stern said. "There's evidence that the human brain is wired to encourage religious beliefs, some more than others. Skeptics claim it's just biology. Others say God made us so wired in order to discover Him or Her."

"Which is why your questionnaire asked if we were religious or into the occult."

"Yes," Luria said. "We don't want subjects who are

susceptible to paranormal phenomena because they're prone to confabulating NDEs from something they read in a book."

Or people who think they mind-merge while playing Texas hold 'em. And what about quoting Jesus in Jesus's tongue while comatose?

"If I agreed," Zack said, "how long would I be flat-lined?"

"No more than three minutes."

"Then you'll revive me."

"Yes, by turning off the infusion," Sarah said. "Plus we'll give you a small injection of norepinephrine, which instantly increases the heart rate and blood pressure."

"What are the risks of something going wrong?"

"There are none. Zero."

"How many others have you flatlined?"

"Many," Luria said.

"And they all were revived," Cates added.

"And all the same as they were before being flatlined?"

"Yes, no problems or side effects," Luria answered.

Zack was silent for a moment as he processed it all. Then he asked, "Why me and why not my friend Damian?"

Dr. Luria's birthmark darkened. "Well, as Morris said, some people are genetically predisposed to NDEs, which is why we did that helmet test on you. Your temporal lobe is highly sensitive to dissociative experiences. Damian's wasn't. In fact, most people's aren't."

Dissociative experiences. Is that what happened at the blackjack table?

"May I ask how you're funded?"

"Privately."

But she did not elaborate. And clearly this was not research that was supported by university grants or the government.

"Any chance of me checking references—you know, talk to other test subjects?"

"We can't do that because of confidentiality agreements," Luria said. "But to reassure you, we have some videos of past NDE subjects in suspension and being revived."

She turned the monitor around and clicked on a video, which lasted maybe half an hour. There were three separate subjects, two males and a female. Their faces were blurred, but Luria said they were in their twenties and thirties and all healthy. Each was lying on a gurney and speaking with Luria and others as technicians hooked up IV lines and wires to their head and chest. When they said they were ready, a technician administered something into their IVs, and almost instantly they fell into a deep sleep. In clear view of the camera were electric defibrillator paddles. The video ran for a few minutes while Luria and others watched the monitors. Then the subjects were awakened, each appearing groggy for a spell. One man seemed to relapse into suspension and was given a second injection of norepinephrine. Then, following a time jump, Dr. Luria was shown interviewing each—asking how they felt. All said normal. Then a short list of questions to assess their memories: Name the date, the current president, the state and its capital, and so forth. Luria turned off the sound while the interview continued.

"The rest involves their experiences, which we're keeping confidential. We also don't want to prejudice your own responses should you agree. Any questions?"

He didn't seriously believe in the NDE stuff. His main concern was coming back from the chemical cocktail. "What's the drug, by the way?"

"It's called tetrodotoxin."

That told him nothing.

"It's a natural ingredient and perfectly safe," Sarah said. She patted his arm. "I promise you'll be just fine."

"I should add that if you agree to volunteer, you'll be paid an additional two-hundred-and-fifty-dollar signing fee—a total of five hundred dollars."

Zack could feel lines of expectation converge on him. He glanced at the nondisclosure and waiver forms. Then his eyes returned to the computer image of the last NDE subject, frozen at the point where he said he felt perfectly fine. "You're asking me to be sent to death's door, so I'd like to think this over, if you don't mind."

Luria's expression sagged. "Of course, but it's perfectly safe."

He made a move to the door. "I'm sure, but I can't just sign my life away."

"But you're not," she said, struggling not to be too insistent.

"I'll get back to you."

"Fine. We hope that you'll let us know soon." Luria went to the desk and called Bruce. When she finished, she pulled Zack aside, and in a low voice she said, "While you're deliberating, you should know that this project is on the cusp of a great scientific discovery. Perhaps the greatest. And you can be part of it."

34

....

Two days later, they began to put the pressure on Zack. Dr. Luria sent a letter thanking him for his initial participation in the "tests" and saying that she understood his concern. Sarah also sent him a note saying that she hoped they could continue working together. To ease his mind, she had sent him a link to a secure site on which there were more video interviews of subjects who had emerged from suspensions. Their identities were blocked, their faces smudged, but they were clearly in the Proteus lab being interviewed by Dr. Luria and Sarah Wyman.

They all identified themselves as college students or young professionals in their twenties or thirties. Notwithstanding the selection of videos, the half dozen or so test subjects unanimously said that they experienced no side effects other than feeling a little sluggish. After the sedative had worn off, they claimed to have felt perfectly normal. Two expressed regret about coming back to the real world. One had likened the return to Dorothy leaving the land of Oz for black-and-white Kansas.

What interested Zack particularly were their descriptions of the actual suspensions. While one recalled nothing from his suspensions, most of the others claimed that in their NDEs they had remarkable feelings of peace, unity, and unconditional love:

> I saw a light—not blinding but a wonderfully nurturing, peaceful light.

> I can't recall exactly the environment, but I remember it was very peaceful and very beautiful. I was aware of colors—more pure than any colors I had seen in life. I also felt light emanating from me, a warm bright light that accompanied a profound feeling of peace and safety and love.

> I had a sense of great unity with all things. Also, I remember a very powerful and profound presence.

The next day, Luria did a follow-up call to ask if he had watched the videos.

"Yes, they were fascinating," he said.

"And all very positive reports, as you noticed."

"Yes."

"And all very safe, obviously."

"So it seems." He knew he was playing coy.

"So," she said, "I hope you're agreeable to undergoing a suspension with us."

"I'm still thinking about it," Zack said.

"Well, you should know that I met with the others and we unanimously agreed to raise the suspension fee to seven hundred and fifty dollars."

A $250 raise. "That's great," he said. "But what's the reason?"

"Well, frankly, because in neurological terms you're quite special. As I said the other day, the activity structure of your brain appears especially sensitive."

He wondered if he should feel flattered or apprehensive. "Just one question," he said. "How come no one in any of the videos claimed to have met dead relatives?"

"Well, maybe you'll be the first."

35

....

Zack tried to suppress his anxiety as Bruce drove him to the lab the next Tuesday night. He tried to lose himself in the Vivaldi CD, thinking about those people who had been flatlined and crowed about spiritual transports of loving light and tranquillity.

When he arrived, the core team met him, and Sarah gave him a warm hug, wishing him a belated happy birthday. Yesterday he had turned twenty-five. That made him feel better. He signed the various waivers and non-disclosure forms. They then led him into the MRI room, where he changed into pajama bottoms and lay on the gurney. They connected him up to an IV and several electronic monitoring devices. Along one wall was a viewing window, behind which were the computer workstations where scans of his brain would be projected.

Sarah positioned a videocamera on a tripod. "Once again, we're going to record the whole procedure and catch any movements."

"Like breaking into the 'Hallelujah' chorus."

She laughed. "That would be something." She then put a mask across his brow, ready to be lowered. He felt a nervous flare in his chest.

When they finished, Dr. Luria came over. She was beaming with expectation. "Ready?"

"I think so."

"How do you feel?" Sarah asked.

He looked up at the faces, the lights, IV stand, tubes connected to him, thinking that he was a syringe away from near death. "Nervous."

She patted his arm. "Of course, but you'll be perfectly safe. You're just going to sleep."

"Easy for you to say."

"I'll be monitoring every second you're under. Then in an hour we'll bring you back."

"You've done this before?"

"Yes, of course."

"And everyone came back?"

"Absolutely."

"And whole?"

"And whole and healthy." She patted his arm again. "All set?"

"Want to come with me? I may be going to paradise."

She laughed. "Love to, but I don't have your brain."

She lowered the mask and fitted the earplugs and muffler, cutting off the outside world. The gurney moved headfirst into the tube and he felt a twinge of claustrophobia. "How long will it take to fall asleep?" If anyone responded, he never heard. His brain went instantly black.

....

"Hey, Zack, you're waking up."

A female voice.

"Zack, can you hear me?"

He grunted. Shards of sleep were falling away as awareness gradually returned.

"He's coming to."

A male voice.

"Come on, Zack, wake up."

He forced open one eye.

"That's it, Zack, open your eyes."

Then the other.

"Welcome back. How do you feel?" asked a pretty woman with short hair.

He licked his lips.

"If your mouth and tongue feel tingly, that's normal. Can you tell me your name?"

He looked at her dumbly without response.

"Okay, you're still a little foggy."

"Can you tell us your name?" an older woman asked.

He shook his head.

"No? Sure you can. It's Zack. What's your last name?"

He hesitated a moment. Then he muttered, "Kashian."

"What was that?"

"Kashian."

"Right. Good. And do you know where you are?"

"Magog Woods?"

"Where?"

"Magog Woods."

"His voice sounds different," someone said.

"Where's Magog Woods?"

"Where I live."

"And where's that?"

"Maine."

"Maine? No, you're in Massachusetts. You remember."

Zack shook his head.

"Yes, you're in Massachusetts, not Maine. And you live in Boston."

He looked around dumbly. Then his mind slowly began to clear, and the trees faded and it became bright, and he saw people standing around him in a large white room with all the electronic equipment and tubes and wires attached to his head and arms.

"Do you know why you're here?"

"Mmm. Guess I was dreaming. Sleep test."

"Good. Can you tell me your name?"

"Zack Kashian."

"Great. And the date?"

He thought a moment, then it came back to him.

"Very good. And what state are we in?"

"Massachusetts."

"That's better. And the capital?"

"Boston."

"Do you remember my name?" asked a younger pretty woman.

He felt himself return to the moment. Sarah Wyman, the neuroscientist with the pretty face and short hair. "Joan of Arc."

"Joan of Arc?"

"Look like her. Paul Delaroche, painter."

"Wow. You know your art."

"French history." He spoke haltingly, trying to clear his brain. His mouth felt dry.

"Where?"

She was still testing him. "Northeastern."

"I think he's fine. Zack, it's me, Dr. Luria." She sat beside him with a clipboard, a videocamera trained on him. "I'd like to ask you a few questions about your experience. Do you remember anything while under— people, locale, activity of any kind?"

"No, nothing. Just a blank."

"No sense of where you were? Who you were with, if anyone?"

Zack shook his head.

"Any residual feelings or emotions?"

"Just a blank."

"Any sense of your own physical self?"

"No."

Dr. Luria asked a few more questions, then gave up, looking disappointed that he could recall nothing. They helped him to the screen, where he changed into his clothes.

"How about a coffee to help you wake up?" Sarah asked.

"Something cold. My mouth's dry," he said through the screen.

"We have some Poland Spring in the fridge."

He pulled up his pants and tucked in his shirt. "Got anything else?"

"Such as what?"

"Root beer?"

"Root beer?"

He slipped on his shoes, then stepped out from behind the screen. They were all staring at him. "You said root beer?" Sarah looked frozen in place.

"If you have any."

"Any particular brand?" Dr. Luria asked.

Did they stock a whole variety in their fridge? "I don't know . . . A and W."

"Is A&W root beer something you usually drink?"

"No. Any brand'll be fine. What's the problem?"

Luria approached him. "Zack, please bear with me. When was the last time you drank an A&W root beer?"

Zack's head still felt buzzed, as if insects festered in his skull. "Huh?"

"Please, just answer the question. When was the last time you had an A&W root beer?"

"I don't know," Zack began. "I can't remember the last time. Maybe when I was a kid . . . fifteen years ago, if ever. Why? What's this all about?"

"Do you live near any stores, billboards, fast-food places, with A&W signs visible?"

"No."

"Can you recall anyone in the recent past mentioning A&W or ordering one anywhere?"

"No."

Luria turned the laptop toward him. "Is the A&W logo an image that's familiar to you?"

"I think so, but I can't tell you what it looks like."

"But you'd probably recognize it, right?"

"I suppose."

"But it's not fresh in your head."

"No." The dark expectancy in Luria's eyes set off a small charge in him. "What's this all about?"

Luria nodded to Sarah. But instead of leaving for the drink, she produced a stepladder and moved it to a tall cabinet against the wall. She climbed up and removed a laptop flattened open on the top. When she got down, she turned the screen toward him, and on it was a shot of a frothy mug of A&W root beer.

"I don't get it," he said.

They were still staring at him. Then Dr. Luria said, "I think, my friend, you had an out-of-the-body experience."

36

....

"A what?"

"An out-of-the-body experience. Do you know what that is?"

"Like when people have accidents and watch paramedics give them CPR or whatever?"

"Precisely. Or in an operating room, patients will report floating over the scene."

"What does that have to do with root beer?"

"We conducted a test while you were in suspension," Luria said. "You couldn't see it from where you were, nor could we. But on top of that cabinet we placed that laptop with its screen opened to the ceiling. On it was an image randomly selected from hundreds. We had no idea what it was until you awoke. Your first request was for root beer, preferably A and W—the very image the computer had selected, visible only from above."

The cabinet was about seven feet tall with nothing visible on the top. The ceiling about three feet above that was made of nonreflective panels, so there was no way he could see even if he stuck his head out of the MRI tube. "Couldn't it be just a coincidence?"

"Statistically very unlikely, since you said you can't recall the last time you had that brand," Luria said.

"What about those images from the other day? Maybe it was one of them and stuck in my mind. I woke up thirsty, and that was the first thing I connected with."

"Except that in suspension, your brain cells were anesthetized from communicating with each other. Your memory bank was dormant."

"You mean even if that logo was in my head, I wouldn't have remembered it?"

"Precisely."

The skin on his scalp tightened.

"Another thing," said Luria. "The resolution power of this machine can record minuscule variations in cell-pattern activity from visual stimuli. Those brain scans we did the other day allowed us to identify discrete neuropatterns with specific images. You follow?"

"Kind of."

"In other words, the machine correlated particular images—kittens, sunsets, exotic cars, root beer logos, family photos—with neuroelectrical activity at the cell level."

"Think of it as a neurostatic fingerprinting," said Sarah. "What we saw in your brain activity patterns specifically correlates with that pattern when the A and W logo was shown to you the other day."

"So you can recognize particular emotional states of people?"

"Yes, modes of joy, anger, sadness—a full spectrum of emotional states."

"But pictures of birds or sunsets don't create emotional differences."

"You wouldn't think," Stern said. "But actually they do, but on a micro level. The brain creates very subtle

differences, 'microemotional' reactions to particular stimuli. With more personal images, like your pet, girlfriend,
a family member, or favorite vacation spot, there are
more pronounced neuroreactions. Eventually we can develop full neuroelectrical signatures of test subjects' various states. And those help us interpret what goes on
during NDEs.

"Also, some of these individual signature patterns coin-
cide with those of other test patients. In fact, some of these
patterns are standard and give us a boilerplate code."

"But I thought you said the anesthetic stopped the
electrical activity in my brain."

"That's right."

"Then how did you detect electrical patterns in the
scans?"

"That's the key question," Stern said. "There's a bio-
chemical explanation. Part of your brain didn't respond
to the anesthetic. Possibly there's an undiscovered so-
dium channel that did not react to the tetrodotoxin but
still kept you in a flatline state."

"I don't follow."

"Well, that specific neuroelectrical pattern regarding
the root beer logo could only have been there had you
woken up and climbed out of the MRI and up a ladder
to the cabinet."

"But that didn't happen," Zack said.

"That's right," said Dr. Luria. "The other explanation
is that in the state of suspension, your consciousness
transcended your brain. If you will, your spirit left your
body."

Zack's mind felt stunned. "But how . . . ?"

Sarah came over to him with a bottle of water. "Are
you okay?"

"I don't know. I'm having problems with what you're
telling me."

"Of course. It's a bit incredible to me also."

"But how do you explain that?"

Dr. Luria's face looked like a polished apple for the excitement she was trying to contain. "That's also what we're trying to determine and the reason why we'd like to run another test on you, if you wouldn't mind."

"You want to put me under again?"

"At another time. You need to rest up and let the sedative leave your system. We also need time to analyze all the data. But, if you're willing to have another session, we'll pay you another seven hundred and fifty dollars."

The group looked at him with faces full of expectation. He felt his Armenian merchant gene kick in. "How about a bonus for good behavior?"

Luria smiled. "Would eight hundred make you feel better?"

"Not as much as a thousand." He held his breath as Dr. Luria thought that over.

"You drive a hard bargain," Luria said. "Okay, one thousand. And we'll come up with a mutually convenient date."

Yes!

Then Luria took Zack's arm. "Zack, I want to remind you that nothing that occurred here tonight can be shared with anybody else. This is all still very confidential."

"Of course," Zack said, wondering how and when they'd reveal their findings. "How exactly are out-of-the-body experiences related to near-death experiences?"

"More than fifty percent of those having NDEs claim to have out-of-the-body experiences. They're part of the same phenomenon."

"What if it happens the next time?"

"Then it would all but eliminate coincidence," she said, "and would confirm that you acquired information while in suspension—that your unconscious mind left your body."

Zack made a move to follow Sarah to the exit. But Luria stopped him. "Zack, you may be interested in knowing that the heightened neuroactivity we recorded is located in the very sector associated with religious and spiritual experiences. It's known as the 'God lobe.'"

"The God lobe? But I'm not even religious."

"And that's what's so interesting."

Zack gathered his things. Then Sarah walked him to the door. "How are you doing?" Her eyes glowed warmly, and he liked the feel of her hand guiding him to the door. He was still a little shaky on his feet.

"A bit dazzled."

"Of course. It is very exciting," she said. "Oh," she added, and handed him a check.

He slipped that into his pocket and followed Bruce to the car. The chauffeur got into the driver's seat and closed the door. Before Zack got in, he turned to Sarah. "When you're not looking for the afterlife, do you ever go out for beer and pizza?"

"Are you inviting me?"

"Yeah."

"I'd be happy to."

"How about Friday night?"

"Sounds fine."

He got in the car. If this was his postcoma afterlife, he was beginning to enjoy it.

37

....

Roman entered La Dolce Vita restaurant feeling a little giddy. From what he surmised, Cola, Pomeroy, and company were conducting experiments that would have gotten them burned at the stake a few centuries back. Today, they hired Roman to do the job.

He ordered a seafood risotto and a glass of Chianti. His next assignment was a Roger Devereux, a research neuroscientist from Boston University School of Medicine. According to his scant information, the man was also a regular at this restaurant, coming in a couple of Monday evenings each month. He usually showed up for a seven o'clock reservation, window seat. It was six forty-five, and Roman had a table at the rear of the main room with a view of the empty reserved table by the window.

Through the windows, his eyes fell on a large Gothic church in red brick across the avenue. What a difference from the squat yellow brick structure of St. Luke's on a side street off of Franklin Avenue in Hartford. He still remembered Father Infantino's hellfire sermons about what would happen to sinners when they died—resurrected in body and mind and dumped into hell to suffer hideous punishment forever without the relief of death. The good father had claimed that there was a punishment tailor-made for every kind of sinner. Those who blasphemed God would be hanged by their tongues. Adulterers would have liquid iron poured on their genitals. Liars would be forced to chew their tongues while vultures pecked out their eyes. Women who had abortions would be made to wallow in excrement up to their chins. Murderers would be cast into pits of poisonous snakes. Those who turned their backs on God would be impaled on spits and roasted over blazing fires. And these torments would go on for eternity.

"And how long is eternity?" Father Infantino would howl. "Imagine a mountain thirty thousand feet high and that every ten thousand years a giant bird would fly to the top and rub its beak but once on the rocky peak. How long would it take before that wore the mountain to its base? Not a billionth of the time you'd burn in hell." And the awful magic of hell was that you wouldn't die. You wouldn't burn up—just suffer forever and ever, torment without end.

Even as a boy, Roman didn't understand how anyone could believe in a God who'd torture His disobedient children for all eternity. Wasn't God supposed to be good and loving and all-forgiving? Or was He such a raging sadist? If so, it was hard not to question His moral integrity. Also, how did Father Infantino know that hell was like this? Was that stuff really in the Bible? And wasn't the Bible written by a bunch of old guys thousands of years ago? Even if hell was really like that, why bother? Why not wipe out all of it? Blotto. Once you're dead, you're dead. No second chance, no hellfire. Hell was just not going to heaven where the good guys went.

Some years later, Roman would tell himself that Father Infantino's rants were the product of a sexually frustrated middle-aged guy who couldn't find a real job and who got off scaring the shit out of little kids. Probably diddled a few behind the altar.

But over the last few weeks, Roman began reexamining the possibilities beneath all the thunder. And what he had concluded was that there was a God after all. He wasn't sure that heaven was a city of gold and precious stones, or if God sat in a throne of light, or that you got to hang out with your dead relatives, saints, and Jesus himself for eternity. But he had come to believe that life did go on. And for some reason, these doctors were in league with Satan. So what did he have to lose by knocking them off? Nothing. And maybe an eternity to gain.

A little before seven, in walked a guy who matched the cell phone photo of Roger Devereux. He looked less like a professor of neurology at BU and more like someone behind the counter at Ace Hardware. He was short, chubby, and bald and was stuffed into a too tight blue blazer and blue shirt. He entered alone and was led to a window table. After maybe ten minutes, a woman appeared in the entrance and joined him. Devereux's wife, a former lab associate.

Roman had taken a table where he could not be seen by the Devereux, nor near the restrooms should either need one. He ate slowly and had a second cup of decaf while the couple finished their meal and left. Roman paid the check and followed the Devereux, who lived in a high-rise condo complex a few blocks from the restaurant. He kept his distance and waited for them to take the elevator to the fourteenth floor. Then fifteen minutes later, he rang the intercom for 1404. A male voice answered. "Dr. Devereux?"

"Yes."

"My name is John Farley. I'm from the Boston office of the FBI, and I'd like to ask you a few questions."

"FBI? What's this all about?"

"Well, I'd rather explain in person. If you'd like, we could talk down here or go someplace else, or I could come up."

"I'll be right down."

"Fine." The guy was smart. A minute later, he came down, still dressed in chinos and blue shirt. He opened the security door and stepped into the foyer. Roman smiled and flashed a phony photo badge fabricated a few years ago on another case. "I'm sorry to disturb you, but we'd like to talk to you about a former colleague of yours, LeAnn Cola."

"LeAnn? What about her?"

Roman looked around the bleak entryway. "It's a rather sensitive matter, and I'd rather not do it here. We could go find a coffee shop if you'd like."

Devereux studied Roman's sincere blue eyes. "No, come on up."

"Really, there's no need to disturb your family."

"No, that's fine." And he unlocked the security door and led them to the elevator.

Hook, line, and sinker, thought Roman as they stepped into the elevator.

Nothing was said in the ride up, and at the floor Devereux unlocked his condo door. "Ruth, we have a guest," he called out.

The wife appeared, and Devereux introduced Roman, who flashed his badge again and apologized for the intrusion. "Our office is investigating the death of Dr. LeAnn Cola," Roman said, then expressed condolences for the death of their friend.

Mrs. Devereux asked if he'd like coffee or something else to drink, and Roman politely refused. Then she disappeared into the other rooms, leaving him and Devereux on facing armchairs. To Roman's right was a

wall of built-in dark-wood shelves with books and photographs, including a large one of a woman and two
young children. Roman nodded at the photo. "Beautiful
children."

"Thanks. My daughter and her kids."

"Again, I'm sorry about the death of your associate."
Devereux thanked him as Roman reached into his briefcase by his feet and extracted a clipboard pad. "Does
the name Thomas Pomeroy mean anything to you?"

Devereux's face clouded over. "Yes, Tom was a friend
and colleague."

"You know that he died recently also."

"Yes."

"How did you know them?"

Devereux hesitated for a moment. "I worked with
them."

"Well, we have reason to believe that your colleagues
didn't die by accident or natural causes as reported but
were murdered."

"Murdered?"

"Yes. That their deaths were staged to appear like a
heart attack and gas leak."

"That's awful. Who would do such a thing? And why?"

"That's what we're hoping to learn." Then, with a
woeful expression, Roman added, "We think the deaths
are connected to some research they were doing. I'm
sorry to say that we picked up intelligence of a contract
on your own life."

"What?"

"Yes, someone wants you dead, and I'm hoping you'll
give me information that could help us prevent that."

Devereux's mouth went slack. "What?"

"Our sources tell us that the contracts may have come
from somewhere in the Catholic Church, believe it or
not."

"The Catholic Church?"

Hearing the squeal in Devereux's voice, the wife came out of a back room in her bathrobe. "Is everything okay?"

"Tom Pomeroy and LeAnn Cola were murdered," Devereux announced.

"What?"

"Mrs. Devereux, I'm afraid that's true and that your husband's life is in danger, maybe your own. And we think it has to do with the research you all worked on." Before either of them could catch their breath, Roman turned to Devereux. "I'm wondering if you could tell me about that project, because I think it'll help prevent more killings." Then he turned to the wife. "And Mrs. Devereux, please join us, since I understand you assisted."

In shock, the woman lowered herself onto the sofa. "We were doing research on sleep, what happens in the brain in various states," Devereux said.

"Sleep?"

"The project was confidential by contract, but we worked on imaging software."

"Can you tell me a little more, like why someone would want to stop you?"

Devereux stared at him for a long moment. "I think it might be a good idea if I contacted my lawyer before we continue. We're entering sensitive areas. I'd also like to notify the local police if my life is in danger."

"You don't need the police. You've got the FBI. We're working to protect you."

"You keep on saying *we,* but there's only you."

"I don't like this," Mrs. Devereux said. "I'm scared." She shot to her feet and started to move away.

"Where you going?" Roman asked.

"To call the police." She headed for the telephone on a corner desk.

"That's not a good idea," Roman said. But she didn't

stop. So Roman pulled a silenced pistol from his brief-case and shot her twice in the back. She crumpled in place. But before her husband could move, Roman low-ered the gun to his face. "Move and you're dead."

A yelp rose from his throat as he stared at his wife's body.

"Tell me what you were doing on that project."

For a long moment Devereux struggled to control himself, looking from Roman to his wife to the gun aimed at his head. "Who—who are you? Why did you shoot her?" His voice warbled with horror and disbe-lief.

He started to get up, but Roman flicked the gun at him. "I'll kill you."

Devereux settled back in place.

"Tell me what you, Cola, and Pomeroy were working on, and no more sleep research bullshit, because I know where your daughter and her children live. And if you give me any double-talk, I will kill you and visit them, *capice*?"

Devereux nodded, his face a bloodless bag of loose flesh. His voice choked as he glanced at his wife's lifeless body, blood spreading across her blouse. "Near-death experiences."

"Near-death experiences?"

"They were bringing people to flatline to detect elec-trical activity."

"Keep going."

"To see if there was anything to the claim—dead rela-tives, heaven, whatever."

Oh my, Roman thought.

Devereux continued, gasping for air. "Or just neuro-biology."

"What does this have to do with Satan?"

"Satan? I—I don't know what you're talking about."

"Why is the Church opposed to your research?"

"The Church? I didn't know it was."

"You were trying to prove if the afterlife was for real or just in the brain, right?"

Devereux nodded.

"And what did you conclude?"

"I don't know. It's still ongoing."

"Where was your research done?"

"I don't know. It was all freelance. I know nothing else about it, I swear on my life."

"How much did they pay you for your work?"

"Five thousand."

"Are they still doing the experiments?"

"I think so."

Roman studied Devereux squirming in the chair. He looked as if he was telling the truth. "Why does the Catholic Church want you dead?"

By reflex, Devereux sucked in his breath. "I don't know. Please let me go."

"Think."

"I don't know. Maybe because we were trying to prove that religious experience was just brain chemistry."

Roman felt a small jab to his solar plexus. "You think they're on to something?"

"I don't know. Please don't kill me."

"What else do you know? Who else worked with you?"

"All I know is they got a test subject with positive results."

"Meaning what?"

"He's neurosensitive. I don't know. I just worked on the imaging software. His name was in the paper a while back. He woke from a coma and people thought Jesus was talking through him or something."

"You got a name?"

"No. Some college kid. That's all I know."

"What happened to him?" Roman slipped to his knees and pushed the silencer near his mouth. "Tell me the truth. Tell me names of any others. Or where I can find them, and I'll let you live."

"I—I don't know any others. I worked on the side and gave the results to Morris."

"Morris who?"

"Morris Stern. That's all I know. I swear I know nothing else. I swear."

"Anything else about this kid?"

"No."

Roman studied him for a moment as he sat shuddering in the armchair, his face colorless, his mouth panting, his eyes twitching. Roman then jammed the silencer into Devereux's mouth and pulled the trigger. The bullet exited the back of his skull, splattering blood and brain matter onto the back cushion and far wall.

Roman had been careful not to touch anything. He put on a pair of surgical gloves, removed the silencer, and wiped the pistol clean of his prints. He then pressed the gun in Devereux's hand and let it fall as if he had committed suicide after shooting his wife.

Before he left the apartment and took the exit stairs to the street, he looked back on the scene of the dead Devereux.

Nearer my God to Thee, he thought, and slipped away.

38

....

"It's going well. I sleep and they pay down my Discover card, thanks to you."

"Glad it's working out," Damian said.

"So the good news is this dinner is on me."

Damian looked down at his chicken burrito. "Hell, we could have been at Davio's."

"Next time."

Zack had met Damian at Qdoba, a Mexican eatery that bordered the Northeastern campus and sat at the same Huntington Avenue intersection where five months ago he had hit a pothole on his bike and landed in a coma.

"So what are they testing for?" Damian asked.

"They wire my head and measure the activity while I'm dreaming." He didn't like being vague, especially since Damian had gotten him the gig. But he had signed the nondisclosure forms, and Dr. Luria was insistent that what they did in the lab had to remain in the lab.

"Any interesting dreams?"

Yeah, gasping for air and chewing sand.

"Just fantasies of a hot neurobiologist on the project."

"That gives you something to look forward to."

"Yeah," Zack said, thinking about the eddy of emotions that had swirled in him since the helmet episode. No doubt aftereffects of the stimulation, deep sweet memories of his father would poke through the resentment that had stratified over the years. Like this morning while at the library. He was working on his thesis when his mind clicked back to a silly game they'd played when he was maybe four years old. He would slip under his little-boy blanket with the goofy cats, and when he called, "Ready," his father would come into the room. "Where's Zack? Where, oh, where can little Zack be?" And he'd hear his father look in the closet, under the bed, in bureau drawers, all the while saying, "Where's my Zack? He's got to be here somewhere." And this would go on until Zack couldn't hold in the giggles anymore and threw back the blanket and announced, "Here's your Zack!" And his father would slap his chest in mock surprise and say, "There's my Zack!" And he'd jump on the bed and smother him with kisses that turned into a tickle attack that left Zack giddy with laughter. The memory was as fresh as yesterday, and it had left him hollow with yearning.

When they were finished eating, Damian offered to give Zack a ride home. "Thanks anyway. I'm being picked up just down the street."

"More sleep?"

"Something like that. By the way, can I borrow your car this weekend?"

"A date with the hot neurobiologist?"

"If there's a God."

"There is," Damian said, and flashed his saintly smile. "Unfortunately, I'm going on a retreat in Vermont. But any other time. Going to be great weather, so go for a walk with her." Then he added, "Live in light, go in faith."

It was one of his little salutations, born more of habit than stubborn efforts to convert him. "Thanks, I'll try."

....

At six o'clock, Bruce showed up and drove him to the lab to Beethoven's Third. By seven thirty, he was changed, on the gurney, and hooked up to the IV and monitors. Then they rolled him into the fMRI machine. When Sarah asked if he was ready, he nodded. And the last thing he remembered was her depressing the anesthesia into his IV.

"Zack, can you hear me?" A female voice.

He woke up with a mouthful of sand.

"He's coming to."

He couldn't catch his breath. Throat was clogged. Lungs were sacs of concrete.

"Come on, Zack, wake up."

He pushed against the weight, trying to free his hands. With every ounce of strength, he loosened them and clawed his way out. The cold night snapped against his skin. He rolled onto his knees, his diaphragm racking for air, his mouth drooling grit.

"That's it, open your eyes."

His eyes. They were swollen slits and lined with sand. His mouth, nostrils, and ears were clogged. His hair. Gritted. And mites were eating him all over.

"Push, Zack. You can do it."

Through the gloom, he could make out the water's edge—black curls lapping the shore. Like a crab, he scuttled toward the surf and lunged in. The salt water stung his eyes and skin, but he forced himself to stay under until the bugs and sand washed away.

Then he was lying on his back, filling his lungs with sweet, cool air.

"That's it. Push a little harder. Open your eyes."

Light. The moon had broken through the cloud cover and set the sky in motion.

"How you doing?" A woman was peering down at him.

Then others.

He had no idea who they were. His body jolted. He had no idea who he was.

"Welcome back."

His lips and tongue were numb. His eyes were burning. Their faces hung in watery blurs.

"Zack? Are you all right?"

"What are you doing?" Fear jerked his body. He tried to get up, but his limbs were wooden blocks. And his arms and chest were tangled in something.

"Don't be afraid," the younger woman said. "You're doing fine."

"Who are you?"

"Zack, it's me, Sarah Wyman." The woman pushed her face forward. "You remember me. And Dr. Luria and Dr. Cates."

He tried to sit up but was heavy with wet sand and vegetation. And his head was thick with sludge. He flopped back down on the sand and looked up at the people. This woman and two others, one an older woman and the other a younger black man. He had no idea who they were. He had no idea why they were calling him Zack.

With help from the younger woman, he sat up and blood drained from his head.

"Don't you remember?" the older woman asked.

He shook his head. He remembered nothing.

"Tell me your name," she said, her face looking tight and pale but for dried blood on her cheek. She looked vaguely familiar.

For a long moment, he stared into her eyes. *Your*

name. Your name. "I don't know." He looked around but couldn't see the beach or water. And the sky had been replaced with a ceiling, and the moon was panels of fluorescent lights.

Your name. He knew he had one. A history. A presence. Yet it was just beyond his grasp.

"You'd been asleep for an hour, don't you remember? This is Elizabeth Luria and Morris Stern and Byron Cates. And me, Sarah. We were doing tests on you."

The night beach had faded into a large white room with electronic equipment attached by wires to his head and arms, where the seaweed had been. Behind him was a large machine with a round opening. And three people. Then, like a Polaroid image developing, it all came back to him. "Zack . . . Kashian."

"Good," Sarah said, looking relieved. "Do you know why you're here?"

"Yes." And they asked him the usual questions to test the state of his memory.

Then Dr. Luria began a battery of other questions. "Do you remember anything—images or experiences, locales, other people—from when you were in suspension?"

Suspension? He wasn't in suspension. He wasn't asleep. "I think I was on a beach."

"A beach?" Luria said.

His mind was foggy, and his recall faded rapidly. "Got sand in my face."

"You were kind of spitting when you came through," Sarah said.

"Recall what you were doing at the beach?" Luria asked, her face stiff with concern.

"No."

"Any movements of any kind—walking, jumping, swimming, interacting with people?"

"I don't recall anything."

"What about the presence of other people?"

Zack shook his head. "I was alone."

Byron Cates came over from the computer. "Zack, can you characterize your emotional state while at that beach?"

"My emotional state?" He thought for a moment, trying to summon the experience. Then he shook his head. "Not really. Just a blank."

Cates glanced at Luria for a moment. "No sense of anxiety or fear?"

"No."

"Are you sure?"

"Yeah, I'm sure. Why you asking?"

"Because your blood chemistry registered a high level of cortisol, which is a stress hormone secreted by the adrenal gland."

Dr. Stern cut in. He had been studying feedback from the computer monitor he was at. "Zack, we've been doing these kinds of tests for a while, matching blood and neuroelectrical activities with subjective reports. There's every indication your unconscious experience was borderline violent."

"But I don't remember any of it."

"Just as well," Stern said. "Because it appears you were fighting for your life."

39

"Zachary Kashian," Roman Pace whispered to himself. "Gotcha!"

The morning after his visit to the Devereux, Roman went to the Providence Public Library on Empire Street, where he Googled "coma," "woke," and "Jesus." He came up with over 277,000 hits. He refined the search by adding "Massachusetts," reducing it to 5,000 hits. At the top were recent reports about a Northeastern grad student who had gotten into a bicycling accident back in January and ended up in a coma for nearly three months, waking up this past Easter Sunday.

What held Roman's attention was that during the coma, the kid had mysteriously muttered snippets of Jesus's Sermon on the Mount, including the Lord's Prayer, in the original language. That and how a lot of miracle-seeking religious fanatics had crashed his hospital room and had to be removed by security.

One of the doctors remarked that "given the severity of his trauma and the coma level," his odds of recovery were "very slim"—borderline miraculous. Others were convinced that Kashian was channeling Jesus Christ. According to all reports, the kid had never been exposed to Aramaic. He was also a member of some college atheist club.

What made Roman's heart leap was that a nurse's aide, so taken by the "miracle," had captured the mutterings on a cell phone video. She was subsequently fired for breach of confidentiality. But the clip had made it to YouTube, and Roman watched it over and over again.

Of course, the kid was emaciated and his head had been shaved and had wires coming out of it. And with his eyes closed, he looked like something this side of a corpse. Roman could not tell what he really looked like, but he froze the video and printed up a frame.

The likeness was made worse by the graininess. But it would do.

40

....

Sarah lived just off of Harvard Square in a second-floor apartment on Harvard Street, across from the Penny-packer dormitory. She met Zack at the door that Friday night, and they walked down the street to Massachu-setts Avenue and to the Grafton Street Pub & Grill, where they got a table in view of the bar.

She was dressed in jeans, a cream-colored shirt, and a matching jacket. With her short auburn hair, she looked more like a French fashion model than a neuroscientist. A waiter hustled over and took their drink orders. Zack asked for a Guinness and Sarah a sauvignon blanc.

"So, what's a nice girl like you doing in near-death experiences?" he asked her.

She chuckled. "Now, there's an original line. Well, my grad work was with Morris Stern in his neurobiology lab at Tufts. He was working on enhancing molecular MRI imaging and ended up as my thesis adviser. He signed up with Dr. Luria, and later he asked me aboard."

"What was your thesis on?"

"Neurotheology."

"Ah, yes: 'The Role of Serotonin . . . Receptors in Spir-ituality.'"

She nodded. "The neurological mechanisms active in spiritual and religious experiences."

"Kind of what you're doing with Dr. Luria—seeing if we're hardwired for God."

"Yes. We know that mystical experiences originate from the same mechanisms that produce hallucinations—you know, people who claim to see the Virgin Mary, dead grandmothers, even space aliens. When the parietal lobe is stimulated, that region reports a sense of another's presence."

"What happened to me in the booth."

"Yes. We stimulated your parietal lobe, and you sensed your father's presence."

"But it felt so real."

"As we knew it would. The challenge was to find a diagnostic means to distinguish these from actual experiences."

The waiter returned with their drinks.

"Before she got the fMRI prototype, Elizabeth was restricted to interviewing hospital patients who claimed NDEs. Now we can do it in the lab under controlled conditions."

"So how long have you been flatlining people?"

"Only three months, but the project's been going on for a few years."

"How many others have you suspended?"

"The data's confidential, but a few."

"Can you say what you've determined so far?"

"Nothing conclusive, but Elizabeth's very excited about your testing."

"Because I've got a hot God lobe."

She sipped her wine. "Yes."

"So how come I get a craving for root beer instead of a tunnel to the pearly gates?"

"Maybe next time."

And how come I have flashes of digging myself out of sand? another voice cut in. But he pushed it down, and the waiter came for their orders. Sarah requested the shrimp risotto and Zack the blackened tuna.

"One of the other problems," she said, "is trying to separate actual near-death experiences from confabulations. People make all sorts of claims, some the result of autosuggestion—what they think they should experience: moving down tunnels, life reviews, meeting beings of light. Claims that don't match with neuro and metabolic activity."

"So it's easier to verify out-of-the-body experiences because they either identify images or they don't."

"Yes, and reports of NDEs are nearly untestable. All we can see is activity and blood chemistry, which tells us something about the emotions of the experience."

"Do people ever report bad NDEs, something other than light and peace?"

"On occasion. Why?"

"Just wondering. All you hear about are blissful ones."

"The literature cites a few cases of unpleasant experiences. But nothing I've seen."

Zack sipped his beer. "You're a scientist, so where do you stand on all this? Do you think my mind actually separated from my brain and floated to the ceiling?"

"The short answer is maybe. But that's the big question—what sits at the heart of the whole science-faith debate: Is the mind reducible to neural networks, or is there something beyond the physicality of the brain? And if so, does it exist in another realm—heaven, nirvana, the afterlife?"

"Yeah, all of that."

"Well, I'm also a former dyed-in-the-wool Roman Catholic. I used to believe that religion was a leap of faith, untouched by rationalism. But the more I studied, the more I began to lapse in faith." She took another sip of wine. "Yet this project raises other possibilities."

"Like what?"

"Like maybe there's something to the spiritual world, though not in the biblical sense."

"So, you believe in God but you don't."

She smiled. "I like how you word things."

"One of the few benefits of being an English major: saying things to impress a date."

"I'm impressed. Let's say that I'm still skeptical, but if there is a spiritual sentience, I don't believe it's the Judeo-Christian-Muslim paternal figure who watches over all life and answers prayers."

"You're not quite a born-again NDE-er."

"No, I'm still stuck in the materialist school—you know, that consciousness is a function of the living brain—and once the brain is dead, so is sentience. So an NDE is a shut-down mechanism of the brain telling the body to die."

"Then how do you explain all the reports of heavenly light and great peacefulness?"

"Possibly evolutionary strategies to make death easier to accept—buffers to the horror of one's dying."

"Pure neurobiology," he said, using Stern's phrase.

"Yes. For an NDE to be real, one would have to scientifically demonstrate that consciousness survives clinical death. And the only way to do that is for someone to acquire information when their unconscious mind leaves their body."

"Like my craving for root beer."

"Maybe."

"But that could also be a coincidence, or recall of the photo tests."

"Except that you couldn't have remembered it. Also, we've seen other OBEs before."

"Maybe more coincidences."

"Or maybe evidence that the mind *can* separate from the body."

"Do you believe that?"

"I'm open to the possibility, but not there yet." Then she leaned forward, her face glowing as if a light had clicked on inside. "But if true, what an awesome possibility—that in the end, we experience a transformation in states, from physical to nonphysical sentience. In short, there's no such thing as death. And that once we die, our minds merge with a cosmic sentience—the Overmind."

The intensity of her manner sent a ripple through him. "The Overmind?"

"Another sci-fi term. Some think that mental telepathy is a glimpse of the Overmind. Also that some of us are genetically programmed for such."

For a shuddering moment, his head filled with the face of Winston glowering at him across the poker table.

"And that telepathic people are evidence that we all merge with the Ovemind—which is what all religions talk about. If that could be demonstrated—a huge *if*—it might be *the* discovery of all time. As Elizabeth says, what we need are secrets from the grave."

"Such as?"

"Such as information known only to the deceased and not the subject."

"Like meeting your dead grandmother, who says there's treasure buried in the backyard. And lo and behold, you take a shovel and voilà."

"That would do it."

Zack was enjoying the suppleness of her mind and the vigorous enthusiasm in her manner that lit her eyes and lent a resplendence to her beautiful face. He could also tell that she was enjoying being with him—and that gave him relief that there was life after Amanda. When

they had broken up last year, Zack had nearly convinced himself that his best options were behind him,
that he was not destined to find a woman who was as
fascinating, smart, and attractive. "I get the feeling that
Dr. Luria is more open to spiritual possibilities."

"Yes."

"And Dr. Stern is pure neurobiology, kind of like yourself."

She smiled warmly at his name, as if he were more
than a mentor, maybe a father figure. "He's a hard-core
rationalist, a geneticist by training, who takes an evolutionary interest in the phenomena. He believes that a
small number of people have a bent toward spirituality,
but that's as far as he goes."

"That we're wired to believe in God," he said.

"Yes, which has the evolutionary advantage of forg-
ing communities based on belief systems, at the heart of
which are shamans, priests, and other specially wired
people."

"But that's not the same as saying there's a God."

"No, just that some have neurological hankerings for
a God."

"And visions of tunnel light and dead relatives are the
brain's way of softening death."

"Yes. Interestingly, when the brain dies, the optical
center creates illusions of moving down a tunnel toward
light."

"I can see why some would consider that sacrilegious."

The waiter came with their orders, and they ate quietly
for a few moments. Zack could not remember having such
a satisfying first date—if that's what this was. "When I
was a kid, I used to ask God for a sign—make a weird
noise, cause an animal to step out of the woods, send a
meteorite across the sky. Something out of the ordinary.
But I never got one." And when his father died, Zack

prayed for him to show himself, whisper to him, brush his cheek. He drew a blank there also.

"We all do that. Every time I get on a plane, I whisper a prayer we don't crash. When my mother got cancer, I prayed to save her. But if God intervened whenever we asked, there'd be no science. In fact, the world would be a frightening place with nothing predictable."

The waiter came by. Sarah ordered a second glass of wine. Zack had another beer. He looked around the restaurant. It was mostly a young crowd, college kids and young professionals. "I've got a feeling not a lot of other people in here are talking about whether there's an afterlife."

"They're probably more concerned about the Red Sox."

"Now *that's* important." On the bar monitors, the Sox were behind Toronto 6–2. As Zack scanned the bar, his eyes fell on a man sitting alone and reading a newspaper. Their eyes locked, then the man went back to his paper. Zack leaned into Sarah. "That guy with the newspaper and the Patriots hat. Does he look familiar to you?"

Sarah glanced over her shoulder. "Not really. Is he someone famous?"

The man was white and in his fifties, with an oval face partially hidden by the cap and glasses. "I don't know, but he's been eyeing us since he came in."

"No one I've seen before."

"Maybe he's checking out good-looking women."

"Or good-looking men."

"He'd do better with option one." Zack paid the check, and they got up to leave. Meanwhile, the guy behind the paper paid them no attention as they walked outside.

It was a pleasant evening, and the Square was alive with people. They walked to Brattle Street, then back up Massachusetts Avenue. Zack enjoyed the Square, although it had lost its renegade charm, funky little shops and eateries giving way to mall franchises. They cut through Harvard Yard, which took them back to Harvard Street and Sarah's apartment, where he had locked his bike.

Zack hoped she would ask him upstairs, but she didn't. Maybe this was just a professional tryst rather than a bona fide date. It crossed his mind to give her a kiss, but he didn't want to push matters. So he thanked her for the pleasant evening and extended his hand. She took it and, surprisingly, gave him a hug. "See you Tuesday."

Zack was so happy for that gesture that in his distraction while unchaining his bike at a nearby telephone pole, he failed to notice a man in a blue shirt and Patriots hat watching him from the silver SUV across the street.

41

....

Bruce dropped off Zack at the lab around seven that next Tuesday, and Sarah met him at the entrance and walked him to the lab office. "Where did you find that guy?"

"Bruce?"

"Yeah. Not exactly Hoke Colburn."

"Who's Hoke Colburn?"

"Morgan Freeman in *Driving Miss Daisy*. He's got the personality of asphalt."

Sarah laughed. "I'll see what I can do."

"Also, see if you can arrange a bona fide tunnel."

"We'll work on that, too."

"My luck, I'll end up in the Ted Williams with no money and a maniacal toll collector."

"You're in good spirits," she said.

"For a guy who's going to die."

"You're not going to die," she said. "And thanks again for Friday night. I had a good time."

"Enough to do it again?"

"Sure."

She opened the door to the MRI room, where Drs. Luria, Stern, and Cates greeted him. He then changed and got up on the gurney, where Sarah and Cates hooked him up to the monitors and IV. He could feel his heart pounding in anticipation. As Sarah adjusted a connection, he whispered, "In case I don't come back, you're gorgeous."

"You are, too," she said. "See you soon."

Zack smiled and passed out.

His first awareness was of moving through a tunnel toward light. No, not a tunnel. A hole above him with a dim slice of light glowing through the opening. And the walls were made of sand, and he was pushing his way upward. But he had no idea who he was or where he was. A dull, filmy moon hung overhead, and he was covered with sand and chilled to the bone and burning from stings of things needling into his flesh. His mouth was numb and his fingers stiff, as if his blood had turned to wax.

He pulled himself out of the hole and began to shuffle across the sand toward the water, guided by some raw instinct. His feet were bare and half-numb to the rocks and shells, too distracted by the chilled air.

"Hey, sport, want to hit a few?"

He stopped and looked behind him, and coming toward him across the sun-warmed sandbar was his dad, with a bright yellow bat and bucket of whiffle balls. On the beach sat his mom in a lounge chair, with Jake on a blanket with the kid from the next-door rental.

Instantly, the world was sunny and good. *"Sure."*

His dad was five feet ten, but he looked twice as tall standing before him on the flats, his big hard body glistening from sunscreen and his gold crucifix winking at him from the chain around his neck.

"What about Jake? He can play field."

"He said he'd rather get some sun."

"Did you ask?"

"Yeah, but he's not the baseball type. But you are, sport. And you're a hitter, right?"

"Right."

With the bat, his dad scratched a home plate in the sand, then moved some feet away and drew the pitcher's mound. When Zack said he was ready, his father made an underhand pitch. Zack swung mightily but missed. *"That's okay. You'll get it."* His dad made three more pitches, and each time he missed.

"You're swinging like a girl. You're chopping at it. Make a straight easy swing."

Mortified, Zack tried again, and again he missed.

His father came over to him and crouched down. *"I think you've been watching your brother too much. The secret of hitting the ball is how you hold the bat."* While Zack held it in his hands, his dad positioned his feet and got him to choke up. *"And keep your upper arm parallel to the ground. Know what parallel means?"*

"Sure." He could smell his dad's sunscreen, a scent he loved and one he always associated with him. *"Like this?"* Zack raised his arm, the bat at a stiff angle over his shoulder.

"Perfect."

His father beamed and patted his shoulder. And a ripple of pleasure passed through him as he got ready to show his dad.

"Okay, now hold it just like that." He went back to the pitching line. *"Ready?"*

"Ready." When the next ball came, Zack swung but missed again. And he smacked the sand with the bat. *"I stink."*

"No, you don't. You swung too soon. Keep your eye on the ball."

One more went by, and he tipped it. *"Now you're getting it."* Before the next one came, his dad said, *"You're a hitter, Zack."*

And he smacked the next one, sending it far over his

father's head. "*There you go!*" his dad shouted, and he shot his fist into the air.

He hit several more.

Then they were walking down the flats, which glistened in the late morning sun as if the sea had been sprinkled with diamond dust. Seagulls wheeled overhead, sometimes landing on the sandbar to squawk hysterically over a dead fish.

"*Dad, you like Jake, right?*"

"*Of course I do. Why do you ask that?*"

"*Just wondering. You know what?*"

"*What?*"

"*I wish you never had to go back to work and it could be summer all the time.*"

"*Me, too.*" And his dad put his arm around his shoulders and kissed him on the head.

They picked up shells—huge ashtray-size quahogs, whitened by the sun. They skipped stones. They skipped quahog shells. And the sea sparkled with frenzied glee.

It was the happiest moment of the summer.

They continued down the sun-warmed flats of the sandbar for a few more minutes, then his father stopped. He looked back toward the beach, toward where their cottage hunched on dunes above their umbrella. Gray clouds were rolling in from the mainland.

"*I have to tell you something,*" his father said. "*It's important.*"

His father had gripped him by the shoulders, and his face was serious. "*What?*"

"Time to wake up."

"That's it, Zack. Open your eyes. How do you feel?"

It took him a few moments to catch up to his awakening. He blinked around the bright lab, taking in Sarah, who was standing there with a clipboard. Dr. Luria was next to her, and Drs. Stern and Cates were at their computer monitors. Two technicians were watching from the other office through the windows.

"Are you all right?" Sarah asked, handing him a cup of water.

Her voice sounded as if it came from a mile-long tunnel. He nodded.

"Unless you prefer root beer."

He shook his head and sipped the water.

"Do you recall anything?" Luria asked.

He felt himself adjust to the moment. "Just scraps."

"Like what?"

"The sandbar of a beach. I think it was Sagamore."

"Sagamore Beach?" Luria said.

"Kind of vague," he said. "With my father, hitting balls."

"Go on," Luria said.

He struggled to find the words. From what he recalled, it was a strange double vision, and he didn't know how to explain seeing himself as a boy through his own eyes, then through someone else's in weirdly shifting perspectives. He remembered seeing his father pitch to him, then from a distance he saw himself in baggy green trunks swinging the bat.

"I was hitting whiffle balls, but I can't remember anything else."

"How would you characterize your emotional state?"

"Happy." Instantly he felt himself choke up. He squeezed down, reciting pi.

Sensing his struggle, Sarah cut in. "Zack, did you have a sense of other people?"

He wanted to thank her for changing the subject. He shook his head.

"No other people on the beach?" Luria asked.

"A few down the sandbar. I think my mother and brother were on the beach."

"But you remember playing ball with your father."

He felt himself gain control again. "Yeah, and it felt very real, not like a dream—like I was there on that sandbar." He could still feel the warmth of the sun on his skin as Dr. Cates began to peel off the electrode cups. He could still feel the soft, fine sand of the flats, his father's hand in his as they walked along.

"Did you feel yourself detach from your body?" Dr. Luria asked.

"No, I was in my own head," Zack said, trying to get back. But the experience was fading fast, as if he were pulling away from the scene.

"Anything else happen in the experience?" Luria asked. "I mean besides hitting balls with your father, then walking down the sandbar? Did he say anything?"

"He said he wanted to tell me something."

"What exactly did he say?"

"Just that, then I woke up." He could still see the expression on his father's face—serious, time for "a big-boy talk." From nowhere the phrase shot up. *Big-boy talk.*

"That's it?"

"Yes."

They continued interviewing him, going over the same ground. He could see their disappointment, especially Dr. Luria's. "What did the scan and blood show?" he asked.

"We still have to analyze them," said Dr. Stern at his computer. "But the secretions show that you had a pleasurable experience, unlike the last time."

"If it's okay with you," Luria said, "we'd like to do another run this Friday if that's good for you."

He still felt a dull jab of anxiety but agreed. But this time it wasn't the thousand-dollar fee. He felt an agonizing yearning to get back to the flats with his dad.

42

....

Warren Gladstone loved the Lord. He loved the Lord with all his heart and soul and mind. He loved the Lord more than anything else in his life, because he knew that God loved him. And with God's love all things were possible.

Warren had asked the Lord God for water, and the Lord God gave him a river. He'd asked the Lord God for light, and the Lord God gave him the sun. He'd asked the Lord God for a flower, and the Lord God gave him a garden. He'd asked the Lord God to show him the way to defeat the enemy, atheistic science, and the Lord brought him this video.

"Who is he?"

"His name is Zachary Kashian," Elizabeth said. "He's a grad student at Northeastern University here in town."

"Well, this certainly beats a bunch of drug addicts and illegals."

"We had to start somewhere," Elizabeth Luria said.

"Except they found hell instead of paradise."

They met in an elegant suite on the tenth floor of the Taj Boston at the corner of Arlington and Newbury. Because of the commanding view, this was Warren's favorite venue for their meetings where Elizabeth and Morris Stern would apprise him of their progress. For too long, *progress* had been an overstatement, with mediocre results at best, sometimes outrageous failures such as the mental impairment or death of test subjects. Some committed suicide, others suffered relapses of suspension because of excessive dosages of tetrodotoxin. Only in the last few months had true progress been made, and Elizabeth had called this meeting to recap the turnaround.

"So, tell me what I'm looking at." Stern and Byron Cates had brought laptops.

"We're looking at images from the functional MRI machine whose resolution power is unlike any other on the planet, thanks to your generosity, Reverend."

Warren cringed whenever Morris Stern addressed him as Reverend, because all he heard was sarcasm. Stern was a hard-nosed scientist whose expertise alone qualified him for the project. He held no spiritual beliefs: He lived in a universe where nothing was sacred. He had been heard saying that religion was the enemy of free thinking and more about death than peace. He had once claimed that all religious conflict reduced to "My imaginary friend is better than your imaginary friend." His antireligious stance was rooted in his secular Jewish upbringing. So, having him run the diagnostics was like hiring a blind man to invent a better light bulb. But he knew that Stern would soon prove himself dead wrong and end up singing "Amazing Grace." Warren lived for that moment.

Stern brought up images on the two separate monitors. "The left shows interaxonal activity from Zack's brain while in suspension. On the right are brain images of others during flatline. You can see the clear differences." He scrolled through several different images. "Each of these subjects was flatlined. When we woke them, they claimed to have no NDEs."

"You're saying that none of the others had near-death experiences?"

"Correct," Elizabeth said. "This one is special. Very. His brain electricity is extraordinary." She nodded for Morris Stern to continue.

"The first time we put him under, he claimed to have no discrete NDE." Stern moved the mouse, and a video image of the MRI of Zack Kashian's brain appeared with moving blotches. "A few days later, we put him under again, and you can see the different patterns move from flatlined inactivity to a full OBE. Whatever was going on, his mind appeared to be functioning independently from his brain. Of course, we have to do more work with him before we can draw any conclusions."

Warren nodded. The godless bastard wouldn't give an inch. He looked to Elizabeth for a more enlightened interpretation.

"Warren, what we can tell you is all good news. Zack has had three different experiences while in suspension. And the last—his most coherent yet—appears to indicate the presence of another mind—one independent of his own. It's only in scraps of exterior data, and we still need to run more analyses. But it's the first time we've seen anything approaching something like an external sentience."

"Hal-le-lu-jah!" Warren said, drawing out the syllables with glee.

"Yes, hallelujah," Elizabeth said as if taking an oath. "At this stage, he still doesn't have clear recollections of his NDEs, but the diagnostics indicate great intensity."

"And we still have a lot of computations to do before drawing any conclusion." It was Stern, muttering to nobody in particular.

Warren disregarded him like a gnat and glared at the colored mottlings imposed on the schematic of Zack Kashian's brain. "This fellow may be a godsend . . . literally."

"Yes," Elizabeth said. "He's got the most active God lobe we've ever seen. Last week, he positively identified a root beer logo hidden from view. Then he had two more NDEs that he couldn't recall but which showed high activity. What distinguished the last one was the emotional profile. His bloodwork showed secretions of chemicals associated with fear followed by serotonin tranquillity."

"Dare I suggest that he crossed over to heaven?" Warren could see Stern rub his nose in disdain at the suggestion. The man was a godless fool, locked in his own steel-clad tunnel with the cold light of reason burning at one end, a sealed tomb at the other.

"A lovely thought," Elizabeth said, "and maybe so. But he reported none of the classic experiences: no tunnel, bright lights, no sense of tranquillity. Just playing ball with his father."

"And his father is dead, correct?"

"Yes," Elizabeth said.

"So maybe he was interacting with his father's spirit."

Before she could respond, Stern cut in. "Or maybe a flash dream just before he woke up."

Warren nearly spat at Stern.

"We still have more tests to run before we can draw conclusions," Elizabeth said.

"The point is," Stern continued, "we haven't got enough data to determine if sensing a dead loved one is a so-called spiritual experience or long-term memory rising from stimulation of the temporal lobe—the more likely case."

"You don't give an inch, do you?"

"I would if I saw the evidence."

"It's still very encouraging," Elizabeth said, trying to end the scrapping.

Warren nodded. "Okay, so what do we know about him?"

"He needs the money."

"That hardly distinguishes him," Warren said.

"No, but his father abandoned him and his mother when he was about ten, and he claims to have sensed his presence in the booth test. He hasn't said it in so many words, but I think he wants to make contact."

"Don't we all," Warren said.

"She means he wants contact with his biological father," said Stern.

"We would all do well to seek our Heavenly Father, you included," Warren said. Then he turned to Elizabeth. "So, what's the next step?"

"To suspend him again. We've scheduled him for this Friday."

"I'd like to meet this young man." Warren checked his watch. He had a meeting with his accountant in an hour. But there was something in Elizabeth's face.

"I hate to be the bearer of bad news," she said, "but we lost another of our colleagues, Roger Devereux. He and his wife, Ruth, were found shot to death—a case of murder-suicide, according to the police."

"Good God. How horrible!"

"Yes. We didn't know of any problems," Elizabeth said.

"Roger was a good man," Stern interjected. "He helped design the imaging software. His wife was also a neurologist who worked with him. It's a terrible loss."

"The police have no motive so far. We don't know what went wrong," Elizabeth said.

"That's the third person associated with the project who's died in the last month."

"I'm afraid so."

Although he financed the project and met regularly with the principals, Warren didn't know others whose work on the project had been contracted for specific tasks. And only the principals and a couple of technicians knew the big picture. It was their way of maintaining security until they had conclusive evidence that he could broadcast to the world. "Could be an unfortunate coincidence," Warren said. "But you can still carry on without him, right?"

"Yes, of course," Stern said. "Sarah Wyman is very competent."

"The other possibility is that these deaths are the result of foul play," Warren said.

"Foul play? Tom Pomeroy died of a heart attack, and LeAnn Cola from a gas leak."

"Yes, but those could have been cleverly staged, like this one."

"But why?"

"Warnings for us to desist."

"But who would do that?"

"I'm not sure," Warren said. "But there are enough fundamentalist crazies out there who oppose what we're doing." Like every televangelist, he received an occasional nasty letter, telephone call, and e-mail mostly from unenlightened oafs who complained that they made contributions and still had miserable lives. But ever since Warren had begun broadcasting his Day of Jubilation message, he had received scathing responses suggesting an awareness of their research. Possibly some had drawn conclusions from Warren's online exhortations that Christians embrace science, not fear it; that while atheists look at the rational universe and see accident, the enlightened look at the universe and see the handiwork of a rational Creator. Maybe someone had connected the appeals to his NDE books. "Just in case, I think we should take every precaution. I need not remind you how much is at stake."

"We have cameras all over the compound. And no one can get in without IDs."

"Then it might be time for a security service—armed guards, whatever."

"Okay."

"If these deaths are deliberate warnings," Stern said, "it might be wise to back off on the broadcasts. Sending out more sermons about the Day of Jubilation might only fuel the fire."

Warren looked at Stern, wondering if the man was a wolf in lamb's clothing. He pretended to be a Jewish rationalist, but he could be one of those Opus Dei or Fraternity of Jesus loonies who had posted threatening, scathing blogs against his NDE writings. The real question was how they knew. "That probably makes sense. When we reach our goal, we'll come out in full force."

"In the meantime, we'll look into security guards," Elizabeth said.

"Good," Warren said, and he could see Elizabeth begin to fret.

"Of course," she said, "that means we'll need more resources."

"You're as subtle as a train wreck, Elizabeth. Send me a bill. In return, I want to know who leaked."

43

....

Zack was again back on that beach, but the tide was up, the air was cold, and fog was closing in. Also, the perspective was wrong. Instead of crossing the sandbar, he was looking down from a set of wooden stairs at the far end of the beach and climbing to the cliff top. He knew the area, but the stairs seemed much higher than he remembered. And the beach appeared to stretch forever. Somewhere in the distance was their rental cottage, but he couldn't make it out. And farther down was the vague impression of the canal. Through the mist, he could hear the muffled groan of the foghorn and see the blinking red eye of the channel marker. Just below, the bay spread into the mist like a sheet of rippled iron.

"Almost there."

He looked up. His father. He was maybe ten steps ahead of him, climbing to the top. *"Dad, wait."*

But his father kept climbing without looking back. *"This way."*

Zack's legs were tired, but he had to keep up because his father had to tell him something. *"Dad, slow down."*

But his father didn't seem to hear him. Or maybe it was the sea breeze in his ears. Winded, Zack fought the heaviness in his legs and pushed on. When he looked up again, the top was only a dozen stairs away. But something was different. His father's clothes had changed from the swimming trunks and bare back to a brown robe. Where did that come from?

Stranger still, the top was not a clearing with ocean-view homes like he remembered of the Manomet cliffs, but a thick forest. His father's head was covered with a pointed hood, giving him a disturbing appearance. He turned, but his face was lost in shadows. *"This way."* And he cut into the trees.

Zack didn't actually hear his father's voice, only in his head. But he was out of breath from the long climb and stopped for a moment. *"Wait up."*

But his father continued into the dark thicket.

"Dad, wait, I'm going to lose you." Panting, he stumbled after him, trying not to lose the figure, trying not to get his feet snagged in the underbrush. *"Dad, don't leave me."*

But his father continued fading into the woods.

"Dad? It's me, Zack."

The brown figure disappeared behind trees, then emerged again, moving deeper. With a shock, Zack wondered if his father wasn't hearing him on purpose. That he didn't want to tell him something but was trying to lose him. *"I'm your son, too!"* Suddenly he was filled with hot anger. They killed Jake and left his father a loveless shell of a man. *"Why won't you wait for me?"*

He moved as best he could over fallen branches and tree stumps, trying to keep up, not knowing where they were or how these endless woods got up on the Manomet cliffs, and where all the fancy houses went. He kept losing sight of the figure that cut soundlessly through the trees.

Several times Zack called, but his father neither stopped nor called back. And horror filled Zack that he'd never catch up or find his way out of the woods as the sky darkened.

Then Zack lost his father for good. He stopped, hearing nothing but his own panting. No birds or insect sounds. Nothing but the stirring of the wind through the treetops.

For a long moment he stood there, hugging himself against the chilled air.

Suddenly a large winged bird swooped overhead from its perch and sliced through the trees. Some kind of hawk. Zack followed it to a small clearing, where he saw the hooded figure. He was standing motionless, his face lost in opaque shadow, his arms folded into the sleeves. Behind him was a large granite outcropping.

"*Dad?*"

"How you doing?"

"*What?*"

"How you feeling?"

Zack squinted at the bright lights of the MRI lab. Sarah, talking from a muffled distance. He tried to sit up, but his head thudded painfully.

"Don't move until the sedative wears off a little," she said, peeling the contacts off his chest. At nearby computer terminals sat Drs. Stern and Cates.

"Welcome back." Dr. Luria's face appeared above him. Behind her was a videocamera on a tripod, recording everything.

After a few moments, his head cleared and she began asking him the usual questions to test his awareness—his name, where he was. He answered them to their satisfaction.

Then she said, "We recorded some neuroactivity while you were under. Do you remember any of it?"

"I was on a wooden staircase." He wanted to get it on record while it was still fresh in his mind.

"Did you recognize the locale?"

"Sagamore Beach. The set of stairs at the end leading up to the Manomet cliffs."

"Were you alone?" Luria asked.

"No. My father was there. He was ahead of me, climbing." Sarah finished removing the contacts and brushed his hair out of his eyes. He liked the feel of her warm hand. "Then it all changed."

"Changed? How so?"

"The top of the cliff was all woods—thick trees and scrub." And as best he could, he described the area.

"Did you recognize it?"

"No, just thick woods. But there aren't any woods like that on the cliffs."

"So it wasn't a place you recognized."

"I don't know, but it's not the cliff."

"Did it feel like an out-of-the-body experience?"

"No, from my own perspective. But it didn't feel like a dream, you know—things happening in fragments, no timeline. It felt real, like I was in those woods."

"Following your father."

"Yes."

"Did he say anything?"

"No, but I think he wanted me to follow him."

"How do you know?" Luria asked.

"I don't know how I know. Just a feeling." Then Zack turned to Dr. Stern, who was at his computer terminal listening to him intently. "Was it a real NDE?"

"I don't know for sure," Stern said. "There was activity in the temporal and parietal lobes, suggesting stimulation from outside."

"So it's an NDE? Not a flash dream thing?"

"At this point, it looks as if you weren't dreaming," Dr. Luria said. "The dream centers of your brain were dormant, yet there were electrical stimuli that appear to have come from outside your brain."

"I beg to differ," said Dr. Stern. "But it could still be a flash dream just as you woke up. Most of the activity takes place at the very end of your suspension."

Zack could see Luria bristle at Stern. "We'll have to do another run."

"Another suspension?" Zack asked.

"Yes. But some other time. It takes twenty-four hours for the sedative to work itself out of your system. Would you be willing in a couple of days?"

If there was anything to the narrative flow of these visions, they were getting darker. He could feel his hesitation, in spite of another $1,000. "I guess."

"Good. Let us do the analysis, then we'll call."

After he got dressed, Sarah walked him to the limo out front. As they walked up the stairs, Zack stopped. "I was there, Sarah. That was no dream, flash or otherwise."

"I'm sure it felt that way."

"Except real dreams always have some margin of awareness. Not this. I could smell the pines, I could feel the sand on my feet. I'm still chilled from the cold air. It was a total sensory thing, not a dream."

"The preliminary data do show a lot of sensory activity."

"But?"

"But so did other suspensions that turned out to be flash dreams after we ran the math."

"So when will you know?"

"In a day or so."

Bruce was in the car and waiting for him in the parking lot alongside the building.

"She keeps asking me if I was alone in these dream

visions or whatever they are. Is that something you can determine?"

"That's what we're hoping. Which means separating out the neuroelectrical signature of your own mind from other data we've picked up. If the other neurodata can be identified as an external sentience, it would be a major leap. Are you okay for another run?"

He really didn't know. Standing in those woods and facing that mute hooded figure was not something he was yearning to return to. Yet he felt compelled by a bizarre sense that these suspensions had produced a queer narrative—but one that seemed to be growing darker, more secret.

Secrets from the grave. Luria's words swooped across his mind like that bird. "I suppose."

"See you soon." She gave him a hug, and he left with the driver.

44

....

Roman's weapon of choice for assignments was the 9 mm Beretta 92FS Parabellum. Its name derived from the Latin, *Si vis pacem, para bellum,* meaning "If you seek peace, prepare for war"—which could have been Roman's own motto these days.

What he liked about the Beretta was its accuracy at high distances. The manufacturer boasted a flat trajectory for a hundred meters, but Roman didn't need that in his trade, since most kills were up close. And the 9 mm had lethal stopping power. Especially important was the long barrel, which added to the noise suppression provided by a silencer. Silencers didn't really silence the way they did in the movies, they only reduced the gunshot to maybe a hundred decibels. Like car mufflers, they contained and dissipated the hot gases from the exploding propellants, suppressing a much louder escape blast. Thus, the longer the gun barrel, the better the suppression.

Every couple of weeks, Roman would bring his Beretta to the Pawtucket Rifle and Pistol Club to shoot off a box of rounds. He had done this for years, even after officially retiring. He'd love to fit the weapon with one of his suppressors, except that they were illegal for private

ownership in Rhode Island or Massachusetts. Only the
military or police could use them. So he wore his ear
mufflers and fired full blast at various distances. He did,
however, bring his own special-order paper targets, which
came in a wide variety, from the dart target board to
deer silhouettes to human silhouettes. Today he was
shooting at a slightly demonic blackened skull with the
bull's-eye on the forehead. He liked that because it reminded him of the devil. No matter what the target,
range shooting was great therapy—pure eye–hand coor-
dination and a chance to clear his mind of the usual debris.

But his thoughts today kept coming back to that fucking Kashian kid.

What he knew confused him. Here's this kid who
quotes the Lord's Prayer in the original while half-dead.
A bunch of people flock to him for miracles, some feeling Jesus in the room, some smelling roses of the Virgin
Mary. Yet Devereux claimed that they were testing him,
hoping to confirm the spirit world was real—and maybe
the reason Roman had been hired to pop the scientists.
That made no sense.

He went online and looked up "near-death experience,"
finding hundreds of reports. Most accounts were first-
hand testimonials of people who nearly died in hospitals
or in accidents, then went sailing down tunnels to a bright,
happy paradise where they met with the spirits of dead
loved ones and holy ghosts.

He also found Christian Web sites dealing with NDEs—
Web sites that outright condemned attempts to contact
dead relatives or saints, claiming that "great spiritual
dangers" awaited those who made such attempts. Apparently those interactions weren't with dead loved ones or
Jesus, but with demons—or Satan himself, hoping to lead
victims away from dependence on God. The worst offend-
ers were NDE charlatans who exploited victims of grief.

One blogger claimed that the death of a loved one should drive us into God's loving arms, not New Age books full of lies and false hope.

The complete disparity in claims not only quickened Roman's curiosity, but blurred his theological mission. He took aim at his target and put five holes in the skull's forehead, thinking that he'd better check out this kid at close range.

45

....

"We have a little surprise for you," said Dr. Luria on the phone the next Tuesday. "No suspensions tonight, and please come dressed up."

That was all she told him, except to meet at the usual pickup spot near Symphony Hall.

Zack's sole dress-up wardrobe consisted of a blue blazer, a pair of chinos, and a blue shirt. His one tie was balled up with a pair of dress socks. He ironed that, and at six sharp he was at the corner of Huntington and Massachusetts Avenues, picked up this time by a Lincoln Town Car, not Bruce in the SUV. And the driver came with a personality.

"Where we going?" Zack said, getting in.

"The Taj Boston."

He had heard of it and knew it wasn't exactly a grad student hangout. "Sounds good."

"I take it you're not from around here."

He didn't want to sound dumb, given that he was born and raised just ten miles out of town. "Nope, just arrived."

"Where from?"

"Maine." He had no idea why he said that.

A few minutes later, the driver pulled up to the corner of Arlington and Newbury at the doors of the most elegant hotel Zack had ever been to. When the driver let him out, Zack fumbled for money, but the man said that was all taken care of.

"Tenth floor." He handed him a card: "Commonwealth Suite." "Enjoy your stay in Boston."

Zack thanked him and went inside, instantly aware of his have-not status. The lobby was bustling with people dressed in high-end clothing and looking as if they had stepped out of travel posters. Along the foyer were glittering shops and window displays of designer clothing and jewelry and a fancy café. The interior of the elevator looked like a jewelry box. At the tenth floor, Sarah greeted him, wearing an emerald green sheath that nearly knocked the wind out of Zack. "Dazzling," he whispered.

She grinned and gave him a warm hug. "You're looking pretty good yourself."

She took his arm and led him through a fancy door and into an elegant suite with floor-to-ceiling windows overlooking the Boston Public Garden. Several well-dressed people sat on floral sofas or stood around with cocktails. He recognized a few faces from the lab, including Morris Stern dressed in a blue blazer and Byron Cates in a smart gray suit. Uniformed staff moved through the crowd with drinks and hors d'oeuvres. Along one wall lay a sumptuous buffet elaborately arranged.

When Dr. Luria saw him, she waved expansively for them to join her small clutch of people. "Here he is," she chortled, and gave him a hug as if he were a favorite nephew. "I want you to meet a very special person. Zack Kashian, this is Dr. Warren Gladstone."

Gladstone was tall and lean, with a tight, boyish

face that contrasted with the loose skin of his neck, making Zack think that he had had cosmetic surgery. His chocolate brown hair, which was perfectly coiffed and parted with optical precision, looked artificially colored against the gray sideburns. A bright, toothy smile lit up his face. He looked like someone you might have seen in movies.

"I can't tell you how pleased I am to meet you," he said, pumping Zack's hand. "You've been a real asset to our program. And by the way, I'm not a medical doctor. Doctor of theology."

"A pleasure to meet you," Zack said. *Theology?*

Elizabeth put her hand on Gladstone's arm. Beaming, she said, "Warren is a very accomplished writer and tel-evangelist. He has so graciously supported our research. In fact, I don't know what we'd do without him."

"The pleasure is mine and the rewards are great," he said. "So, you're at Northwestern."

"Northeastern."

"Of course. And what's your major?"

"I'm doing grad work in English."

"Marvelous. English was my favorite subject at UT in Chattanooga. That's where I discovered Shakespeare, a heaven-inspired man if there ever was one."

Zack nodded politely as Gladstone continued non-stop to tell him about the courses he took and dramatic productions he was in, quoting various lines.

"My favorite was *Hamlet,* of course. I played Polo-nius."

"Of course," Zack said, thinking, *Typecasting.* Polonius might be the biggest windbag in Western world litera-ture.

"I ended up second in my class in English studies. I wanted to be a poet and minored in English but decided to go into the seminary."

A waiter came by with a tray of champagne and wine. Thankfully, Elizabeth spotted him. "Warren, why don't we let Zack get a drink, then we can chat some more."

"Of course. 'A man cannot make him laugh; but that's no marvel; he drinks no wine.' Recognize that?"

"Sounds like Falstaff," Zack said.

He patted Zack on the back. "Very good. *Henry the Fourth, Part 2.* Now go wet the whistle and we'll chat later."

Sarah joined him for a refill. As they made their way to the waiter, he whispered, "Second in his class for non-stop talking."

"Can you imagine who took first?"

"Some kid named Tourette."

She snickered. They got their drinks and found a private corner by the window. "Be nice," she said. "He's Elizabeth's sugar daddy. That fMRI machine has his name on it."

That made sense, since no university, government agency, or legitimate scientific institution would sponsor NDE research. "Who're the rest of these people?"

"Friends and associates of his."

"He must have a pretty good-size ministry."

"Plus a few bestselling books."

"On what?"

"Near-death experiences."

Then the name clicked. Reverend W. G. Gladstone. "You mean like *Tunnel to Heaven*?"

"That's him."

"How about that?" He had read up on NDEs, and Gladstone's book was one of the few that had hit the *New York Times* Best Seller List. Zack remembered that it had included several reports, including Gladstone's own, claiming to have died during an asthma attack some years ago—an experience that led him to his ministry. He also had recorded accounts of NDEs from blind people, atheists, even children whose brief encounters with death triggered paranormal experiences. What distinguished Gladstone's book was its unabashed nondenominational interpretation of near-death and afterlife experiences. It also celebrated the healing powers of a loving nondenominational "Being of Light."

Zack also remembered scathing reviews condemning the use of Gladstone's ministerial authority to sell books with anti-Christian notions: that no one need fear death; that God was a nonjudgmental wimp; and that heaven was an open door. One reviewer railed, "In Gladstone's heaven, you can have a garden party at the same table with Mother Teresa and Adolf Hitler." As expected, most of the criticism came from religious conservatives.

While they chatted, a large, bald-headed man whispered into Gladstone's ear. As he stretched, Zack noticed a bulge under his jacket. "Who's the guy in the gray suit?"

"I think he's an assistant to Gladstone," Sarah said. "Why?"

"Just wondering." *The guy was armed.*

The buffet consisted of lobster tail, shrimp Newburg, scallops, and a lot of other fancy dishes. He and Sarah ate at one of the stand-up tables located throughout the suite. He went back for seconds on the lobster. Later, Gladstone wandered over and asked Zack to move to the window where they could talk. The bald guy and another closed in on them, making a wall. Across the room, Sarah made a shrug.

"I just wanted a chance to chat privately." He handed Zack a business card with shafts of light through a cloud. Embossed in gold was "GodLight," under which were contact numbers and a Web site for Gladstone's sermons. On the reverse side, an inscription:

OURS IS A COVENANT WITH THE LORD GOD
ALMIGHTY TO SPREAD THE GOSPEL OF THE
MESSIAH BY MEANS OF MASS COMMUNICATIONS
TO THE WHOLE WORLD.

"Elizabeth has told me all about your remarkable test results."

"I guess she's pleased." The wattle under his chin didn't go with the smooth face.

"As you may know, I've researched NDEs for years and heard all sorts of inspiring claims, hoping to find hard evidence to substantiate them."

Zack nodded, knowing where this was leading.

"Zack, I'd like to hear it directly from the horse's mouth." He leaned closer. "How do you explain reciting words from Jesus's Sermon on the Mount in Aramaic?"

That was not what Zack had expected. "I really can't."

"Did someone teach that to you?"

"No."

"Did you learn it in school or Sunday school?"

"Not that I remember."

Gladstone stared at him with wonder. "You can well imagine my interpretation," he said. "You're making phenomenal history in neurology, biology, theology, and every other -ology. Because of *you*, we—Elizabeth and her team—may be on the cusp of the greatest discovery of mankind ever. Can you appreciate that?"

"Probably not."

"Well, who really can? But if subsequent tests are as encouraging, we have an obligation to share this with the world. Don't you agree—to let the world know that science has confirmed the continuation of the spirit?"

Zack was beginning to feel uncomfortable. "I guess."

"You guess? Zack, we're talking about singular

evidence for the existence of the afterlife and, by extension, the Lord God Almighty."

Zack sensed a lecture coming.

"Zack, the Bible tells us that 'faith is the assurance of things hoped for, a conviction of things not seen.' But the reality is that for thousands of years people have believed in the Lord by putting faith not in things unseen, but in the trust of others, people who claim to know God—family, friends, ministers, priests, rabbis, imams—you name it. For Christians, it's trust in the character and teachings of Jesus Christ.

"But that's not the same as belief based on hard evidence. And that's the bugaboo—the reason why faith is considered nonrational. And the heart of the age-old debates between science and religion. Also the reason why atheists rant against religion: There's nothing to stand on but faith in the faithful."

His face swelled. "But you're changing all that. You're giving us hard evidence that your mind transcended your body and passed through the tunnel into the realm of spirit."

Zack saw himself crawl out of a sand pit in the middle of the night and end up on a sunlit sandbar. But he was dead certain that was some kind of hyperdream, the result of all the electrical and chemical juicing of his brain. "Okay," he said to humor the guy.

Gladstone clapped him on the shoulder. "Good. After the introductory fanfare, I see video interviews of people proclaiming how their passage into God's light changed their lives forever. One testimony after the next, all climaxing with footage of your own remarkable journey."

Zack had forgotten about the release agreement on recording his suspensions.

"But videos alone can't convey the enormity of the truth. I'm saying that I would like you to bear personal testimony before the GodLight congregation—nay, the world."

"You mean you want me to go on your show?"

"Precisely, and I'd be honored to share the pulpit with you."

Zack felt a prickly discomfort. Gladstone had invested millions of dollars to prove the existence of the afterlife and now wanted Zack as his pitchman. "But I've got nothing to tell."

"Not just yet, but you will." Then Gladstone took Zack's arm, pushing his face so close that he could taste his bourbon fumes. "I'm just setting the stage."

Zack didn't like this at all. An alleged out-of-the-body experience, and Gladstone was setting him up to sell books, his ministry, and himself as the second coming. "I'll think about it."

"Fine, and remember that it's more than a privilege. It's a moral obligation to share our success with a world that's suffered thousands of years of uncertain belief in things unseen."

Zack made another noncommittal nod, thinking that the only unseen thing he believed in was the next thousand-dollar check.

"In the meantime, live in light, go in faith," Gladstone said.

Zack walked away to join Sarah, thinking how he had heard those words before but couldn't recall where. Nor did he bother to rummage for a connection because Sarah held another glass of champagne for him; and with her back to the afterglow of the sun and her emerald sheath hugging her like spring, she looked like a beatific vision.

46

....

The kid was climbing the social ladder. A two-hour stop-off at the Taj and a chauffeured limo. Roman never graduated from college, but even he knew that students didn't meet with their professors in the fanciest hotel in town.

Nor did the kid strike him as a high roller. He had unremarkable clothes, lived in a university-owned apartment, and took his bike or public transportation everywhere.

Unless it was the foxy girlfriend. She had arrived separately but came out of the hotel with him, all decked out in shiny green. The Town Car was waiting for them. Maybe it was a wedding. Maybe some other kind of celebration. But it didn't look like a date, coming separately like that.

Roman had parked just down Arlington Street, so he followed the Town Car for Storrow Drive and westward until it crossed over the Larz Anderson Bridge to Harvard Square. The limo pulled up in front of her place on Harvard Street, and the two of them got out and went into her three-decker.

Roman checked his BlackBerry for the time. Five hours

of surveillance, and all he had learned was that the kid and the girl had attended some fancy event and then shacked up at her place. *A friggin' waste of time,* he thought as he looked at the small screen.

Or maybe not.

47

....

Sarah's apartment was on the second floor. They walked into the living room, which was done in white and beige with accents of color, and nothing was out of place. Against the bank of windows overlooking Harvard Street sat a deep, cushiony sofa with a coffee table supporting a vase of fresh tulips. Two white-and-gold lamps sat on end tables, filling the room with a warm glow. Across from the sofa were two white French chairs. On the opposite wall were posters of French café scenes. It looked like a space Sarah would occupy.

"How come your place looks like it was just attacked by *Architectural Digest* and my place looks bombed out?"

"Maybe because I was expecting company."

"Tell me I'm it."

She smiled. "Besides, you're a guy."

"And I've never been more grateful."

On the fireplace mantel were photos of her parents and a graduation shot of her in cap and gown with a smiling Morris Stern beside her. He followed her into the kitchen, her sensuous body making the emerald sheath look liquid as she walked.

"Red or white?" She directed him to a small wine rack on top of the refrigerator.

He removed a bottle of cabernet sauvignon and opened it while she got the glasses from a cabinet. Then he filled the glasses and they clinked. "Lovely, dark, and deep."

"The wine?"

"Your eyes."

"You're sweet." She took his arm and walked him to the couch. "So, what did you think of Reverend Mr. Gladstone?"

Zack settled beside her. "Besides his capacity for wind, he seems to carry a lot of weight."

"Without him, there'd be no lab."

"He also believes he's about to find the Promised Land."

"I suppose that's the televangelist in him."

"Except he expects me to point the way," Zack said. "Just what kind of NDEs does he hope for me to have?"

"I don't think anything in particular."

"I mean, I've been suspended four times, and all I can remember is crawling out of a sand hole and playing ball with my father, then following him into some woods. Not exactly a life review and angels of light."

"Except each run yields new data about what goes on in NDEs."

"That's my point: if I had bona fide NDEs. I mean, I didn't feel separated from my body, looking down at myself like a seagull. And I didn't pass through any tunnels toward godlight."

"You also said that they didn't feel like regular dreams."

"Yeah, I still wouldn't say they were supernatural. Just very realistic dreams."

"Elizabeth thinks you experienced transcendence."

"But everything I've read, including Gladstone's book, talks about unconditional love and tranquillity. I didn't get that. Plus I was younger and so was my father, and he wasn't any being of light."

"So what are you saying?"

"That maybe Dr. Stern's right. Maybe it's all from inside my own head, and nothing else." His only explanation for the root beer logo thing was sheer coincidence—that the image had been buried in his brain, tweaked while in suspension, so that he came out thirsty and craving a frosty A&W. As for the nightmares of being buried in sand, he blamed that on the anesthetic—that and how his brain had suffered trauma from the bike accident, followed by weeks in a chemically induced coma.

"That's entirely possible, which is why she wants more tests, if you're still willing."

"I've got bills up to here, so I'm willing." But he still felt torn. Despite the wide-eyed speculations about the afterlife and cosmic sentience, he couldn't help thinking that he was part of a very expensive exercise in pseudo-science. It reminded him of those Discovery Channel shows about alien visitations, with scientists holding forth with sweet-smelling endorsements. Of course, he didn't say that. Nor did he mention how he'd like to get back to those woods and find out what his dream "father" wanted to tell him.

"Let's see how you do on Thursday."

After a second glass of wine, Sarah lowered her head onto his shoulder. In a few moments, they were kissing and fondling each other. After a spell, she began to unbutton his shirt and kiss his chest. "You know what?" he whispered.

"What?"

"I'm starting to believe in transcendence."

48

....

At six P.M. on Thursday, Sarah pulled up in front of Zack's apartment to drive him to the lab. "Bruce, you never looked better," he said, getting in.

Sarah smiled. "He's got the night off."

She headed down Huntington toward the MassPike. But instead of the usual turn off Route 109, Sarah proceeded to the next right and then another, cutting behind the lab building where construction was being done. Because of the high evergreens, Zack had not noticed the large white church on the other side of the woods behind the lab. A sign in front read, "The GodLight Tabernacle." As they passed the church, construction crews were finishing a security fence around the lab. "It's on the same property as the church."

"Yes. Gladstone owns all the acreage around here, including the lab."

She continued past a low white parish house through more hemlocks to a new security gate at the entrance of the lab. Because of the trees, the fence was not visible from the church, and it was topped with razor wire. Also new was a guard shack with an armed uniformed man. Sarah showed her ID and guest pass for Zack. The guard looked at Zack and let them go through. "Is there something I should know?"

"Just that a lot of crazies don't like what we're doing."

"Any actual threats?"

"Just some nasty communications," she said. "As you can see, the guards are new."

"Guards, plural?"

"There are others around the compound."

They parked against the building, then moved through the front entrance, where a barricade had been erected and where a technician scanned them for metal and checked Zack's backpack. All this in just a few days. "Just how serious are these communications?" he said as they walked down the hall to the lab office.

"It's more precautionary than defensive."

Dr. Luria was talking to Dr. Stern and a technician when they entered her office. They greeted Zack, then walked him down the hall to the MRI room, where he changed and got hooked up on the gurney.

Sarah patted his arm. "Ready?"

"If you don't bring me back, the Discover people will be really upset."

She smiled. "So will I."

"Be still, my foolish heart." He closed his eyes on her smile as she powered him into the MRI tube.

His last thought before Sarah depressed the plunger was, *Dad, be there.*

....

Zack did not recognize the car. Or the street. Nothing about the locale meant anything to him. Nor did the fact he was driving somewhere in the country with very few houses and deep forests right up to the road. Nothing had any meaning except for the figure far down the road. A woman jogging in a pink outfit.

She wore headphones and was pumping hard along the same side of the road. Sunlight splashed through the canopy of leaves. He slowed to the speed of the jogger, who was too lost in her music and running to notice him pace her a hundred feet back.

Two cars came the other way and disappeared in his rearview mirror. Ahead, the road was a straight cut through the trees with no houses or cars approaching. He pulled alongside the woman. Without breaking her stride, she turned her face toward him. She wore sunglasses with large white frames. He lowered the passenger window as if to ask directions.

It took a few moments, but her face registered fear and she stopped in her tracks.

In a lightning move, he put the car in reverse and then jammed it into drive. Before she could move, he turned the wheel sharply and drove into her. She let out a cry as she tumbled onto the soft shoulder. When she saw him back up and then shift into drive, she let out a scream, cut off as he drove over her body and felt the heavy crunch of bones beneath the wheels.

He woke up to the sound of his own scream.

....

But nobody in the lab heard it.

Sometime later, he was in a chair in the lab office, drinking black coffee. Sarah, Luria, Stern, Cates, and a technician at the video camera listened to him.

"Did you know the woman?" Luria asked.

"I never saw her before."

"Or where you were?"

"No."

"Or why you hit her?"

"No. It didn't even feel like me driving."

"What do you mean?"

"I can't explain. It just didn't feel like my emotions." Silence settled over the room like fog. "It was like someone else's nightmare."

On the computer monitors, colored splotches danced across the schematic of his brain. After a moment, Dr. Luria said, "Zack, you didn't have a dream or nightmare. Your brain was incapable of dreaming on the anesthetic."

He looked at her without response.

"Every indication points to a transcendence. The data's still raw, but at the intercellular level the sensory centers of your brain experienced external stimuli—vision, hearing, touch, spatial maneuvering."

"We still have hours of analysis ahead of us," said Dr. Stern.

"But you think it was a transcendence?" Zack asked.

"I'm not ready to jump to conclusions yet."

Sarah said nothing, but Zack suspected that she agreed with Stern. Luria made a dismissive gesture with her hand and moved to another monitor beside Byron Cates. "Your blood profile shows a dramatic spike in epinephrine, another name for adrenaline. And that means your brain experienced a fight-or-flight response signaling your heart to pump harder and your blood pressure to increase. Do you remember feeling any fear?"

"No. Not at all."

"What about anger or rage?"

He stood up. "I think I've had enough." He looked to Sarah. "I'm ready to go."

"Zack, I understand how this may be upsetting," Dr. Luria said. "Maybe next time—"

But he cut her off. "I don't think there will be a next time."

"What? Why?"

"I'm not sure I want to do this again."

"Why not?" Luria protested. "We're making great progress with each run."

Zack shook his head. "Sorry."

"If it's the money, we'll pay you more."

"It's not the money." Zack got his stuff and headed toward the door.

"Zack, please don't go," Luria wailed.

But he continued out the door and into the security area of the lobby. Sarah was right behind him. So was Byron Cates, who caught up to him and handed him a slip of paper. "Just in case," he said. It was a prescription for Haldol.

Sarah had her belongings and was ready to drive him home. Right behind her was Dr. Luria. "Zack, listen to me. You may have experienced total transcendence." She took his arm. "Don't you understand? You may have glimpsed the afterlife and returned. You owe it to us . . . to the world." She stammered in disbelief and anger. Her eyes were huge, and her face filled with blood.

"If there's an afterlife, I'll take my chances the traditional way."

And he walked out the door with Sarah behind him.

49

....

"I don't know what to tell you," Sarah had said as she drove him home. "Yours is the first suspension that comes close to possible transcendence."

"What about all the other subjects?"

"I've only been on the project a few months."

"But you must have seen the records."

"A few and nothing very promising. Only one or two were possible OBEs. But no follow-ups like yours."

That was far from comforting. "So you're saying my mind separated from my body and experienced me running down that woman."

"I'm saying the raw data shows a highly intense experience. As for the hit-and-run scenario, that could be something created in your own head—a flash dream."

"And what about the possibility these suspensions are fucking up my brain? Did anyone think of that?" he snapped. "That all the toxins and flatlining are making me loony."

"You've had bad nightmares before, we all have. But you didn't lose your mind because of them, right?"

"So you're saying it could be some weird nightmare vision."

"I'm echoing Morris here, but yeah. Stuff in your unconsciousness got activated just as you emerged from flatline."

He couldn't tell if she really believed that or was trying to placate him. "But you said the stimuli was recorded in real time while I was suspended."

"Yes." She was silent for a moment. "Zack, I really don't have a good answer."

"But if you were me, would you submit to another suspension?"

"I can't answer that. It depends on how disturbing the experience was and how much of a risk you want to take of having another."

In a flash, he saw his father in his monk's robe standing in the woods before a large rock. *Time for a big-boy talk*. "I'll think about it."

By the time she dropped him off, he was feeling more settled. Before he got out, she gave him a hug.

"Want to come up?"

"Not tonight. I've got a ton of work."

He kissed her good night and went up to his apartment. He took two sleeping pills, and before fading into a dreamless night, he again saw his father standing in the long brown robe before a large rock outcropping. *Big-boy talk*.

The next day, Friday, he called Sarah to say he would submit to another suspension next Tuesday. She was free that night, and Damian didn't need his car all weekend, so Zack took Sarah to the waterfront, where they took a ferryboat cruise of the Boston Harbor.

Over the weekend, he worked on his thesis. At Byron Cates's suggestion, he filled the prescription for the antipsychotic Haldol, which apparently did the trick—no more dreams of crawling in sand. No psychotic visions of running anyone down in a car. No weird out-of-the-blue flashes.

That Tuesday night, Sarah picked him up and drove to the lab. Everybody was delighted, especially Dr. Luria, who could barely contain her relief.

He was prepped and ready to be rolled into the MRI machine. His last thought was, *Dad, please be there.*

50

....

This would be a night to remember for Billy—one he'd mark the calendar from. Breaking his own personal best.

He had converted his garage to a home gym, adding a rack of free weights, two benches, one tilted, one that lay flat. He also had a used Cybex machine for his back and shoulders.

He still belonged to the local health club, but he liked having his own workout space where he could do his routines without a lot of other people around. In fact, he preferred to work out alone. His wife was visiting her parents in Albany, so he had the place to himself and could pump in peace and quiet. His hope tonight was pushing his bench press to the next plateau.

Billy was proud of how his upper body was bulking up. He was doing forty-pound curls and seventy-pound shrugs. But he had to work on his chest. He wanted bigger, chiseled pecs like some athletes and movie stars. And the way to do it was to bench regularly and increase his maximum, which meant finding the weakest part of his lift and focusing on that.

His weakest was at hoisting the weight off his chest, so he'd concentrate on lifting the bar no more than six inches. Workout videos recommended going slowly, bringing the bar negative all the way and not cheating by bouncing off the pecs. His goal was to get ripped for the beach now that summer was here. His favorite uncle was a lawyer who owned a place on Martha's Vineyard where he and his wife stayed for a week every July.

He warmed up at two hundred and forty, doing three sets fairly easily. After a rest and some water, he did a set at two sixty. That went well, and he felt strong. So strong that he slipped another two ten pounds on each end of the barbell, bringing the total to two eighty—twenty pounds higher than his max. Yes, he was pushing it, but all he wanted was one full lift to break his record.

He planted his feet firmly on either side of the bench, then raised his arms and gripped the bar as it sat in the spotter stand. This was more weight than he had pushed, and he was aware of the effort to hold it in place at arm's length. So much of bodybuilding was in the head. The trick was to be totally in the moment, to focus on particular muscles to take to the next level.

Toward that end, he turned off his cell phone, dimmed the lights, and inserted earplugs to block ambient noise—cars going up the street, dogs barking, planes overhead. So as he lay on the bench, gripping the bar, he concentrated like a laser on his pectorals, tuning out everything else until he became those muscles.

He closed his eyes in total concentration, feeling his arms extend, his pecs harden. As the training videos said, he imagined a stronger, more powerful Billy. He imagined himself leaving his own body and entering his ideal body.

As he pressed shut his eyes, Billy thought, *Strong. Powerful.* He thought, *I can do this. I am my all-muscle self.*

He adjusted his grip on the cross-hatchings until he was fully comfortable. He lifted the bar from the spotter above his face, feeling the full exertion, then lowered it to his chest, where he let it rest a moment.

When he was fully psyched, he pushed with all his might to raise the bar to full extension, where his bones would lock in place. His arms shook as the blood swelled his arms and shoulders and bulged the arteries along the sides of his neck.

Just as he reached that position, a voice cut through the earplugs.

"Billy."

His eyes opened as his heart nearly burst from his chest.

In the dim light, he saw a reflection in the mirrored wall at his feet—a dark figure standing directly behind his head. "Wha-wha-wha," was all Billy could say.

Then he heard a whispery voice mutter something else.

But before it registered, his arms collapsed to his sides, slamming the bar onto the ridge of his nose and eyes, then rolling down his face to rest on the soft pocket of his neck.

It happened in such a violent blur that he could barely process that the bar was crushing his windpipe, pressing impossibly hard toward the floor, instantly cutting air from his lungs and blood to his brain.

He could not scream. He could not see for the blood flooding his eye sockets. He could not breathe.

He thrashed with his arms and bucked with his hips, but the bar weighted impossibly against his throat, pinning him to the bench. And the more he struggled, the more his brain dimmed and the strength seeped out of his muscles.

In the microsecond of awareness, he tried to see the face of his killer, but he was not even certain anyone was there or if the figure was in his head. It made no difference, because night filled his brain, and the next moment he was dead.

51

It took several minutes for Zack to break through.

They had given him a shot of norepinephrine, but he was still stuck in a small, dim space, staring at the face of the man he had killed.

He could smell the terror in his breath, like burned garbage. He could still hear himself utter the man's name. He could still feel his hands locked in a grip around the bar, spaced outside of where the man's hands bent backward, trying to push the bar from his throat.

Zack focused on the man's eyes, which bulged like hens' eggs from jagged sockets of bone. The more he pressed, the more the hydrostatic pressure forced blood to spurt from the eyeholes and nostrils, mixing with snot. His lips moved as if to say something, but there was no sound— just the slapping of his shoes against the floor as he danced in the last throes of his life.

Zack watched as the kicking and flailing came to a halt and the man's mouth went slack and strings of red saliva dripped to the floor, his tongue protruding through his bloodied teeth like a slug.

Zack made a final full-weight heave on the bar and with grim satisfaction watched the man die, his final breath caught in a deep-chest gurgle from a collapsed throat, blood streaming from the rut across his eyes and nose and puddling on the floor.

Zack bolted upright into a sitting position on the gurney, his face snapping around the room, eyes sucking in the bright fluorescence to flood the horrible images in his head.

Four faces stared at him—Sarah, Luria, Stern, and Cates.

"You all right?" someone asked, maybe Sarah. "What happened?"

He looked down at his hands, still frozen in their grip. He shook his head but couldn't answer.

"You're still coming out of it," Luria said.

Zack rubbed his eyes. A soupy horror filled his head, as if he had just returned from the scene of a murder. One he had committed.

He lay back down on the gurney. His hands were trembling uncontrollably. He could see the concern on Dr. Luria's face. He wanted to say he was all right, but he felt that at any moment he might break down.

He glanced at the heart rate monitor, which read 138 beats per minute. His blood pressure was registering at 185 over 105. The EKG machine was spiking like crazy.

"Give him some time to settle down," Stern said.

Zack closed his eyes again and recited pi to fifty places, then started over again. He recited the lyrics of songs in his head, the Gettysburg Address, which he had memorized in the fifth grade, the Pledge of Allegiance, stanzas from Poe's "The Raven."

"He's coming down," Byron Cates announced after a few minutes. "One forty over ninety-four. Pulse ninety-two."

After several more minutes he felt calmer, more centered. He opened his eyes. Sarah was by his side. She took his hand.

"Zack, what happened?"

He filled his lungs with air, then let it out slowly. He sat up again. Luria and Stern were staring at him on the other side of the gurney. Byron Cates was glancing at him from the computers.

"What is it?" Sarah asked.

Bad trip. "Still groggy."

"Take your time," Dr. Luria said. "Can you recall anything?"

He shook his head, trying to force his face into neutral against the assault of those images. "Nope. Nothing."

Dr. Luria moved closer to him. "Zack, tell me what you experienced."

He shook his head again. He didn't want to put it into words. He didn't want to fix it with images for fear of haunting his brain with them. He just wanted to go home and fall into a deep sleep. "Want to leave."

"Okay, that's fine," Sarah said.

But Luria cut in. "In a moment." And she shot Sarah a sharp look, then poured herself a cup of black coffee. She took a sip while studying Zack, then clicked on the overhead monitor and moved the mouse until an image of Zack's brain filled the screen. She hit some keys and ran the images of neuroactivity from the moment he went under until he was awakened.

Sarah got him a bottle of water while he waited. A weird buzzing in the fore of his brain was creating a sense of vertigo. "I'd like to go."

"You crossed over." Dr. Luria's words were barely audible. "This time we're sure."

"What?" He looked at Stern. "Is that right?"

Stern took a deep breath and let the air out slowly. "What I can tell you is that there's parity with the last few sessions, but of greater intensity. The activity in neuron clusters of your frontal and parietal lobes don't appear related to unconscious neuroelectrical activity."

"Meaning what?"

"This may be a first," Stern said, "but your consciousness appears to have separated from your brain."

"A near-death experience."

"Yes, but there's anomalous data we need to crank through the algorithms."

Zack was almost too numb to let that sink in.

"Do you remember anything more specific while you were under? Any sense of place or who was with you or what you were doing?"

"No." Zack's sense of unease was mounting. He slid off the gurney and went behind the screen and changed. "Someone take me home or I'm going to call a cab."

"I'll take him," Sarah said.

Something crossed Luria's face. "Fine. I'll call you in a few days, Zack." She stuffed a check in his shirt pocket.

The woman was relentless, but Zack said nothing and left with Sarah.

52

....

"I killed a man."

"*What?*"

"In suspension, I ended up in some guy's workout room and choked him to death with a barbell."

It was sometime after eleven, and Sarah was driving in the northbound lane of Route 128.

"Why didn't you say something?"

"Because Luria would have pumped me the rest of the night."

"But that's the point—to learn what you experienced."

"Except I'm not doing any more."

"Was it that bad?"

"Yeah, and as real as riding in this car. What scares me is how I felt. Volcanic rage. I wanted to press the life out of him. I can still feel it. And I haven't got a clue who the guy is."

"How awful."

"It's also the second time. I didn't know that woman either, not a clue. But I wanted to kill her, too."

"I don't know what to say."

"That's the other thing. These weren't some eye-in-the-sky OBEs. My hands were on the friggin' barbell, the guy's face staring at me upside down because I was behind him. I saw him die up close and from my point of view—the killer's point of view. Same with the woman. I looked her in the eye, then turned the car on her. What the hell happened?"

"I don't know, but now I'm getting scared."

"Yeah, and I've had enough tunnel visions for the rest of my life," Zack said. "I don't need the money this badly."

Sarah put her hand on his leg. "I understand. I'll tell Elizabeth."

"I'll call and explain myself. Sorry if this screws up your research, but I'm not going around wondering if I'm a killer."

Or worse.

Zack didn't believe in the supernatural. He didn't believe in the afterlife. He didn't believe in spirits, ghosts, ESP, or other paranormal phenomena. Miracles were just good luck, like his waking from a coma. All else was fantasy, driven by ignorance, including good poker hunches, root beer logos, and reciting Jesus. But he was beginning to wonder if maybe he did cross over and tap into the psyche of some homicidal maniac.

Please let there be a more rational explanation.

"Maybe it's just a bad reaction to the anesthetic," he said. "That's possible, isn't it?"

"Yes, it's possible."

Sarah kept her eyes on the road, but in the flickering light of the traffic Zack could see that she wasn't convinced. After a few moments, he said, "Sarah, what's turning over in your head? And please, no more bullshit."

She continued driving without response. Then she said, "I don't understand it, but given the neurological activity and your running blood chart, whatever you experienced took place in real time."

"What?"

"It wasn't a flash dream just before you woke up."

"You mean an OBE."

She nodded. "That's one of the things we'll be looking for—the possibility you encountered another awareness."

Another awareness. Zack felt a frigid ripple pass through him. "Jesus!"

"I know how you don't want to go through another suspension. I really do."

"No."

She looked at him. "Might be the only way to figure out what's going on."

"You mean you don't want me to blow your chances for an article."

Sarah flared instantly. "That's not my motive, Zack. I'm not doing this to get published. This is virgin territory, and that's why I'm here, dammit."

They rode in silence for a few moments. "Sorry."

"Accepted."

It was a little after midnight when he entered his apartment. He was exhausted and anxious and dreading going to bed for fear of being assaulted by more homicidal flashes. But Luria was right. This had none of the feel of a dream, even more so than the beach visions. It was disturbingly real and raw, and he feared it would all rise up as soon as he fell asleep. So he forced himself to stay awake.

His brain was too weary to allow him to work on his thesis or read. So he turned on the television and tried to lose himself in *David Letterman*. But every time the camera focused on someone's face, his brain tripped on flashes of that guy's eyes popping out of a bloody, ruined face. He could also still feel his fingers clawed around the bar and pushing against the man's windpipe. It was awful—as if his brain had been infected by some psychic miasma.

Worse was the alien rage that had surged through him as the guy flailed and kicked. He had murdered the man with hot satisfaction. And while he had no idea who he was, just beneath the threshold of awareness he sensed a disturbing familiarity. But nothing he could grasp.

He shuffled around the apartment, walking from room to room. His bedroom was a mess, so he put away clothes and straightened out the bed, fussing to make hospital corners and flatten the covers. When he finished, he cleaned up the kitchen and then moved to the bathroom, where he washed the tub and folded towels. When he felt himself grow sleepy, he took a Haldol and a double dose of Lunesta. It was probably dumb to combine the two, but he wanted a night of oblivion.

He began to wash his face, but as he looked into the mirror, another face stared back at him. A whimper rose in his throat, but in a blink the stranger's face was gone and staring back at him was his own, looking gaunt and tight with fright. "What the hell's happening to me?" he said aloud.

What did they put in that drug?

What did they do to my brain?

He wiped his face and returned to the living room and sat at his laptop to read e-mails. Notes from Damian, Anthony, other friends, one from his mother. University notices and spam. He opened the latest from Damian, who wanted to know where he had been, how the sleep study was going. One from Sarah apologizing

for tonight's run. He appreciated that. Luria was ob-
sessed, intent on proving her theories and telling the
world.

But he'd be her guinea pig no more.

53

....

Roman found a listing for Zachary Kashian on a site devoted to "miracle people."

He scanned through a bunch of newspaper articles, including "Miracle? Coma Victim 'Resurrected from the Dead.'" And "He Spoke the Words of Jesus from a Coma" and "Doctors Baffled by Miracle Man."

He also read blogs from people who had been at Zack's bedside, some claiming to see images of Jesus in wall shadows or smelling roses of the Holy Virgin. These were nonsense examples of autosuggestion, of course. Besides, nobody knew what Jesus looked like or Mary's favorite flower. However, some claims couldn't be dismissed.

"We believe that signs and wonders were evident with Zack. He manifested unexplainable wounds on his body like those of Jesus Christ. His hands and feet. The bruise on his side. I felt the presence of Jesus in that room."

Another claimed, "St. Paul has told us that suffering is our way of continuing Christ's redemptive suffering. . . . I believe that Zachary was doing this for us—uniting his suffering to Christ the Lord."

"I came because my daughter has leukemia and I wanted Jesus to help her. When I entered Zack's room, I felt the Lord's presence. . . ."

"I believe the Lord spoke through Zack, giving us a sign of hope and mercy. And he chose Zack because he was broken in body and in a state of total purity of spirit. Jesus spoke through him. I believe this with all my heart."

There were many more of the same.

But down the Google list were other, darker responses—warnings that these miracle-seeking faithful were being brutally misled, and not by wishful thinking or autosuggestion, but by Satan himself.

"Remember the warning of the scriptures, Second Corinthians 11:14: 'Satan disguises himself as an angel of light.' And let's not forget that Zachary Kashian is a professed atheist and member of the Secular Humanist Society of his university.

"I'm telling you that Satan's deceptions are much like a kaleidoscope: As the tube is rotated, the same bits of colored glass will form a new design. Those who claim seeing Jesus in that young man's room are the devil's dupes. That was not Jesus or the Blessed Virgin, but Satan himself—the Great Deceiver."

The words sounded familiar to Roman, but he dismissed them as stock religious attacks—theological chestnuts. Likewise the name of the blogger meant nothing to him: Norman Babcock, director of the Fraternity of Jesus.

But what kept pecking at him was that the kid was born on the sixth of June, 1986. Were Roman a superstitious man, he would have wondered at the significance of those numbers: 666. The number of the beast.

For a moment Roman, too, was lost in the possibilities

of what may have transpired in that hospital room—
whether Zachary Kashian was channeling Jesus Christ
or the Antichrist. Whichever, maybe it was time to meet
this "miracle" man.

54

....

"We think he's merged with another mind."

"What? *What?* Who?"

"We don't know who. And there's no way that can be determined," said Morris Stern. "But we're certain it's a bona fide merger."

"Glory hallelujah," Warren Gladstone said. "Thank you, sweet Lord. Thank you."

They were back in Warren's suite at the Taj. Morris Stern maneuvered the mouse until a video image of the MRI of Zack's brain appeared. "Here are images of the electrical activity in his first NDE. You can see discrete signature patterns consistent with the mathematical analysis. Now look at this." The next screen showed other pulsing blotches superimposed on the first.

"Oh my," Warren said.

With a pen, Stern pointed out the new configurations. "This activity here and here and here were not present in the original NDE. They're a completely foreign imprint."

"We're looking at the mind of God," Gladstone declared.

"More likely the mind of someone else."

"But from the other side."

"That I don't know," Stern said.

That was the most he was going to concede. "Why not God?"

"Because we don't have God's profile on file."

"But you're telling me that the boy was in communication with someone from the other side. So why not God? Why couldn't his mind have merged with the Lord's?" Warren could barely contain himself.

Stern shook his head. "I didn't say from the other side—"

"Warren," Elizabeth broke in, "what we picked up was clearly an intrusive electrical presence imposed on his own activity. It's a huge leap to claim merging with God. More likely he mind-merged with someone now deceased, which is nonetheless still remarkable. A first!"

"Hallelujah."

Warren had seen the videos of the other test subjects, including several college kids; he had listened to their accounts of near-death experiences, some so full of detail and passion that he was nearly convinced. He had even allowed Luria to set up their lab in his own minister's home, which they'd had to gut to install their MRI machine. He had spent $10 million of ministry money, an investment that had turned some board directors against him. And after all the years of expense and false hope, after all the brain scans and videos of people in suspension—this was the first time that Elizabeth Luria and company had shown actual evidence of spiritual contact.

Yes, more tests would be needed, as Elizabeth had said. But he felt a near rapturous anticipation of the day he could grasp the Holy Grail and show the world that the Lord God Almighty exists.

And the possibilities were endless. No longer would

belief be simply a leap of faith. No longer would death be final. His would be evidence of things unseen. Evidence that all the world would embrace. Gone would be barriers that separated Christians and Jews, Muslims, Hindus, Buddhists, and the rest. All would be joined in one unifying belief system, at the core of which would be Warren Gladstone and his tabernacle. Yes, there would be cries of trickery, even heresy, perhaps even temporary backlashes—the inevitable resistance and protests against any pronouncement from Evangelical Christianity. But he'd cross those bridges when he got to them, fortified by the realization that he was at the vanguard of the greatest revelation ever: that he had found God.

"And you'd said he declared no religious affiliation?"

"Sorry. He entered 'NONE' on the questionnaire."

"Sorry nothing," Gladstone chortled. "All the better. He'll be our own Doubting Thomas who not only sees the light but sheds it on the world." Then he added, "Guard him well. This young man is manna from heaven, a gift from the Lord God Almighty Himself."

"It couldn't have happened without your generosity."

"Worth every penny." Warren stared at the images from the fMRI. "And delicious irony abounds. Deus ex machina."

Elizabeth Luria smiled. "That may be, but we still have more computations to do before we claim vindication."

"Then do them."

And as Warren lost himself in those pulsing colors across the schematic of Zack Kashian's brain, he felt the breathless promise well up in his soul. He knew he was looking at the mind of the Creator—but he also knew in his soul that he would indeed live in the house of the Lord forever and ever.

Amen.

55

Zack had called Dr. Luria two days ago to explain that he was not interested in any more suspensions. It was taking too much of his time, and he had to finish his thesis. His manner was polite and his tone neutral. And he said nothing about the murder flashes because she would use that to fuel her insistence that he return for more tests.

As expected, she did not take kindly to his announcement, beseeching him to reconsider, proclaiming that they were on the cusp of a great discovery, et cetera, et cetera. She had enlisted her best appeals short of begging. To soften the blow, he said that he would get back to her if he changed his mind.

In the meantime, he worked on his thesis, occasionally flipping through library books on NDEs. Most reports described the standard experiences—tunnel rides, total serenity, a oneness with the universe. And the standard presence of light and spiritual beings. A great number of claimants reported how NDE changed their lives for the better, making them more faithful and caring. But none reported anything like his horror shows.

As he did most mornings, Zack headed for an isolated table in the student union café that Thursday. It felt good to be back at his thesis without distraction. He worked steadily for a good part of the morning, until a voice startled him.

"Hello, Zack."

He looked up from the screen, and out of a half-glimpsed premonition there stood Elizabeth Luria. She was holding a tray with two coffees and croissants.

"I wasn't sure if you liked cheese or chocolate, so I got one of each."

Zack had seen her only in a white lab smock, but she was dressed stylishly in a pink blouse, tan slacks, and black blazer. Her hair was done up, and she wore a silver locket around her neck.

"May I join you?"

"Sure," he said. He got up and pulled over a chair for her. "How did you know where to find me?" He tried not to let his irritation show.

"It wasn't easy." She sat down. "Working on your thesis?"

"Trying to."

"Well, I won't be long."

"I mean it's just hard to get back the enthusiasm."

"I'm sure it'll return." She took a sip of her coffee. "You probably suspect why I'm here."

"Yes, and I'm not interested."

"Because you had an unpleasant experience, and I'm sorry that happened."

Had Sarah told her? He didn't think she'd betray him. But maybe she had. Luria was her boss after all. "Whatever. I just don't have the time."

"I understand."

She reached into her handbag and pulled out an envelope. From that she extracted a photograph and turned it toward him. It was a studio shot of a handsome young boy smiling broadly at the camera. Behind that was a shot of the same boy with a golden Labrador and an older man. "This was my son, Kevin, and his father, my husband. They were killed in an automobile accident some years ago. He was twelve at the time."

"I'm very sorry, Dr. Luria." It was the same child in the photograph on her lab desk.

"Thank you, and please call me Elizabeth." Then she continued, "I'll be straight with you. When I first started working on the project, I regarded all NDE claims as the brain's defense against the onslaught of death. But I've seen growing evidence that points to transcendence. And your sessions confirm that."

He could see that she was fighting back emotions.

"Zack, I believe that we are on the threshold of validating the existence of the afterlife."

He nodded, beginning to feel sorry for her.

"We've analyzed all the MRI data from your last session and, like the first run, everything points to the conclusion that you crossed over."

"Uh-huh."

"I was brought up in a religious home, but from a young age I didn't believe in the soul or God. I saw no evidence that the supernatural existed. But now I do. And my investment in this project goes beyond science. Frankly, I'd like to know that my son and husband are in a good place—that they're all right."

"Dr. Luria, what are you asking me to do?"

"I want you to submit to another session," she said, her body ramrod straight, her voice steady, without inflection, her eyes wet. "I want to confirm that the afterlife exists. I want confirmation that my child may still be alive in some form."

After a long moment, he said, "With all due respect, I'm not some kind of medium or swami."

"No, but you're the only person who technically died and returned with evidence that our essence goes on."

"What evidence?"

"The brain patterns, the electrical activity, the bloodwork—they all verify that your mind had actively separated from your brain, that your sentience continued even in flatline. That you had a near-death experience unlike anything we've seen before."

From nowhere rose the image of that man's ruined face under Zack's hands.

"This may be the greatest discovery ever: that we don't die but continue in some conscious form. Think of the hope that knowledge would afford people."

"Can't you use another test subject?"

"None of the others come close to your results."

"You mean I'm your only test subject?"

"At the moment, yes."

Tears began to flow, and she caught them with a napkin. *Shit.* He felt himself soften.

"I don't have the words to tell you the kind of grief and guilt I've experienced. Nor do I want or expect your pity." Then her face stiffened. "Did you have another unpleasant experience in the last run?"

"It's not worth talking about."

She glared at him as if trying to read his mind. Then from her purse she removed a checkbook. "If you don't care to discuss it, fine. But I'm willing to pay for your time, knowing full well your other responsibilities."

And in a fine hand in blue ink she wrote a check and handed it to him. "I'm hoping this will convince you how important it is to let us test you again."

Zack looked at the check in disbelief. It was made out to him for $10,000.

His first thought was that this was the largest check

he had ever seen with his name on it. The second thought was that he could clear all his debts and have money left over to give to his mother. The third thought was that for ten grand he could take the chance of another three-minute suspension. "This is a lot of money."

"You don't have to make a decision right now. All I ask is that you please think it over before saying no. Will you do that for me?"

"What do you want me to do?"

"To agree to let us test you a few more times."

"To put me in suspension."

"Yes."

"How many more times is 'a few'?"

"Until we get certain confirmation."

"But you already said you have confirmation."

Her face hardened and she said simply, "We need more data."

"And how will you know when you get what you want?"

"The mathematical analysis is complicated. It has to do with probabilities—which Morris can tell you more about."

She was being purposefully vague again. Nonetheless, he saw no point in having her twist in the breeze. "I'll do it on one condition: that I decide when one more suspension is too much."

"Fine," she said. Her eyes fell on the photograph of her son, and they filled again. In a moment, tears were flowing down her cheeks. "I know I can never have my son or husband back." She dabbed her face with a napkin. "But there would be great consolation to know that there's something beyond and the possibility that I may be with them again."

"Okay."

"I'll be in touch," she said, and thanked him. Before she left, she said, "His name is Kevin. Kevin Luria."

Then she turned and walked away, leaving Zack staring at the photograph and the check, thinking how she wanted him to give her hope in something he could not get his own mind around—something that perhaps should remain beyond human grasp.

56

Roman Pace lowered the student newspaper and watched the woman walk away.

He didn't know who she was—maybe the kid's mother. Maybe one of his professors. She had slipped him an envelope, which could have been a homework assignment or a letter of recommendation. Anything. But it looked like serious business. Not light talk.

When she got up to leave, Roman was tempted to follow her but decided to stay with the kid. He did get a couple shots of her on his cell phone.

As for that younger, good-looking woman from the Grafton Street place, they seemed to be more than friends. He had overnighted at her place last week.

Whoever she was, he'd find out.

57

....

Tetrodotoxin is a powerful neurotoxin found in puffer fish and is 10,000 times more lethal than cyanide. Twenty-five milligrams could kill a 165-pound man. There are no known antidotes for the toxin, which kills by causing respiratory failure. For 70% of the victims, death follows within four to 24 hours. The toxin works by shutting down electrical signaling in nerves. Nonlethal dosages can produce dizziness, headaches, and hallucinatory effects.

The last two words jumped out at Zack as he glared at his laptop later that evening.

He was staring at three options:

Behind Door One: He was brain-damaged and had hallucinated murder scenes. Door Two: He was an actual killer who murdered two strangers while in a trance. Door Three: He had crossed over and linked up with some homicidal psyche.

In spite of Elizabeth Luria's pleas, even Morris Stern's concession that he may have had out-of-body experiences, Zack did not buy the supernatural, no matter what their fancy MRI recorded. He didn't believe in ghosts. And he didn't think he was nuts.

That left the puffer fish toxin.

And there it was: "Nonlethal dosages can produce dizziness, headaches, and hallucinatory effects."

He had gotten nearly 470,000 hits from Googling "tetrodotoxin." Aside from all the data on how it was probably the deadliest substance in the natural world, he learned that the prime source, the puffer fish, though outlawed as a menu item in America, was a coveted Japanese delicacy called *fugo* that when prepared by an expert sushi chef produced a psychedelic high for the diner. "In the skilled hands of an expert *fugo* chef, if just enough tetrodotoxin is left in, the preparation of puffer fish flesh leaves the customer with a pleasant tingling sensation to the lips and a slightly mind-altering buzz."

"A thrill without the kill," proclaimed one *fugo* blogger.

Before he logged off, he noticed a link to *The Boston Globe*. Dated four months ago, the story described a homeless man murdered by another with a baseball bat on the Harvard Bridge. According to a witness, the murder appeared to be a bizarre mercy killing. The Massachusetts State Crime Lab reported traces of tetrodotoxin in his blood. Either the guy had exotic taste and a bad cook or a new drug had hit the streets. Yet a Boston Police Department spokesman said, "I don't know how a homeless man ended up with puffer fish toxin in his liver. It's a first for us."

According to another site, a nonlethal dosage dropped one's temperature and blood pressure to the point of inducing a deep coma. In a few accidental food-poisoning cases in Japan, victims recovered days later after being declared dead. In Haiti, tetrodotoxin was known as the "zombie drug," used by voodoo priests to fake the deaths of victims who were revived hours later to the dismay of others.

In the United States, tetrodotoxin was on the "select agents" list of the Department of Health and Human Services, meaning that the drug could be used only by registered research scientists.

58

....

Mitch turned onto Connecticut Route 84 and headed north for the Vernon exit. It was Saturday night, and he had been at the Outback in Manchester, celebrating his promotion to floor manager at the Buckland Hills Sears. And, of course, he'd had a few beers and was wiped out and dying to get to bed.

He was driving a 1992 Mitsubishi 3000 VR-4—one of the few all-wheel-drive sports cars on the road and one of the best looking. He had bought it used four years ago and had it repainted and detailed. Today it was in mint condition, even though it had seen 162,000 miles. He loved the sculpted design, the wide wheel base, the low-slung macho look. And with three hundred horses under the hood, the Mitsu had balls.

He was maybe two miles shy of the exit when he heard a deep rumble. "Shit!" he cried, and slammed his hand on the wheel. His muffler had blown a hole. He growled down the highway, sounding like something out of a NASCAR race. He had gone maybe half a mile when he heard the connector pipe hit the ground and drag, no doubt leaving a trail of sparks. "Fuck!" The car began filling with fumes.

He opened the window and took the next exit down Bolton Road to a clearing among trees. There were no streetlamps in this area, but he had a flashlight and some rope in the hatch to tie up the pipe. Luckily it had happened only a few miles from home.

He pulled the flashlight and a fishing knife from the glove compartment and got out. He looked under the car. The muffler was still intact, but the pipe was on the ground. He opened the hatch and removed the jack, then raised the car maybe a foot so he could slide under.

The hangers that held the pipe to the muffler had come loose. But it had cooled enough to be roped to an opening. Unfortunately, the pipe had rusted through and would have to be replaced. By the time the Midas people got through with him, he'd be talked into a whole new exhaust system, putting him back at least a thousand bucks. And given the year of the car, it might take a week for parts to arrive, which meant he'd have to get a rental. Hell, he didn't need this.

Even though the air was cool, it was hot and cramped under the car, and his arms tired working the rope. Worse, he was exhausted and yearning to be in bed.

He had worked for maybe twenty minutes when he heard something. He didn't know if it was the wind or the traffic, but it sounded as if someone had approached the car. He looked down the length of his body, then to the right and left. Nothing. He squirmed to face the rear of the car, maneuvering the flash in the tight space. Still nothing. Just the underbrush and shadows.

Yet he had a sensation that he was no longer alone.

After a few moments, he dismissed the feeling and continued tying the pipe to the car's underside.

A minute or so later, he again thought he heard something. And again he looked around, half expecting to see feet out there. Nothing. Probably the sound of the engine cooling, the metal contracting in the cool night air.

He was just finishing the last makeshift rope hanger when he heard some scuffling just to his right.

"Who's there?"

Nothing.

Mitch waited until he was sure it was only in his head. He continued securing the rope to the pipe.

"*Mitchell.*"

His name. Someone had whispered his name. But it was so soft, it could have been the wind in the trees.

The next moment, he heard the jack cranked down a notch. The sound shot through him like a bullet.

The car had lowered on him.

He turned the flash toward the jack, expecting to see a pair of feet, but only the jack lit up. Before he could move to squirm out, another snap of metal, and the underside of the car came down an inch closer to his face. He could feel the searing heat of the engine. He could smell oil and rust. He could taste terror.

Before the car came down another notch, he squirmed out from under. He fanned the flashlight around, but no one was there. Just the trees and scrub, making shadows against the light. He pulled himself to his feet, then moved around to the other side of the car. Through the passenger window he reached into the glove compartment, where he kept a loaded .38-caliber Smith & Wesson. "Okay, you son of a bitch." He turned a complete circle, holding the gun straight out.

Nothing. Nobody was there. A couple of sets of headlights came down the road, and he lowered the gun so he wouldn't draw attention.

The cars passed and he stood there in the silent black, a flash in one hand, the pistol in the other. The only sound was that of the crickets. He sprayed the trees again with light. Nothing.

Your imagination, he told himself. He was tired and edgy from a long day, sore and pissed from having to crawl in the dirt to fix a muffler pipe.

But he hadn't imagined the car being lowered on him.

He inspected the jack. It was still in place, but the tire iron was gone. He had used it to crank up the car and thought he had left it on the ground by the jack. But it wasn't there. Maybe he'd brought it with him when he slid under the car. He dropped to one knee and shone the flash under the car. No tire iron.

As he pulled himself up, he heard that whispery voice again. *"Mitchell."*

By reflex, he shot in that direction. The explosion filled the night air, and in the flash of the gun, he saw a hooded figure like the Grim Reaper.

"Wh-who are you?"

"Go to hell, asshole."

In a flicker of light, a blackened figure stood with the raised tire iron in hand. Before Mitch could scream, it crashed down on his head.

59

"*Okay, time to wake up.*"

"*That's it. Open your eyes.*"

"*Can you tell me your name?*"

Disembodied voices through the fog.

He could not answer. He cracked open his eyes against the bright ceiling lights. He rolled his head, taking in stacks of electronic equipment, computer monitors, the desks, shelves of books. Faces of the lab scientists and technicians. But across his mind flashed images of a black metal tire iron smashing the head of some faceless guy in the shadows.

In disconnected image bursts, he saw the curved bend of steel whack the man on the crown, then again on the back of the neck, then the man crumpling to the ground like a broken marionette.

Someone said something to him, and he stooped over the man's body and smashed him again on the shoulder and his rib cage until he no longer moved.

"*Zack, are you all right?*"

He didn't answer but kicked the man so that he rolled over, one knee raised to his chest, the other leg broken at a weird angle on the ground.

"*Would you like to sit up?*"

He shook his head and stomped on the guy's chest . . . again and again until he felt the rib bones crack into his lungs and blood spurted from his mouth and nose.

"*I think you're still a little foggy from the drug.*"

He touched his left side where the bullet had entered. It was still tender in the area of his liver. But remarkably, there was no blood.

"*Does your side hurt?*"

He did not respond, but the gunshot rang in his head.

Somebody handed him a bottle of water. The pretty woman with the short auburn hair. He drank from the bottle and looked around the room stupidly at all the equipment and the four people staring at him.

Another woman asked him his name. He couldn't remember. He was too intent on getting away.

Once again he heard the older woman say, "Do you remember your name?"

And he heard himself whisper, "I don't know."

"Your name is Zachary Kashian. Remember?"

Zack. Zachary Kashian.

For maybe a full minute in real time, he stared at nothing. His head was clearing of the attack. He drank more water, hoping to flush away recall.

Then the moment came back to him.

Yes, Zack Kashian.

The brightly lit room—the people, computers, beeping monitors, IV drips, oxygen tanks, cabinets, defibrillators, medical cabinets, shelves. He looked at them, the fading images leaving him spent and trembling.

"You were in suspension, remember?" Sarah said. Sarah Wyman.

He nodded.

They had put him under again. They had flatlined him

and sent him someplace awful that left his mind full of venom and his side aching.

"Want to go home." His voice was a jagged whisper.

"Of course, but we'd like to ask you a few questions first." The older woman. Dr. Luria.

Call me Elizabeth. The one with the dead kid she wanted him to find. Questions. She always stoned him with friggin' questions.

"Only because the experience may still be fresh in your mind."

Sarah brought him a bolster, and he lay back on it. He felt too spent to protest.

Dr. Luria pulled a chair beside the gurney while Dr. Cates turned on the video camera.

"Zack, do you remember anything from being under? Anything at all? Where you were? What you were doing? Who was with you?"

"No."

"Do you remember where you were? Any sense of place?"

"No."

"Or what you may have been doing?"

Go to hell, asshole. He could still feel the rasp of those words.

He shook his head. He could see from the expression on Dr. Luria's face that she was not happy with his responses.

"Take your time and think. I know you're still a bit foggy. But relax and search your memory."

He closed his eyes as if he were rummaging through his memory banks. That was the last thing he wanted—to be back on that night road. All he wanted was for this to be over so he could leave and never come back. They were screwing up his brain.

Sarah could see him struggling and suggested that he

go to the restroom to change and freshen up. She helped him off the gurney, and he headed for the toilet with his clothes.

When he returned he felt better, his mind less raw. He decided to play dumb so they'd let him go. But Luria and Morris Stern were waiting for him, like twin vultures on a tree branch. Sarah handed him a mug of coffee.

Luria sat at her desk and Stern next to her by the computer monitor. The others were standing on the sidelines. Zack took a seat to face them.

"Feel better?" Luria asked.

He just grunted.

She nodded, then kicked into interrogation mode. "Zack, let me go back and start again. Do you recall any sense of the locale?"

"No." Something flitted across her face, as if she knew he was lying.

"Were you outside? On a beach? In a room? Woodlands? Just some sense of the setting?"

He shook his head and felt a twinge on his left side.

"Okay. Any sense of the presence of other people?"

"No." He could hear the hollowness of his own response.

"Don't rush your answers. Think, try to relax and recall the experience."

He looked at Sarah, whose eyes were large and staring at him. The same with the others. The room seemed to be holding its breath. He nodded at the computers. "What does it show?"

Stern and Cates looked to Luria to take the question. "It shows heightened sensory stimulation coming from the outside."

"Like the last time," Stern added. "The activity in the limbic area was wild."

"I don't remember."

Luria's eyebrow shot up like a polygraph needle. "You don't remember. Well, frankly, I find that hard to believe. Your blood chemistry was teeming with cortisol and epinephrine. Your brain was in fight-or-flight response. How can you not remember anything?"

His heart was pounding so hard that his diaphragm throbbed visibly. This was like a psychic striptease. They knew he was lying.

"I'll ask you again," Luria said, her eyes black and intense. "Do you recall anything from suspension? Any sense of activity, of emotions—fear, anger? Of another's presence?"

The pain in his side kept flaring at him. Again he checked it.

"Are you okay?" Sarah asked.

He nodded. The skin wasn't broken, no bruises. But it felt as if the bullet were lodged inside.

Before Luria could launch into him again, Morris Stern cleared his throat. "Zack, a couple of weeks ago we explained how the machine can detect individual neuroelectrical signatures. Remember? Well, your brain contains one hundred billion neurons, so it's like listening to conversations of every person on the planet fifteen times over. From all that chatter, complex algorithms help us eliminate those common to all other people from your own discrete signature. Okay?"

Zack made no response, but Stern went on as if he had.

He turned the computer monitor so Zack could see multicolored scintillations and patterns. "This may mean nothing to you, but that's the axonal electrical activity in a region of your parietal lobe. Just before we woke you, we recorded a sudden change in patterns. We need to analyze more of the data, but preliminary results indicate an anomaly."

The patterns flickered and changed color and meant nothing to Zack.

"These splotches flashing across your hippocampus indicate that the visual cortex and sensory centers were being flooded with data from the outside. In short, you were not manufacturing a near-death experience, you had one."

"You said that the last time."

"Not me, because I wasn't convinced, but now I am. Your mind left your brain and took in an experience of its own. There's more data to analyze, but we've got enough for confirmation."

"Confirmation of what?"

Stern pushed up the glasses on his nose and looked directly at him. "That you merged with another mind."

"What?"

"Like the last time. We finished those analyses, and found a signature that's not yours—that belongs to another entity. Frankly, this is phenomenal."

"In addition to that," said Elizabeth, "your blood analysis shows spikes in adrenaline commensurate with the intense activity in the rage center of your brain. What you experienced was violence—like the last two times."

A rat uncurled in Zack's gut. *I'm not buying this,* he told himself. It was just a bad trip, a 3-D nightmare. The tetrodotoxin crap caused hallucinations. It was like what Stern said the other day—his brain put together scraps of memory, some wish fulfillment things from the day, and produced another killer flick inside his head. "If anything comes back to me, I'll let you know."

"You're lying," Luria said. "You are bloody lying. I can see it in your face. Tell me the truth, goddamn it. What did you experience?"

The others froze in place, but he could see Sarah wince in anticipation.

"I killed a man."

"What?"

"I killed a man. I beat him to death with a tire iron while he was fixing his car."

Sarah looked horrified. Luria's face was a blank of itself. "You killed a man?"

"He was under his car fixing something. I waited until he crawled out, then smashed in his skull. And the last time I strangled a guy lifting weights. And before that I ran a woman down with a car." He got up to leave.

"Wait, please," Luria pleaded. "Do you know these people or why you attacked them?"

"No. And I don't want to. You've fucked up my head something wicked."

"Please don't go just yet," she begged.

"Lady, I may have permanent brain damage. You got that? I'm fucking out of here."

"Fine, fine," Morris Stern said. "You've been through enough."

Sarah agreed. Dr. Luria glanced at the others. "Okay." She took Zack's arm. He could feel trembling but couldn't determine if it was him or her. "Why didn't you tell us before?"

He pulled his arm free but didn't answer her.

"I'm very sorry. We can give you something to help you sleep peacefully. I promise. But you have made an extraordinary breakthrough. You—"

He headed for the door. Sarah caught up to him. "Sorry, Zack."

He pulled out his wallet and laid Luria's $10,000 check on her desk, then passed through the door.

Luria ran to him, begging him to take it. "Please, Zack. Take a week off to rest. But please let us continue. Please. We're almost there."

He didn't know what she meant and didn't care. "Leave me alone."

"But you made contact with another sentience."

"I made contact with hell and I'm not going back."

60

....

Roman played the Warren Gladstone video for the third time.

The guy had a big cartoon happy face, and he was making claims about the Day of Jubilation as if it were the second coming itself. He carried on about a whole new way of life for the world—a way of life that would unite people of all faiths and of no faith; a day when there would be no more fear of death. No more fear of hellfires.

A day of rejoicing. A day that will live forever and ever, world without end.

The guy sounded pretty convincing—so much so that Roman felt a little tickle of inspiration.

But there were dissenters—bloggers railing against him for going "soft on sin" and reducing the gospel to a lot of left-wing self-help bullshit.

Making God an extension of New Age desires trivializes His divine sovereignty and fails to explain the place of good and evil in His divine plan. He teaches people to believe that with God you can do anything you want. God helped them win the lottery, get a job, afford a new car. But that trivializes God to handouts.

What snagged Roman's attention was what one commentator said about near-death experiences:

Some claim they've encountered a being of light that was Jesus. Appealing as that may sound, this is a false Jesus who teaches that death is good; that sin is not a problem. That there's no hell to worry about since all people go to heaven, regardless of whether one has faith in Christ . . . that all religions are equally valid. . . .

The only conclusion is that this "Jesus" is the lying spirit warned against in the Book of John. And those who believe are the devil's dupes.

Remember that Satan can appear as an "angel of light" and "servant of righteousness" (2 Corinthians 11:14– 15). His goal is to mimic Jesus and to lead people away from the true Christ of scripture.

Beware! Such claims of tunneling into the afterlife are the work of Satan's henchmen. . . .

And at the bottom of several blogs was the name of the same organization, one he had never heard of: the Fraternity of Jesus.

He logged off as the words echoed and reechoed in his head: *Devil's dupes. Satan's henchmen.*

61

....

Zack was shaking uncontrollably by the time Sarah dropped him off. Very little was said during the ride. She apologized several times, and he nodded acceptance. But it wasn't her fault.

Nor was his mind on resentment or anger or disappointment. He wanted to say something conciliatory, sensing that she felt blameworthy. But it wouldn't come out, constrained by the singular emotion that made his chest pound and his ears click and his mouth turn spitless with dread. He muttered a good night and jumped out of the car.

And he knew why.

And like a force of gravity, that knowledge yanked him out of the car and up the stairs to his apartment.

He tried stalling the pull by drinking a glass of warm milk and slipping into bed. He even fingered what was left of the Lunesta and Haldol in the dark, his body feeling as if it had turned into a giant cardiac organ, throbbing wildly.

Why are you stalling? Get up and get it over with.

He shook away the voice and popped the pills with the milk. Then he rolled over and tried to shut down his mind.

Impossible.

He tried to focus on absurd things like floating through the air, sailing across Boston. He ran pi to fifty places twice. Nothing. It was still there, pulling at his brain like a bungee cord. And he knew it wouldn't let up until he knew for sure.

God, I don't want this, he thought. *I don't want to know.*

But it was now or tomorrow or the next day. *Might as well get it over with,* he told himself. *Might even be wrong.*

He threw off the covers and padded out of the bedroom and into the other room, where he stumbled to his desk and flopped into his chair.

Years ago, when he got his driver's license, his mother had said that she had to go to Mount Auburn Hospital for a procedure. He'd pressed and pressed until she'd revealed that she had a lump in her breast. For days he'd prayed that it not be malignant. As he sat in the dark, all that rushed back.

"Don't let it be," he said to the dark. Then he turned on his laptop.

Shaking, he clicked on Google and wrote in the name. He got two dozen hits. But at the top was an item from the *Hartford Courant* that he read as if in a premonition:

The body of Mitchell Gretch, 34, of Cedar Road, Manchester, was buried yesterday in Cedar Hill Cemetery in Manchester. He was found bludgeoned to death four days ago on Bolton Road, lying in a pool of blood. He had apparently been attacked with a tire iron while fixing a broken muffler pipe on his automobile. . . .

Gooseflesh shot up his torso and across his scalp.

Thirteen years ago, Gretch was exonerated from a charge of murdering Jacob Kashian, from Carleton, MA, but that case was dismissed by the judge for insufficient evidence.

Coincidentally, his alleged accomplice in that homicide, William Volker, died last week from an accident in his home in Waltham, Massachusetts. Local police have ruled out foul play.

Manchester police believe that Gretch was murdered by an unknown assailant who used the tire iron from Gretch's 1992 Mitsubishi sports car.

Police have named no suspect or suspects and say they are continuing to investigate the circumstances of Gretch's death. . . .

As if on autopilot, he Googled William Volker. Instantly a dozen hits came up, at the top of which was an article from *The Boston Globe:* "Freak Weightlifting Accident Claims Life of Waltham Man."

Zack's brain could barely register what he was reading. Jake's other killer. He didn't have to double-check on the dead hit-and-run woman. He knew.

62

....

"Volker and Gretch killed my brother. And the woman was Gretch's cousin—one of their witnesses who claimed they saw nothing." Zack handed Sarah the obituaries he had printed up.

"What?"

It was sometime after two in the morning, and he had called her to come over, terrified at his discovery.

"And these were the same people you saw in your NDEs?" she said as she read them.

"Yes." Photographs were included with the obits. "I recognize them."

"Maybe it's just bizarre coincidences."

"What, that my brother's killers got murdered and I was there each time? Sarah, I saw them. I felt their deaths. I was there. Jesus, I'm either losing my mind or I killed them." He had been drinking a glass of warm milk and had to hold the glass with two hands, he was shaking so badly.

Sarah looked at the obits. "I don't believe either."

"But that tetrodotoxin is lousy with side effects," he said. "What if I blacked out and went after them? Killed them and don't remember anything?"

While she read the printouts, he moved to the sink to steady himself, looking into his glass of milk and thinking that maybe he had lost his mind—that maybe the combination of head trauma, the coma, and the zombie anesthesia created some weird brain damage that had turned him into an insane stalker bent on vengeance. He had had nightmares throughout his life like anybody else. But these had been like no others—intense, brutally vivid, and through the eyes of someone else—of that he was almost sure.

Sarah's voice jarred him back into the moment. "But this says Volker died on June tenth. That's when we were at Grafton's. A neighbor says he always worked out after supper."

"Yeah, and we left around nine. I could have gone over there after we split and killed him . . . and blocked it from my memory."

"But he lived in Waltham. Even if you took the T, it would take over an hour," she said. "Do you even know where he lived?"

"Yes." Volker moved from Allston to Waltham after the court decision. Zack's mother hadn't wanted to know where, but Zack had looked him up. And even before he'd gotten his driver's license, he'd fantasized about driving to Volker's apartment and firebombing it while he slept. Later he would sometimes drive over and follow Volker to work or the supermarket or to friends' places. "I had my bike, and it's only seven miles down the river."

"Do you remember doing that?"

"No."

"Not exactly something you'd forget," she said. "Remember pedaling home?"

"No. Just walking you back to your place."

Sarah picked up another obit. "This says Gretch died

in Vernon, Connecticut, on Saturday the twenty-fifth, eight days ago. Do you remember where you were?"

"The library."

"Can you verify that?"

"I checked out a book." From his desk he pulled out a collection of essays on Mary Shelley. The slip inside gave the date and time—same date as Gretch's death.

"What time?"

"Four eighteen."

"There you are. A motorist found him around one in the morning a hundred miles from here. There's no way you could have biked down there."

"Except I had Damian's car that weekend."

Her face stiffened. "Do you remember going down there?"

"No."

"So how can you remember borrowing his car?"

He removed his wallet and pulled out a slip of paper. "Receipt from the Gulf station on Huntington. I put in forty-three dollars' worth of gas at five that afternoon." No MassPike receipt, but the entrance was a mile east down the avenue.

"And you don't remember where you went?"

"No." Fear shuddered through him as if there were a core of ice in his chest.

They were silent a long moment as Sarah stared at him, probably afraid for her own safety, he thought. Then she said, "But that means you'd have to have looked him up, where he lived, worked, what he was doing that night. That's a lot of unknowns."

He nodded.

"Remember doing any of that?"

"No," he said. "But sometimes I'd wake up in the middle of the night and be at my computer and not remember getting there."

"Sleepwalking. Is that something you've done?"

"Not until recently." He downed the rest of the milk, which had done nothing to calm him down. "He worked at the local Sears. Maybe I called and got stuff from a coworker." Even as he said that, nothing inside clicked.

Sarah said nothing. She looked scared.

He picked up the obit notice on Celia Gretch, the jogger. She was run down on a rural back road in Reading, fifteen miles north of Boston, on the afternoon of June 25—the same day her cousin Volker was found dead in his garage.

"Wouldn't Damian have mentioned damage to his car?"

"Not if she was just knocked down."

"But she died by getting hit."

"She died by being crushed under the wheels."

Her eyes were dilated with fear. "So what does this all mean?"

"It means I don't have an alibi for three murders I saw myself commit."

Sarah backed up to the kitchen sink, her arms folded protectively across her chest. "You're scaring me, Zack."

"I'm scaring me."

63

....

Roman arrived at the confessional early that morning. He had called two nights before on the secure cell phone and insisted they meet. Father X was not pleased but agreed when Roman said he had something important to propose.

The church was empty when Roman slipped into the booth. At ten sharp, Father X entered the other side. "God be with you, my son. You did good work."

"Thank you."

"So, what are you proposing?"

"I'm proposing we cut the Father-son bullshit and get real."

"I beg your pardon?"

Roman punched his fist through the grate. He reached in with one hand, grabbed the man, and pulled his face to the window. "You're no more a priest than I am. You're Norman Babcock, and I want to know what the hell this is all about."

The man made an involuntary grunt as his fat bald head flushed like a ripening tomato.

"I'm not on some mission for the Church. You hired me to settle some pissant little scores for you."

"What? That's not true."

"Then tell me what the fuck is going on or I'm going to come in there and pound you till you stop moving."

"Please lower your voice."

With the other hand, Roman whipped out his gun and poked the barrel with the silencer through the window. "This better?"

"God, don't. Please."

Roman tightened his grip on Babcock's shirt. "Then tell me why you want these people dead."

"Okay, okay."

Roman yanked the white collar off his shirt and tossed it at him.

"H-how do you know . . . ?"

"How do I know you're Babcock? 'Satan's henchmen,' 'dupes of the devil.' Your pet phrases are all over your Web site."

He looked at the silencer aimed at his chest. "What do you want?"

"I wanna know why I'm killing these people. And don't give me any mission-for-the-Church bullshit." Roman would have loved to choke the fat bastard to death out of sheer rage—rage at being Babcock's patsy, rage at himself for having nearly fallen for the setup. For wanting to believe that he was on a genuine quest to eliminate the enemies of Christendom and, in so doing, opening a path to heaven.

"You *are* on a mission for the Church. For the Lord Jesus Christ himself."

"They're a bunch of fucking doctors and computer geeks."

Babcock hesitated, probably wondering how much Roman knew. He had been hired to kill and not ask why.

"Yes, and what they are doing is evil."

"They're doing near-death experience research."

"So you know. But you know what they're trying to do?"

"I've read your Web site."

"They're committing blasphemy. They're violating God's demand not to practice divination. And that's what their research is—defilement of God's Word."

Babcock's Web site was a nonstop rant against near-death experiences—"the Great Cosmic Lie," another favorite phrase. "So some people say they see dead loved ones. What's the big deal?"

"The big deal? The test subjects are innocent. It's those running the tests who are violating God's prohibition, leading them to believe that they're encountering beings of light, glimpsing heaven. But that's all deception—fabrications of Satan. . . ."

Roman snorted. "Yeah, yeah. I read all that."

"Then you also know that stopping them is a sacred mission for the Lord and the Church."

In his heart of hearts, Roman wanted to believe him. "But this mission's not sanctioned by the Church. It's for you and your Friends for Jesus."

"No. The Fraternity of Jesus is dedicated to the belief that every member of the Church is called to holiness—to a sanctifying life of doing God's work. And fighting God's enemies is the highest mission and an aspiration to sainthood."

Roman snickered. "So, I keep it up, they'll make me a saint?"

"I didn't say that. Your work in defense of the Church is a blessed mission. History will decide if your success is worthy of sainthood. But this is not some little personal payback thing."

Nothing in Babcock's manner suggested that he did not believe in his own words. And he had put forty-five grand where his mouth was. Roman pulled the pistol out of the smashed-open window between them. "What's your beef with Warren Gladstone? And don't go stupid on me. Your rants are all over the Internet."

"I think he's behind the NDE project."

"You mean he's bankrolling it?"

"Yes. And throwing his moral weight behind it. He's a disgraced Evangelist minister who's trying to get back in the limelight."

"Why not take him out of the picture?"

"He's not important unless he has his so-called proof. Eliminating that will be the better strategy—exposing him: the emperor with no clothes. Also, eliminating him risks making him a martyr—and that'd be counterproductive."

"Okay," Roman said. "So why's this miracle kid so important?"

"What kid?"

"Zachary Kashian."

Babcock's face did not struggle for an expression or pretend ignorance. "What they're doing is converting him into Satan's dupe in order to parade him before the world as evidence they've found the afterlife. It's their grand illusion: Science finds God."

"Does the kid know what he's doing?"

"No, but they're conditioning him to channel the devil."

"But he quoted Jesus from a coma."

"That wasn't Jesus. That was Satan. That's how he works. That's his modus operandi—to lie," Babcock whispered, his face all flushed. "That young man has become Satan's mouthpiece, his channel, and he doesn't even know it. At least not yet."

"What do you mean, 'not yet'?"

"Once he operates on his own, he'll achieve their mission."

"What mission?"

"Bringing to earth the Antichrist."

"You got to be kidding."

Babcock pushed his face into the jagged hole from Roman's fist. His face was full, fleshy, and burning. "Do I look as if I'm kidding, Mr. Pace? He's their secret weapon."

"How do you know all this?"

"We have our contacts."

In spite of himself, an electric glow in Roman's chest had its source in something close to conviction. Maybe it was wishful thinking, but Roman began to settle into a strange solace. "You going to want me to go after him?"

"Not just yet. They may self-destruct before we get to that."

"How's that?"

"Only those nearest the project know who's been eliminated. Either they'll take the hint and stop, or they'll continue. Either way they'll fail. And there won't be any going back."

Roman didn't understand what he meant, so he remained silent.

"But you'll hear from us in due time."

"Meanwhile . . . ?"

"Meanwhile do nothing but pray for your soul."

Roman slipped the weapon back into the shoulder harness and pulled his jacket forward. He nodded at Babcock and left the booth. The church was still empty.

Instead of going outside, he stopped at the end of the nave and stared into the church. The day was partly overcast, so stray sunlight played through the colors of

the stained glass, filling the floor with splashes of reds,
greens, blues, and gold.

He looked upward from the stone floor and followed
the direction that the architecture pulled the eye to—the
circle of colored light over the altar and upward to the
vaulted ceiling. The people who designed these churches
knew what they were doing, Roman thought. The eyes
were drawn from stone-cold mortal earth to heaven.

Roman admired the colors and the art, but he didn't
feel the presence of God. Nor was he sure what that
would be like. But standing there, he could sense something higher than himself. And that made him feel good.
So did the reassurance that he was still on a mission. He
knew he didn't have it in him to become a regular church-
goer. He didn't like crowds. He didn't like people. He was
divorced with no children and few friends. So he couldn't
imagine sitting in packed pews with someone in the pulpit
booming away in Latin. That was not him. His relationship with God was strictly private.

He dipped his fingers into the holy water and crossed
himself.

Thank you.

Then he walked outside into the shafts of sunlight
with two thoughts humming in the fore of his brain.

One, that the Reverend Warren Gladstone was a bank-
roller.

Two, that some just plain college kid might be pitting
heaven against hell.

64

It was nearly three in the morning, and Zack and Sarah were still sitting in his apartment, the obits in a pile on the kitchen table between them. "There's another possibility," he said.

"What?"

"That I crossed over and linked up with something evil on the other side."

"Evil? Like supernatural?"

He nodded. "Sarah, my mind feels violated, like I'm psychically bonded to a psychopathic killer."

"But that's impossible."

"Is it? You all said I experienced transcendence, right?"

"Yeah, clinically. But—"

"And my blood showed spikes of rage?"

"Well, the adrenaline—"

"And that I merged with another mind?"

"Possibly."

"What if that other mind is my dead father?"

"What?"

"I know how crazy that sounds," he said. "But what if I crossed over and released his spirit, and it's hot with vengeance, and he went after those bastards. And somehow

I mind-linked with him. I've been feeling his presence since that first day in the lab."

"You mean his ghost came back and killed them?"

"Got a better explanation?"

"No. And I don't believe in ghosts."

"Neither did I, and now I'm afraid of them."

"Zack, even if ghosts exist, I doubt they can overpower a weightlifter or drive a car."

"If I didn't do it myself, then what the hell am I picking up?"

"I don't know, but I don't believe you killed them."

"That's a relief." She didn't want anything, but he went over to the refrigerator for another glass of milk. *Milk,* he thought as he stared into the glass. *So innocent and ordinary.* It wasn't long ago when his own life was innocent and ordinary. "So, if it wasn't me, how the hell did I see those murders?"

"I don't know. I can't even explain transcendence, and every metric says your mind left your brain. But I can't tell you how."

Zack sipped his milk. "I feel like that kid in *The Sixth Sense.* He sees dead people. I watch them die. It'd be funny if it weren't so friggin' real."

She thought for a moment, then looked up at him. "Maybe you really did have a paranormal experience. Really."

"That works in books and movies, but how do you explain telepathy or astral projection or whatever the hell in rational terms?"

"Something I've been wondering since I started. But if you picked up someone else's sentience, it has to be through one of the four known force fields—nuclear, atomic, gravity, or electromagnetic. The first two don't count—the ranges are too small. And as far as we know, gravity doesn't carry information. That leaves EM waves."

"Like light and radio waves."

"Yeah, but to pick up thoughts of someone five miles away, you'd need a power source that would cook your brain. And Gretch was in Connecticut."

"So how do you explain it?"

"I can't, but Elizabeth would say you experienced the supernatural."

"But what do you think?"

She shook her head. "I'm still a skeptic. Either it's an unknown medium—something we've never seen before. Or we're missing something in the diagnostics. Don't get excited, but the only way to know for sure is more suspensions."

"Well, that's not going to happen."

"Can't say I blame you."

"But what if she's right? What if there's a whole other level of awareness—what mystics have been talking about forever? Some kind of mind pool I tapped into." He finished his milk and walked to the sink. "My head feels haunted. And it's been this way since I started these friggin' tests."

"Did you ever, you know, ever have psychic experiences before?"

He could hear the guardedness in her voice. "Once." And he told her about the night at the Foxwoods Resort Casino.

"How come you never mentioned that?"

"Because I thought it was nothing but a weird coincidence."

"I don't know. Maybe you made a freak connection or something. That's something you should have told Elizabeth and Morris."

"Elizabeth and Morris have done enough damage." He moved to his desk and removed some papers and handed them to her. "Three homeless people were found dead with tetrodotoxin in their bloodstreams over the last two years." He poured himself another glass of milk and warmed it in the microwave while she read the articles. "Each of them died bizarre deaths. One guy was mercy-killed with a baseball bat. Another threw himself under a truck. The third, a woman, rammed a screwdriver through her ear into her brain."

"What?"

"According to friends, each complained of headaches and bad visions. One guy claimed he was possessed by demons. Another said bugs were eating out his brain. Whatever, they were tormented to death because of their suspensions."

Sarah continued reading.

"The kicker is that each of them had tetrodotoxin in them—nothing the police had seen before."

"Because it's a research drug."

"That's my point."

Her face clouded over. "All our drugs are under lock and key, and we've never had a break-in. 'Least not while I've been there."

"I think they were test subjects before you came aboard."

"No way. If subjects complained of a side effect, they'd stop the tests. Besides, volunteers came from local colleges, not homeless shelters."

"But you've only been there a few months."

"So?"

He turned one of the articles toward her. "The guy who threw himself under a truck had a friend who said he began to complain about beetles and terrible pain in his head after some scientist guy offered to pay for sleep tests."

She read where he pointed. "This doesn't have to be us."

"How many labs you think are doing sleep tests using tetrodotoxin?"

She stared at the paper. "I don't believe this."

"Tell me about it. Since you started, how many subjects have you suspended?"

"I don't know, maybe fifteen out of a hundred interviewed."

"You know how many since they started?"

"I never checked the records."

"You might want to, because I think you'll find a bunch of illegal aliens and bogus names."

65

....

Sarah left, saying that she would drive to the lab first thing in the morning to check the records.

Meanwhile, Zack took two sleeping tabs and turned off the light, hoping to shut his mind off from speculating on the hideous options. Like Sarah, he did not believe in ghosts. And his mind refused to accept insanity or the possibility that he had murdered three people and repressed the acts from conscious memory. That left some psychic awareness he had tapped into—some alien sentience that had left his mind feeling contaminated.

After several minutes, he slipped into a drowsy twilight, feeling himself fading into a dreamless void. He didn't know if at first he was imagining it, but he thought he heard something outside his bedroom door.

His first thought was Sarah. Maybe she forgot something. Or maybe her car didn't start. He called her name. Nothing. Then he reached over to turn on the light when a bright flash went on in his eyes and a hand with a white towel clamped down on his face.

As he thrashed against the pressure, harsh chemical fumes filled his head. Chloroform. He recognized the odor. He also recognized the bald-headed male as his body pressed across his own, the towel smothering his face.

But before he could connect it, his mind faded to black.

"*He's coming to.*" A male voice.

Zack squinted at the bright light. *The sky*, he thought. *Bright white sky*.

But then taking shape was the textured, translucent panel that covered the fluorescent lights recessed into the ceiling of the lab. He tried to move, but his hands and feet were restrained, and he was wired up with contacts to his chest and an IV line in his arm.

Standing beside Elizabeth Luria in street clothes were two men. One had a hairless domed head and fleshy pink face. A face he had seen before. The other was thin, with glasses and dark hair.

"I'm sorry, Zack," she said. She was standing on the other side of the gurney.

He tried to say something, but she depressed the plunger, and he was gone.

THREE

66

....

"You knew about these deaths. You were there."

Morris Stern was at his desk in his office at the Tufts University School of Medicine, hunched over a cup of coffee he had been sipping before Sarah pushed her way in. But for the twitching tic of his left eye, he stared blank-faced at the photocopied articles of street people found dead.

"They could have come from any number of other labs."

"What, the Zombie Research Center?"

"That's not particularly funny."

"Neither is your stonewalling, Morris."

The teeth in her words surprised even her. Morris had been her favorite professor and thesis adviser. Moreover, she looked up to him as a father figure, someone she could confide in. When her mother had died two years ago, it was Morris who gave her comfort, who helped make funeral arrangements. "I was flattered when you asked me on. Privileged to be working on a great cutting-edge project. But you used these people, Morris. You suspended them and dropped them off on some park bench. No follow-ups. No checking for bad side effects. You used them like lab rats."

"These people were homeless," he said, stabbing his finger on the article and squinting at her in a pretense of outrage. "You know as well as I do that all our volunteers are college students and closely monitored during and after."

"Now they are. Before that you bought people off the street—people no one would miss."

He couldn't hold her gaze and dropped his eyes to the clippings. "They could have gotten the drug anywhere—another lab, the black market, whatever. So don't come accusing me of unethical practices before you know what the hell you're talking about."

"It says that scientists paid them to take sleep tests. That's the same pitch you put up on student bulletin boards all over town. And I checked with the state health agencies—no other research institution has used tetrodotoxin for years. Only Proteus."

"I've heard enough from you." He stood up. "This conversation's over."

"You don't even care, do you? Two committed suicide, another had his friend bash his head in. And who knows how many others. They were plagued with horrible visions, and you people didn't care."

"Sarah, this has turned into an interrogation, and I resent it."

"Would you prefer the police?"

His eye spasmed. "Is that a threat?"

"What you people did is criminal."

"You have no proof and no right accusing me. Now get the hell out of here."

She could hardly believe that he was the same man she had adored—a man of high-minded ideals, a man who had seemingly dedicated his science to raising the quality of life, who had taken the Hippocratic Oath. Suddenly he was a cowardly, pathetic old man denying he was a murderer. Before she left, she removed a wide folder from her briefcase and dropped it before him.

"What's this?"

"One of your skeletons."

He didn't touch it. "I said to get out of here."

She flipped open the folder to reveal downloaded neuroelectrical images taken from the lab archives. "Look familiar?" she asked.

He glanced at the imaged configuration and the name in bold on the sticker.

"You used him, too," she said. Then she turned on her heel toward the door. "Maybe you're right after all: There is no God, only man."

67

....

George Megrichian loved surf casting. He had been doing it most of his fifty-six years.

He had fished everywhere, but this was his favorite spot because no one was around and because the sand was shoring up. In fact, this beach was the only one on the Massachusetts Bay that was growing in volume, because the lower Cape was eroding and sending all its sand to this sandbar. Twenty years ago, the beach was segmented every hundred yards by stone breakwaters that stood so high in high tide that kids would jump off the ends into deep water. Now, not a single granite boulder was visible in the five-mile stretch. Two decades and millions of tons of sand had been washed onto the shoreline, pushing the sandbar maybe a full quarter mile into the surf. He joked that were he to live another thousand years, he'd be able to walk to Portugal.

Because it was a private beach, you'd never find more than twenty people on the stretch of sand, even this week of the Fourth of July. Of course, more than a mile to the east was Scusset Beach, which was public and packed on summer weekends. But not here. And no matter which way you looked, not another soul was in sight.

The tide was in and the sun had just broken the bank of clouds hanging over the horizon.

He cast his line into the gentle surf and stuck the grip end of the pole into the holder buried in the sand. Then he sat in his folding chair with a mug of coffee and stretched his bare legs to take in the rays of the morning sun. Out at sea, sailboats cut across the horizon, their jibs bellying against the wind and glowing against the azure blue. *This is as good as it gets,* George thought. *What heaven must be like.*

Suddenly something moved out of the corner of his eye. He looked to the right. It was just above the storm line, where a continuous brow of seaweed had been pushed back during winter storms, now sun-dried to black.

His first thought was that it was a trick of the rising sun. But the surface of the sand seemed to be moving. Crabs. Except crabs didn't live in high, dry sand, only the wet stuff.

As he sat up to see better, a hand pushed its way into the air.

"Jesus Christ!" George cried. He scrambled out of his chair, knocking his mug over. A moment later, a second hand pushed its way out. Then arms. Suddenly the top half of a man rose out of the sand, rubbing his face and spitting sand.

For several seconds, George was too frozen with horror to move—too stunned by what his eyes were registering. The man rolled to his side to free his legs, then pushed himself onto all fours, drooling sand and gulping in air. He was wearing shorts, but no top or shoes. George gasped as he watched.

The hole was maybe two feet deep—far too deep for the sand to have covered him naturally, like if he got drunk the night before. He had been buried.

The guy struggled to push himself to his feet, wavering

and spitting and looking like one of those movie zombies. At one point, he clamped his hand to his side and groaned as he nearly doubled over. Then he checked his hand as if looking for blood.

Then before George knew it, the guy began to stumble toward him. George yelped and grabbed his pole to defend himself, gripping it like a baseball bat. But the guy shuffled by him down the beach, rubbing his face and hands, moving at a weird angle as if he had a stitch in his left side.

He headed toward the wooden set of stairs that led up to the top of the Manomet cliffs. He said nothing, nor did he look back, just climbed the steps one by one to the top, where he disappeared, leaving George wondering how he would explain this to his wife.

68

....

"They were all premonitions," Zack said. "I kept seeing myself being buried alive."

Sarah looked at him. "But how could you see something in the future? That's impossible."

"I don't know how. I don't understand any of this, except the bastards flatlined me, then dumped me in a hole on that beach."

It was nearly noon, and he had stumbled up to the White Cliffs complex of condos and golf course. In his print boxer shorts, he looked as if he had just come up from sunbathing. At the top, he found a greenskeeper and asked if he had a cell phone he could borrow. Two hours later, Sarah picked him up on Route 3A.

His brain still felt fuzzy and slow, and his side ached, although there was no wound or bruise. "What about Stern?"

"He denied everything. He just stood there and lied point-blank. I still can't believe it."

"Because it's the truth and he's scared shitless."

"But he wasn't at the lab last night, was he?"

"I didn't see him. Just Luria and Gladstone's choirboys.

But he may know they came after me. He no doubt called Luria about your visit, which means she's probably at the lab erasing the evidence."

"Or at her office at school," Sarah said. "We have to go to the police."

"It's our word against theirs," he said, thinking how he wanted to get Elizabeth Luria alone.

"Maybe not," she said.

After leaving Morris Stern's office, she told him, she had called several of the local hospitals to inquire about any patients who had had bloodwork showing signs of tetrodotoxin. She fabricated a claim that some of the compound was missing from their lab following a break-in and that she was working with authorities from the State Medical Board to help locate victims. Claire Driscoll, an old friend from nursing school who worked at Jordan Hospital, called back to say that a nurse colleague might have some information for her. Sarah then called the woman, who said to come in anytime today. Her name was Karen Wells.

"I think we may have something to show the police. But first we have to get you some clothes."

....

They drove to Independence Mall in Kingston, where Sarah ran into Sears and bought Zack some jeans, a top, and shoes. Also muffins, juice, and coffee. He ate and changed in the car. His head still buzzed, and he felt slow and heavy. He was anxious to file a police report against Elizabeth Luria, but he consented to go along with Sarah, who was convinced that this might be more evidence to build a case. And Jordan Hospital in Plymouth was on the way.

They found Nurse Wells at the desk of the emergency

room. She was a pleasant-looking woman around fifty with quick intelligent blue eyes and a take-charge demeanor. Sarah introduced herself and Zack and reiterated what she had said on the phone.

Nurse Wells had a folder on the John Doe in question. "I have to tell you it's a first," she said. "I've been here for almost twenty years, and never did we have a misdiagnosed death. We had a whole triage team on him and still got it wrong."

"So, you're saying that it actually was a misdiagnosis," Zack said.

"That or the guy was a zombie."

"So how did he show up here?"

She checked her folder. "An ambulance unit brought him in around three A.M."

"What date was that?"

"May nine, 2008. They picked him up on a 911 call. I guess some people returning home from a party found him under their bushes."

"Where was this?"

"Plymouth County, just south of the White Cliffs in Manomet."

"Manomet. That's near Sagamore Beach."

"Yeah."

"What was his condition when they brought him in?" Sarah asked.

"Dead. No BP, no pulse, temp at eighty-two. But the paramedics said he had a pulse when they found him. We tried to revive him with CPR and defibrillators, but those didn't work. Then we injected him with resuscitation drugs, but that didn't work either. So we officially declared him dead."

"How do you explain his getting up and leaving on his own?"

"Beats me, because I can tell you we didn't fail in our

diagnosis. We had all the monitors on him and the guy was flatlined."

"Any chance we can see the security video?" asked Zack.

"I pulled it out, in fact," she said. "Because we never got an ID on him, there's no breach of patient confidentiality. Besides, it's too grainy to make out his face."

She led them into a small office with video equipment and closed the door behind them. "Like I said, it's absolutely creepy," Karen continued. "The guy was dead on arrival." From a plastic case she removed a DVD and inserted it into a computer monitor. She made some adjustments, then sat back so Zack and Sarah could watch.

On the screen a nurse with a clipboard walked down a quiet corridor. Karen fast-forwarded to where paramedics burst through a door wheeling a man into one of the bays.

"Okay, I'm going to jump a couple hours," Karen said.

The same ceiling shot of the corridor running the length of patient cubicles. Nothing moved but for an orderly pushing a cart. After a few seconds, a man emerged from one of the cubicles. His face was aslant from the camera, and he was naked from the chest up. Round monitor electrodes were pasted to his shoulders and chest. He moved unsteadily in bare feet down the corridor, disappearing through the exit.

"I really can't explain it, but there you are," Karen said.

"Did you order a blood test for toxicology?"

"Yes, but since he was misdiagnosed, we didn't bother to do a follow-up." She pulled a pad out of her pocket. "As it turned out, he had no alcohol or standard drugs in his system, but he did show traces of ketamine and that tetrodotoxin you asked about."

Sarah shot a look at Zack, who was still staring at the monitor.

"Ketamine we use all the time. It's a sedative for patients undergoing surgery. It reduces the trauma and helps them forget the ordeal. But frankly, I'm not familiar with tetrodotoxin, at least I wasn't until you called."

"It's the so-called zombie drug," Sarah said. "What voodoo priests use in Haiti to fake people's deaths, then revive them hours later."

"Which may explain why we couldn't get a pulse or heartbeat."

"The right dosage lowers body temperature and reduces the pulse, heart rate, and blood pressure to a minimum—probably below what your machines could detect."

"He looked it, stumbling out of here like he was moving on brain stem impulses alone," Karen said. "So where the heck did he get puffer fish toxin? It's certainly not anything we stock."

"Because it has no medicinal benefit. It's strictly a research compound."

"So you think he broke into your lab?"

"Possibly."

"Can you run that again?" Zack's eyes were still fixed on the monitor.

"Sure," Karen said, and restarted the video from the beginning.

When it got to where the man emerged from the bay, Zack hit the pause button.

The video stopped on a frame of the man in profile as he headed down the empty corridor toward the exit. It was grainy and hard to make out. "And you never got an ID on him?"

"He didn't have any. Just pants and T-shirt. No wallet of IDs. No shoes or socks. His feet were bloody. He was also covered with bug bites and sand."

"Sand?" Zack said.

69

....

Roman's first impulse was to follow the woman out of the Neuroscience Research Center building. She was beautiful and shapely, and it would be fun tailing her butt. Except he knew who she was—Sarah Wyman, a postdoctoral research assistant at Tufts. Also a part-timer at a lab that, according to Norman Babcock, conducted the NDE project in a converted preacher's home on the grounds of Gladstone's church in Medfield.

It was the old guy in the office upstairs who held his interest. The name on the door said, "Dr. Morris J. Stern." He didn't know the nature of her relationship with him, but the way she looked when she left suggested that they'd had something of a dustup.

Whatever, Roman had some time on his hands, and keeping tabs on Stern seemed like a good idea. So he went back down to the lobby, where he hid behind a book he'd picked up on near-death experiences. He had never experienced one but wondered if there was anything to them. What he read sounded pretty silly—people floating around, looking down on their near-dead selves, and feeling love-happy. They all sounded similar yet deadly sincere. Nearly every one claimed that their dying wasn't awful but wonderful, using words like "blissful," "sweet," "tender," "sensuous," "tranquil"—as though it felt so good, they didn't want to go back to life.

But Roman was confused. While he gladly took Babcock's money, he couldn't understand Babcock's outrage. Nearly every account went on about glorious encounters with beings of light, communicating mind to mind with "a loving omniscient presence," which some called God and others Jesus. And they all claimed that the experiences transformed their lives for the better—made them more spiritual, loving, kinder, more in tune with the universe. Some NDEs even turned agnostics and atheists into believers.

So where was the blasphemy? Where was old Satan in all this?

70

They couldn't go to the police without first gathering evidence linking the test victims to the lab. They would also need proof that Sarah had joined Proteus after they stopped using street people as guinea pigs. But that would take more time than they had. So Zack had Sarah drive them to Zack's place, where he showered, changed, and packed some overnight clothes. Then they headed up Commonwealth Avenue to a dealership just beyond the BU campus, where he rented a Nissan Murano and drove to a parking lot on Longwood.

While Sarah waited in the car, he climbed to the third floor of the Goldenson Building on the Harvard Medical School campus. And just as the secretary had said when he called, she was in her office. Without knocking, Zack opened the door.

Elizabeth Luria jerked visibly in her chair, her face draining of color around her birthmark.

"Looks like you've seen a ghost." He closed the door behind him.

She let out a small squeal as her mouth quivered for words.

He walked to her desk, which was covered with paperwork. "Back from the dead, and hotter than ever."

"I can explain."

"What, how you kidnapped me, then buried me alive? I'd really like to hear that, Elizabeth."

"W-we needed just one more run to confirm merger, just that one, but I know how you refused. We were so close, I—I just felt desperate."

"So you force-flatlined me and left me for dead for real. But I bet you got your data."

Her face lit up. "Yes, yes. It's remarkable. Really. It confirms—"

"Blah, blah, blah. Then you buried me alive."

"That was an accident, I swear. We couldn't revive you. Something went wrong. Maybe it was too early for another suspension. Maybe the sedative was still in your system. I don't know."

"But you tried, of course."

Her face exaggerated itself. "Oh, God, we tried. Of course. Of course—injected you with epinephrine. Used defibrillator paddles over and over. Nothing worked, I swear. You had no heartbeat no matter what we did."

"So, what I'm wondering is how hotshot neuroscientists with the most sophisticated MRI machine on the planet couldn't see that my brain was still alive."

"We couldn't get a reading. Something went wrong."

"But you confirmed that I transcended and merged with another sentience."

"Yes." Beads of perspiration had formed in the pockets under her eyes.

"And you buried me on Sagamore Beach."

"Because that's where you said you felt most spiritual."

"A little déjà vu all over again."

"Pardon me?"

"Just like my father." As soon as he said that, he felt a sharp jab in his side.

"What?" She froze for a moment. Then her hand jerked toward the desk phone. But he reached over and yanked the wire out of the wall.

"If you yell for help, I'll fucking kill you."

"What do you want?"

"I want you to tell me why you killed my father."

Again she hesitated, trying to gather herself. "We didn't kill him. He died on the gurney."

"He was still alive when you buried him."

"What?"

"He clawed his way out," he said. "EMTs brought him to Jordan Hospital with tetrodotoxin in his blood."

Her mouth quivered as he described the security video. "We didn't know."

"Like you didn't know with me."

She made no response, looking overwhelmed.

He picked up a bronze brain-shaped trophy. According to the pedestal engraving, it was the Department of Neurology award to Luria for teaching excellence. He felt its solid heft, smacking it against his palm and thinking how it would feel to bash her face if she screamed.

"That was three years ago, before we had the MRI machine. We had no idea his brain was still alive. And that's the truth." On a shelf behind her was another photo of her son posing on a pony, with Elizabeth standing next to him beaming.

"So you just drove to Sagamore Beach and buried him in the sand."

"Because that's what he wanted. He entered the same place on the questionnaire."

In spite of himself, Zack felt his throat thicken. Where they had felt most connected with the universe. Where they'd been the happiest as a family. "Except he dug himself out." And Zack had relived it all in his head, then last night for real. "This was all a setup from the start. You had my father's brain patterns on record, and when he died you went after me, hoping if I crossed over, I'd contact him. All because you wanted secrets of the dead. Well, you got it," he said. "And the secret is he wasn't dead."

She looked at him blank-faced and said nothing.

"Whose ashes are those on my mother's fireplace?"

"Nobody's."

"Nobody's? Then who was Brother Albani?"

"Bruce."

"Bruce? So, you buried my father alive, then sent that fucking creep in a monk's robe to give my mother some bullshit story how he died in his sleep, clutching his crucifix. And for three years we thought those were his remains when it's probably charcoal from one of your friggin' lab cookouts."

"I don't deserve that."

"No, lady, you deserve a lot worse. You destroyed people's lives in pursuit of cheesy glory."

"It wasn't glory. The activity in your father's brain was off the charts. So was yours with identical circuitry. We hoped you'd transcend and make contact with him."

"I did," he said. *But he wasn't the father I had hoped for.* Again, the stabbing pain to his left side. He winced and straightened up. "How did you end up suspending him?"

"He volunteered."

"Don't give me more bullshit."

"I'm not. We began scanning people who claimed to be spiritual. That brought us to religious groups, including Carmelite nuns and the Benedictine monastery where your father was. When we told him what we were doing, he volunteered to be suspended."

"Why?"

"Because he wanted to contact your brother."

Zack couldn't quite define it, but his heart clutched in a primal reflex of jealousy. His father had always favored Jake. *Smooth, smart, confident Jake*, he thought sourly.

"We never determined that he did," Luria continued. "When we read about you, we saw an opportunity to test the genetic possibilities, hoping that you'd merge with him."

"I did." *And he's a psychopathic killer.*

"And that was incredible." Her eyes lit up again. "Zack, our intention wasn't to harm people. We weren't conducting some kind of Nazi experiments."

"Then what about these, *mein Führer*?" From his back pocket he pulled photocopies of the articles of people who had killed themselves or died—all with tetrodotoxin in them.

She scanned the articles. "These deaths were not intentional. I swear."

"Right." He felt another jab in his side. He had to leave. Time was running out. "How does the good reverend reconcile these deaths with the Word of God?"

"These were technical accidents."

"That doesn't answer my question."

"He wasn't pleased."

"And what about last night?"

"He has no idea."

"But it was his men who kidnapped me."

"They're security guards working for the lab. I called them."

"How did you turn Damian into a fucking Judas goat? Thirty pieces of silver?"

"We paid him nothing. We read about you in the papers, and he agreed to put us in contact with you. He knew nothing more than we were looking for people with spiritual powers to scan. And that's the truth."

"How did you find him?"

"At one of Reverend Gladstone's sermons."

Pieces were snapping into place as if magnetized. On some level, Zack wasn't surprised. From the first day, he had felt that he was participating in someone else's game plan. "Did it ever occur to you that what you did in that lab was wrong? That maybe you were going after forbidden fruit? That you were playing God?"

"I was playing God. I was hoping to find what every person who has ever lived wanted: hope of going on. Hope that there's more to this life. Hope of seeing loved ones again. And last night you gave us conclusive evidence that your father still exists in some realm. That nothing ceases to exist. Nothing! With all my heart I believe that now."

"And you didn't let kidnapping and murder stop you."

"But they died only in body."

"So, you're a savior, too."

He put the statue back on the desk and left.

Nothing ceases to exist. Nothing!

Her words hummed in his head like a chord struck on a church organ as he walked out of her office and down the corridor to the stairs leading to the parking area.

Sarah was still in the car behind the wheel of the Murano. When she saw him, she climbed into the passenger seat and he got behind the wheel. "We have to go," he said, and checked his watch.

"Where to?"

"I'll let you know when we get there."

71

....

That same morning, Roman heard back from Norman Babcock with his next assignment. The drop this time was at the Fresh Pond Mall parking lot near Whole Foods at seven A.M. In the bag was the usual $15,000 in packs of hundreds and another secure cell phone. And the next hit lived with his wife in a historic red farmhouse in Arlington, Massachusetts, with a sign that said, "Circa 1706."

He found the man two hours later on his knees, on the other side of a stone wall, weeding a bed of flowers. "Dr. Morris Stern?"

The man looked up. "Yes." He stood up, wearing a red Tufts sweatshirt and old jeans, the knees of which were stained with grass and mud.

"My name is John Farley, and I'm with the Boston office of the FBI." He leaned over the stone wall to show the phony ID. "We're investigating the deaths of Roger and Ruth Devereux. I'm wondering if I might ask you a few questions." He pulled out copies of the obituaries and articles on the Devereux and handed them to Stern. They flapped in the breeze.

"Yeah, sure." He peeled off his work gloves.

"We can do it out here or someplace else." And he gave a quick glance toward the house.

Stern seemed wary and said, "Out here is fine."

"No problem." Roman pulled out a small laptop and placed it on the wall. He clicked a few buttons and moved his finger on the pad. "I don't know if you can see this in the light, but it's a photo of Roger Devereux. Is he someone you recognize?"

Stern squinted at the too bright screen, trying to shade it with his hands. Then Roman attempted to make an awning with the obit photocopies, but they flapped uselessly in the breeze. Finally Stern said, "Maybe we better go inside."

"Are you sure? We can sit in my car."

"No, it's cooler in the house."

"Fine. And may I trouble you for a glass of water?"

"Sure." Stern led the way through a side door into the kitchen, where he poured Roman a glass of water and then invited him to sit at a table in a small sitting area by an ancient fieldstone fireplace.

"Great place. I noticed the sign saying it's on the register of historic homes."

"The oldest place in town. Some say this fireplace dates back to the 1690s."

Roman could see the wrought-iron fixtures embedded in the stone. "Wow. The 1690s. Wasn't that the time of the Salem witch trials?"

"I think so."

"Amazing. The original inhabitants of this place may have witnessed the actual burning of witches."

Stern's expression changed a little. "Possibly, though they didn't burn witches. I think most were hanged."

"How about that?" Roman sat in a red armchair as Stern sat across from him with a coffee table between them. "History was always my weak subject. Do you live alone?"

"My wife's visiting our grandchildren. So, what exactly are you investigating?"

"Well, the local police have ruled their deaths a murder-suicide. But we're investigating the possibility that the Devereux were both murdered." He pulled a small notepad from his sport coat pocket and, for effect, squinted at his writing. "The names Thomas Pomeroy and LeAnn Cola mean anything to you?"

"You wouldn't ask unless you already knew the answer."

"Got me there. So, they were associates of yours."

"Yes. And maybe you can tell me what this is all about."

"Of course," Roman said. "Information came to our Boston office that the Devereux, Pomeroy, and Dr. Cola were murdered because of a secret scientific project they worked on. Unfortunately, your name came up as a coworker. I don't mean to upset you, but we think your own life may be in danger."

"What?"

Roman then unzipped his attaché case. "And there's some pretty solid evidence." He extracted the silenced pistol and aimed it at Stern's midsection.

"W-who are you?"

"I'm here to ask questions, and you're going to answer them. Be straight with me, and this will be easy for you. Give me bullshit, and this will be a very bad day. *Capice?*"

Stern nodded, stunned in his chair.

"What's so special about Zachary Kashian?"

"How do you know about him?"

"He was your prime test subject. Tell me about him and why he's so special."

"Who are you working for?"

The Lord. "I want to know about him. I want to see

the files and videos of him in suspension."

"How do you know these things?"

"That's not important. I understand you taped experiments with him. I want to see them."

"I don't have them."

Roman aimed at a spot between Stern's feet and snapped off a shot. "The next will be between your eyes."

Stern stared at the hole between his feet. "Okay, okay. But please, I've got children and grandchildren."

"A deal. You show me the stuff, and I'll let you live."

"Swear on your life."

"I swear."

Stern stared at Roman for a long moment. "They're in my laptop." He got up and led Roman into the kitchen and to a narrow set of stairs leading to the second floor. In a small corner office with a window was a desk with a computer monitor and stacks of papers.

"Play it."

Stern clicked the mouse and ran the first video of Zachary Kashian in a soundproof chamber wearing a motorcycle helmet with wires. Stern explained how they had stimulated parts of his brain and how he had emerged claiming he sensed his dead father. The next video showed Zack in suspension, shots of the various monitors, computer images of his brain. Then his awaking and requesting root beer, which proved the kid had an out-of-body experience. Then clips of him coming out of near-death experiences, claiming he'd killed people. Stern explained that the other scientists believed that Kashian's spirit had merged with that of his dead father.

"Is that something you believe?"

"I think it's some kind of paranormal thing like ESP. But I'm not convinced."

"So you're not buying that his spirit merged with his dead father's."

GARY BRAVER

"No."

"Even though the others claim he's got this hot God lobe."

Stern nodded.

After reviewing more videos, Roman packed Stern's laptop and slung it over his shoulder.

"What are you going to do?"

"You're coming with me."

"Where?"

"Your cellar."

"My cellar? What for?"

"To keep you from jumping on 911 soon as I walk out of here." He jabbed the pistol into Stern's back. "Downstairs."

Stern led them to a door that led into the basement, a small dim place with one wall of granite boulders that formed one flank of the foundations. The other walls had been finished off. The ceiling was maybe seven feet high, consisting of beams and wallboard. Some beams looked original, with hooks for drying meat in the olden times.

From his briefcase Roman pulled out a length of rope. "Turn around." He wrapped the rope loosely around his hands. Then he removed a sleep mask. "And where exactly is the lab?"

Stern rattled off directions as Roman jotted them down. "Who else works there?"

He named names, beginning with Sarah Wyman.

"Do she and Kashian have a thing going on?"

"Not that I know of."

"And Elizabeth Luria's in charge."

"Yes."

"Back to Zachary Kashian. Is he special?"

"How do you mean special?"

"Is he divine?"

"Divine?" Stern gave him a perplexed look. "No. He's a neurological anomaly, at best maybe psychic. But he's as mortal as you and I."

"Then how do you explain his channeling Jesus?"

"I don't know. Maybe it was a paranormal experience. Maybe he memorized it as a child."

"Any reason to believe he was lying about his experiences?"

"No."

The man had settled into the charade as his body relaxed. And that was good. "Would you say that he's evil?"

"Evil? No, he's not evil."

Roman slipped the mask across Stern's eyes. "Two more questions, and then we're done. Do you believe in God?"

There was a moment's hesitation as his body appeared to stiffen. "No. I don't."

"Well, you're wrong. God exists."

Stern said nothing.

"What about the devil? Do you believe in Satan?"

"No."

And in a flash Roman slipped a length of clothesline over a beam hook and a noosed end around Stern's neck. With all his body weight, Roman pulled the rope, causing Stern's body nearly to lift off the ground. The man kicked and twisted as the rope dug into his neck, cutting off blood to his brain. In less than a minute, he stopped twitching as his body went limp. With a few quick twists of the loose end around the hook, Stern's body weight did the rest.

"Well, you're wrong there, too," Roman said, and left.

72

....

"You don't even know if he's alive," Sarah said.

"I think he is," Zack said as he drove. "And I think he's dying."

"Based on what?"

"The last NDE—Gretch shot him in the side. And I felt it. I still do." He pulled up his shirt to show clear, unbroken skin. "But it hurts, and I think he needs help." He headed down Huntington Avenue and took a left onto Forsyth and from there to Storrow Drive, heading east, feeling a dim hum in his mind just above the threshold of awareness.

"This is crazy. You said yourself the toxin creates delusions."

"That was him in the video."

"But it was grainy. You couldn't see his face. Besides, that was three years ago."

Zack felt a blister of petulance rise. "Sarah, I recognize the shape of his head. I also saw him dig himself out," he said. "And I saw him kill those people." At the end of Storrow Drive, near Mass General Hospital, he turned into the lane for Route 93 North. "I felt the bullet go into him, like it was me."

"You heard Morris. They could be just scraps in your unconscious—things you put together. Flash dream stuff."

"He also said my mind merged with another."

"But that wasn't confirmed."

Her insistence that he was yielding to some mystical instinct was making him anxious. "Then tell me how I knew about those deaths?"

"Your suspensions happened after they died. So maybe you read about them and forgot, and maybe you thought you experienced them in suspension."

The traffic had slowed to a crawl just before the turn-off to 93 North. To their right was Massachusetts General Hospital. Except for the coma, the only other time Zack had been in a hospital was at his birth twenty-five years ago. His mother said he had been born with a caul. She also said that according to legend, people born with cauls were supposed to be mystical, have special powers. "Maybe."

Not so long ago, Sarah had sat across from him at the Grafton Street Pub & Grill and talked about the wondrous possibilities of transcending the physical world, of there being no death. And now she was telling him it was probably delusions. And that whatever instinct he was following was just his imagination. "Then how do you explain Luria's claim? She said they'd identified his neuroprofile and that I merged with him last night."

"I wasn't there. I didn't see them."

"So she's delusional, too?"

"No, but it's possible that she's lining things up to fit a predetermined conclusion." Then she added, "Look, Elizabeth Luria came into this project hoping to prove there's an afterlife, and she got huge support from a televangelist. So scientific objectivity may not have been her bottom line, okay? Yes, they had your father's neuropatterns. But what they found could also be an anomaly."

"So if a tree falls in the forest and Sarah's not there, it didn't fall."

"I didn't say that, and frankly I don't like your tone."

"And frankly I don't like your automatic dismissal of other possibilities. I'm getting painful flares in my side, so how do you explain that?"

She looked out the window for a moment to cool the air. Then she said, "Since there's no evidence you got injured, I'd say you're experiencing some kind of psychosomatic effect. You imagined or dreamed your father was shot, and this is just a case of autosuggestion or sympathetic delusion."

Autosuggestion. Sympathetic delusion. Such silky words, such silky reasoning, he thought. *After all that talk about telepathy and the Overmind. Now it's all New Age crap.* "You've got a rational explanation for everything, haven't you?"

"And so did you once."

"Well, maybe this card-carrying reductionist is seeing other possibilities." He felt another flare in his side, and he shot through the tunnel onto the northbound ramp of 93 and straight up the Zakim Bridge.

"Will you please tell me where we're going?"

"I think I'll know when we get there." Ahead was the sign for a down-ramp that would take them back to Cambridge. "Still want to come?"

"Only if you tell me where."

"Call it ESP, call it telepathy, call it cosmic fucking sentience—but I want to get to him before he dies for real. If I'm wrong, I'm an asshole. If not, I get to see him one more time." He slowed down and pulled into the right lane for the turnoff. Sarah saw it approach.

"What's up 93?"

"Maine."

"Maine? Zack, will you please tell me something definite?"

"Okay," he said, trying to flush away the festering irritation that she might be right: that he was talking himself into believing his father was beckoning him. "When my father was young, his father purchased a tract of land in the woods of southwestern Maine. He built a little hunting and fishing cabin on the property, where my father was taken as a kid. When he got older, he'd hole up there for weeks on end."

"By himself?"

The exit was upon them. "Should I turn?"

"No."

He swerved back into the ongoing lane heading north on 93. "There's another exit two minutes up." Then he continued. "Yeah, by himself. He was a loner, and he loved the wilderness and learned survivalist skills. After college, he lived there for a year without seeing another person. It was his hideaway."

"Have you ever been there?"

"Once, but I was four or five. All I remember is woods and a small cabin. My mother didn't like it because it was too isolated and primitive—no electricity and well water."

"Do you know where it is?"

"Off of 95, somewhere in the vicinity of the New Hampshire border."

"Gee, that narrows it down nicely."

He let her sarcasm pass. "I think I'll know where to go when we get there." They drove for a few more miles without saying anything. Then he turned his head toward her. "There's one more exit before we get to 95. I can still take you home."

"Do you want me to come?"

"Yeah, I do. And if I'm not delusional, he'll need medical attention."

"I was a nurse for only ten months, and that was five years ago."

"Beats my experience."

"Does this place have a name?"

"Magog Woods."

"Magog Woods? Sounds vaguely familiar."

"That was the name back then. It may not even be called that or on any map."

"So, it's been twenty years. Chances are old landmarks might be gone."

"Most likely."

"Then how will you know how to find it?"

"I'm not sure," he said. "I'm hoping I'll just know."

"I feel like a character in *Close Encounters of the Third Kind*." She looked into the cargo space, where Zack had packed sleeping bags for them and a duffel bag of clothes. "All I have is what I'm wearing."

"You can get what you need up there. There are outlets everywhere." They were closing in on Exit 36, Montvale Ave./Stoneham. "I can still take you back."

Just short of the turnoff, Sarah said, "Keep going."

Zack felt his internal organs unfist themselves. "Thanks," he said, thinking, *Oh, one more thing.* Yesterday, on a hunch, he had found an online obit for Raymond Perkins, the hotshot lawyer who had gotten Volker and Gretch acquitted. Billy Volker's uncle, in fact. He was found four weeks ago with an ax embedded in the back of his head.

Zack kept that to himself and shot into the passing lane.

73

....

The Kashian kid was missing.

After dispatching Morris Stern, Roman drove to Kashian's apartment on Hemenway Street in Boston—a four-story redbrick building for college students. When nobody answered, he hit other buttons on lower floors until someone blindly let him in. Before that party came out to investigate, Roman was already above and jimmying the lock to Kashian's door.

The apartment was dark and looking as if the kid had left in a hurry. Bureau drawers were open, and underwear and tops were strewn about. His laptop was on his desk. No toothbrush or toothpaste in the bathroom. The kid was planning overnights.

He left and drove to Harvard Street in Cambridge. Sarah Wyman was also nowhere to be found, and the downstairs neighbor said she had seen her leave the building before eight that morning.

An hour later, he was at the address given him by Stern. GodLight Tabernacle Church sat at the front of a wooded compound in the suburbs of Medfield, about an hour southwest of Boston. A large empty parking lot separated the church from the road.

Roman pulled in and drove to the rear of the structure. Sitting behind a shiny new chain-link fence was a large white house with an extension on the back. Its blandness masked the kind of research that apparently went on below—Warren Gladstone's personal Manhattan Project. That explained the guard shack and barbed wire atop the fence.

The shack was empty, and the gate was closed and padlocked. Because of the weekend, the place was abandoned, except for a single blue Volvo against the building.

Roman had rented a Ford Explorer with a grille guard, which could have pushed his way through the fence. But that might set off an alarm. He had packed sundry paraphernalia in the back, including flashlights, rope, duct tape, and a variety of tools, including a long-handled cable cutter capable of snipping through half-inch steel wire. It took him only seconds to cut through the padlock.

He drove through the gate and parked beside the Volvo, which was unlocked. On the upper corner of the windshield were parking stickers for Harvard Medical School faculty. He cut around to the main entrance, which to his surprise was unlocked, although he could have cut his way inside. The door opened to a security desk and gate with no one in attendance. Behind it was a door leading through a corridor to another entrance leading to the basement.

With his pistol drawn, he descended the stairs.

Halfway down, he detected a faint high-pitched electronic sound. At the bottom of the stairs was a corridor lit by a bank of fluorescent lights. Coming off either side of the corridor were rooms, some with windows. But the only one that was lit was toward the end—and the source of the electronic squeal.

It got louder as he approached the room, his pistol gripped in both hands.

The sound was some kind of alarm, and the piercing shrill was making him anxious.

He reached the knob of the door, turned it, and, gripping the pistol, kicked it open.

The alarm was emanating from a rack of electronic equipment that sat beside a gurney on which lay the body of a woman. She was hooked up to an IV and the various monitors on which alarm lights pulsed with the squealing. Clutched in her hands was a photograph of a young boy.

From the various video images, he recognized Elizabeth Luria.

And like the Kashian kid in the videos, she was hooked up for suspension from an IV. But unlike in the Kashian videos, the monitors were blinking red and squealing because all the vital function lines on screen were totally flat.

The woman had suspended herself to death.

74

....

An hour later, Zack and Sarah were passing through Portsmouth, New Hampshire. The earlier heat of irritation had cooled, leaving him grateful that she was with him.

As they moved to the right-hand lane, Zack pointed out the submarine base in the distance where his father had brought him when he was maybe seven.

"What do you remember about him?"

"Not a lot. He wasn't around much," Zack said. "He was a project engineer and worked long hours. I saw him mostly on weekends. Then my parents separated after Jake's death. Sometime after that, he dropped out of sight."

"That must have been rough."

"It was."

"But you have some good memories of him."

"Until I was about ten. After he left, I saw him on a few occasions, which were mostly me telling him about what I was up to, but little about himself. Funny thing, as I got older, I thought of myself as not having a father, just a mother."

"That's sad."

"To compensate, I made up stories about him. He was something of a photographer, so I'd tell kids he was on assignment for *National Geographic* and was off covering animal migrations in Kenya. Or helping build a refugee camp in Biafra. I once claimed he took me to Hawaii, where he saved me from a shark attack. Pretty pathetic."

"I guess that's how you dealt with his absence."

"And all along he was a Benedictine monk praying and making jellies for tourists."

They crossed the Piscataqua Bridge. Although he had passed this way fifteen or more years ago, he felt nothing overt—just a vague sense that he was pursuing some kind of directive. Or maybe it was just dumb autosuggestion after all. And the very possibility made his heart slump.

"If he's really still alive, what would you say to him?"

"I'd ask him why he left me and my mother." *And if God is in him and talking to me.*

They soon passed a sign reading, "Welcome to Maine. The way life should be."

"Now what?"

"We keep going."

"Until?"

"Until I come to the right exit."

"Do you know which one?"

"Not yet."

Please give a sign, he whispered in his head. *I believe. Please give a sign.*

75

....

For several minutes, Roman didn't know what to do. Elizabeth Luria was dead. So were Stern and others who had put together that lab. He didn't care about those he didn't know about. The project was dead.

And the Kashian kid was missing.

Roman had spent the previous night and that morning poring over data in Morris Stern's laptop. The mathematical stuff meant nothing to him. But the videos and explanations of the neuroimages of Kashian kept playing in Roman's brain. And as he drove back to Boston, an idea began to grow. A very good idea. No, a brilliant idea. In fact, an *epiphany*.

Epiphany.

The term had shot up from the recesses of his memory. From his fretful days at St. Luke's. *Epiphany*. As in Day of Epiphany. A revelation. A vision. A sudden miraculous insight.

When he was a kid suffering through sermons, he remembered one Sunday in January when Father Infantino held forth on the meaning of the Day of Epiphany, when Christ's divinity was revealed to the Magi. He went on about how each of us must find meaning in our lives and must listen to the yearnings of our souls, just like a lot of famous people who had made a difference in the world—Mother Teresa, President Kennedy, Martin Luther King. He hammered on about how each had experienced a revelation of how they should dedicate their lives—of how they were driven by higher missions from the rest of us. But the only difference between them and ordinary people was that they had discovered a clear purpose that they had embraced with fierce determination.

Back then, Roman's only yearning was for Father Infantino to wrap up so he could go to Goodwin Park and play ball with the other kids.

But as he headed north on 95 toward Watertown, Roman experienced his own little epiphany, and it flickered in his head like a votive candle.

76

....

The sensation was back.

They were only a few miles into Maine on the northbound side of the turnpike. They had passed a long stretch of marshland that gave way to forests of pine and deciduous trees. Maybe it was the thick claustrophobic woodlands that triggered some recall or premonition, because a strange awareness hummed in the fore of his brain. And it was stronger.

He thought about telling Sarah but decided against it. He didn't quite grasp what he was experiencing—if it was real, some quirk of his imagination, or if he had slipped into another neurological ditch. But the longer he drove on, the more he felt that he was following an invisible beacon beamed at him by some unknown source.

He kept his hands on the wheel, moving with the turns of the highway, half-certain that if he let go, the car would proceed under some weird remote control.

He was also convinced that whatever pulled him was not a matter of recall. None of the landscape looked even vaguely familiar. Nor was it some kind of déjà vu. In fact, it seemed like déjà vu in reverse. Instead of being compelled by things familiar, Zack felt propelled by a prophetic rightness. A prescient awareness maybe like the kind that inspired saints of old to take up spiritual quests—pilgrimages to sacred places.

"*Zack!*" Sarah screamed.

"What? What's the problem?" He looked ahead, expecting to see a car in their path or an animal. But the road was wide open. "Why'd you yell?"

"You were driving with your eyes closed."

"What?"

"I looked over and your eyes were closed. You dozed off."

"No."

"You did," she insisted. "Want me to drive?"

"No, I'm fine," he said. *Dozed off? Did I really blank out?*

"I think maybe we better take a break. The sign said there're outlets at the next exit. I have to use the toilet, and maybe you can get some coffee. I can also pick up some overnight stuff."

He didn't like the idea, but a couple of miles ahead he turned off and merged with Route 1. They found a strip mall with several clothing outlets, and he pulled in and turned off the engine.

"Aren't you coming in?"

"I think I'll just rest a little." And he lowered his seat back and rested his head.

"Sure you'll be all right?"

"Just a little tired." He watched her get out of the car. "I won't be long."

"Good." *She doesn't have a clue,* he thought, and he followed her with his eyes into the entrance of L.L. Bean. This wasn't some serotonin country ride. This was a mission of salvation. Something bordering on a religious pilgrimage. He closed his eyes. A stabbing shock to his side made him gasp out loud.

A sign.

His eyes flipped open, and his heart started racing. He didn't have much time. *Where the hell is she?* he thought. In there buying clothes while his father was dying by the minute.

Jesus, why did he bring her?

77

Roman Pace sat in his rental across the street from the neat white Victorian house on Mt. Auburn Street in Watertown. From the outside, it could have been another late-nineteenth-century private home with a manicured lawn, a full red Japanese maple tree, and a variety of rhododendron and hydrangea. The only sign that it was not a private residence was a plaque by the front door: "Fraternity of Jesus Christ—Second Floor."

Roman had called on his way in from Medfield, saying that he had big news to share. Babcock said he'd meet him at his office at eleven thirty. Roman arrived early. Since he had nowhere to go, he sat in his rental and went online to search some Google maps.

At about eleven fifteen, a black Mercedes S550 pulled into the driveway. Two men got out—Babcock in a red polo shirt and chino pants, looking as if he'd been summoned from a golf game. The other man was unfamiliar but wore a white shirt and black blazer and matching pants. He dropped off Babcock and pulled the Mercedes behind the building, then emerged a minute later in a silver BMW 328i sedan and left. Babcock let himself into the front of the building, disappearing upstairs.

At eleven twenty-five, Roman crossed the street. An accountant's office occupied the first floor through a separate entrance. The door leading up to the Fraternity of Jesus offices was locked, so he pressed the button. Moments later, a male secretary opened the door. Roman introduced himself, and the guy nodded and led the way upstairs to a front office. He picked up the desk phone and announced Roman's arrival. Then he led Roman down a hall to an office that clearly used to be a master bedroom before the place was converted.

Babcock was behind a mahogany desk, his face pasty against the bright red shirt. He shook hands and invited Roman to take a seat across from him. A brass plaque on his desk read, "The Lord Be with You."

"Nice office," Roman said.

On a table beside the desk was a computer monitor. On the desk were photos of his family and a gold crucifix mounted on a marble base. On the walls hung religious pictures as well as photographs of Babcock with other people, including clerics in robes.

"It's small, but comfortable. So what do we have?"

"We'll need your computer," Roman said.

Babcock agreed and let Roman come around. Over the next several minutes, he showed Babcock some of the video of Zack Kashian's suspension and the imaging data. "They claim he had a near-death experience and merged with his dead father."

Babcock studied them quietly, his face seeming to fill with blood.

"I gotta say, they're pretty impressive," Roman said.

"Charlatans usually are."

"Well, I mean, some of these people are convinced he's crossed to the other side."

"Mr. Pace, these people are necromancers, who've crawled out of the sewers of science to seduce the masses and get filthy rich. They're willingly working for the devil, proselytizing his evil." He pulled the black leather Bible off his desk and flipped to a page, stabbing a passage with his finger. "'And the Lord proclaimed, "Do not practice divination or sorcery. . . . Do not turn to mediums or seek out spiritists, for you will be defiled by them."' Leviticus 19:31."

Roman glanced at the page. It hadn't taken Babcock long to get home. His flushed face looked like an extension of his golf shirt.

"And that's what they're doing. That's what that bastard writes about in his books, on the God lobes and God spots and finding the light at the end of the tunnel. It's what they're doing in that bloody lab of theirs." Babcock continued full steam, whipping through the pages for another passage. "Here! Second Thessalonians 1:8, 9: 'And for those that do so, "In flaming fire take vengeance on them that know not God, and that obey not the gospel of our Lord Jesus Christ: Who shall be punished with everlasting destruction from the presence of the Lord."'" He turned the book around so Roman could read. "That is what our role is. Your role is. *Vengeance.* What more proof do you want?"

Babcock was on fanatical fire about Gladstone and his scientists. But Roman did not want to send the guy into cardiac arrest before he completed his purpose here. "I get it. But the kid was quoting Jesus, reciting the Lord's Prayer in God's own language. That's not exactly words from a horned demon."

Babcock rubbed his face as if he were weary of Roman's thickness. "No, but it's how your horned demon gets people to listen. Then once he's got followers, he does his evil. That's how Satan works—by deception. Here he disguises himself as a poor comatose kid and spouts off scriptural passages. And that's the deadliest weapon in his arsenal—what he's done since seducing Eve in the Garden of Eden. What you're seeing in those videos is Lucifer masquerading as a follower of Jesus. Do you get it? Lucifer, God's onetime light bearer. That's the bloody devil in disguise."

Babcock's face looked as if it would burst.

"Look, I explained this to you several times. Their so-called NDEs are supposed to be tunnels to the afterlife—that everybody goes to heaven and there's no hell—which means that even fucking Osama bin Laden and every other heathen bastard would live forever. Hell is the other rock of the Catholic Church, okay?"

"Let me ask you something," Roman said. "I'm still trying to sort things out, and I've been reading stuff. You've got this big organization . . ."

"We're not a big organization," Babcock interjected. "We're a small, elect few."

"Well, you got this office and I don't know how many numbers, but you got resources."

"Your point?"

"Even the pope isn't worked up over these NDEs. With all due respect, it's like you've got this radical thing about Gladstone and what they're doing with this kid. What's the archdiocese say about this, or the local bishop and cardinal? They crying blasphemy, too?"

Babcock took a deep breath and rocked back in his chair. "Mr. Pace, let's just say that ours is a radical theology, and one that's not subscribed to by the diocese or the local cardinal or the so-called Holy See. And it's their fundamental failing. Our fraternity stands firmly on the true teachings of the Lord and to true Roman Catholicism. And if others don't subscribe or persecute us, then it only confirms that we're the elect, the true defenders of the Church. Period."

"Did you know the Kashian kid's father was one of their test subjects?"

"What?"

"A few years back, they ran him through the same tests. Seems he was some kind of lay brother. I guess he had the same hot God lobe the kid has."

"So what?"

"Well, they put the kid on TV saying he merged with his dead father, channeling him or whatever, and they show all their fancy neuroimages and stuff and the brain images overlapping and all, back-to-back with his talking Jesus video—the kid's gonna be bigger than the pope and all the saints put together."

Babcock looked as if someone had stuck his finger in a light socket. He glared at the computer monitor with a split screen of Zack's brain and the A&W root beer logo. He muttered something to himself. Then he turned to Roman. "What are you proposing?"

"To take care of him. To take out the Kashian kid."

His head bobbed. "Yes. Except he's fallen off the face of the earth."

"I have an idea where he is."

"How do you know?"

Roman said nothing, just stared at Babcock.

When Babcock got the message, he said, "Are you sure you can do it?"

"Have I let you down?"

"No, but I want him dead and untraceable."

"No problem."

"But I want hard evidence."

"How about his head?"

Babcock blinked a few times, then said, "That'll do."

"Okay. Which brings up the question of how desirable."

"What are you asking?"

"One million dollars."

"*What?* That's ridiculous."

"Is it? I'm offering you a threefer."

"What threefer?"

"Father, son, and unholy ghost."

Babcock put his hand to his head, flustered. "I can't make a decision on that kind of money just like that. I have to talk to people."

Roman looked at the expensive furniture and statuary around the room. The building itself had to be worth three or four million. "Fine. But the longer you take, the deeper in hiding the kid goes. And the cooler I get."

"Meaning what?"

"Meaning you have four hours to talk to your associates and raise the cash."

"Cash?"

"Five hundred up front, five hundred for his head."

Babcock leaned back in his chair. After a long pause, he said, "I'll call you tomorrow."

"No, by three forty-five this afternoon."

"I can't raise that kind of money in four hours."

"You're the true defender of the Church. Bet you can."

Babcock was speechless.

But Roman could hear thoughts churn in his head. He glanced at his watch. "Three forty-five, and I call and tell you where."

Babcock stood up. The meeting was over.

Roman extended his hand. Babcock hesitated at first, then extended his, which felt like a damp puff of fat. "The Lord be with you."

....

Fifteen minutes later, Roman was riding down Storrow Drive toward Boston. It was a beautiful day, and dozens of sailboats were cutting down the river in bright white sails. Across the river, the Cambridge skyline seemed to stand out in high-def clarity.

The way he looked at it, the Kashian kid was either divine or the Antichrist. Either way, Roman won. If, as Babcock claimed, the kid was some kind of talking head for the devil, killing him would not only fatten Roman's bank account but would help win his way into God's graces. That was how warriors of God were rewarded, right? On the other hand, if the kid was divine, then protecting him would be Roman's service to God.

Faith was all. But faith could swing both ways. The same with service to God.

What Luria, Stern, and company had created was some kind of religious Manhattan Project. The project was dead. But Roman wanted that bomb.

78

....

"What the hell were you doing in there?" Zack said when Sarah emerged from the store.

She tossed two bags into the rear and handed him a coffee. "What's the problem?"

He put the coffee in the holder and pulled the car out of the slot with a jerk. "The problem is we're running out of time."

"It was crowded. And a line for the coffee." She turned her face out the window.

He pulled back onto Route 1, thinking that she was probably regretting she had come with him. "Thanks for the coffee," he said, hoping to clear the air. "What did you get?"

"A change of clothes." She glanced over her shoulder. "You brought sleeping bags. I'm not overnighting in the woods."

"We'll be fine." They drove without saying any more, but a prickly silence filled the car. He pulled back onto the turnpike.

"You have a compass?" she asked.

"What for?"

"If we're going to be walking in the woods, we'll need one."

"Yes, I have a compass."

She glanced in the direction of his duffel bag. "You sure?"

"Yes, I'm sure." *She doesn't believe in you,* he thought. *She doesn't believe any of this. But that's okay. She's blindsided.*

He merged with the turnpike, which was heavy with weekend beach traffic.

The sun was still high in the sky. It hadn't begun to tilt to the western tree line yet. But it would soon enough. Then night would fall.

Let there be time, he whispered in his head. *Let this be so.*

79

....

A little after twelve-thirty, Warren Gladstone entered the bar at the Taj, and Roman recognized him instantly. Except that he wore a gray blazer over a white shirt instead of the sky blue robe in his broadcasts.

Earlier, Roman had left a message for Gladstone at the Taj desk to call him for important information regarding the whereabouts of Zachary Kashian. As expected, Gladstone complied and said to meet at the bar instead of his private suite, playing it safe.

Roman introduced himself as John Farley, showing his bogus ID. Gladstone had a shiny, pink face with sincere blue eyes. He ordered a Scotch and water, and Roman asked for seltzer on the rocks.

"So what exactly is the FBI's interest in Zachary Kashian?"

"Let me begin by saying what we both know—that Zachary Kashian is missing and you want him back, correct?"

Gladstone took a sip of his Scotch. "What makes you think that I'm interested in him?"

Roman opened his briefcase and pulled out a folder with several images downloaded from Gladstone's Web site as well as images of Zack's brain and stills of mathematical data from Morris Stern's computer. "Because he's your great Day of Jubilation, and without him you're blowing in the wind."

Gladstone thumbed through the pages, which also included photos of Zack arriving and then leaving in a limo with Sarah Wyman. Also shots of Gladstone's church and the lab behind his tabernacle.

When he was through, he closed the folder. "You know a lot. Who else has seen this?"

"No one."

"And you say you know where he is."

"I'm saying I can bring him back to you."

"Why do you think we want him?"

"Because he is your ticket to heaven and because others want his head."

"Who does?"

"Reverend, please let's cut the bullshit, okay? People have been gunning for you and your GodLight thing ever since you started with the Day of Jubilation promises. It's all over the Internet. The point is there's a contract on his head, so he's on the run. And I'm the only one who can bring him back to you alive, *capice*?"

Gladstone flicked through the folder again. "How did you get all this?"

"Our office has been investigating the deaths of three other scientists who'd worked on this project of yours." And from his briefcase Roman produced the obituaries of Thomas Pomeroy, LeAnn Cola, and Roger Devereux.

Gladstone stared at the write-ups. "Then your office knows about Kashian."

"They've never heard of him. They've never heard about NDEs or your lab. Just these deaths."

"Then you're here on your own."

"That's right. And if you're thinking of contacting the

local field office, they won't have heard of him. And he'll end up in his own obit within the next twenty-four hours. And I will deny ever meeting you."

"And who's out to harm him?"

"Not harm him, kill him. The same people who think he's the Antichrist who's going to bring down the Catholic Church if you put him on your show."

Gladstone swallowed more of his Scotch and ordered a second. He was silent for a few minutes as he processed Roman's claim and thumbed through the folder material again. Finally he whispered, "Nothing can happen to him. He's very special."

Roman leaned back and sipped his bubbly water. Gladstone was beginning to see the light. "Let me ask you something, Reverend. You really think he made contact with his dead father?"

"All the evidence points to that."

"Then would you say he's divine?"

Gladstone's brows arched like a church window. "Divine? No, he's mortal, but I believe he was in contact with his father's spirit and glimpsed the realm beyond. He's living proof."

"What about the scientists? Do they think he had a spiritual experience—you know, been to heaven and back?"

"Why are you so interested?"

"Just wondering."

"Are you a religious man, Mr. Farley?"

"Yes."

Gladstone smiled approval. "Well, some prefer calling it a 'paranormal' rather than spiritual experience."

"What's the difference?"

"The difference is that paranormal avoids religious interpretation—no acknowledgment of God."

"You mean like that New Age astral projection crap?"

"Yes. Maybe some kind of telepathy thing. Essentially heaven for agnostics and atheists."

"And you don't buy that."

"No."

"So you don't believe that someone can have a soul without there being a God?"

"I'm saying that we all have a God-given soul, which is what makes us His children, and that if you believe in the Lord Jesus Christ, you'll have everlasting life in heaven."

"Some of your enemies say near-death experience claims are blasphemy—that anyone can get into heaven, any sinner and nonbeliever. That they're all tricks of Satan."

"That's ridiculous. Having a near-death experience doesn't mean they automatically go to heaven when they die. God is still the final judge of that. Because you can see the moon doesn't mean you can fly there at will."

"But what about the claim you're practicing sorcery?"

"That's selective theology. You don't hear these people calling the visions of Saint Teresa or the Lady of Fatima sorcery. No, they're revered and the stuff of sainthood." Gladstone took another sip of his Scotch. "In fact, Jesus himself was accused of performing his miracles by the power of Satan—miracles that bore visions of heavenly beings and feelings of peace and love. He himself warned against attributing to Satan works of the Holy Spirit. The very critics who claim that NDEs are works of Satan are themselves blaspheming the Holy Spirit—a sin that Jesus said is beyond forgiveness."

Roman was all the more confused. No matter what you believed, you could find passages in the Bible to back yourself up.

"Okay, let's get back on track," Gladstone said. "You say you know where he is."

"Yes, and I can bring him to you."

"For a fee, I presume."

"Tell me you work for free."

Gladstone gave him a toothy grin. "Okay, the ugly stuff."

Roman finished his seltzer and leaned forward so that his face was inches away from Gladstone's. "One million dollars in cash, fifty percent up front."

Gladstone did not flinch. "And you'll bring him in alive and well."

"Alive and well," Roman said, wishing he had asked for more.

"How long do I have to think this over?"

Roman checked his watch. "Two hours, cash in hand."

"That's not much time, Mr. Farley."

"There are banks all around here where you can get money transfers. And while you are, these people are scrambling to find that kid and put a stake through his heart. If they do, we both lose—you more than me."

"And how do I know you won't take the money and run?"

Roman laid his hand on the folder. "First, I'm the only one who knows what this kid is worth. Second, I want that other half million."

Gladstone nodded, then pulled his iPhone out of his pocket and said to the party who answered, "Bruce, bring the car."

"I'll meet you across the street in two hours under the statue of George Washington. Two forty-five sharp."

"Make that three. I have to buy a suitcase."

....

At three o'clock, Gladstone walked up the flowered path from Arlington Street with a leather carry-on bag in his hand. He was alone.

He gave the bag to Roman, who laid it on a bench near the statue to inspect the contents. When the area was clear of strollers, Roman backed up and asked Gladstone to open the bag himself and tilt it toward him to see the contents.

Gladstone cocked his head at him. "You think I've got a bomb in here?"

"If you refuse to open it, I will."

Gladstone snapped open the bag and tilted it toward him. It was full of bound hundred-dollar bills. Roman walked over and reached randomly into the bag to check the packs. All Franklins in packs of ten thousand. He didn't have to count them. He closed the bag.

"When will I hear from you?" Gladstone said.

"Within the next twenty-four hours."

Roman then watched Gladstone walk the same flower-lined path to Arlington Street. To be sure Gladstone left, he cut across the grass to where the Lincoln Town Car waited at the curb. While Roman watched through some bushes, he saw the driver get out and open the rear door for Gladstone. With a shock, Roman took in the face of the chauffeur. It was the same guy who had ridden to the Fraternity of Jesus with Babcock.

Son of a bitch! Roman thought. Bruce was burning his candle at both ends, too.

80

....

About two hours after stopping, Zack came upon the Biddeford/Route 5 exit. Nothing looked familiar, but he turned off.

"Is this it?"

"Yes."

"Are you sure?"

"Yes, I'm sure."

There was a new motel complex just off the exit ramp that still had scaffolding on one wall and construction machinery in front.

"But that's all new, and you haven't been here in twenty years."

"Believe me, this is the right way."

"I'm trying to."

There was a clutch of fast-food restaurants on the access road.

"Maybe we should stop for directions and get something to eat."

"We'll find a place when we get closer."

"Closer to what?"

He didn't say anything because he didn't want to startle her. But the sensation was now electric. She wouldn't understand, and he couldn't put it into words that made sense.

But he really should thank Sarah for helping to lead him out of the tunnel and into the light. If it hadn't been for the suspension tests, he'd still be stuck in the gray materialist world. Although he had long denied it, something had gotten into his head that first day with the stimulation helmet, then burned like a pilot light throughout all the nasty flatlining; and now it was a discernible beacon.

Ironically, the only one in that lab who had insight was the same person who tried to kill him. Funny how he was now coming around to respecting that woman. She had had her eye on the prize. And the prize was just ahead.

He turned onto Route 5.

Just a few more miles.

81

....

At three fifteen, Roman called Norman Babcock to tell him to meet him in half an hour and named the drop spot. Babcock agreed.

At three forty-five, from his rental car, Roman watched Babcock drive his Mercedes to a deserted corner of the Watertown Mall. Roman pulled out of his unseen slot and moved to within fifty feet of Babcock, who, as instructed, stood in front of his car with a travel bag. When he was certain no other cars had accompanied Babcock, Roman called him on his cell phone, instructing him to approach his car. As he did, Roman rolled down the driver's-side window.

But Babcock did not hand him the bag. "How do I know you won't just disappear yourself?"

"I didn't do that for the last four assignments, right?"

"Yeah, but this is half a million."

"And I want the other half."

"And when will I see the results?"

"Twenty-four hours," he said, and pulled over an empty backpack from the passenger seat.

"What's that for?"

"Today the money, tomorrow his head."

Babcock nodded. He handed Roman the valise. But Roman shook his head. There were no cars nearby. "Step back ten feet and open it and show me the contents."

"What? Why?"

"Just do it."

Babcock froze for a moment as Roman raised his weapon so it was visible and rolled up his window to watch.

Then Babcock unzipped the bag and tilted it toward Roman's side window. He even pulled out a pack of hundreds and fanned it with his thumb.

When Roman was satisfied, he rolled down the window and let Babcock hand him the bag. He unloaded each pack of hundreds and transferred them to his backpack, leaving Babcock with the original gym bag just in case it had a homing device on it.

"Twenty-four hours," Babcock said, still looking torn.

"'"Believe in me," saith the Lord.'"

"But you're not the Lord."

"No, but I'm the best warrior he's got."

82

....

Roman drove from the Watertown Mall to a Bank of America in Watertown Square to deposit the cash from Babcock and Gladstone in a safety deposit box.

The parking lot was nearly abandoned because the bank was closing shortly. He had a few minutes and pulled to the rear of the building. Before he got out, he slipped the DVD of Zack Kashian's first suspension into his laptop. Something in that first interview had stuck in his mind like a thorn. And for the third time he reviewed the kid's emergence.

"Hey, Zack, you're waking up." The voice came from a woman off camera. *"Zack, can you hear me?"*

He grunted.

"He's coming to," said an unseen male.

"Come on, Zack, wake up."

The kid opened one eye.

"That's it, Zack, open your eyes."

"Welcome back. How do you feel?"

"If your mouth and tongue feel tingly, that's normal. Can you tell me your name?"

Kashian gave the woman a blank look but said nothing.

"Okay, you're still a little foggy."

"Can you tell us your name?"

He shook his head.

"No? Sure you can. It's Zack. What's your last name?"

After a moment he said, *"Kashian."*

"What was that?"

"Kashian."

"Right. Good. And do you know where you are?"

At that moment, Roman paused the video. From the far entrance, he spotted a silver BMW sedan with Bruce behind the wheel and some guy he didn't recognize. Before they could block him in, he spun the car around and pulled into the street.

He shot up Mt. Auburn, and the BMW kept right behind him. Roman pushed the bag of cash onto the floor and raced up the hill with the BMW still on his tail. The sons of bitches had followed him from the drop. It was a setup from the start.

Ahead he saw Watertown High School and turned down the side street and into the large parking lot. Because it was the weekend, the place was abandoned.

He cut a half circle so that his car faced the entrance from the street.

A second later, the BMW pulled in. Before he could give Bruce a target, Roman turned hard to his left, then cut a sharp right. He could see the passenger aim a gun at him. But Roman zigzagged his car, floored the accelerator, and rammed the BMW broadside with the grille guard, crushing the passenger door and pushing the car to a screeching stop.

Roman jumped out with his silenced pistol and ran around the rear of the BMW. Before Bruce could recover, he smashed in the driver's-side window, shot dead the passenger, and rammed the gun into the soft of Bruce's neck.

"Don't, please. I didn't mean anything."

"Yes, you did." And Roman pulled the trigger.

Ten minutes later he was back in the bank parking lot, but it had just closed. Furious, he pulled out his cell phone and called Babcock. "You send any more of your frat boys after me, and you're dead. You got that?"

"Roman, I swear I had nothing to do with that. They must have followed me. I swear. They were acting on their own."

"Well, it won't happen again. They're permanently flatlined. And if you want this kid taken out, don't fucking mess with me." He clicked off.

All the banks were closed and he had $1 million in cash with him. He'd have to drive home and drop it off.

In the meantime, he went back to his laptop and turned on the DVD again.

"Okay, you're still a little foggy."

"Can you tell us your name?"

"No? Sure you can. It's Zack. What's your last name?"

"Kashian."

"What was that?"

"Kashian."

"Right. Good. And do you know where you are?"

The kid responded.

Roman paused the video, went back, and played that part again. Then he thumbed through a folder of data he had gotten from Morris Stern. After several minutes, he found what he was looking for.

"Oh my," he said aloud.

He turned on his GPS. There was no time to head home. Suddenly this had turned into a religious pilgrimage, he thought. And he pulled onto the street and into the fast lane.

83

....

It was a little after six when Zack turned off Route 5 and onto 202, a two-lane blacktop that cut through dense woodlands.

The indefinable instinct was like having a GPS system on the inside of his skull. They entered the center of Farrington, a strip of houses, a volunteer firehouse, and a small service station attached to a general store. Zack pulled up to a pump. Sarah got out to use the restroom and grab something to eat.

When nobody came out, Zack got out and removed the pump. As he did, a man in an orange top and black cap emerged from the store. "Second door to the left. No key needed," he said to Sarah, who thanked him and walked to an outside entrance.

"I wasn't sure if it was self-serve or not," Zack said.

"Ayuh. This ain't Massachusetts. We give you either option up here."

It came out *uhpeeyah*. They really did talk that way. *Ayuh*. The guy had a salt-and-pepper beard, the mustache part curling over his lip. In a side pocket of his mind, Zack wondered why he didn't trim it and tried not to think of him eating an egg-salad sandwich. He handed the pump to the man and asked him to fill it.

"Just wondering if you ever heard of Magog Woods."

The guy cocked his head. "Ayuh."

"Are we going in the right direction?"

"Depends on your direction."

Because of the location of the pumps, their car was pointing west. "North."

"Ayuh, 'cept the sign's been down some years now."

"Any landmarks?"

"Trees."

"That's all there is up here."

"You got that right."

Except for this minivillage, impenetrable woods girdled the roads. "How far would you say?"

"To what?"

"Magog Woods." Zack was beginning to feel that the guy was either playing games with him or just slow.

"Fourteen, fifteen miles."

"Is there an entrance of sorts?"

"Not of sorts."

"How will I know I'm there?"

"Prob'ly won't, 'less you know what you're looking for. Just a cut in the trees, if it's even there anymore. I don't go up that way much myself." Through the rear window, he glanced at the rolled sleeping bags and backpacks in the cargo space.

When he finished pumping, Zack handed him $60. The guy inspected the twenties as if suspecting counterfeits. When satisfied, he pulled out a roll of bills, licked his thumb and forefinger, and slowly peeled off four singles. While the man went through the motions, Zack noticed two people inside the general store studying him.

"Is that where you're planning on camping?"

"Why do you ask?"

"Because there ain't anywhere to lay down a tent, 'less you walk a fair distance. Thick as barbed wire. A pond or two deep inside, but nobody goes there anymore."

"How come?"

The guy cocked his head again. "If you ain't got business there, I'd move on."

Zack felt the rat in his gut claw at something.

"Plenty of good campgrounds down Fryeburg way, Kezar Lake. Running water, and they're safe."

Just then Sarah walked out of the store with a bag of food and drinks.

"Got some maps of local campsites." He looked at Sarah. "The lady who sold you those will be happy to assist."

Sarah glanced at Zack. "What about motels?"

"Got those, too, and some nifty B and Bs made special for Massachusetts folks. Just ask Marianne."

Sarah went back inside. Zack waited until she was out of earshot. "Are you saying there's a problem at Magog?"

"Specially for the folks that went in."

"What happened?"

"Never came out again."

Zack nodded; it was all local rumor. "Any idea what became of them?"

"Hard to say. Maybe got lost. Maybe got hurt. Maybe fell into quickmud. Maybe worse."

What could be worse than sinking in quickmud? "You mean like animals?"

"Got lots of those about." He bobbed his head as if running through an inventory of creature dangers. Then he added, "Could be something else."

"Like what?" The rat began gnawing on something.

"Hard to say. But even the IFW agents don't go in there, and they carry more guns than the state police."

"IFW?"

"Inland Fisheries and Wildlife. They make sure wildlife is healthy, nobody poaches."

"What's the problem?"

"Problem is some folks up here aren't like you Massachusetts people. They don't have regular paying jobs and civ'lized lifestyles. Live in the woods, live off the land, don't come out but once a year, if that. Eat what they kill. They jack a moose, the IFW looks the other way." He pulled out a rag and began to wipe his hands. Then his nose.

"I still don't see what the problem is."

"Well, some would say they be a little light on top— maybe too much isolation, maybe too much livin' in the wild. Whatever, we leave them alone, they leave us alone."

"You're saying there are dangerous people up there?"

"I'm saying drop your bags somewhere else."

Sarah stepped out of the store with a small guidebook and some sheets with motels and B and Bs. She thanked the man and slipped back into the passenger seat.

The woman came out after her. "Here's the rest of your change, ma'am." And she handed Sarah some coins.

The woman was large and had her hair pulled back in a long ponytail. She had a wide mannish face and was wearing a bright pink sweatshirt that said, "Maineiac Momma." When Sarah said to keep the change, the woman said, "Thanks, but we don't take charity." She moved beside the pump man and watched them leave.

Zack waved and buckled his seat belt while the two watched them without expression, looking like an overweight version of *American Gothic*. Just as Zack was about to pull away, the man made a gun with his fingers and aimed southward down 202. Sarah didn't see him, and Zack turned the car northward. In the rearview mirror, the man stood there with his wife and watched them drive away, shaking his head.

When they were about a quarter mile up the road, Sarah handed Zack a tuna sandwich that had melted through the bread. "It's all they had," she said. "Guess there was a run on the good stuff."

"Yeah, a foodie's mecca."

Zack put the sandwich in the hold between them. He had no appetite. He took a sip of the iced tea and drove on, feeling the rightness of his direction in spite of the guy back there making like one of the villagers in *Dracula. Surprised he didn't offer me a crucifix,* he thought with grim bemusement.

"Your recall's amazing," Sarah said, biting into her sandwich. "I asked the lady, and she said Magog Woods is about fifteen miles up the road."

Not recall.

"You must have been up here a few more times than you remember."

Ever rational to the end, Zack thought. "Maybe so," he said to humor her. "Soon as we hit that center, it all came back."

"Still, you have a great memory."

"Or maybe I had no reason to remember, and now I do."

"I'm not sure I follow."

"Not important."

Out of the corner of his eye, he saw her turn to him. "What's not important?"

"Nothing." Purple shadows of the setting sun made a pall over the road ahead.

"Zack, I don't like this."

"You don't like what?"

"Being up here. The way you're behaving. The way you're talking. I'm getting creeped out."

"Well, I'm sorry."

"I want to go back, okay?"

No! She's trying to lead you astray. Deflect you from your mission. "Look, it's only another ten miles or so. If we don't find it, we'll go back. I promise."

"You don't even know what you're looking for."

"If you want, I can drop you back at the store and go myself."

"Be serious."

"Then trust me."

"If you don't find whatever it is, we turn back. Promise me."

"I promise."

But in the back of his mind, there was a flicker of guilt.

84

....

About a dozen miles beyond the gas station, Zack slowed the car. The thick wall of trees on either side made of the road an unbroken, darkening corridor. Since their stop, he had counted only one other vehicle on the road, coming from the opposite direction.

"Is this it?" Sarah asked, the fear audible in her voice.

He didn't answer, but his chest was pounding so hard that his breath came short. After half a minute more, he pulled over. In the heavy scrub was an opening to an unmarked dirt road, nearly indistinguishable but for the narrow cut through towering pines, oaks, and dense brush. Zack pulled the car into the lane. No other cars were on the road, which faded into gloom in either direction.

"What are we doing?"

"We're here."

Zack turned on the headlights. The rutted dirt lane was one car wide, with weeds growing down the center line, some spilling into the tire troughs. It hadn't been used much and brooded ahead of them as it disappeared into the depths. Zack checked that the doors were locked. "I just want to go in a little way, then we'll come right out."

"I don't like this."

"We'll be fine." His brain was humming like a hive of hornets. He inched his way down the lane as brush scratched against the car, and the overhang of trees made a tunnel of the path, closing down on them as they moved deeper. Something really weird was about to happen.

"Zack, please turn back. I want to get out of here."

"Okay. We'll find a clearing to turn around."

"Just back out."

But he paid her no attention and rolled a few more yards ahead until it was clear that they had reached the end, the headlights falling on a wall of trees with no opening wide enough to accommodate a car. "See?"

"See what? There's no room to turn around."

He had no idea how far they had come—maybe a hundred yards. But she was right. He had only two or three feet on either side of the car to turn around. And no easy way to back out with only the backup lights.

Sarah seethed to herself while he worked the shift from drive to reverse, advancing a foot or so each time. The sides were scraped, and he'd have a handsome bill to cover the scratches. But after several minutes, he had the car pointed the way they had come down. Sweat poured down his face and back.

"What's that?" gasped Sarah.

He turned toward her, thinking she had spotted something in the woods. But she was staring straight ahead.

Through the windshield he could see nothing but the dirt road and wall of trees. Then he flicked on the high beams. Something flashed back at him, and his guts knotted. Maybe thirty yards ahead, filling the width of the road, was a black van.

"Who is that?" Sarah whispered.

"I don't know."

The van's lights were off, and in the high beams Zack could see no one behind the windshield.

"We're trapped."

Whoever had followed them did so in scant light, because Zack had come down this road with one eye ahead and the other in the rearview mirror. Without lights, the driver had to have followed them in near total darkness. And given the time it took Zack to turn the car around, whoever it was either knew the way or could see in the dark.

If the van was empty, the driver could be anywhere watching them.

"We're sitting ducks," she said.

Zack undid his seat belt.

"No, don't get out."

"Just getting something in the back."

"No." She was beginning to panic and grabbed his arm. "Don't get out, please."

"Then come with me." He got out, and she climbed over the center and got out beside him. He led her to the hatch, where he grabbed his backpack and pulled out two flashlights. He didn't turn them on but handed one to Sarah. He slipped on his backpack, pulled up the carpet, and raised the false floor over the spare tire. In the repair pouch was a foot-long crowbar. It would have to do. He closed the hatch, gripping the black torch in one hand, the iron in the other. In a flash, he saw himself smashing Mitchell Gretch's skull.

Sarah pulled him around the side to get back. "Let's get inside."

The woods were dark and full-throated with the chittering of bugs. What there was of sky had turned opaque, with a few stars blazing through the thick canopy. "What for?"

"Maybe we can push it off the road."

"Too many trees." They grew right up to the road, with no opening to shove the van.

Sarah was trembling. "What are we going to do?"

Zack had no idea who drove the van, no psychic familiarity. His heart was pounding, but he wasn't afraid. He opened the driver's door. "Okay, get in. Lock the doors and start the car."

"What?"

"Just do as I say. Please."

"No, Zack. Don't."

He nudged her inside, closed her door, and moved up the dirt path in the Murano's high beams, gripping the crowbar in his right hand, the torch in his left. As he approached the van, he saw no one in the front seats but couldn't see into the rear. He sprayed the surrounding trees with the torch but saw nobody.

He reached the van, an old beaten-up VW with no front license plate and a two-year-old Maine inspection sticker. The engine was warm. He held his breath and gripped the crowbar. Then he pressed the torch against the windshield. The van was empty. The doors were locked. No key in the ignition. Nothing in the front seat. In the rear he could make out some nondescript boxes and plastic jugs on their sides. Some piles of clothes or rags, he couldn't tell which. But his heart made a little surge when his light fell on a gun rack mounted on the ceiling behind the driver. It was empty.

He flashed around, knowing he was being watched. As he started toward the van's rear to look for markings, Sarah screamed.

He tore back to the Murano, barely registering his feet contacting the ground. He could see no one at the vehicle, just the white face of Sarah inside. When he reached the driver's door, she unlocked it.

"Someone's out there," she said, barely able to catch her breath. "I saw him."

"Where?"

"My window."

"Did you see his face?"

She shook her head. "Just a flash."

"Did you recognize him?"

"No. It was too fast."

"What did he look like?"

"I don't know. Just a dark shape."

"He say anything?"

"No. What are we going to do?"

The engine was purring, and in the headlights they could just make out the van up ahead. "Probably locals out to spook Massachusetts folks."

"The gas station guys?"

"Yeah. Backwoods version of Friday night fun."

"It's moving," she said.

Zack flicked the lights. The van *was* moving, but not toward them. It was backing up. In a moment it receded without lights into the black as the trees closed around it like a drawn curtain.

"Get going," she said.

Instead, he turned off the headlights. The woods were a solid black. No receding light from the van. No distant lights from the road. Nothing but uncompromising black. He turned off the car's engine.

"What're you doing?" she squealed. "Let's get the hell out of here."

"They're gone." He opened his door.

"Zach, get back in and take me home."

"That's not what we came for." He snatched the keys and got out.

"Goddamn it, get in."

As she continued protesting, he said nothing and

sauntered to the end of the lane where he had turned the car around.

Above, the stars still winked through the treetops. But he could see a thin layer of cloud begin to haze the light. He could also feel a drop in temperature as the wind picked up, laced with the scent of rain.

Sarah got out of the car and slammed the door. "What the hell are you doing?" she said, coming up to him.

"We're not finished." He felt the crowbar pulse in his grip.

Suddenly the woods filled with a hideous otherworldly cry that raised a yelp from Sarah and nearly stopped Zack's heart.

"What's that?" she cried.

"Only a loon." Someplace else, another answered in the same hysterical warble.

She grabbed the front of his shirt. "I want to get out of here. Now!"

"Then go." He dangled the car keys in front of her. "Take the car and leave. You're free, the road's clear. I'm not turning back."

"Why are you doing this?"

"Tell me, Sarah, what exactly do you believe in, huh? Is everything serotonin and God lobes?"

"What?"

"Isn't it possible that there are things unseen in this world?"

"Zack, please . . ."

"I'm asking you a real question. Isn't it possible you could be wrong? You want hard evidence? Well, you're looking at it: me."

"But . . ."

"But what? I'm delusional? Psychotic? Crazy?"

"I didn't say that."

He put the keys in her hand. "Go home, Sarah. Go

back to clean, well-lighted Cambridge." Then he turned and walked away, his head filling with the musky, piney odor from the trees and decaying leaf mash. And something else.

Man sweat.

And something else.

Wood smoke.

Zack froze in place and turned his head as if it were an antenna looking for a signal.

They were surrounded by a continuous wall of trees making a chiaroscuro thicket around them against fading starlight. He slipped the crowbar into his belt and moved into the tiny clearing where he had turned the car.

"I'm not leaving," Sarah said.

He said nothing but stopped in his tracks. Then, inexplicably, something in the depth of his brain made a click. He turned to his left and stared at the black ground.

"I can't see a thing," she muttered.

He aimed the light at a spot on the ground. "This way."

85

....

"How will we find our way back?" she whispered.

"No problem."

"What do you mean, 'no problem'? And where's your compass?"

"I've got it."

"Where?"

But he didn't answer. Instead he turned off his torch and led them on while she kept hers trained on the path in front of her. Through the canopy, the fading starlight made a vague diorama of branches and tree trunks. Ground visibility was minimal. Yet Zack moved through the thicket of brush and trees as if radar directed. And Sarah plodded behind him, saying nothing.

As they moved deeper, he felt the temperature drop even more. In spite of their movement, a chill cut through his jacket and sweatshirt. It occurred to him that if they got lost, no one would find their remains for years. If ever. The woods were crawling with night creatures—coyotes, bears, bobcats—that would strip them to bone in no time. And anything left over would be consumed by bugs and worms. Death and total recycling.

And he could hear them—the chittering and trilling

and chirping, an occasional grunt or wheezing breath. In the distance, the hysterical yodels of loons. And in the even greater distance, coyotes yowling at the heavens.

God, give a sign.

When Sarah tugged at his shirt to ask where they were going, to beg to go back, he simply said, "Trust me."

The path was narrow and covered with tender shoots like the hope pushing up in him. Silently he led Sarah through the growth. At one point, she let out a cry when some ground-nesting birds were startled up from nowhere, the flurry of their wings reflecting in their flashlights like banshees.

But something else was out there. Something alive and aware. He could feel its presence even if he couldn't hear it. Every so often, he would stop and listen.

The woods were electric with the scrapings of a million metallic cricket legs, charging the air with a fierce expectancy. Unfortunately, the air was also alive with stinging flies that got in their eyes and ears and turned the Maine woods into a buzzing hell. And they had no repellent. But the wind had picked up and blew them away.

A sign? Maybe the wind, he thought.

Against Sarah's protests, they moved deeper. "Sarah, we're fine."

"I'm not fine, goddamn it."

But he disregarded her and moved through the brush like a bloodhound. He wished he could explain. He wished he could find the words. But this was beyond language. And she was too much the rationalist, living within the confines of Cartesian logic and Newtonian physics. The way he used to be. But something had happened— something not dreamt of in her philosophy. For the last several hours—or weeks, come to think of it—things had come together with a sublime inevitability, like the working out of prophecy, that was culminating in these woods where the trees rose like cathedral spires.

Suddenly Zack stopped in his tracks.

"What?" Sarah gasped.

"Listen."

Everything around them had become utterly silent— as if someone had turned off the audio. No chittering of crickets; no rustling or chirps of night critters; no squawking flutter of startled birds; no coyotes yowling. Not even the hush of the wind in the treetops. It was as if the forest were holding its breath.

"What's happening?" Terror was strangling her voice.

"Nothing." Zack looked behind them. Even if he wanted to go back, they could never make it, not in this muzzy dark. Besides, the trampled brush behind them was already snapping back into place. And a cold drizzle began to fall.

"We're lost," Sarah whispered. "We're fucking lost, and you don't have a compass. You lied." She was crying.

Sudden doubt clenched his heart. What if he was wrong? What if he had talked himself into believing? What if the instinct pulling him along was a figment of a brain rotted on tetrodotoxin? What if she was right, that it was all in the head—that nothing lay beyond all this? No transcendent mind. No higher awareness. Just the cosmic joke of hope.

"Zack!"

He turned, and behind them the ground was burning with green fire—as if alien lava were seeping out of the earth. The path in front of them was still black, but behind them their tracks left an incandescent trail, as if they'd been walking in liquid radium.

He pulled Sarah forward. The stuff stuck to their shoes and the bottoms of their pants like phosphorescent mites. The ground was aglow with millions of them. She stomped her foot, and her running shoe lit up.

"What the hell is that?"

A sign. Thank you.

He gripped her shoulders. "Sarah, calm down. It's called fox fire. Will-o'-the-wisp. A chemical reaction that takes place in fungus and wood rot. A chemical phosphorescence. Pure biology."

"What? How do you know?"

"Faerie fire," his father had called it, and it all came back to him for real. The last time he was up here, his dad had walked him and Jake down this same path one night. He had turned off his flashlight to show them the phenomenon. "My father."

They moved ahead. Behind them the fox fire followed them, silhouetting sods of dirt, saplings, and fallen limbs and splashing with each footfall as if just below the surface were a thin lake of Day-Glo fire.

"You see?"

She nodded, looking back at their glowing trail, fading slowly in the dark.

"You okay?"

She didn't respond. He took her hand, which was cold and wet, and he pulled her along. The drizzle was making a cold aspic of his skin. They went another several feet when she stopped dead.

"I can't go on. I can't."

"I understand," he said, and hugged her. She didn't understand. How could she? "We're almost there."

"You keep saying that. I wanna go back."

"Please trust me. Just five more minutes. I promise for real."

They stumbled on, and soon the faerie fire disappeared, leaving only black woods. He followed his flash as a worm of doubt slithered across his chest again.

Please, don't abandon me.

Suddenly Sarah stopped. She was trembling, and in the light her face was a tight white mask of itself. Tears were rolling down her cheeks. "No."

"Just a little ways more."

"No, and you're scaring the shit out of me."

"Smoke."

"What?"

He snapped his head around. "I smell smoke."

"I don't fucking care."

He walked a few feet into the dark. "There."

In the distance was a dull orange glow. He looked back at her. She was standing with her hands clutched to her breast, her hair matted by the falling rain. She looked as if she had turned to stone. He went to her and held out his hand.

For a long moment she stared at him, then she put out her hand. They walked maybe another thirty yards, following his light.

"My God," he whispered. "I'm home."

86

....

"Is this it?"

Zack looked at the cabin with a shock of recognition. "Yes."

He could barely believe what his eyes were recording. He hadn't been here since he was a child, and the trees had probably increased their girth, but it all rushed back. The cabin—a dark brown box of vertical wooden planks, the pitched roof—the rough, thick tangle of woods, the old oak stump for splitting logs, a long-handled spiked ax embedded blade down, a sharpening wheel beside it, the stack of wood alongside the cabin. Also an artesian well his father had built, drawing water from an aquifer from the nearby creek.

To the right of the front door was a small window, glowing from interior light. Smoke rose out of a chimney pipe someplace in the rear. As he was taking it all in and trying to sort out recall from psychic flashes, Sarah whispered his name. He looked, and she was aiming her torch on something. He moved to her. Sitting in the circle of light was the same black van.

Zack moved to the front door and tapped. No answer. He tapped again. "Dad, it's me, Zack."

Nothing.

He tapped again. "Nick Kashian. It's your son, Zachary. Please open up."

Someplace in the distance a loon cried out.

"It's locked," Sarah whispered.

A stainless-steel combination lock hung from the latch. He slipped his fingers under it and held it up to Sarah's torch. He tried the tumbler. Then, as if his fingers had a mind of their own, he turned it to the right three times to 24, then once left to 8, then twice right to 14, and the lock opened up.

"How did you know?" Sarah asked.

He shook his head. The numbers just came to his fingers. He removed the lock from the eyehole and pushed open the door.

The interior was lit by a single kerosene lantern. And the immediate impression was clutter. Stuff collected over years of occupancy. Empty plastic kerosene containers hung in clusters from a ceiling support beam maybe ten feet up. From another beam hung slabs of dark dried meat and fish wrapped in cheesecloth.

A makeshift bed sat against the left wall, a gray pillow and rumpled soiled bedding covering it. A small wood-burning stove sat at the far wall. He could feel its heat.

The air was laced with the odor of sweat, smoke, and musty wood. One wall held shelves full of canned goods, jars of food, cooking pots, a few hand utensils, dry goods. His father's old Nikon. Telephoto lenses sat in cylindrical cases.

On another wall were three racks, two holding shotguns. Boxes of ammo sat on a nearby shelf. Near the door hung sheathed knives and a machete. And from wall pegs, hooded jackets, tops, and a pair of wading boots. A small workbench and chair sat in the rear right across from the bed. Several tools were lined up on a pegboard.

"Zack."

Sarah shone her flashlight on some discolored photographs pinned to the wall above the worktable. Photographs of him and Jake or the four of them—the same family portrait that sat on his mother's fireplace mantel. One of them was a shot of Zack as a young boy proudly holding up a brook trout nearly as big as he was, a body of water in the background. He'd never seen that photo. It had to have been taken someplace around here.

But what caught Zack's attention sat on the wall over the bed. It was a water-stained drawing of Jesus preaching to his followers, below which in triptych was the Lord's Prayer in English, some foreign script, and an alphabetic transliteration. Zack pulled out his cell phone and played what he had muttered in his coma.

Avvon ð-bish-maiya, nith-qaððash shim-mukh
Tih-teh mal-chootukh. Nih-weh çiw-yanukh:
ei-chana ð'bish-maiya: ap b'ar-ah.
Haw lan lakh-ma ð'soonqa-nan yoo-mana.
O'shwooq lan kho-bein:
ei-chana ð'ap kh'nan shwiq-qan l'khaya-ween.
Oo'la te-ellan l'niss-yoona:
il-la paç-çan min beesha.
Mið-til ðe-ði-lukh hai mal-choota
oo khai-la oo tush-bookh-ta
l'alam al-mein. Aa-meen.

"Word for word," Sarah said.

Zack nodded. "Except that's not my voice."

Before Sarah could respond, the cabin door slammed open and a figure stumbled inside.

87

He could barely recognize him behind the shotgun. "Dad, it's me, Zack."

His father's face was shadowed under a gray hooded slicker. Stringy hair hung over his brow, and the bottom of his face was buried under a scruffy beard. But those eyes were the eyes of his father—piercing green gemstones that Zack had inherited.

He glared at Zack, the shotgun wavering at him.

"Dad, it's me, and this is my friend Sarah. We're here to help you."

For a frozen moment, Zack could not tell if anything was getting through the wild glare in his father's eye. He could be totally demented and blast them for intruding.

Some would say they be a little light on top—maybe too much isolation. . . . Whatever, we leave them alone, they leave us alone.

His father jerked the barrel upward toward Zack. Then Sarah. "Who're you?" His voice was scratchy from disuse.

"This is Sarah Wyman. She's a nurse. We came to help."

He kept the shotgun barrel aimed at her midsection. He was wavering and grimacing, his mouth moving under the gray-and-black scruff as if he were carrying on a conversation inside.

He gaped at Zack, squinting and wincing as if trying to register recognition. The shotgun swayed from Sarah toward Zack, sending a shock to his midsection. *He doesn't recognize me,* Zack thought. *His mind is gone and he hasn't got a clue who I am—just a midnight intruder here to rob him.* In a chilled moment, Zack wondered if he had through some deep recall stumbled upon the demented, shabby remains of someone who used to be his father and who might turn the next moment into bloody mayhem. As he watched the black hole of the barrel jerk in the air between them, he considered making a grab for it. But if it went off, they could be hit by the blast. "Dad, please . . ."

Before he could finish, his father let out a pained cry and slumped to his side, landed on one knee, wincing and gasping. The gun clunked to the wooded floor. Zack caught him by one arm as Sarah took the other. Slowly they moved him to the bed. He groaned as they removed the slicker and raised his feet onto the bed. Gently they laid him on the mattress, a thin, stained pad that was sour with body smells. Sarah grabbed an old sweater for a pillow, and Zack lowered him onto it.

"Jesus," Zack muttered. The right side of his father's pullover was dark with blood.

Zack didn't know if the shock rose from the realization that his father had in fact been shot as presaged in the NDE or from the hideous wound the bullet had left.

He tried not to react to the rancid odor of decay as they removed a dressing made of a rag and duct tape. The bullet was probably still lodged inside of him, and where it had entered was a fetid puckered hole of draining pus, haloed by a raw, angry swell of discolored flesh.

Zack's first thought was gangrene. His second thought

was that it had spread to his father's brain, rendering him delirious and incapable of recognition. He was shaking with fever and dehydration. Without antibiotics, he probably wouldn't make it through the night. "We have to get him to a hospital."

"No hospital." The syllables scraped out of his father's throat.

"But the infection's spread," Sarah said.

"Not dying in a hospital," his father said in a wheezing voice. It was the first lucid statement he had made.

"Okay," Zack said, relieved. From his jacket pocket he removed a vial of Percocet he had brought, left over from his release from the hospital. He slipped two tabs into his father's mouth and raised the water bottle to his lips. "This will make you feel better." His father swallowed the pills.

Meanwhile, Sarah removed Nick's shoes and pulled the blanket over him. She added some wood to the stove to take the chill out of the air.

As they waited for the drug to take effect, Sarah shook her head to say that Nick's condition looked bad.

Zack held his father's hand while he closed his eyes, wincing occasionally against the pain and waiting for the medication to kick in.

As Zack studied his father, things came back to him. The way the blue vein on his forehead was visible, now pulsing with a labored heart. The small chip on a front tooth, the result of a fall from his bicycle when he was a boy. The slightly crooked third finger on his right hand, which he had broken in college during a fraternity prank. Little features he had forgotten. Yet the green eyes still blazed with a fire he could never have forgotten. They stared back at Zack every time he looked in a mirror.

He could also see how he had aged—the deeply scored crease lines around his eyes, the cleft between his brows.

The liver spots on his forehead and the backs of his hands. Various cuts and scars on his arms. His chipped and blackened fingernails, the grime in his matted hair. The whitened scruff of a beard. He had lived in this wilderness, renouncing the "civilized" world like some latter-day Thoreau, subsisting on the land that he loved—this sanctuary of Magog.

But what squeezed Zack's heart was the certainty that these were the last hours he would spend with the father he barely knew. So much to say, so much to ask, so few heartbeats left.

In a few minutes, the drug took effect. Nick opened his eyes and nodded that he felt better. He drank more water.

Sarah got up to give them some privacy. The interior was small, but she moved to the other side of the cabin, where she found some napkins and duct tape to make a clean bandage.

"I knew you'd find me." He spoke in a feathery rasp. "Felt you coming."

"Me, too. I saw them bury you alive on Sagamore. I saw you dig yourself out. I was with you."

His father's eyes filled up. "You have the gift, too."

"The gift?"

"You see the unseen. You touch the spirit."

"But how?"

His father began to speak but got caught in a coughing jag that turned into a fusillade of wheezing gasps. Sarah shot over, and they raised him up and held him until he could catch his breath. Sarah poured him a cup of water from a five-gallon jug rigged up in the far corner. Nick took small, pained gulps. When he was finished, they propped him up with pillows. For a few minutes he lay still with his eyes closed.

From a table against the opposite wall, Sarah returned

with a thick cardboard box with a strip of silver duct tape across the top and ZACK printed in a bold hand.

Inside was a photo album containing black-and-white shots, the first of which showed Zack being handed his B.A. diploma at graduation. It had been taken not by the official school photographer, but through a telephoto lens in the crowd, probably from one sitting on that shelf beside the old Nikon F.

And there were others, all of Zack—playing pickup softball at the field on Columbus Avenue; high school graduation shots of his accepting a scholarship check from the principal; Zack pinning opponents in high school wrestling matches; Little League shots of him catching a pop-up. There were dozens of them—each an event from Zack's young life and all shot from a distance. His father had been there, unseen.

"You made me proud," his father whispered.

"Why didn't you let me know?"

"I didn't belong in your life."

"That's ridiculous. You were my father. I needed you. We needed you."

"Not the man I should have been." Tears squeezed out from the corners of his eyes. "Couldn't handle things. Your brother's dying . . . bringing you up, being married. Too weak. Too weak. I wasn't worthy of being your father."

"You were worthy."

He shook his head. And in a failing whisper he muttered, "Couldn't live in a world I didn't understand."

"So you joined the monastery."

"For God to forgive me, help me understand . . . My penance."

"For what?"

"Jake's death, bad father, bad husband. All my weakness."

"Why didn't you at least answer my letters?"

"I did." He pointed to a wooden cigar box on the shelf with books and shotgun shells. "I have them all. Something else."

Sarah moved to the shelf and got the box for Zack. Her eyes were wet.

Inside were all of Zack's letters sent from the time he'd learned where the monastery was. They were bound together with string. Also unsent letters addressed to him from his father. No stamps on the envelopes. Also a small, ledgerlike diary. When Zack removed that, his father whispered, "No. After. . . ."

Inside was also a thick manila envelope addressed to Adam Krueger at a Boston address. "Adam Krueger. I know that name. He's an insurance guy."

Nick shook his head. "Lawyer."

"The guy who signs all the checks to Mom. We thought it was insurance money after they said you died." They regularly received payments from two separate sources, which his mother had assumed were from two different life insurance policies. "Where'd the money come from?"

"Luria," his father whispered. "Wanted to find Jake. They kept paying me."

"And you paid Mom."

He nodded. "Also, when I pass . . . where to put me. 'S'all in there." He could barely talk and winced against the pain.

Zack moved closer to his father's ear. "Dad, I saw the deaths of Volker and Gretch."

His father turned his head a little but said nothing.

"I saw them get killed."

Still no reaction.

"Was that you?"

After a moment, he nodded. "In the letter to Adam. He'll know what to do."

"You killed them."

"Revenge is the worst evil," he whispered. "Why I became a brother."

"You joined because of them?"

"Wanted to find peace. Forgiveness. But couldn't protect me from myself. Maybe He was angry I abandoned you and Mom."

"Who?"

"God."

"Why . . ."

"Maybe killing them was my penance for not being your father." Then he added, "Not blaming God. Should have forgiven them. But couldn't. Also couldn't forgive myself . . . abandoning you."

"I forgive you."

He nodded as tears ran from the corners of his eyes. "You're a better man than I ever was." He struggled to catch his breath. With what little strength he had, he squeezed Zack's hand.

Zack kissed him on the forehead.

"Love you, sport."

"I love you, Dad."

"Take good care of your mother. Good woman."

Then he nodded at the cigar box in Sarah's lap. He wanted Zack to flip through the photographs. He did, and when he reached a particular one, Nick stopped him. The shot was of a granite pinnacle in the woods. Zack recognized it—a place he had visited with his brother and father years ago. What he had glimpsed in suspension.

"Where you take me when it's time."

Nick again motioned for Sarah to find another photo. When she reached the correct one, he fingered it from her hand. It was a duplicate of one pinned to the cabin wall above his bed—a shot taken in front of their Carleton home. The four of them: Nick, Maggie, Jake, and

Zack, who was maybe eight at the time—all beaming from a happier era. With shaking fingers, he slipped the photo into his breast pocket to be buried with him.

Zack kissed his father's forehead, a great ache racking his heart.

Maybe another hour passed as Nick's breath became shallow, and he closed his eyes for the last time, his chest laboring for air.

They sat with him in silence, holding his hands, Zack on one side, Sarah on the other. And after several minutes, he fell into a deep sleep.

Maybe an hour before dawn, it was over. His last breath was a gentle *Ahhhh*—as if he had found something that he'd once lost. Then his chest ceased moving, his heart silenced, and his pulse faded to nothing.

Zack waited several more minutes, still holding his father's hand. Soon it lost its warmth as his body became something ceremonial.

Then Sarah moved to the other side of the room as Zack washed his father's body with a towel and water from the dispenser. They redressed him and wrapped him in a blanket. One more time, Sarah read the burial instructions.

Then they opened the cabin door to the chilled gray air.

Somewhere beyond, a loon screamed.

88

....

Zack was numb as they headed out.

It wasn't just grief. On some wordless level, he felt abandoned. All the preternatural glimmerings seemed to have vanished in the morning chill. His father had died, and something had left Zack's soul—a small glow that had burned in the background of his consciousness like a filament.

Overhead, behind the black snarl of trees, the iron gray light began to seep out of the sky.

Zack carried his father, now a swaddled bundle, through the woods, following Sarah with the flashlight. Nick had lost so much weight from dehydration that he felt like a child in Zack's arms. Probably the way he had felt when his father had carried him so many times up to his bed when he had fallen asleep on the family room couch.

They moved along a vaguely worn path through the brush and fallen tree limbs, guided by Sarah's flashlight. The air was heavy with predawn moisture and the mustiness of the soggy ground. Out of the mud and muck of decay, new shoots were coming up.

After maybe ten minutes, they arrived at a huge granite outcropping that rose maybe twenty-five feet in the air to a conical peak, looking something like a hooded figure hunched up out of the scrub. He knew this monolith. He had climbed it in his little-kid sneakers. Tabernacle Rock. The name came to him from nowhere. He didn't know if that was the name given by earlier settlers or his father. But he had brought Zack and Jake here as children.

At the base of the rock was a pile of dead branches and leaves. Beside it sat a pile of dirt covered by a plastic tarp. Zack laid down the body of his father, then he and Sarah removed the covering. Below was the grave hole his father had made—about six feet long, a couple of feet wide, maybe three feet deep. It had been dug with functional intent—roughly squared off, though not lined with rocks or pruned of stray roots.

Zack removed the plastic tarp to reveal the overburden as well as a short-handled military-surplus shovel. With a small shock, Zack realized that his father—a man who had no friends, who had hermitted himself away up here in the middle of nowhere—had dug his own grave with the sole purpose of relieving Zack of the unpleasant task. More than that, its careful planning anticipated Zack's journey here—maybe even his summoning. There were so many unknowns, so many unseen things.

Before they lowered the body into the hole, Zack folded back the blanket to reveal his father's face one more time. Perhaps he was imagining it, but it seemed to hold a look of peace.

He kissed him on the forehead again. "Good-bye, Dad."

Then, with tears blurring his eyes, he folded the blanket over again. Sarah pulled him into a tight embrace. They both were crying now. For a long moment they knelt beside his father's body, pressed against each other.

Sometime later, Zack picked up the shovel and began to bury his father.

Sarah stood beside him with the flashlight. Overhead, birds were awakening to the dawn. He could hear their chirps and twitters as he covered his father's feet and legs, part of him in disbelief, another part feeling a strange fulfillment.

He was almost finished when he turned toward the path, half expecting to see something emerge from the cut in the trees.

"What's wrong?" Sarah said.

"Nothing." The trees made a dark inert wall. "Just a deer."

Zack went back to the shovel.

He buried his father while Sarah sat silently on the tarp, her knees pressed to her chest as she watched. Neither of them said anything. The gray light grew steadily brighter.

When he was finished, Zack covered the mound with fieldstones, making a small cairn. According to his father's wishes, he did not place a cross of sticks on it. Instead, with Sarah by his side, her arm around him, he said a silent prayer.

"Good-bye, Dad. May you find peace wherever you are."

"How touching."

Sarah screamed.

Out of the trees behind them stepped a man with a gun.

89

....

"Who are you?"

The man emerged from the shadows, pistol raised at Zack. "The real question is, 'Who are *you*?'"

He was dressed in a camouflage jacket, pants, and hat. Over his shoulder was a backpack with something protruding from it ending in a black handle. And aimed at Zack's chest was a long-barreled pistol, exaggerated by what appeared to be a silencer. Nobody went hunting with a silencer.

The man moved into the clearing, his eyes wide. "So, you're the miracle man."

He looked vaguely familiar. "What do you want?"

"They told me you'd split. But Morris was kind enough to show me your videos. Which is how I found you. Magog Woods—not exactly a tourist trap."

"What did you do to Morris?" Sarah said.

"Morris? You mean the late, great henchman of Satan? Let's just say I relieved him from his life of blasphemy."

"You bastard."

He disregarded her and looked at Zack. "Some say you can perform miracles. Others say that you're the devil in disguise. I'm just wondering which it is."

"I don't know what you're talking about."

"You recite Jesus's words in the old language. You see things that aren't there. Maybe got God talking through you. That's pretty awesome. You could also be the Antichrist."

The man's face suddenly connected. The guy at the bar at Grafton Street Pub & Grill in Harvard Square. He had been stalking them.

"What do you want?"

The man stepped closer. "What I want to know is, which is it—are you angel or demon?"

The expression on his face said his question was dead serious. And he glared at Zack with the same look of wondrous expectation that he imagined lit the faces of those who had gathered around his hospital bed. Except this guy had a gun, just in case Zack turned out to be the wrong one—or neither.

"You'll have to decide that yourself." He felt Sarah looking at him in horror, wondering why he was baiting the guy.

"Demon or angel, you can do things the rest of us can't. Isn't that right?"

Zack didn't answer.

"I mean, maybe you've got some heavy-duty powers. So, either you're working for the man upstairs or the guy down below. Which is it?"

"If it's money you want, we can go to the nearest bank."

"You're worth more to me than whatever you can get from a bank."

"Meaning what?" Zack said.

"Meaning people will pay big-time for you—alive or dead." He stepped closer. "Come on, show me your stuff." He bent down and picked up a rock from the grave. He felt the heft of it, then tossed it at Zack's feet. "Turn that into a loaf of bread."

Zack looked at the rock. "Be serious."

The man flared up and jabbed the pistol at him. "I *am* serious. I've got serious up to here. You got Jesus in you, do it!"

"I can't."

"No?" He then picked up a branch from the ground and tossed it at his feet. "How 'bout a serpent?"

"I don't do magic tricks."

"I'm not asking for magic tricks. I want the real thing. You're supposed to have supernatural powers. I want you to show me them. I want to see a miracle."

Zack said nothing.

"Come on!" he demanded. "Make the sky cloud over. Make the mist lift. Make something happen—a fucking pillar of fire or something. Show me what you are and why everybody is fucking hot for you—willing to pay millions."

"I can't—" began Zack.

The man snapped the gun at Sarah and shot her.

She screamed and grabbed her arm. The bullet had cut through her sweatshirt just above the elbow. She pulled up the sleeve to reveal a bloody stripe in her flesh.

"Come on, miracle man, heal her. You can do it. You've got the God brain or whatever. Do it!"

"You son of a bitch," said Zack, and lunged at him.

But the guy stopped him at gunpoint. "You want to live? Then heal her. Do it. You channel the powers of God, so do it. Goddamn it. Show me you're God."

Sarah groaned in pain as blood seeped through her fingers. Without saying anything, Zack removed his jacket, bit a hole in the sleeve of his shirt, and tore it off his arm. He wadded up the cloth to stanch the blood. It was only a flesh wound, though bleeding steadily.

"Think this is a joke?" he yelled. "I want you to make her wound go away, not a fucking bandage."

With his belt, Zack made a compress on Sarah's arm. "Sorry," he whispered.

"I'm telling you to fucking heal her wound."

"I can't."

The man aimed the gun at the grave and fired twice into the dirt mound. "What about raising the dead, huh? Jesus did that with what's-his-name . . . Lazarus. Come on, raise up your old man." The intensity in his eyes was fierce. "Bring him back."

"You're crazy."

"Crazy, am I? Yeah, maybe I am." He looked at Sarah as if thinking about shooting her dead.

"What the hell do you want from me?"

He swung the gun at Zack. "I want you to show me you're for real, not some fucking rumor. But that's what I think you are—a fucking rumor." He shot at a spot between Zack's feet. Sarah screamed.

"A fucking lie like the rest of it. And God's the biggest lie of all. Might as well believe in Santa Claus. Because you know what? There's nothing else." He raised the pistol at the sky and fired. "Not fucking up there!" he shouted, saliva spraying from his mouth. "It's all bullshit. All fucking liars—Father fucking Infantino, the saints, the pope. All bullshit. No fucking heaven. No fucking salvation. No God, Jesus. All empty fucking frauds is all."

He jabbed the gun at Zack and shot another hole in the dirt before him.

"This is the real hell," he continued. "We're living in it. There's nothing else. And when it's over, it's over. A black hole in the dirt forever."

With one hand he reached over his shoulder, gripped the black handle protruding from the backpack, and pulled out a machete. He then aimed the gun at Zack's chest. "You're worth more to me dead."

"No. Don't!" screamed Sarah.

The man held up the machete, the long shiny blade like a large sliver of light in his grip. "Who hired you?" Zack said.

"Some asshole who thinks you're the devil. But you couldn't light a fucking match."

"Tell me his name."

The guy looked at him with dead eyes. "Norman Babcock."

"You killed Tom Pomeroy," Sarah said.

"Yeah, and now you, you fucking fraud." He raised the gun to Zack's chest.

"No!" Sarah screamed.

The gunman suddenly turned toward the thick of the woods. His face was taut, his eyes shocked open. He dropped the machete and assumed a two-handed stance, taking aim at something just behind the dark wall of trees. He fanned the area, trying to fix his target, moving the gun to the left and then the right, then up into the treetops. Suddenly he froze his arms straight out and squeezed off three shots in quick succession.

Small branches and leaves blasted in all directions. But Zack could see no one—just scrub and trees and small birds flapping away. Still in a two-handed stance, the man swiveled to another position and emptied the clip, then shoved in another from his pocket.

Zack pulled Sarah to him. "What's he shooting at?" she asked.

Zack had no idea. The guy was tracking something unseen in the trees, swinging this way and that. He fired off more rounds, emptied the clip, then slammed in another. More flashes of tree debris, and the only sound was that of startled birds. If there were hunters or even police, they'd have made themselves known or returned shots.

With the last wild volley, a shriek rose up. And out of

nowhere, a large hawk shot out of the sky, wings fully extended.

In reflex, the gunman took aim and fired.

The bird flapped awkwardly out of the sky and hit the ground with a muffled thud maybe twenty feet away. One wing was spread unnaturally, the other half-folded under it, maybe broken, its head at an odd angle. Zack glimpsed a flash of red, but he couldn't tell if it was blood or tail feathers. From the rumpled heap, an open eye stared at Zack.

Without thinking, he raised his hands toward the bird. *"Avvon d-bish-maiya, nith-qaddash shim-mukh."*

"What?"

"Tih-teh mal-chootukh. Nih-weh çiw-yanukh:"

"The hell's he saying?"

"ei-chana d'bish-maiya: ap b'ar-ah."

"He—he's . . . ," Sarah began.

"Haw lan lakh-ma d'soonqa-nan yoo-mana."

"It's Jesus," she whispered.

"What?"

"It's Jesus. He's speaking through him."

"O'shwooq lan kho-bein: ei-chana d'ap kh'nan shwiq-qan l'khaya-ween."

"Cut the shit."

"Oo'la te-ellan l'niss-yoona: il-la paç-çan min bee-sha."

"No, for real," she said. "Jesus is speaking through him. Those are his words. It's Jesus."

Zack heard the syllables trip from his mouth, not knowing where they came from or how he could pronounce the alien sounds, but he continued uttering the incantation, while the gunman stood before him, stunned in place, the pistol in his hand still aimed at Zack's heart.

As the words continued flowing from Zack, the man gazed at him in wide-eyed wonder, as did Sarah. Perhaps to test him, the gunman raised the gun to within inches of Zack's face and poked the air before his eyes. But Zack did not flinch, he did not cry out, but continued reciting the ancient prayer.

"*Mid-til de-di-lukh hai mal-choota—*"

"I don't know if he's in a trance or fucking faking it." Then he aimed the gun at Sarah. "This is some kind of bullshit act."

"*oo khai-la oo tush-bookh-ta l'alam al-mein. Aameen.*"

"Son of a bitch." He thrust the gun at Zack's heart.

"No!" cried Sarah.

Suddenly rising from the ground, the hawk flapped up toward the man. In reflex, he wheeled toward the bird and fired. He missed, and the bird flew off. But before he could turn on them, Zack leapt for the machete and with all his might he swung. The blade sliced through the man's gun arm. In disbelief, he cried out as blood geysered from the severed stump, his dead hand lying in the weeds still gripping the gun.

Zack stepped on the gun and drove the man back with the machete. Gripping his stump, he stumbled down the path toward the cabin, yelping in pain.

Zack helped Sarah up, then they moved after him. They cut down the path, still heavy with morning shade. Because of the thick brush and the man's camouflage, they couldn't see where he had gone. Nor could they hear him.

And all was silent.

Soon they came to the clearing where the cabin sat. No wind in the trees. No twittering of morning birds. No buzz of insects. The place looked like a still life. Nothing moved.

Nothing but the dripping of blood.

Sarah made a faint gasp, and it took a moment for

Zack's mind to catch up to what had startled her. The gunman was draped across his father's splitting stump. His arms were splayed by his sides, his legs open, blood pooling on the ground from the severed hand.

From all appearances, he had stumbled over the stump, impaling himself on the exposed spike of his father's ax.

For several minutes they searched the area where he had unloaded his clips. They found white scars on the trees and shattered branches from the bullets. But no footprints. No trampled new growth. No signs of any other presence. From what they could tell, the man had been shooting at nothing.

Nothing visible.

EPILOGUE

....

SEVEN WEEKS LATER

"To Zack, on the acceptance of his thesis," Maggie said, raising a flute of champagne. "Congratulations."

"To Zack."

And six glasses clinked over the table.

It was a mild August evening, and they were sitting at an outside table at Daisy Buchanan's, a trendy restaurant on Newbury Street. Zack had gotten the good news from his adviser two days ago. And celebrating with him were his mother, Sarah, Anthony, Geoff, and Damian.

"So, you get your degree in December, then what?" Anthony asked.

"Then I find a teaching job," said Zack.

"I'll drink to that," Maggie said.

He knew that would make her happy, since she had spent twenty dedicated years in the classroom. Although his adviser encouraged him to pursue his doctorate, he decided to apply to high schools and community colleges within an hour's drive of Boston to be close to his mother and Sarah.

For nearly two months, he and Sarah had been seeing

each other exclusively, and in that time Zack had felt warm possibilities fill his soul. It helped that Maggie had grown fond of Sarah.

"To education and a life of poverty," Zack said.

"Well, there's that," Maggie said with a chuckle.

"At least some things won't change," added Damian.

"But the hounds are off my back."

"And you don't have to sell your blood and soul for the good folks at Discover."

So much had happened since the events in Magog Woods.

Elizabeth Luria left no formal suicide note, just the blood and neuroelectrical activity recorded during her self-suspension. Although she would never know the diagnostic results, the analyses of the data indicated that she had experienced momentary transcendence. As an act of redemption for all the harm done to others, she had left most of her estate to a homeless shelter in Boston. She also had sent Zack a Treasury check for $10,000. It was Zack's hope that she had found the union she had long sought.

Because Byron Cates and Sarah had joined the lab after the deaths of the street people, they were not incriminated in the police investigation.

As for Norman Babcock, he was arrested as an accessory to murder. The evidence was overwhelming since, as insurance against betrayal, his hired assassin, Roman Pace, had recorded their conversations in which they discussed the killing of project scientists. The large sums of money found in Pace's rental car matched the cash withdrawals by Babcock.

Police were still investigating the Fraternity of Jesus to determine if any others were complicitous in supplying funds for Pace's hire. That investigation was still ongoing. Authorities had questioned Timothy Callahan,

pastor of St. Pius Church of Providence and nephew of
Babcock. In an interview with the local media, Callahan
denied knowing anything about Babcock's criminal activities, claiming that his uncle was a misguided loner
whose online diatribes against Warren Gladstone and
the near-death experience research were private obses-
sions not to be taken seriously. According to the bishop
of the Boston archdiocese, the Fraternity of Jesus was a
"disturbingly reactionary" splinter group of sedevacan-
tists who rejected the current Church policy of ecumen-
ism and religious tolerance as well as the last eight popes
and, thus, was not recognized by the archdiocese or the
Vatican.

Maggie, of course, had been shocked to learn that
Nick had been alive and living in Magog Woods. She
was doubly shocked that he had killed four people in
revenge for Jake's death. A letter of apology was for-
warded to her from his lawyer, explaining how Nick
could not defeat the darkness and how he had entered
the monastery in part to shield Maggie and Zack from
his own corrosive despair. He asked for forgiveness and
said that his consolation was to cherish his brief bond
with Zack. Maggie did not understand that last statement, and Zack did not attempt an explanation.

The waitress and two male assistants arrived with their
orders. Since the young woman had first taken them,
Zack had sensed her attention. In fact, he'd picked up
on it as soon as they put in for a table with the hostess.
As they waited for their champagne, he felt lines of awareness converge on him from the wait staff and a few cus-
tomers.

When she placed his dinner before him, she could not
help but ask, "If you don't mind my asking, is your name
Zachary Kashian?"

"Yes."

Her eyes lit up. "When I saw the name on the reservation, I thought it was you. I read about you in the newspaper." She smiled nervously. "Nice to see you, and enjoy your dinner."

"Thanks," Zack said, noticing a gold crucifix around her neck. And before she left, she repositioned his plate of salmon, brushing her fingers against the back of his hand. It wasn't an accident.

During the one interview he'd granted—to a reporter of the *Boston Phoenix*—Zack had admitted that he didn't fully understand how he had recited that excerpt from the Sermon on the Mount while comatose. He guessed that his father had taught it to him as a child and it somehow came out of his memory after he'd slammed his head into the light pole. But he didn't believe he was channeling Jesus. And no, he still couldn't say that he believed in God—at least not the God of religious writings. But he did say he believed there was something greater than humankind—a spiritual essence that may be felt in human life.

In spite of the NDE tests, he still didn't know if there was an afterlife. But he did think that it was probably better to believe than not to believe. When asked to explain, he said believing not only got you through the hard parts of life, but made it easier to face tragedies with more than mere resignation. If you saw life through a lens of hope, you were less afraid of crises, less afraid of death. It was what motivated Elizabeth Luria and that professional killer and a lot of people in between. We all sought eternity.

When asked if clinging to hope of the hereafter made people more effective in helping others, he said that depended on the person. His mother didn't believe, yet she was a good and caring person who helped others out of the goodness of her heart, not from the hope of rewards in the afterlife.

As for Luria's project, he reminded the reporter of the message of *Frankenstein*: Don't tamper with natural forces. Believing in the afterlife was fine, but trying to prove its existence may be venturing where we shouldn't.

Zack did not tell the press that sometimes while lying in bed he would send up thanks for his mother, Sarah, his friends, and his own life to whatever phantom deities might be listening. He could never say for sure if what happened in those woods was an accident or something higher, but he also thanked his father, just in case.

Perhaps believing made it so. Perhaps wanting to believe was the essence of faith.

And with that thought, Zack glanced across the table at Damian, who for a moment closed his eyes to say grace to himself. When he looked up, Zack caught his attention and nodded. "Me, too." And Damian smiled.

"Okay," Anthony said, downing the rest of his champagne. "The papers and TV are off your ass. So I gotta ask, what really happened up there?"

"What do you mean?"

"I mean how did you get a jump on the guy? He was a professional hit man who went to a pistol range every week. According to the papers, the guy was Annie Oakley."

"I don't know what happened," Zack said. "My guess is he just snapped."

"The cops found cartridges everywhere. So what was he shooting at?"

"I haven't got a clue. Maybe he was hallucinating."

"Did he look like he was on drugs or something?" Anthony asked Sarah.

"No, he looked crazed."

"So, you're saying he got distracted by this hawk that flew down."

"Something like that."

Half-consciously, Zack fingered the silver chain around his neck. It wasn't his father's crucifix. That they had buried with him. The chain he had purchased at a local shop that did custom work; and hanging from it was a small red tail feather. Only Sarah knew that he wore it. If anyone asked, it was only a good-luck charm.

He and Sarah had been over the events of that morning, telescoping the moments and parsing each movement to understand what had really transpired. To this day, and in spite of his memory, Zack could not recite more than the first few syllables of that Aramaic prayer that had held the killer spellbound. Where those words came from, he couldn't explain—though Sarah's quick thinking had distracted the killer. Nor could he explain how that bird appeared to have died and come alive again. Nothing could settle him on a conclusion that made total rational sense.

"I don't know, bro," Anthony said, shaking his head. "Either you're one lucky dude, or someone up there likes you."

Everybody else nodded and returned to their dinners.

Everybody but Sarah. She raised her eyes to Zack's. It was fleeting so as not to draw attention, but he knew in the depths of her eyes what she was saying.

"Maybe so," he said, and felt her hand slip under the table and give his a squeeze. "Maybe so."

TOR

Award-winning authors
Compelling stories

Please join us at the website
below for more information
about this author and other great
Tor selections, and to sign up for
our monthly newsletter!